MW00887300

51 SLEEPLESS NIGHTS

THRILLER SHORT STORY COLLECTION ABOUT DEMONS, UNDEAD, PARANORMAL, PSYCHOPATHS, GHOSTS, ALIENS, AND MYSTERY

TOBIAS WADE

HAUNTED HOUSE
PUBLISHING

This is a work of fiction. Names, characters, organizations, businesses, places, events and incidents either are the product of the author's imagination or are used fictitiously. Any resemblance to actual persons, living or dead, or actual events is entirely coincidental.

51 Sleepless Nights
First Edition: June 2017

PUBLISHING

Copyright © 2017
Haunted House Publishing
TobiasWade.Com

All rights reserved. This book or any portion thereof may not be reproduced or used in any manner whatsoever without the express written permission of the publisher except for the use of brief quotations in a book review.

CONTENTS

FOREWORD

IN DEFENSE OF FEAR

Why horror? Isn't there already enough fear in the world?

Yes there is, and that's exactly why horror entertainment is so important.

Some people will try to focus on "positive emotions" such as love and joy while repressing their fear, anger, jealousy, and other "negative" emotions.

I think this is an extremely dangerous thing to do because pretending they don't exist doesn't make the other emotions go away. It only inhibits our ability to understand and control them—and when we aren't controlling them, they're controlling us.

Without control, we are easy victims for any politician to use our fears to manipulate our vote. We are helpless to the holy man who uses our fear of the afterlife to control our values. We are even inept to confess to the girl we love, or follow our dreams, or anything else where fear stands as a boundary between us and our goal.

There is no such thing as a "positive" or "negative" emotion. Everything we feel contributes to making us human, and all emotions have an equal capacity to improve or destroy our lives and the lives of those around us.

How many times has love been our justification for obsession and greed?

Hasn't the pursuit of joy caused some of us to waste our lives with selfish hedonism?

Even empathy for your neighbor has been used as grounds to start wars or ostracize entire races and cultures that seem different from us.

So do not judge fear as evil just because it can be used for evil means. It is silly to blame a knife for a murder that its wielder committed.

By appreciating the beauty of fear—fear as an art-form—by accepting it is part of the human experience instead of trying to run from it, we're able to better equip ourselves to handle the fear in our daily lives.

That's why I've decided to write horror. My goal is to dig down to all the nameless terrors rooted in your subconscious and rock you to the bottom of your psychology. I'm going to let all the monsters out from under your bed until you finally get a good look at them and realize that fear can't hold you back anymore.

That it can even be fun.

CONFESSIONS OF A SERIAL KILLER

This letter is from a confessed serial killer to his thirteen-year-old daughter.

Dear Samantha,

I'm sorry I haven't been around for a while, but you're going to have to be strong, just like I'm trying to be strong for you. I don't know how much your mother has told you, but sooner or later you're going to hear about what Daddy did, and I want to tell you why I did it. They're going to tell you I killed those 7 kids. That I tortured them first, chaining them in that shed in the woods. You remember the place—you used to build a fort there and play princess of the castle. You'll always be my princess, even after everything that has happened there. You're going to hear about how the victims were starved and forced to eat the one who came before them, and how they'd be chained until the next one came 'round to eat them up too.

You're going to see my name brought up on websites and social media. Photos of the murders are going to be uploaded, and you're going to have to see those corpses stripped of flesh and put on display for the whole world to see. You're going to hear priests condemning me to Hell, and news stations using my name as propaganda for whatever self-serving platform they can find. And worst of all, you're going to be feared because of your association with me.

But you have your whole life ahead of you, and no matter how bad it seems now, this is NOT your defining moment. These weeks or months until everyone forgets won't last forever. These killings will not determine who you are. I won't be coming home again, but someday after years have stretched this memory thin, it's going to be like none of this has ever happened.

That's why I did it. That's why I confessed, so you could move on and forget. That's why I never told the police that you were the one who led them into the woods. That's why I turned myself in as soon as I found the bodies. I don't care how many of them you got, there's only one person I care about protecting, and that's you, my princess.

If this is what you want, then you should have it. You deserve everything in this world. I know you told me that you weren't going to stop leading people into the woods, but at least try to be more careful next time. Don't take kids—don't take anyone they're going to look for. And when I'm gone, I hope you find someone who loves you as much as your Daddy does. I hope they love you so much, they confess for you and you can keep playing forever.

Don't ever stop playing, Princess. The world is yours.

Love, Daddy—My name is Detective Mathews. I was led on the "Killer Miller" serial murder case. This letter was confiscated after an inmate tried to smuggle it out of the visitation room. Samantha Miller is currently missing, last seen in Los Angeles County. The station is offering a reward to anyone who can provide information regarding her whereabouts. Samantha is considered to be a danger to herself and others. If you have any information, please call (323) ***-**** and ask for Mr. Mathews.

MY MOTHER THE SPIDER QUEEN

People think they're being discreet when they whisper from the side of their mouth. They think just because they're not making eye contact, that somehow I won't know they're talking about me. Even when they're able to restrain the thoughtless dribble from their faces though, I still know what they're thinking from the thousand others who couldn't be bothered to spare my feelings.

Disgusting child.

Attention whore.

They shouldn't let her out of the house like that.

And of course I grin and stare back until they are more uncomfortable than I am, but I still feel compelled to write this and defend myself, so here goes. This is the story of my mother the spider queen.

She isn't my real mother. I don't know what happened to my real mother, but I like to think of her as an actress involved in some celebrity scandal which made it impossible for her to keep me. I imagine the death threats she received from my father, the tearful nights and the decision which would rip her world apart, and the love which made her disguise herself and leave me in the care of Mrs. Willow.

The woman who raised me was part hyena and part boa constrictor by nature although she successfully spun a mask of white lace and perfumed curls which might be mistaken for sophistication at a distance. She was adamant about the punishment fitting the crime although I would argue being forced to drink dirty mop water isn't proportional to a soiled floor. Of course her own son Jeff wasn't subject to this parenting style, but as she often liked to remind me, I was her obligation, not her child.

Mrs. Willow was too disdainful of real work to get her hands dirty with me though, and I wasn't afraid of anything her bird-arms could hurl my way. It was Jeff who made my life there a living Hell. Three years older than me and at least twice my weight, Jeff made a sport out of tormenting me since he couldn't hope to compete in anything else. Glue in my sandwiches and shampoo bottles, broken glass scattered around my bed, profane words cut into my clothes that wouldn't be replaced—it's amazing that a boy with his creativity and work ethic could still be failing in school.

Retaliation was impossible. The slightest hint of resistance would send him howling to his mother. I think Jeff could have murdered me, and she would have still blamed me for getting him in trouble with the law. When I was 10, some teachers sat down and talked with my mother about my injuries, but she found it more convenient to convince a psychiatrist that I had Asperger's and was abusing myself rather than intervene with her angelic boy. It didn't help that I almost never spoke back then, but that's just because staying quiet always seemed to bore my tormentor more quickly.

I spent a lot of my time hiding in cupboards, trying to stay out of everyone's way. It was too dark to read or anything, but it was quiet, and I could listen to myself think without being interrupted. If I was lucky, then Jeff would get distracted and forget about me, and I could spend a whole day sitting peacefully in the dark. Then came a weekend when I was 12 years old when Mrs. Willow was going out of town for a spa retreat. It was just going to be me and Jeff, and I knew no corner would be remote enough to hide from him.

I'd been sitting under the kitchen sink for about an hour before I was blinded by the sudden light of the opening door. I tried to crawl away from it, but Jeff's hand latched around my ankle.

"Stop being weird and get out of there."

I managed to wriggle free for a second, but then he got hold again. Both hands this time—it felt like he was going to rip my leg right off. I groped through the darkness and clung onto something, immediately letting go when I realized it was the pipe for the garbage disposal. Whatever I got wouldn't be nearly as bad as the sanctioned violence for breaking her precious kitchen. Jeff was still tugging relentlessly on my leg. I allowed myself to go limp, closed my eyes, and waited for the inevitable to come.

"Oh shit what was that?"

He let go of my leg, and I felt a rush of cool air replace his hulking presence. He was reeling back as though something hit him. Then I felt it—the soft tickle of a spider crawling down my arm.

"Smash it and get out here," he said. Jeff was already half-way across the kitchen, actually trembling. I couldn't believe my eyes. 15 years old pushing and 200 pounds, and he was actually scared of an insect. I gently cupped my hands and let the fuzzy little guy wander into them.

"I told you to kill it!" Jeff shouted.

I let it meander up my arm, enjoying the sight of Jeff squirming in discomfort. I pretended to swat the thing, then scooped it up again and placed it in my hair. I giggled—not from the soft tickling of its legs, but rather at the white bleached horror spreading across Jeff's face. I cautiously climbed out of the cupboard, waiting for him to attack me at any moment, but he was absolutely frozen with terror.

"You can't just leave it there," he finally spluttered. "It's going to bite you."

But it didn't, and why would it? Animals aren't like humans. They need a reason to cause suffering; humans only need an opportunity. Jeff followed me, but remained a respectful distance for the rest of the day.

What I had anticipated being the worst weekend of my life was actually the best I can remember. The spider and I were inseparable, and I named it Swish because of the feeling of its fuzzy legs on my skin. Jeff wouldn't even get close to me, and it didn't take long before I figured out how to use Swish as an excuse to control him completely.

"I wouldn't sit there," I'd say. "Swish was hiding between the cushions."

Or

"You sure you want the last donut? Don't you see the little footprints?"

It was like a miracle. He locked himself in his room for two days straight, and I had complete freedom. First thing I did was make a fly trap out of some honey and glue, then fed Swish for his hard work. Then I got to take a shower in the bathroom with hot water and let it run for as long as I wanted without being yelled at. I even used real shampoo and everything. Swish waited for me on the sink, so I rewarded him with another fly.

It was a dream to think that kind of respite could last. Before Mrs. Willow had even set down her luggage, Jeff was already spinning the most incredible lies.

"She chased me with it! All over the house, wouldn't leave me alone. She put it in my food and wouldn't let me eat—I had to starve the whole time you were gone. I think it's bitten me, look!"

Mrs. Willow had come back earlier than I expected. I didn't have time to hide Swish. After everything it had done for me, it was my fault what happened. Mrs. Willow grabbed me by the hair and dragged me all the way to the bathroom. I told her it wasn't still in there, but she wouldn't listen. She chopped off all my hair with a kitchen knife, then shaved the rest of my head down to the scalp. I didn't struggle, because I knew that would just give her an excuse to cut me.

After that, she tore my room apart until she found it. I'd built Swish a home out of a shoe box and some twigs. Mrs. Willow didn't want to touch it, but Jeff was howling so badly that she just dropped the whole nest in the bathtub and lit the thing on fire. I squeezed my eyes shut, unable to watch the poor creature struggling to escape. I knew exactly how it felt, wanting so desperately to get out but having nowhere to go, and when it burned alive, I couldn't help but envy it for finally being free.

After her trip and that ordeal, Mrs. Willow was too tired to do anything more to me that night. Tomorrow though—she gave me her word like she was swearing her righteousness before God—I was going to pay for what I did to her son.

"Girls with Asperger's," Mrs. Willow said as she closed me in my room for the night, "have been known to do horrible things to themselves. I even heard of one cutting off her own ear with a pair of scissors. I don't think anyone will be surprised by what happens to you."

I lay awake the whole night, imagining what may be in store for me. Mrs. Willow didn't usually like to break the skin with her punishment, but between her zealous worship of her son and the wild look in her eyes, I didn't rule out any possibility. Worse than anything though, was the feeling that I betrayed Swish. I hadn't built the house for him at all—I built it to keep him trapped so he wouldn't run away and leave me alone. It was my fault he'd been in there when Mrs. Willow found him. Maybe I should have tried to run away too, but I was convinced she would find me again, and it would only make matters worse.

If I'd learned anything from living here, it was resistance always made things worse. I just had to close my eyes, try not to cry, and let it happen. I wish she could have just done it tonight. The anticipation was the worst part. If I could just fall asleep it would be morning, and then it would pass, but no. All night long I lay awake, listening to the soft swish of little legs no doubt scurrying to flee the house.

I must have fallen asleep at some point, because next I knew I was woken by the midday sun flooding through my window. I couldn't believe she didn't wake me. I quickly patted myself down, making sure she didn't cut off anything in the night. Then I crept from my room, peering around the house. All the doors were closed. All the lights were off. It was as though no-one had woken up at all. Maybe this was part of the punishment—she knew I hated the waiting. She was just going to let the fear keep building until I least expected it and then— KNOCK. I gently tapped on her bedroom door. The lights were off, but the door swung open, and I saw her sitting on her bed. Fully dressed, white lace straight, hair perfectly curled. She waved at me and smiled, and I immediately shut the door. So she is awake. This is just a game to her. Well it wasn't fair, and I wasn't going to play. I couldn't just sit and wait for it to happen. I couldn't just be quiet and still forever. I was going to tell her what really happened. I was going to tell her that her son is a liar who hurts me whenever she isn't looking. I'm going to scream it in her face, and if she hits me, then all the better. At least I can let her anger out and get it over with.

Opening the door again took all the strength I had.

"Mrs. Willow," I said it loud and defiant into the dark room. "Your son is the one who deserves to be punished. Not me."

Her head tilted to the side as though unable to support its own weight. She turned to face me in small increments, unable to believe what I'd just said to her. All my instincts roared at me to close my eyes and hide, but I stared her fiercely in the face. She'd burned Swish alive, so now she gets to see my fire.

"He's a sadistic brat, and the more you lie to yourself, the worse it gets," I said. She stood shakily to her feet and took a step toward me.

"You think you're protecting him, but you're not," I said. "Because one day he's going to go out in the real world where he's accountable for his actions."

She was almost on top of me now. I was going to get it worse than ever, but I didn't even care. I wanted to fight back.

"I just want you to know that you're a terrible mother, and at the end of Jeff's miserable destructive life, he's going to blame you and hate you for it. And if you don't already, you're going to hate him right back."

There. I finally said it. She dove at me, but I didn't try to run. The last of my strength was gone, and my old protective instincts flared up. I closed my eyes. I let my body go limp. I told myself to accept the pain.

Swish.

"You're absolutely right. I'm so sorry, my love."

I felt her arms around me, but she wasn't trying to choke or restrain me. She was... hugging me. It was such an alien sensation that I immediately opened my eyes. That's when I saw them. Hundreds—no thousands of gossamer spider webs holding up her body like a marionette doll. I recoiled immediately, and she let me without the slightest resistance.

Swish.

The spiders were everywhere. Crawling across her face, through her hair. When she opened her mouth, I saw more of them inside her, pulling the threads to work her jaw. Her throat pulsed, and I knew more must be further down to vibrate her vocal chords.

"But he's never going to hurt you again. You have our word."

I was too shocked to fully understand what was happening. The alarm in my mind wouldn't stop, and I still felt like I was about to pay for my rebellion. I didn't want to stare, but couldn't look away. I didn't want to go and see, but my feet carried me there anyway.

I opened Jeff's room and found him on his bed. His hands and feet were bound with countless loops of spider-web. More of it was across his face, tying his tongue securely to the roof of his mouth. His skin was perforated with a thousand holes, and spiders were crawling in and out of them as they carefully partitioned and wrapped each piece for consumption. His eyes blinked at me, although I don't know if that was a sign of life, or simply the successful attachment of yet another internal strand. I quietly closed the door and let them finish their work.

So if I seem strange to you, walking down the street with spiders in my clothes and hair, don't think I'm doing it for attention. They were a gift from someone who wants to keep me safe. I love them, and I love her for it. My mother is the spider queen, and she's the only family I've ever had.

THE ORGAN HARVESTING CLUB

Growing up, I was one of those kids who could be washed with a fire hose and still have dirt between my toes. Mud was the best toy in the world. I used it like Play-Doh to build entire forts, and my twin sister said she could always tell when I was coming before she saw me because of the squelching sound.

Bugs? Bring it on. I'd eat one for a dollar. Painting? My whole body was both brush and canvas. Maybe you'd find me baking a cake with my sister. We looked almost identical, but you could easily tell us apart because she would be wearing disposable gloves up to her elbow, while my whole face was buried in the bowl to lick the batter.

That's what makes it so unfair that she got sick and I didn't. It started with her feet and ankles swelling up. I thought she was just starting to gain weight, and I forced her to jog with me in the morning before school. She kept trying to push through, but she couldn't keep up with me like she used to. I shouldn't have made her feel bad for it, but I was only 17 then. I thought she just wasn't trying. I didn't understand that she was trying twice as hard as me, or that trying sometimes wasn't enough.

A month later, she could barely walk without throwing up. She was exhausted and dizzy all the time, and I felt so helpless watching her drift away from me. She was diagnosed with a polycystic kidney disease which was causing both of her kidneys to fail. She tried dialysis for a while, but it quickly became clear that she was going to need a transplant.

I didn't even have to think about it. She was my other half. If her body was sick, my body was sick, and if there was something I could do to make her better, then I that was the end of the discussion. It was just bad luck for her to express the inherited condition while I didn't, and it could have just as easily been me. It was going to be a routine enough operation though, and once she had one of my kidneys, there was no reason for the cysts to form anymore. We were both going to be okay. Yeah, we'd have to be on medications for the rest of our life, but as long as she'd be taking it with me, it would be fair. Besides, what twin doesn't want to have matching scars?

We were prepared for the surgery together in the same room. We made a game out of drinking the nauseating laxatives which were necessary before the operation: first one to get through it gets to choose which kidney to have. It wasn't even close to fair because she started out nauseous and I had always been the one who could stomach anything, so I made a big show of spitting it up and let her win. Her gloating about beating me was the happiest I had seen her in a long time.

It was so embarrassing because she wouldn't stop giggling while the male nurse shaved the little hairs on our abdomen. I started laughing too, and the nurse looked so uncomfortable that he had to excuse himself from the room to 'check something'.

"Come back!" she yelled after him. "We can do you next. It'll be fun!"

Her smile was glowing despite everything she had to go through. I want to always remember her like that.

The surgery was terminated half-way through. There had been a complication, and her body had gone into shock the moment her first kidney was removed. They said she woke up for a moment and held my hand right before she went, but they might have just been saying that to try to make me feel better. It didn't work.

The doctor said I could see the body if I wanted, but what was the point? All I had to do was look in the mirror. All the pain and loss on my face—hers must have looked the same way. Then the doctor leaned in real close—like he didn't want anyone else to hear—and he whispered something to me.

"Since you're all prepared for the surgery anyway, do you want to still go through with it?"

"She's gone. What's the point?"

"There's someone else who is also a match. You could be saving their life instead."

What did he think this was, a charity? I wasn't just giving organs away. I was only doing this because she was my sister, and I would have given anything for her. I wasn't about to risk my life for—"The recipient is willing to compensate you with 250,000 dollars."

I choked on my reply. It's amazing how quickly you're able to justify something for that kind of money. I had already been prepared to give it up. Was there really anything wrong with selling it? I would be able to help my family with all the medical costs my sister had wracked up from her illness. Besides that, I would be able to help so many more people...

I nodded. The anesthesia mask went back over my face, and I slipped back into oblivion.

I didn't tell anyone about the money which was discreetly wired into my bank account. There was an unwholesomeness about it somehow, but maybe that was just because the whole incident was so close to my sister's death.

I paid off all of my parents bills and told them they were covered by an anonymous donor which I guess was true. Over the next three years, I funneled the rest into a non-profit organization which helped people get their medical procedures.

Three years. It went fast. I'd expected that kind of money to be able to help people for a lifetime, but people came from everywhere to make use of the fund.

Co-pay for cancer medications, necessary operations which were denied by insurance, health screenings for those without insurance –

three years, and the entire 250k was spent. But I received so many letters and gift baskets and people hugging me sobbing about how I saved their life. It was a rough estimation, but I figure in that time I saved the lives of at least 30 people.

30 people for a kidney! I was a 20-year-old college girl. There was nothing special about me at all. But knowing that such a small sacrifice had made such a huge impact—I couldn't just stop now.

I went back to the doctor who performed the operation, and he confided that there was a constant market for other organs. I asked about harvesting from cadavers or something, but he said only live donations or incredibly fresh harvests would bring that kind of money.

Getting volunteers though? Next to impossible. And it was illegal to advertise buying that sort of thing. Even if I managed to raise awareness about it around campus without getting arrested, then people would probably keep the money for themselves instead of helping others. If I wanted my foundation to continue, I was going to need to get the organs myself.

It made me angry to even think about how greedy people were. The potential for good each body contained was astronomical. It was selfish—almost criminal—to think that they valued their own life over the lives of dozens of others. I had several meetings with the doctor trying to brainstorm ideas to collect, and that's when he told me a secret which he had sworn to keep for life.

The man who had my kidney killed my sister. He'd paid the nurse 100,000 to do it so he could get my kidney instead. The doctor had found out too late to stop him—his own life was even at risk if he didn't extend the offer to me.

I finally found the first person to join my Organ Harvesting Club.

I tracked him down with the doctor's help and waited for him to come home. Getting in was easy—I just rang the doorbell, and he opened it.

My plan was just to get information on him and his house on my first visit, but I couldn't hold myself back. His blood was flowing through my kidney. My sister's blood was on his hands. I punched him square in the face and tackled him straight to the ground.

He was twice my size, but he was fat and old, and I was an animal. If I had prepared better, I wouldn't have gouged my fingers into his eyes (worth $750 each). I wouldn't have broken his teeth with my elbow (about 1,000$) or spilled so much blood when I slit his throat with my switchblade ($337 a pint).

I didn't even get his body to the doctor in time to get top dollar on the rest of the organs, but I'll be more careful next time. I expect to get close to 600k for the nurse who killed her.

Can you think of any other club which can potentially save hundreds of lives with each new member that's added? I hope my sister is watching somewhere, and that she knows how much good has come from her death. She can stay pure and clean and perfect, but I was never afraid to get my hands dirty.

PAINTING THE ROSES RED

My neighbor Dr. Gregovich suffered both of life's greatest calamities. The first was falling in love, a rebellious and generally discouraged affliction to which he accidentally exposed himself when he was just five years old. Elaine, age four at the time, had given him a snow white rose (doubtlessly obtained unlawfully), and if Gregovich's account is to be trusted, then he was helplessly within her power ever since. The fact that his first instinct was to eat the rose apparently did nothing to lessen the potency of this gesture.

Fortunately for Gregovich, he thrived despite his adverse condition. By some miraculous trick which he swore he never anticipated, Elaine even came to love him back. It didn't happen all at once, but rather as a cumulative study told by the years of his devotion.

He told me that he used to carry her school bag between classes, often finding himself on the wrong end of a rod after he absent-mindedly stayed to watch her rather than attending his own schedule. He had stolen his first kiss in second grade by convincing her that she was a flower while he was a visiting bee, and by their junior year in high-school, they were already engaged.

It's hard to imagine promising your life to someone when you still don't have the faintest concept of what life entails, but perhaps things were simpler in 1941 when they were married. The world must have been jealous of their love, but two wars, seven children, and seventy five shared years of illness, grief, and weariness which infiltrate even the happiest life proved insufficient to destroy their bliss.

It was last month of this year when Elaine finally slipped beyond the capacity of his care and into that great freedom where care is no longer required. I saw the old man tremble so violently as he wept that I anticipated a second grave before the first was excavated, but it is the second of life's great calamities which forced his body to linger even after his soul had perished.

At 94 years old, Dr. Gregovich left his house for the first time in almost twenty years to follow her last black procession. Since then however, I have seen him outside every day, kneeling upon the ground and mumbling through dried lips which have almost already returned to dust.

Rain or storm or howling wind, I would see him there without fail when I returned from work. It was obvious what he was doing, but I asked anyway because it had been too long since my heart felt the warmth I knew his reply would bring.

"I'm planting roses," he told me. "One for every year I borrowed her for."

"I'm sure you are making her very happy somewhere," I told him.

"I don't want her to be happy somewhere, I want her to be happy here. I want the smell to lead her back home to me."

The roses flourished like nothing I had ever witnessed. Seeds the size of a corn kernel would begin sprouting the next day, and a week of growth conjured up a wild thorny expanse which I couldn't have traversed with a ladder. And the roses! Magnificent white blossoms, pure as starlight, beamed through my bedroom window each night as though the whole tapestry of the heavens had fallen to settle in his garden.

"I've never seen a flower grow like that," I told him. "What's your secret?"

"I'm not planting flowers," Dr. Gregovich replied. "I'm planting memories. The older the memory is, the deeper the roots and the more precious the bloom."

The next night I was woken by a terrible scream which my weary mind struggled to comprehend existing outside of a nightmare. I rushed to the window and saw Gregovich kneeling once more in his garden. The moon cast a net of light which caught the blood covering his body, and I rushed at once to his aid. What was he thinking gardening in the middle of the night? He must have cut himself with the shears, and I more than half expected to discover one of his frail hands, skin thin as rice paper, clipped straight from the stump.

Down the stairs, out the door, breath course in my lungs, I stopped suddenly short. Gregovich sat calmly washing his hands with the gardening hose. Beside him lay a dead goat with a savage wound across its neck. No—there were three of the animals here. The first two were already hung up by their feet with buckets placed below them to collect the draining blood. The sticky sweet air from the flowers was tainted with the pungence of death, and I could see that two rows of his flowers were already dripping with their bloody varnish.

"Are you out of your mind? What on Earth are you doing?"

"It occurred to me," he said, now washing congealed blood from his paint brushes, "that white roses are a lie. I can't entice Elaine to return by pretending all our memories are pure. I must show her the truth: the pain, the brutality, and the suffering of life, but remind her too that such sacrifice is still part of what makes it so beautiful."

I was so bewildered by his explanation that I couldn't find anything to reply. I even helped him string his third animal above the buckets before going back inside to take a shower. He promised me that he didn't need to slaughter any more goats to finish his garden, and that he would later prepare the meat in a stew so that nothing was wasted. It was certainly the most peculiar way of dealing with grief I had ever encountered, but besides the initial shock, I didn't see anything especially more abhorrent about the situation than if the animals were killed by a butcher.

Perhaps I was only making excuses to get back to bed though

because the next morning I was appalled by the sight outside my window. While the mask of night had subdued the color into subtle hues, the sun revealed the devastation of his sloppy work. Blood pooled upon the ground where it dripped from the flowers, leaving them unevenly streaked and stained like a field of open wounds. Bloody footprints invisible in the night crossed to and fro across his yard, and the swarming buzz of flies and stench of death made me feel as though I'd woken inside a battlefield.

I crossed his yard delicately to confront him, careful not to tread in any of the tributaries of blood which snaked through the irritation to coalesce into a small river which flowed into a nearby ditch. As I passed through the garden, I noticed a staggering array of signs which punctured the sticky red soil around each plant.

Goat

Rat

Chicken

Cow

Dog

I was covering my nose with my t-shirt when I pounded on his door. The flowers beside the house were stained much darker than the others, and the dry soil told me he had been doing this for far longer than I knew. We both lived on the outskirts of a small town where no visitors were likely to trespass without warning, and if it wasn't for my intervention, he might have cut his way through an entire farm.

"Do you like it?"

I nearly added to the menagerie by jumping straight out of my own skin. He was standing behind me, grizzly shears in hand, still soaked from his perversion. There weren't any footprints upon his doorstep, so he must have been attending to his macabre work all night long.

"It's the most vile thing I've ever seen," I told him honestly. "And I'm sure Elaine would think the same and turn straight around even if she was coming back. This has to end."

"Do you see her? Elaine? Where are you?" The poor creature's eyes bulged from their sockets with unrealized expectation.

"She's not here you dithering old bat."

"Then how can you say this is the end?" he asked, swaying danger-ously upon his feet as he pivoted to face me again.

The slick shears gleamed evilly in his hand, and though I discounted him for his age, the magnitude of destruction around me proved some fire still burned within him. For both of our safety, I resolved to notify the police instead of handling the situation myself. I turned and marched swiftly away from Gregovitch. I held my breath for as long as I could, but released it with an involuntary gasp before I had cleared the garden.

A single white flower remained unsoiled at the edge of his garden. Planted in the soil beside it was a sign:

Human

It was still white, but I had to act fast. If I called the police now— But I was already too late. I heard a loud pop like a firework going off, and then something sharp stung the back of my neck. At first I thought it was one of the biting flies drawn by the blood, but then I heard the sound again and a second needle pierced my thigh. Tran-quilizer darts. I plucked them out and hurled them down although the ground already seemed much closer than I remembered. My throat closed down to a pinhole and the field of red roses swam across my vision. The flowers danced like living things in a sordid parody of the animals which painted them red.

But he was so old! If I could just crawl into the road, I could get away and someone would find me. I plunged my hands into the bloody soil and dragged myself into the ditch. The thick liquid from the fields flooded over me, offering at least some concealment. I choked on air as thick as the river which flooded into my lungs. The red surrounding me was more than color. I felt it course over me, heard it pounding beneath my skin, feeling as though I was part of that stream which pounded through the veins of a giant.

I didn't even hear the third pop when another needle pierced my back.

When I woke up, there was no longer any distinction between me and the blood pouring over my face. I tried to wipe my eyes, but the second my vision cleared, a fresh stream bubbled over them. I was disoriented, but I could vaguely sense that I was hanging upside-down. My throat burned like I was being choked with a red-hot wire. I struggled to reach my feet which were tied above me, but my feeble lurch only served to send a fresh wave of blood from the gash in my neck to splatter in the bucket beneath me.

I tried to scream, but all that came out was a wet splutter. I felt myself slipping out of consciousness again, but I held on and rubbed my eyes clear once more. There! Something was moving beside me, although the state of my overburdened senses and my reversed perspective made it almost impossible to distinguish the blurred shapes.

"You did all of this? For me?" A voice. A woman's voice.

I squinted and rubbed my eyes again. There were definitely two sets of legs beside me. I recognized one as Gregovitch's stained overalls, but the other in a black dress was unfamiliar.

"It's my beacon," Gregovitch said. "I didn't want you to get lost."

My vision slid away from me and I must have blacked out for a moment. Then my body lurched, and I drifted through consciousness again. An old woman in a black dress was cradling me and easing me to the ground.

"Shhhh," she whispered. "Don't worry. When your time has come, someone will call you back home too."

Blackness returned, so deep and peaceful that I seemed to have slipped out of time and space altogether. My pain was gone. My thoughts were as diffused as smoke in the wind, although I did have a vague conception that I was looking for something. Then a bright light pricked my vacuous abyss and forced my attention to focus on the spot. Gradually it grew brighter until with a blinding flash I felt a gasp of cold wind penetrate my lungs.

I was lying on the red soil. My hands raced to my burning throat to feel a thick gauze wrapped around the jagged wound. It took me a full five minutes to stand, all the while unable to process any thought more rudimentary than an awareness of the light.

Finally, agonizingly, I brought myself to my feet. The night was thick around me, and all the lights from Gregovitch's house were out. Gradually my eyes regained their focus and the brilliant white light faded into the pale reflection of the surrounding roses. There was no sign of the blood upon their petals, and each blossom shown with the same incandescent splendor which pierced the darkness I was in.

I managed to call an ambulance before slipping back into oblivion. I had suffered severe blood loss, and the doctor said that it was likely that my heart stopped beating for several minutes. If someone hadn't taken me down and bandaged my wound, there is no chance I would have survived.

There has been no sign of Gregovitch since the police swept his house, although his car remained parked in the garage. I even checked the grave where his wife was buried, but this too remained undisturbed.

I tried to explain what happened, but the condescending explanation I received was that the bleeding and the tranquilizers caused me to hallucinate. That's what I would have thought too, if it wasn't for the field of snow white roses outside of my window. I think that I really had been lost for a moment, until something had found me and called me home.

Of all the worrisome mystery of this situation, there is one thing which most prominently denies my sleep at night. One of Gregovitch's sons stayed at the house last weekend to pack up the old man's things.

After the son had gone, I took another walk through the garden out of a morbid curiosity to try to shed some light on this horrendous business.

All seventy-five white roses are as brilliant as ever, but the son must have still made some alterations in the garden. Instead of the myriad of sacrificial animals once depicted on the signs, there is now only a single word blazoned across every board that stands as stoically as headstones.

Human.

THE POWER OF A SMALL CITY

Four years in the army, and not once did I hear an order from anyone ranked above a Major(O4). Now I've been at the Dalton Power Station for two months, and I've already received three phone calls from James Mattis, the US minister of defense.

It seems like a mundane enough job, right? My stint in the army helped pay my way through a bachelor's in power plant technology after I got out, and I was ready for a reliable income with good honest work. I spent a few years in equipment operations, then checking readouts, and on up to personnel supervisor. Nothing more exciting than a few power lines being blown over in a storm until I was promoted to Plant Operator in Dalton.

"You're going to notice a few anomalies with this plant," the old manager Nathan told me. He was retiring, although by the size of his waste-line and the dull glassy glaze over his eyes, I'd guess he retired about ten years ago and just hadn't left yet.

"But I don't want you to worry," he added. "I worked here 20 years and nothing going on will interfere with your job."

"Looks normal enough to me," I replied. Was this some kind of test? "Single open cycle gas turbines, probably around 140 megawatts, right?"

If I was expecting praise for my perception, I didn't get it. That was the first time I've ever seen a grown man spit on an office floor.

"Not about the output boy, I mean our client. We're just supplying one building up in the hills. The rest of the city is handled by that hydroelectric station downtown."

This had to be a test. It didn't seem fair since they already offered me the job, but there wasn't any harm in playing along.

"No sir, that's impossible. This station should be able to supply around 140,000 homes."

"Or one government building," he grunted.

"Are we not producing at capacity?"

"We are. Hell, they'd take more if they could get it."

"What are they doing up there? I don't understand."

Nathan clapped me on the back like I had just won an award. "And they like to keep it that way. So if you want to stick around like I have, then you'll do what I did and keep your nose out of their business. Besides that, everything should run pretty smooth for you here."

But Nathan was wrong. Right from the start, nothing ran smoothly. First of all, the other plant workers acted mighty strange toward me. Every one of them kept their eyes locked on the floor, all wearing that same glassy eyed complacency I had seen in Nathan. They followed orders readily enough, but they did so without any initiative or individuality.

I caught one guy, Robert, chewing his pencil for ten minutes straight in the break-room. I asked him what he was doing, and he mumbled that his schedule dictated a break every two hours. As soon as his ten minutes were up (to the damn second, I think), he stood up and left the room without another word.

And then there was James Mattis calling every few weeks. Those were the most awkward, forced conversations I've ever had to sit through in my life.

"Acting Manager?" were always the first words out of his mouth.

"John Doe (not my real name) speaking."

"Clearance code?"

I'd give it to him, and then he invariably asked a string of the vaguest imaginable questions. It felt almost like he was being held hostage and had to speak in code to gather information. A few examples:

"Would you consider everything to be more, or less ordinary than normal?"

"Have you had any unusual requests for output to anywhere besides that building?"

"In an emergency, how fast could you shut down power to everything if you had to?"

The financing is another thing that didn't make sense to me. Usually a plant this size will have a couple dozen workers and need its own financing department to keep track of everything. Here we've just got Megan.

"There's not much to do really," she told me. "There's no money coming in. I just prepare a folder every month with all our expenses, mail it to some office down in DC, and they take care of it. They've never denied anything before."

Three days ago topped it all off when I received the strangest question yet from Mattis. He asked: "Have you noticed any of your employees trying to escape?" Then he coughed like he was trying to clear his head, not his throat. "I mean, any of them try to quit or just stop showing up?"

The mystery was unbearable to me, but I was trained to follow orders, and despite everything I could have maybe still accepted the situation if it wasn't for the black van which came by yesterday. "Shuttle service," they called it, although it was only picking up Robert and another technician named Elijah. I watched the van take them up the dirt road winding into the hills.

Yesterday morning they were back at work and I asked them what happened, but they both just laughed and said they went out for a few drinks. Even the laugh felt wrong – like they weren't doing it because they thought it was funny, but rather made the sound in the hopes that I would find it funny and move on.

First thing I learned about working in a power plant is that a pair of professional overalls and a condescending attitude can get you in just about anywhere. All I had to do was strip one of the underground cables leading to the building, file a report on the output fluctuation, schedule my own appointment, and show up. There was a guard post out front, but I showed them my diagnostics appointment and they let me inside (under escort) without complaint.

I called it a building before just because I'd only seen its location on a map. A mine shaft might describe the phenomenon more accurately, or perhaps a crater. The complex was clustered around an abyss located at the bottom of an enormous valley whose jagged slopes looked like the result of a cataclysmic primordial explosion, long since eroded and overgrown with spruce and pine. There was an unusual energy about the place, and I felt compelled to walk gently as though stepping atop a living creature. That was probably on account of the constant vibrations rippling through the ground like something deep below the earth was stirring.

Most unsettling of all perhaps were the rows of black vans parked outside. Four of them were being loaded with long bags about the size and shape of a human body. I caught the eye of the guard accompanying me and noticed its glassy shine.

"Any power cuts have serious repercussions here. Please resolve the issue as quickly as *humanly* possible."

Humanly. Maybe my discomfort had me imagining things, but somehow it seemed like he said that in the same way you or I might say 'He's pretty smart, for a dog.'

The guard led me to a control station about a hundred feet away from the main complex. I couldn't get a good enough angle on the abyss to glimpse what could be down there, but up close the vibrations resolved themselves into the distinct sound of drilling.

"I don't suppose I'm allowed to ask –" I started.

"Won't do you any good," he answered promptly. "I don't know any more than you, and that's already more than enough."

"Have you ever been inside?"

He shook his head, glancing around nervously. Then in a hushed whisper:

"I never seen anything, but sometimes I'll hear things. Like something is down there that don't want to be."

I raised my eyebrow, hoping he'd continue. He opened his mouth like he was going to say more, then shook his head.

"None of my business, none of yours. How long is this gonna take?"

I didn't push my luck by staying long. I traced the power restriction to the cable I striped and followed the line back away from the complex to the spot where I damaged the cable.

I've been keeping an especially close eye on Robert and Elijah all day today. I can't shake the feeling that they're not quite here. I caught Robert chewing his pencil again, but he was doing it so absent minded, that by the end of his ten minute break he had eaten straight through the entire thing.

Elijah was even worse. He was microwaving a cup of noodles in the break room, anxiously pacing back and forth like he was waiting for a bomb to go off. Then it beeped, and he actually collapsed to the floor in shock. I retrieved his glasses for him and helped him to his feet, noticing his eyes were so pale as to be almost completely white. I'm positive they weren't like that before he went into the building.

I searched through the computer databases for any unusual mentions of the two, and found this log written by Nathan dated two months before I arrived.

Robert and Elijah first pickup service today. Good for five rounds each before they're used up. Current staff:

Round 0: 3

Round 1: 5

Round 2: 11

Round 3: 7

Round 4: 2

Round 5: 1

I am the only one at round 5. Requesting replacement for myself in two months after my final round. May God have mercy on our souls.

I scanned back further through his logs and saw a list of similar numbers. It seems like every week another pair of people are sent to the building and their "rounds" are increased by one. Elijah was currently a 4, while Robert was a 3.

There was also a schedule of future pickups. I scanned ahead a few pages and didn't see my name anywhere. It was a relief at first, although the more I searched, the more unnerving it was to be the only one not on the list. Well, here goes nothing.

I edited the next week to switch my name with Megan's (she was a round 1). It seemed like people were returning from whatever was going on there, and I know I'm not going to rest easy until I got a look inside. I don't know what happens past round 5, but after trying to call Nathan's personal number, I'm pretty sure that I don't want to know.

I learned from his wife that he put a bullet in his brain the day he left the plant. If all goes well, I hope I'll get to the bottom of this before I reach that point. And if not, well it's as Nathan said.

May God have mercy on our souls.

"Tell me everything you remember," I ordered Elijah the next day. I had waited until he entered the bathroom before following and locking the door behind us. The black van was going to be here in a few hours, and my excitement was quickly being replaced with dread. I needed answers, and I needed them now.

"I don't know what you're talking about," he replied in a monotonous voice. Forcing myself to stare into his cloudy white eyes was harder than I expected.

"On the nights you're picked up by the 'shuttle service'," I said. "I know you've gone four times now, and I know you weren't just drinking. I want you to tell me what really happened."

A euphoric smile replaced his pallid countenance. Then a frown, as though trying to remember the insubstantial details of a passing dream.

"But that's all that happened," he said. "The shuttle picks us up and they give us something to drink. Then I wake up in my home, and it's time to go to work again."

"And you feel just the same as you did before?"

The frown deepened. Then his eyes stretched so wide I thought they would pop straight out of his head. For a second he seemed about to scream, but then his face reverted back into a blank slate. It all happened in such a flash that I couldn't be sure the expression was there at all, but when he smiled again, I could sense the tension still trembling in his cheeks.

"Better than ever," Elijah replied. "I find it invigorating."

He continued staring me in the face while he opened his belt and dropped his pants around his ankles. I would have liked to ask him more, but I was too shocked and revolted when he began to piss in the sink right beside me. I just turned around and exited the bathroom without another word. Whatever was being done in the building had seriously damaged these people, and it looked like there was only one way for me to find out the truth.

When the van arrived, my name was called alongside Wallace Thornberg. Fat guy in a bulky coat with a hat pulled low over his face – I don't remember seeing him before today. He nodded curtly at me but kept his distance, shoving his way into the van the moment the doors slid open.

"Fransisco with the shuttle service." The driver bounced out from his seat and held the door open for me. He was dressed in the same blue suit as the guard who had escorted me before, but this man's eyes were perfectly clear.

I hesitated. "Where are we going?"

"You know," Fransisco replied. I found his tone overly familiar, and my doubts redoubled.

"What happens if I don't want to go?"

"But you do." The driver grinned and put on a pair of headphones. After that, he didn't speak another word for the remainder of the drive.

I climbed in and sat on one of the two benches bolted to the metal floor on either side of the van. The fat man sat on the other side from me, arms crossed, hat pulled low over his face, looking like he was trying to disappear into himself.

"You been there before?" I asked.

"Wouldn't remember if I did," came the gruff reply. "You're not supposed to be here though. You weren't on the list."

"How do you know?" I asked.

"Because I wrote the damn thing, and I didn't want you to be," Nathan finally looked up. He grinned to see the shock on my face. "Of course I'm not supposed to be here either, so I won't tell if you don't."

Nathan did his best to explain the situation to me as we rumbled into the secluded hills. After each of his first five rounds of procedure, his memory had been wiped clean every time.

"Waking up afterward felt like I was an alien in an unfamiliar world," he told me. "Books, songs, people I had seen a thousand times before, they all started giving me trouble like some sort of puzzle. I even tried to quit once, but the longer I went without another round, the more lost I felt. It became like an addiction, and I couldn't live without my fix. It would have been damn irresponsible for me to keep working when I could barely tie my own shoe laces, so I requested a replacement. That's why I wanted to keep you off the list – so we could have at least one level headed soul to keep everything running."

"Your wife said you put a bullet in your brain."

Nathan chuckled and slid his hat further up his head. A bandage was wrapped around his temple with a great bloody spot like a Japanese flag.

"You blame me? I didn't think I could go on after my fifth round, and this seemed easier than having to manage without it. Next I know, I'm back awake and swearing like the Devil. How's that for clearing your head? Worked like a charm too. I felt more like my old self than I had in years. Now I know they'd never let me walk after a stunt like that, so I let people keep believing I was gone."

"What are you?" I knew he couldn't remember what they did, but the question slipped involuntarily from my mouth.

Nathan glanced at the driver, still wearing his headphones. We were descending at a sharp angle now and must be entering the valley. Nathan moved across the van to sit beside me, speaking in a hushed tone. "I figure there are two possibilities: that they made me into something that isn't human, or the good Lord brought me back. Either way, it's my obligation to stop them doing this to anybody else, so I switched with Wallace to throw a wrench in the cogs. Can I count on you to have my back?"

He caught me staring at the bloody bandage and slid the hat back low over his face. I nodded stiffly, although I hated the idea of committing myself to a war when I didn't have the first idea who was in the right. It didn't seem like people were being forced here, but if they were being manipulated with an addictive drug, then that was just as bad.

The van pulled straight past the control station and stopped in the parking lot where I saw the bodies being loaded last time. The hum of drilling was omnipresent here, and my whole body vibrated like my bones were looking for a way out.

The guard handed us each a pair of headphones as we parked outside the building.

"Wear these," he practically shouted. "It's only going to get louder inside."

Nathan shifted his coat awkwardly, clutching something in his pocket with one hand while he put the headphones on with the other. When he said "wrench", did he mean he was smuggling some kind of weapon in here? The guard didn't seem to be paying any attention and simply walked into the towering structure with us at his heels.

"Can you hear me okay?" Fransisco's voice came through the head-phones. I nodded, absent mindedly walking forward in awe of the gargantuan internal structure. Three, maybe four stories tall on the outside, but it must have been built down into the abyss because the balcony I was standing over dropped down further than I could see. In the distant depths I thought I could make out a faint red glow, but my eyes were repelled from the void by an instinctual terror that I could not overcome.

Endless rows of balconies marched below me into the penumbra of shadow, each containing a massive machine with cables extending downward into the pit. Each machine had a tether of wires extending from the other end which connected with helmets being worn by a men sitting beside it. There must have been hundreds of them sitting so peacefully in repose that they might have been asleep, and hundreds more men in blue suits attending to the machines.

"What the shit?" I couldn't believe my eyes. I took a step back toward the entrance and almost tripped as I walked into something. I turned to see the guard offering me a glass of clear liquid. Nathan was already studying a second glass in his hand.

"You're going to take a drink and sit down at the machine," Fransisco said. "When you wake up, none of this will have happened, but you're going to feel so alive that you might as well be dead now."

"Not remembering it and not happening are completely different things," Nathan said. "But if we ain't gonna remember, you might as well tell us what's going on."

The guard sighed and rolled his eyes, languidly pulling a .44 magnum handgun from his belt and playing with it in his hand. "I've told you every time, Nathan, and I must admit it's getting old. And every time I've told you, you still took the drink, so why not just trust me and do it again?"

Nathan growled and pulled his hat off to reveal the bandage. He reached inside his coat and produced a cellphone with a prominently flashing light.

"Well maybe I'm not as easy to convince anymore," Nathan said. "So why don't you humor me?"

Fransisco calmly leveled the gun at Nathan's face as Nathan lifted the cell to his ear. I took the opportunity to begin circling the guard, but then the magnum pointed my way and I froze.

"Five rounds might keep you alive, but how well do you think your friend will bounce back from a bullet in the face?" Fransisco asked.

"Acting manager?" Nathan spoke into the phone. His voice was different. I'd heard that voice over the phone before, but it had been from the office of the secretary of defense.

"Put the phone down, or I'll shoot," the guard said. "I swear to God Nathan –"

"Clearance code?" Nathan asked. "I want you to shut down the plant the moment I give the word. Are you ready?"

"You can't," Fransisco said. "If we have a power out, every one of these people will die."

"Bullshit. You're just trying to save your own ass," Nathan spat. "Tell me what's really going on."

"He's telling the truth," I interjected. "It happened last time there was a power restriction too."

"I don't fucking care!" Nathan bellowed. He gripped the phone so tight his fingers turned white. "Living like this – they're dead either way. I want an answer. Now."

Fransisco swallowed hard. He nodded. "We're feeding it. If we stop, it's going to be angry."

"What is?" Nathan asked. I caught the guard glancing over his shoulder, and turned to look. Another man in a suit was holding a rifle on the opposite balcony.

"Nathan, watch out!" I shouted.

"Put down the phone, Nathan," the guard said. "You have to trust me."

"What is down there?" Nathan shrieked.

"Nathan put it down!"

The guard beside us nodded sharply. A crack split the tumultuous sound of the drill and blood sprayed from Nathan's face. The rifle bullet had punctured straight through the back of his skull to emerge from his mouth. He looked over his shoulder in bewilderment at the man with the rifle, his whole face splitting open as he turned his head.

Two more cracks rent the air from the handgun. Nathan was staggered to his knees. He hadn't let go of the phone. He spat a mouthful of blood onto the floor and rattled off a rapid string of numbers. Another bullet slammed a hole straight through his forehead, but he didn't even hesitate.

The guard lunged at Nathan, but I blocked him with my body and we both went spinning to the ground.

"Authorization granted. Shut it all down," Nathan said.

My face went numb as the butt of the handgun slammed into my forehead. I groped the air blindly and caught hold of the guard's suit jacket, but he ripped free and dove at Nathan. The former manager scrambled backward, screaming into the phone the whole while.

"Do you hear me? My name is James Mattis. I want the whole station offline right now."

The four bullets in Nathan didn't even slow him down as he scrambled away from Fransisco. I locked eyes with Nathan right as he reached the edge of the balcony.

"Did I save them? Did I do the right thing?" Nathan's voice broke with desperation into my headphones. I pulled myself up from the floor, unable to tear my eyes away from his bloody face.

"You did what you thought was right," is all I could muster. Everyone held their breath, looking around at the lights and the humming machines.

"Connect me to the plant," the guard screamed into his headphones. "Tell them to keep the power –"

And suddenly the silence and the darkness were all there was. Red emergency lights flashed along the walkways for a moment, but row by row they snuffed out as the backup generators were overloaded. The lights on every balcony winked out. The hum of every machine spluttered to a stop. The vibrating pressure of the drills grinded to a halt. In the absence of all other light, my eyes adjusted to see faint outlines visible from the red glare in the pit.

Fransisco roared with frustration and ripped his headphones off. He grabbed Nathan by the coat and rammed him against the railing. I leapt to Nathan's aid, but too slow. Nathan didn't make the least move to resist as he was tipped over the balcony to plummet into the abyss. I ran to his aid – too late. The last glimpse of him I saw was a spiral of blood raining through the air in his wake.

"What's going to happen now?" I shouted.

The guard didn't answer with words, but his message was clear enough. He dropped his gun and started sprinting for the door. I should have just followed him, but I couldn't let all of this be for nothing. My feet plodded pulled me like a moth being drawn by flame until I could directly over the balcony and into the abyss.

Somewhere miles below the earth where the drills once tore

through the crust emanated a baleful glow. I watched transfixed as it shifted, seeming to slide from one side of the pit to the other. I turned and ran from the building. Guards, mechanical technicians, doctors – streams of people poured from the place to fill the black vans. The men tethered to the machines were being left behind, but they couldn't have all been dead. I saw one slide to the ground and begin to crawl, only to be trampled beneath a stampede of men in blue.

I helped the man to his feet and dragged him out of the building with me. His lips kept moving as though he were muttering something, but I couldn't hear it over the sounds of panicked screams and thundering footfalls.

No-one seemed to notice that I didn't have a blue suit in the mad escape. I crammed into one of the vans and huddled in the back while it roared up the valley walls. A noisy rush of speculation surrounded me, but I was incapable of joining the conversation. I stayed quiet though, because somehow even describing what I saw aloud would be enough to make it real.

We were about halfway back up the valley when a deafening explosion knocked half of us from the benches to sprawl on the floor. The van bucked and heaved like a wild animal, but managed to stay upright as it roared down the road. There wasn't a back window, so we all had to wait along the right side until the van made a turn up the switchback road before we saw it. The foundations of the building had been detonated and the entire structure slid off into the pit.

The man I had saved from the machine, haggard fellow with a long beard and eyes as white as starlight, kept muttering along the rest of the drive. He was hard to look at because of the bloody sores on his head. The "helmet" he was wearing had wires which plugged directly into his brain, and when I had torn him free, I had left great patches of his scalp behind.

"It can't die. It's already out. It's inside us all."

No-one else spoke along the drive, so they all must have heard him too. We all just fixed our eyes out the window though, afraid to acknowledge what we all knew. I don't know how many people had looked into the pit before they ran, but I'm sure enough of us knew that the red glow wasn't really sliding like I thought at first. It was opening, and from somewhere in the depth of the earth, I had looked into a colossal an eye staring back at me.

After the convoy of vans exited the crumbling valley, we made a stop about a mile away from the plant. I heard mention that others were continuing on to a nearby army base, but six cars (mine included) peeled away from the rest. The vans parked in a sharp circle, bumper to bumper, with their sliding doors all opening toward the middle.

"Everyone out of the vans and into the circle." It was Francisco. He was holding a rifle now, prodding people as they filed out. "Remove any hats, bandages, glasses – anything which obscures your face. Nobody is leaving here until I get a chance to look at their eyes."

He had to be looking for signs of the treatment. The bearded man I had saved was still in the back of our van with me. He looked so thin and weary – I wonder how long he'd been down there. I caught his eye, and the pure white orbs looked back with helpless pleading.

We both flinched as a gunshot echoed throughout the caravan. Then three more shots, one right after the other.

"Filthy animal. Just die already," Francisco said.

Three of us were left in the van: the driver, the haggard man, and me. I was about to step out when emaciated probing fingers clutched desperately at my shirt.

"Help me. Please. I only did what they told me to."

The driver pushed past us to exit in front. If it hadn't been for Nathan's interference, I would have had my first treatment today. Then I would have been the one to be executed, assuming I hadn't already been killed when the building was detonated. These people had been strong armed and manipulated into obeying orders, and now they were being punished by the same people who made them do it.

Besides that, I still wanted more answers. By the enormity of the thing's ancient presence, I had no doubt that it was still alive down there. The people who had been "feeding" it must know as much as anyone what we were up against. Mankind might be diversive in our values at times, but when a common enemy as calamitous as that whispers our doom, we've no choice but to stand together against its oppression. Anyone like Francisco who sought to divide us had to be labeled as an enemy too.

I saw the car keys poking out of the driver's back pocket as he climbed out of the van. I snatched it, applying pressure to his back to distract him. I was trying to be subtle, but he lost his balance and fell straight out of the van onto his knees.

"Hey, what the Hell man?" the driver was loud. Too damn loud. All eyes fell on me.

"That's the guy who helped Nathan!" Francisco shouted. I launched the van door shut just as he was raising his rifle. The haggard man shoved me to the floor, but before I could fight him off, I heard the metallic clang of bullets punching through the door where I'd stood a moment before.

"Let's move!" the bearded man shouted, practically flinging me through the air and into the driver seat. The van roared to life, smashing into the adjacent van to make enough space for us to escape.

More bullets were raining through the wall, and a spider-web of cracks filled the passenger side window. It must be bullet proof glass, but it still wouldn't hold up for long under this assault. The pale-eyed man grunted as a bullet punched through his door and into his shoulder, but the projectile seemed to barely break his skin before deflecting onto the dashboard.

I slammed the car into reverse, plowing into the van behind me and finally edging out enough room to drive. The car shot off down the road like a stone from a slingshot, the bullets rattling off the back as we went.

"Are you hurt?" I asked the man.

"It'll take more than that to slow me down, so don't let it slow you either. Not until we reach the plant."

"We can't stop. That's the first place they'll look," I said.

"They've all had rounds, and that makes 'em targets now. We have to save as many as we can."

"How do you know about that? Who are you?"

"Dillan, I used to be called. Don't seem right to call me that anymore though. Not much of Dillan left."

We didn't have long to compare notes before I reached the plant. Two of the other vans were close on my heels the whole way. I'm not sure if we can fight them off and escape, but having a whole crew that can take bullets like vitamins seems like a pretty solid advantage to me.

I didn't slow as we passed through the checkpoint – rammed straight through the automated gate. I didn't want to risk crossing any more open ground than I had to, so I drove right through the glass door at the front of the building and parked inside.

A bullet skipped by the ground near my feet the second I opened the door. I thought I had gained some ground on them – they couldn't be here already. Another bullet – this was coming from inside the building. They must have begun clearing the plant before I even got there.

Dillan pulled me from the van and covered me with his body as we sprinted through the building. I saw him take two more bullets, both rattling to the ground after impact. Every room we passed was already strewn with bodies.

Robert is dead. Elijah, Megan – both have been decapitated. Undergoing the treatments seems to have given these people a considerable resistance to injury and death, but there's no coming back from that. Dillan and I managed to get to the security surveillance room to see if anyone is left, but it's only a matter of time before they find me. All the video feeds showed men in suits fanning out through the power plant, most armed with long machetes still stained with blood. There's nowhere left for me to go.

"Look! There's a few hanging on," Dillan pointed at one of the screens. Three plant workers – didn't even have a chance to learn their names yet – were huddled in terror in inside one of the supply closets. Dillan showed no hesitation, already bounding out the door as though he knew the way by heart. I started to follow, but he was quick to close the door behind him.

"You stay hidden," he said. "I've been down there too long. There's nothing they can do to me that they haven't already tried, but you – you'll pop like a ripe melon hit by a hammer."

That thought was vivid enough for me to stay put. I watched him on the security feed as he dashed through the hallways with inhuman speed. If you'd asked me before this started, I would have always told you the humans are the good guys and the monsters can go to Hell. Scanning the familiar workrooms and seeing the bloodbath, watching the men with machetes butchering corpses which still struggled to move, then following the trails of bloody footprints all over the building – well maybe there are no good guys here. Shit, I don't know, maybe I'd even be better off joining Nathan and the thing in the pit.

Even thinking that felt wrong though. The visceral terror I experienced while looking down into that great red eye will be enough to haunt me for the rest of my days. If I could just get out of here, I could let the whole mess of them tear each other apart and stay out of it. I was just about to make a run when the door was kicked open.

Francisco stood alone with a bloody machete in each hand. His eyes were wild, looking even less human than Dillan's vacuous stare. Red hand-prints crawled their way around his legs where his victims doubtlessly clutched at him right before the killing blow fell.

"I thought I'd find you here," he said, his dress-shoes making a wet squelch as they plodded across the room toward me. I backed up against the wall, but I was cornered.

"I'm still human. Nothing's been done to me yet," I said. "You don't have to do this."

"I didn't have to kill the others either," he said. "I wanted to. The moment they were plugged into those machines, they were more beast than man."

"We're both men though – we're both on the same side." I was throwing any words that came to mind into the space between us, but nothing seemed to slow his relentless advance. I picked up the office chair and brandished it at him, but he only laughed. Think again, smart-ass.

I hurled the chair into the surveillance screens and watched it smash them to pieces. Francisco's smirk twisted into a snarl.

"I know where the others are," I said. "You won't find them without my help. Not before they escape."

"Fine – I'll let you live," he growled. "Just tell me who is left."

"Not good enough," I replied. "I want to know what's been going on. I want to know everything you know."

"There's not enough time –"

"Then stop wasting it."

He glanced at the broken monitors, then again at the long track of hallway where he came from. Francisco expelled an irritated sigh, propped the chair up, and had a seat. That's when I finally got the whole story.

The valley had been the result of a primal asteroid smashing into the Earth. A scientific expedition to unearth fragments resulted in the discovery of unusual movement within the lithosphere of the Earth's crust. Two tectonic plates had switched directions and were moving against the surrounding mantel, which resulted in much of the mountainous terrain in the area.

The government deployed a mining expedition, looking for clues as to the buildup of pressure. That's when they discovered IT - the Devil – the beast – the monster – whatever impoverished word man has in the face of such a cataclysmic being dwelling beneath the Earth. The scientists speculated that it was much too large to have been carried on the asteroid, but perhaps a seed or a hatchling had survived the journey and grown through the eons into the monstrous form that was uncovered.

The mining further served to disturb the being, and its increasing activity threatened its pending escape. Nothing short of a nuclear weapon was likely to harm it, and this would be impossible to covertly detonate without radiating the groundwater and devastating the nearby population centers.

The only method which seemed to slow the being down was crudely referred to as "sacrifices". The thing displayed considerable less activity after it consumed the initial miners, and subsequent experiments devised a way to feed it via the network of machines and mental energy which I had witnessed. They had powered the machines for the last 20 years, but the sudden cessation of energy seemed to have woken the creature, prompting the shaft's demolition.

If there was more to the story, I didn't get a chance to hear. Francisco was getting impatient, and I didn't know how much more time I could buy. Luckily, I didn't have to. Dillan returned during the recounting, and while Francisco's attention was still distracted, he pounced.

I say pounced, because only an animal could have flown through the air like that pale eyed Demon. Before Francisco could turn his head, Dillan had wrapped his thin arms around the guard's neck and snapped it like a twig. I would have been grateful if it hadn't been for what happened next.

Dillan bit deeply into Francisco's neck while his limp form was still convulsing in Dillan's arms. Even with human teeth, Dillan was able to rip out great chunks of flesh from the man. The teeth sank through the mesh of veins and arteries, crunching through the spine, and straight out the other side. It took almost a full minute for him to gnaw his way through; I don't think he was even eating it, but simply reveling in the satisfaction of his power.

I didn't say a word. I didn't look away. I just let it happen. Every time I thought I knew what I was doing, the scale of events far surpassed my expectations and I was left a helpless onlooker. After Dillan finished, he gave me a sloppy grin before leading me safely through the building. Heads were separated from bodies everywhere we went, and it was clear which were cleanly severed with a machete and which had been gnawed loose. Dillan had saved the other three people though, and I owed him my life as well. That's how I learned the last part of the story that Francisco had left out.

The people hooked to the machines – they weren't just feeding the thing. It wasn't just the human mind passing down the cables, it was also the mind of the beast passing up into them. With each round of treatment, the subjects became a little less human and a little more monstrous, until they became something like Nathan or Dillan that couldn't live and wouldn't die. Dillan had been one of the original scientists who sacrificed himself to the creature over 20 years ago, and he had voluntarily shackled himself to the machine all that time. He's right though, I shouldn't call him Dillan anymore. Dillan died a long time ago.

As soon as I was out to freedom, I parted ways with the subjects. I got in my car and drove as far and as fast as I could. As far as I know, the creature is still down there, buried beneath countless tons of rock in the hills of Colorado. I don't know whether its body is still trying to get out or not, but I don't think it even matters. The beast thinks with Dillan's thoughts and moves with his body, and like an avatar of some forgotten God, he now freely walks the earth. His zealous protection of the other subjects makes me believe it is the beast's imperative to protect his own, so I can only assume that Dillan is now working to either free the creature, or spread its influence by bringing more sacrifices to its underground lair.

I don't know that he can be killed – don't know that he can be stopped. He must feel some sense of human compassion or he never would have let me go as thanks for aiding him, so one enduring hope still remains to me: that once the beast has risen to the height of its size and power, it still finds enough room for mankind.

MOTHER IS BACK

L ove is blind, and so is hope. But something doesn't become true just because you want it badly enough. I don't know why IT is in my house, but I'm not going to be fooled.

I say IT because she isn't my Mom. She looks like her, and talks like her, and smiles like her, but IT isn't her.

The worst part is, Dad doesn't even notice. I saw them dancing in the kitchen when I got home from school. Frank Sinatra was playing on the stereo, his smooth voice propelling their tangled bodies in a slow waltz across the room. My Dad's eyes were closed as his head rested on IT's shoulder, and he seemed genuinely happy—happier than I've seen him in a long time.

I just dropped my backpack and stared. IT let go of my father and hugged me. I stood stiff as a board. Mom never used to hug me when I got home—she knew I liked having my space. But there's no denying how soft and warm she felt, or the lavender odor of her shampoo washing over me.

We're having homemade pizza with the cheese baked into the crust, my Dad's favorite thing in the world. And seeing him so happy, I didn't have the heart to say anything. I just went to my room like a coward. I just pretended everything was fine.

Maybe if I wasn't a little happy to see her too, I would have fought against it harder. It's been hard for all of us since Mom died, but that was no excuse to let IT into our house, just so we could pretend we were a family again.

But Mom—my real Mom—would put me to bed without staying to watch me fall asleep. She would hold on to my Dad's arm when he talked, but she wouldn't dig her nails in so deeply they drew blood. She wouldn't forget to blink for hours at a time.

Two days have passed. I've been struggling to decide what to do—no, that's not quite true. I KNOW what needs to be done, but it would be so much easier to just keep pretending like my Dad. Maybe in time I would even forget that a drunk driver T-boned my Mom's SUV while she and my Dad were coming home from their date.

I'd forget the bloodstains on the asphalt and the hours I spent waiting for her in the emergency room. Maybe I'd even forget how it felt when she didn't come out.

Then again, maybe those are the memories that aren't real—they certainly don't feel real when my mother—I mean IT—sits between us on the sofa to watch the evening news. But letting her be replaced, even if it was easier for Dad and me, wasn't any way to respect my real Mom. It was for her, not for me, that made me finally speak up. "Dad, we need to talk about Mom."

I'd waited until IT went to the bathroom (which doesn't happen nearly as often as it used to) to corner my Dad in his bedroom. He just kept reading, not even returning my gaze. He knew what I was going to say – he just didn't want to hear it.

"Do you remember what happened last month when she was in that accident?"

"It's getting late. You should go to bed so you'll be ready for school tomorrow," Dad said.

"Dad this is serious. Please tell me that you remember."

I heard a FLUSH from the bathroom. There wasn't much time. I'd never get an answer out of Dad with IT here. Dad was watching the bathroom door too—like a kid praying for the bell to ring before the teacher collected homework. The shower began to run, and I let out a deep breath I didn't even realize I was holding. Dad sighed too—there was no getting out of this.

"Yeah, I remember," he said. He stared back into my eyes—I finally had his attention.

"Do you remember the hospital? And... what happened after?"

"Yeah. It was a pretty bad crash—we're all so fortunate that nobody was hurt." His eyes were keen and sharp. He couldn't have forgotten—he was just trying to get me to accept it without having to admit it. For my real Mom's sake though, it had to be said.

"She died, Dad. We went to her funeral."

He didn't flinch—didn't even blink. He just smiled.

"Don't be ridiculous. She's in the bathroom right now." I ran over to him and grabbed him by the shoulders. I shook him, but he didn't fight it. He just kept staring at me like I was a puzzle he was trying to solve.

"You're lying. You know what happened—I know what happened. Why are you lying to me?"

"Aren't you happier this way?" he asked. "If you think about what happened—really think about it—you'll realize this is the best thing for you." There. That was proof. He wasn't trying to evade anymore. He wasn't even averting his eyes in denial.

The shower stopped running, but he kept his eyes on me. That's when I realized I couldn't remember the last time I saw him blink. Dad had been in the accident too why hadn't I wondered why he came out unharmed? I'd been so busy mourning Mom that I hadn't even stopped to think—He must have seen it in my face, because his smile stretched wider.

"Now you understand. But you mustn't let mother know that I told you. She wants to have a family so badly—I'd hate to think what she would do if she found out you didn't think of her that way."

The bathroom door opened. IT stood there, wrapped in a towel. She walked nonchalantly over to my Dad—or who I thought was my Dad—and gave him a kiss. They both turned to look at me.

"What are you still doing awake?" my other mother asked. "Is everything alright?"

"He was just going to bed," my other Dad said. "Everything IS fine, isn't it?"

I nodded.

"Come, let me tuck you in," my other mother started moving toward me, but she stopped when she saw me flinch.

"Let your mother tuck you in," my other Dad's voice was tense with an unspoken threat. "Perfect parents like us deserve to have the perfect son. I hope we won't need to replace him."

He laughed at his own joke, and she put her hand on his arm as she laughed with him. I turned around and headed for my room so I wouldn't have to see the blood dripping down his arm.

VIRTUAL TERROR

I'm going to tell you a secret that I don't tell anyone. I'm a US veteran of the war in Afghanistan. I was stationed in the Uruzgan province when Taliban militants attacked our coalition base. I stood next to a man I knew since training when an RPG-16 hit the three story building behind and buried us both alive, and I held the flag they sent home to his mother after I crawled out. I've tortured a man for information, threatened a child to coerce his parents to cooperate, and of the seven people I know I've killed, only five were fighting back.

But that isn't the secret, because I was just following orders. The secret is that when I'm lying awake at night thinking about all the things done to me—all the things I've done—I'm not traumatized by it all. The secret is I can't sleep because I miss it.

Adrenaline, fear, excitement—it's all the same thing. I've been addicted to it for as long as I can remember. While other kids were riding skateboards around the neighborhood cul-de-sac, you'd find me grinding along the railings of a rooftop. They threw water balloons; I threw rocks. They learned to drive; I organized street races with my brother. By the time I graduated high-school, I already had a juvie record for fighting. The cop sat me down with an army recruitment officer, and they told me my life had only two possible outcomes left.

"You're going to either keep playing at these stupid stunts until you get locked up for life, or you're going to man up and become somebody."

I told them I had changed, and the officer decided my past mistakes wouldn't disqualify me from enlisting. He was wrong for believing me—I just thought shooting guns sounded like a Hell-of-a lot more fun than sitting behind bars. He was right that I would make a damn good soldier though. Sure it wasn't all excitement, but my life had a purpose and I could finally put my natural affinity to good use. For the first time in my life, I was courageous instead of stupid; a hero instead of a freak.

I didn't come home in a body bag like I had expected, but the wheelchair I got was even worse. The bullet between the 2nd and 3rd lumbar bones is still lodged in my spine, and that was it for me. I didn't know if I would ever get out of that chair, but even if I could, my days of living on the edge were over.

And I hated it.

I hated the army for kicking me out (I would have crawled back into battle if they let me). I hated my brother for the pity he gave me, I hated the boring town I was stuck in, and more than anything, I hated myself for not having anything left to live for. I wheel out to the end of my driveway every month to get the disability check they mail me, but besides that, I just sit at home and watch movies.

War movies. Horror movies. Anything that could make me forget, even for a moment, that the most excitement I was ever going to get was checkup time when the nurse leaned over my chair to measure my stagnant pulse. My brother tried to get me to go out with him more, but I couldn't stand being dragged away from my movies. I wish I could be inside them and never come out. That's when he came up with an idea for a compromise:

"How about you and I go down to the new Virtual Reality Arcade?" he asked. "They've even got some immersive horror ones that are so real you'll piss yourself."

"Sounds like my everyday life," I replied.

I ended up going just to shut him up, and the place was actually a lot cooler than I expected. The arcade was divided into personal pods that looked kind of like spaceships. The assistant was a geeky Japanese dude and spoke with a weird inflection which kept swinging back and forth. He probably spent his spare time making fan-made anime dubs or some nonsense. He helped me get setup with the headset and headphones and made sure the wheelchair didn't get tangled up in any of the wires.

As you might have guessed from my introduction, not much impresses me. But holy shit, this technology has come a long way since the blurry 3D movies I saw as a kid. I found myself confronted with a menu hanging in the air which looked real enough to touch. I selected the horror genre, and then a few more options came up.

Select your difficulty. Are you a:

Grandmother with a heart condition.

Kid with something to prove.

SWAT team looking for practice.

A lost soul seeking forgiveness from GOD.

That last one didn't really sound like a degree of fear to me, but they were organized in ascending difficulty so I selected that. Any hope of a thrill immediately disappeared as a fat cartoon Devil with a pitchfork ran across my field of vision.

"I can see you!" he said, waving his pitchfork at me. "Can you see you?"

"No, because I'm not a stupid cartoon. You sure this game is for adults?" I spoke aloud.

"Just wait and see," the Japanese guy said. It was weird hearing him talk when I couldn't see him. I think he was still speaking, but his words were drowned out by the game music which started playing. It sounded like the bad haunted houses they try to push off on kids: full of rubber spiders, cobwebs, and jars of "intestines" which are just spaghetti and meat-sauce.

My viewpoint was walking along a dark road at night which led to a trapdoor in the ground like a cellar. The cartoon Devil popped up again, and I physically prepared myself for death-by-cringing. I get that my brother felt as helpless as I did, and I know he is just trying his best which is still more than can be said for me. I guess it wouldn't hurt to at least pretend to have fun.

"Through me is the space between you and the Divine; infinite and eternal, inseparable and simultaneous," the Devil said, his voice completely different from his last utterance. The words popped with a confusing static noise. It was almost as though instead of hearing the words, I heard every imaginable sound except the words, and my brain filled in the missing space just like it does with white lettering on black paper.

"Are you scared yet?" I faintly heard my brother's voice through the headset. I shrugged and gave a thumbs up. The trapdoor opened, and I lurched in my chair and something hurt in my back as the viewpoint suddenly dropped into the Earth. It felt impressively real, almost like I was on a roller-coaster which plunged into the darkness. I heard my brother laugh at my reaction. I figure that's enough satisfaction for him. No more looking startled, or I'll never hear the end of it.

I could faintly see phosphorescent mushrooms and rocks lighting the deplorable descent. I was continuing to accelerate as I fell, and I even felt the wind blowing in my face. They must have a fan or something to make it seem more real. The Devil was tagging along with me, but he kept glitching and lagging and getting left behind, only to suddenly reappear in front once more. Then I felt a blast of hot air on my face, and I closed my eyes. Whelp, guess this was it folks. I must be in Hell.

I opened my eyes and squinted against the brilliant glare. I always imagined Hell being darker. Was this Hell-fire? My eyes started to adjust, and I could see the sun reflecting sharply off the wide sandy slopes of... of where? Afghanistan?

Someone was talking behind me in Dari, the most common language used there. I couldn't understand it, but I could tell the person was afraid. I turned my chair to shift the viewpoint until I saw an old man kneeling in the dirt before two US soldiers who had their backs to me. One of them was holding a picture of a teenage Afghani boy.

"Do you know who this is? Have you seen him?" the first soldier asked.

"Is this your idea of a joke, bro?" I spoke aloud.

"Your brother went to use the bathroom," the Japanese guy said faintly.

"What kind of game is this?" I asked, but his reply was drowned out by the VR soldiers.

The old man kept pressing his face against the dirt and shaking his head. One of the soldiers dragged him to his feet and shoved the photo in his face.

"You know who this is, don't you? Why are you trying to protect him? Do you know what he's done?"

This wasn't funny to me. I started to take off the headset, but the cartoon Devil appeared in the corner.

"I can see you!" he said in the silly voice. "Can you see you?" Everything was playing so smoothly it could have been real, except for the Devil which kept lagging and glitching. He was little more than a jumping mass of mis-colored pixels.

One of the soldiers kicked the man on the ground. As he pivoted his body, I caught a glimpse of my own face under the helmet. Suddenly I remembered who the old man was. Abdul-Baser was a Qalandar, or mystic, who was suspected of sheltering Taliban operatives in his house. I didn't need to watch to know what happened next.

I took my headset off and handed it to the Japanese guy. "Did my brother put you up to this?" I asked him.

"I can see you," the assistant replied. He handed the headset back to me, but I pushed it away.

"No duh, Sherlock. How did you get this footage?"

"Can you see you?" he asked. His face froze for a second while he spoke, twisted half-way between words. There were a couple of empty pixels obscuring his mouth, but I could tell he was smiling when he handed me back the headset. I touched his hand – warm and real.

Well, I don't know what was going on, but this certainly captured my attention better than any movie. I slowly took the headset from him, and the assistant nodded and smiled while I put it back over my eyes.

"Hahahaha," the cartoon Devil laughed in a good-natured way. "I played a trick on you: once for what you've done."

Flash—I was beating Abdul-Baser inside a holding cell. Flash—I was back in the desert next to the cartoon Devil. I saw it for less than a second, like a single frame inserted into a movie.

"Yeah, you tricked me alright," I answered. "But you didn't scare me. You think I don't remember everything I saw? I wasn't scared then, and I'm not scared now."

The scene suddenly dissolved, and I was falling through the Earth again. I seemed to be going deeper this time because the tunnel was lit by flowing veins of lava now instead of mushrooms. I sat calmly in my chair, actually looking forward to what came next. I don't know if I was drugged, or having a stroke, or if the Devil really was trying to teach me a lesson, but I was excited to see just how far the rabbit-hole went.

This time it was pitch black when I stopped. Crashed would be a better word though because I felt it. It was like my whole body had slammed into a wall. This trick could make me feel things? Could something here beat me? Or torture me? For a second I actually did start to get scared, but then I reached out with my hands and felt carpet beneath my fingers. That's right, I was still in the VR arcade. I had just fallen out of my chair somehow. Still wearing the headset and seeing nothing but the blackness I landed in, I pulled myself hand-over-hand and crawled back into my wheelchair.

"I can see you," the static-y absence of words said. "Can you see you?" The Devil rose in front of me, but his appearance had changed as much from that cartoon Devil as his voice had. The shape was dark, but it wasn't just like the lights were off. Ordinary dark is the absence of light, but the presence before me was the impossibility of it. In that moment before him, I couldn't even remember what it was like to see, but I could still sense his form through the emotional weight it carried.

His horns were as sharp as being stabbed by the love of your life after you sacrificed everything to bring her joy.

His face was the burden of holding your dying father in your arms while both of you knew you could have saved him if only you'd tried harder.

His body was the shape of a long life spent in quiet desperation after all living matter had wasted away and you alone remained to dwell upon your regret.

"Twice for who you are," the presence said.

He reached out to touch me, but I couldn't let him. Somehow I felt I would become like him, an unreal embodiment of misery and pain, if the presence of his being were to overlap with my own. It wasn't fear that made me rip off the headset—fear is something consciously recognized in the brain. My terror was something much deeper and primitive, the sort of thing which stirred my ancient ancestors into action to prolong their own purposeless existences in the face of some greater dread of the unknown.

I tore off my headset and headphones and threw them into the assistant's face. My brother wasn't there, but I wasn't going to wait for him. I sprinted out of the building, bursting out into the bright clear light of my familiar hometown. Boring? How could anything be boring about this place which brought me into this world and formed me into who I am? I ran as fast and hard as I could, taking in deep lungfuls of clean air which filled my body with hope and jubilation. I had my whole life ahead of me, and nothing I had done or been could ever change that. I couldn't remember the last time I felt this good. Hell, I couldn't even remember the last time I walked outside—And it hit me. I couldn't remember the last time I walked because I couldn't walk. I slowed down and looked at my legs pumping the concrete beneath me. I could feel the blood roaring in my veins and the pressure of my feet on the ground. But I could also see that one leg lagged slightly behind the other even when I stood still, and that it was filled with dead blurry pixels. I walked the rest of the way home, just enjoying how good it felt to move and trying not to look at my glitching legs.

"Three times for what you will do," said the voice which wasn't a voice. My brother was waiting for me in my home, although every instinct within me screamed with the common recognition that it wasn't my real brother.

"Oh but I can't trick you, can I?" his mouth moved, but it was the silly cartoon Devil's voice which came out. "You're not scared of anything."

I reached up to my face, but the headset wasn't on anymore. I turned around and started walking upstairs as quickly as I could. My heart was pounding in my chest like a caged animal trying to escape. My brother-who-wasn't-my-brother followed me up to my room.

"You think you're so strong, don't you? That you don't need anybody. But you know what? There's no-one else here, so you can tell me the truth."

The singsong cartoon voice was grating on my nerves. Wherever I was, I wasn't in control. There was no point in trying to outrun something in my own mind. I turned around to face him.

"I'm not afraid of you or your tricks. What do I have to do to get out of here?" I asked. My voice didn't even shake. I balled my hands into fists, and they were firm and ready.

"Are you sure you want out?" he asked, but it was back in my brothers voice. "Your legs work in here, but they won't out there."

"I don't care, I want out," I said.

"Why? Unless you really are afraid." He smiled, and it froze in a glitch. The face was so warped I could barely recognize him. I couldn't stand to look—I wanted to wipe that smile off. If he wasn't going to be reasoned with, then I would have to do things my own way.

"I'm not afraid!" I shouted. I grabbed him by the front of his shirt and punched him straight across the face. "You're the one who is trapped in here with me!"

"Then what do you feel?" he asked.

The face felt solid and I could feel the bones of his jaw moving from the impact. The instant I hit him however, his face was replaced with Abdul-Baser. The old man started to pull a handgun from behind his back, but I punched him again, almost breaking my hand against his cheekbone. The face changed again, and this time I was looking into my own eyes. That was it—that was the way out. He was reeling from my blows, and I snatched the handgun from his limp grasp.

"That's not going to do anything to me -"

"You're right, it won't," I interrupted, my mind racing with the possibilities, "because you're just pretending to be me. It will however, work on me."

I put the gun in my mouth and pulled the trigger. He jumped at me faster—faster than humanly possible—and knocked my hand aside. The gun went off with a deafening ring, and he fell to the ground in a heap.

"My turn," I said. I put the gun in my mouth, pleased to find that my hand still wasn't shaking, and pulled the trigger.

"I can see you. Can you see you?"

I opened my eyes in the hospital. A doctor was leaning over me, shining a light in my mouth. My head hurt like Hell. I tried to nod, but a searing pain engulfed my awareness and I froze up—almost like a glitch.

My father was sitting beside my bed. He wouldn't say a word until after the doctor left, but eventually he told me what happened. I had entered some kind of fit at the VR arcade and fell out of my chair, probably caused by the bullet shifting in my spine. My brother took me home and stayed with me to make sure I was okay, but I pulled a gun and tried to kill myself. He managed to stop me, but the gun went off and hit him. I shot myself after that, but the bullet went straight through my jaw and missed my brain.

I want to go back to my old life—Hell I want to go all the way back to day one and do it all again, but I'd settle for just a day.

I used to think I had nothing left to hope for. I used to think I wasn't afraid of anything. Now I know I was wrong about both, and that they're both the same thing:

The static sneer, half-contempt, half-agony, glitching across my father's face.

VICARIOUS

Watching my son Andrew kick the winning goal. That's
my dream. Or catching his eye as he holds the science-
fair trophy, head held upright with the pride of our
triumph. I still remember how my own father looked the night my
high school football team won state. Two of my teammates hoisted
me onto their shoulders, and when Dad saw me, it was as though he
forgave himself for every mistake he's ever made – all because he
raised me into the man I had become.

I don't care what Andrew decides to pursue in life, I just want him
to be great at it. Isn't that what all father's want? He's going to be eight
next month, and I know the next generation's best (his future competition) have already begun to refine their talents. Mozart began
playing at 3, Picasso could draw before he could talk, and Michael
Jackson was performing live by 6 years old.

It's taken awhile for Andrew to find his niche, but lately he's
started getting really into mountain and trick biking. His mother
(Amy) thinks it's too dangerous, but I know how important it is to be
passionate about your skillset, so I encourage him every chance I get.
Amy just doesn't understand. She would see one little cut or bruise,

and then suddenly that's all that mattered. I say if you aren't willing to bleed a little to achieve your dreams, then you don't deserve to have them come true.

That's why we started practicing in secret. I'd tell Amy that we were just going to ride around the block. We'd both pedal until the house was out of sight, then we'd blast off toward the hills wearing the same conspiratorial grin. He was good too, fearlessly bouncing down cliffs and rocky slopes that would have even given me pause. Every day he came home a little stronger, and a little more confident than the day before. Every day I knew it was worth all the exhaustion and sneaking around, because he was going to be the best and I was going to be the one who made it happen.

That is, until the day when it wasn't worth it anymore. We'd just gotten home from a trick competition at the skate park, although it was hardly fair since Andrew was still 8 and all the other kids were teenagers. Andrew slipped up while trying a nose-wheelie, and was disqualified before even getting to show off what he'd been practicing. We were both so frustrated, but I was still proud of him for not wasting any time and getting straight back to the hillside to practice.

I could tell he wasn't being cautious this time. It was my fault for applauding and egging him on to tackle bigger boulders and obstacles. When you're disappointed, you can either give up or try harder, and I just didn't want my boy to quit. When he asked if I thought he could ramp off a rock to clear the ravine, I told him what I thought he needed to hear.

"You can do anything you put your mind to," I said.

We were wrong for believing in each other. I shouted when I saw his back tire slipping right before he made the jump, but it was already too late to do anything about. The bike pitched forward and hurled him straight over the handlebars, twisting the bike around on top of him as he flipped. Long before I heard the grotesque snapping of his impact, I knew he wasn't going to walk away from this alright.

Maybe if I hadn't pushed him so hard. Or so soon. Maybe if I hadn't allowed my own guilt and fear to make me hesitate before I plunged into the ravine after him, then maybe I could have saved him. It took a full ten seconds of listening to his agonized groans before I could force myself to gaze down at what used to be my son. He'd landed directly on his head, but the helmet did nothing to prevent his neck twisting halfway around his body under the power of the impact. He'd been jarred so hard that part of his spine ruptured straight through his skin to greet the air with a bloody shine.

Screw competing. If he even survived a trip to the hospital, then I'd still spend the rest of my life feeding him with a spoon. But this was my fault and he was my son, so there could never be a choice. I took the first step of the never ending journey down the slope toward him.

"Let's go home, Dad."

The words should have been enough to bring tears to my eyes, but instead I froze in the grip of absolute terror. It wasn't my son who said it – I didn't even know if my son could talk anymore. I turned slowly, careful not to lose my grip on the pebbled earth and topple helplessly down the ravine.

"I'm okay Dad. Let's go."

Andrew – or at least someone who looked exactly like my son, all the way down to his freckles and the mustard stain on his sleeve – was waiting for me on the top of the hill. Back down the ravine, I still saw the twisted and broken version of the same boy lying there.

"Come on," the unharmed Andrew said. "Race you back."

He hopped on his bike and skidded fearlessly along the hillside. His speed and dexterity surpassed the old Andrew, even on his best days. As beautiful as it was watching him fly over the rocks, the sight was impossible to appreciate with the wet gurgle of coughing blood sounding from further down.

I had to make a choice, and judging by the amount of blood pooling on the rocks below, I had to make it fast. I could go down the treacherous slope and lift my son into my arms. I could drag him to the hospital, burning through my energy and savings in the vain fight toward a subnormal life. I could explain to Amy that I had lied to her, and that it was my fault that our life would never be the same. And if after all that Andrew were still to die, then I know she would leave me and I would have nothing left.

"Don't worry Dad. We're going to win next time. I promise."

Or I could turn around and leave with ... with what? Watching him race up and down the hills, the answer was obvious. I could turn around and leave with my son, and none of this will have ever happened.

"I'll be right there," I said. "First one home gets ice cream for dinner."

Climbing up the hill after Andrew – after my son – it wasn't as hard as I thought it would be. It was abject relief to see his beaming face waiting for me at the top. The only hard part was when I had already lost sight of the ravine and was headed home, only to hear a voice dissipating on the wind behind me.

"Please don't go. I need you Dad."

I gripped my son's hand – my new son – and held on tight all the way home.

For the next few weeks, I wouldn't let Andrew out of my sight. I drove him to school instead of letting him take the bus. I picked him up for lunch, then again when school got out, taking him to his favorite places and spending all of my time helping him practice. I was trying my best to be a good father, and trying even harder not to think about what that meant. I thought about going back to the ravine to at least bury the body, but every time I began to work up enough courage to face that broken corpse, my new son seemed to appear wanting to spend time with me.

By the end of the first month, life had gone back to normal and it was like nothing ever happened. The new Andrew was identical to the old, even sharing the same memories, and habits, and everything. By the second month, I'd even forgotten that horrible day ever passed, although sometimes the echo of those words being torn by the wind still slip into my brain as I lay down to sleep at night.

I need you Dad.

But I was a good father. I did everything for my boy, and I knew he was going to repay me by becoming the best biker the world had ever seen.

It wasn't until Andrew was 12 years old when I began to notice behavioral anomalies that I couldn't explain. But surely the real Andrew – I mean the *old* Andrew – he would have had his own changes by this age. I tried to tell myself that he was just starting to go through puberty, but even Amy began to feel that something wasn't right.

"Do you know what I caught Andrew doing last night?" she told me one morning over breakfast.

"He's going to be a teenager soon. I'm sure I don't want to know."

"He was eating a bug!" she declared. "A big shiny cockroach. Just munching it right up, looking as proud as a kitty cat who caught his first mouse."

Then there was the rustling outside our window late at night. A dozen separate occasions I must have heard it – like someone was in the bushes watching us. Amy wanted me to check it out, but I just kept imagining Andrew running through the field like a wild creature, biting the heads off animals or digging up worms. I think I was happier not knowing.

It wasn't just that either. Some nights we'd catch him awake at four in the morning, face an inch from the mirror, just staring at himself and giggling. Another time he had a butterfly knife – God knows where he got it – and was peeling away the skin on the back of his hand. He'd exposed a strip of bloody muscle and tendons running all the way from the tip of his finger running halfway up his forearm. I took the knife away and demanded what he was doing, but all he said was:

"Just curious what goes on under there, *Dad*."

He grinned when he said *Dad*, stressing the word like it was our shared secret. Neither of us had ever mentioned that day on the hillside, but it felt like he not only remembered, but was actively using it to blackmail me.

The worst was when he was trying to get something out of me, like when he decided he needed a laptop. I told him to wait for his birthday and turned to leave, but then he replied with:

"Please don't go. I need you *Dad*."

Those words were burned into my subconscious like a trigger. Whenever he said it, I couldn't even look him in the eye. I'd just cave and give him what he wanted. It's not because he was the boss of me or anything. There's nothing wrong with me wanting to be a good father.

All the while, he kept practicing with his bike. He was the best I'd ever seen, and anyone who saw him swore the same. He refused to participate in anything big because he "wasn't ready yet", but he blew all the local competitions a new one. People started coming from miles around to watch him perform, and as soon as they found out I was his father, I'd have a dozen hands clapping me on my back or offering me a beer.

"You must be so proud of him," they'd all say.

"Of course I am. He's my son."

This coming weekend is going to be his biggest one yet. Some YouTube personality will be recording the whole thing, and I know the second the world sees what my boy can do, he'll be too big to ever put back in a box. I tried to warn him about how things will change after that, but he wouldn't listen to me.

"Isn't this what you wanted?" he asked. He sat down on his bed, giving me a look of wide-eyed, blameless sincerity as though he was a perfect angel sent here to bless my life. Bullshit act.

"Don't pretend you know what I want," I told him. I was sick of that grin he always wore. "You go if you want to, but you're going alone. I don't want any part in this media circus." I turned to leave, trying to get out of his room quick enough before he said –

"Please don't go. I need you *Dad*."

I don't know why, but that time it really got to me. It wasn't just a little kid trying to get away with something. This was an active taunt, manipulation of the highest degree. I thundered back around to face him, hoping to put my foot down and reestablish myself as the authority figure.

"If I ever hear you say that again, I'm going to beat your ass until –
"

"Until what?" he interrupted. "Until I'm as broken as he was?"

My breath caught as though someone had reached down my throat and grabbed it from the inside. He's never spoken of the other Andrew before. I'd hoped to God he never would. My hands involuntarily clenched into fists, so tight I could feel my muscles trembling all the way up my shoulders.

"It was never about me succeeding, was it?" he asked, that arrogant grin spreading across his face. "You just wanted a little for yourself, didn't you? Only now the light's grown too bright, and you're getting scared."

"I want you out of this house. Now." I've never spoken like that before in my life, so low it was closer to a growl than words.

"You sure Mom agrees with you on that?"

"Don't call her that. Get out. I want you gone."

"Throw away one son, and it's his fault." Andrew wasn't backing down. He was standing an inch from my face now. "Throw away two, and suddenly it's yours."

I threw my fist at his face with everything I got. Maybe I could break his nose, or knock his teeth out. Maybe I could scar him up – anything to make this impostor look less like my son. I hadn't realized just how strong he'd grown though, and when he swatted my fist away, it felt like the bones in my hand were rearranging themselves.

"Don't be like that, *Dad*," he said. "You wanted me to be the best, didn't you?"

I grunted through the pain and swung again. My eyes could barely follow the blur of his movements. He locked my outstretched arm against his side, and before I knew what was happening, he'd spun me around and slammed me into his closed door. I tasted blood, and my arm strained so bad against his pressure that it must be about to dislocate. I bit my tongue, trying not to scream. I couldn't let Amy know her son was a monster.

"What do you want from me?" I had to spit and mumble to push the words through the bubbling blood and the pressed door frame.

He let me go and laughed as I slid to the floor. "I'm not like you. I don't need anything from anyone. I just like being on your side of the world. Where I'm from, we don't have families like this."

I strained for any sign that the words were changing as he spoke. I didn't want to look, but an irresistible urge forced my head to turn. I wanted him to be a monster. Some horrible grey-skinned ghoul with tentacles, or a dozen gaping maws – anything but what was there. Anything but that mockery of my son which grinned down at me.

"What are you?" I asked. "Where are you from?"

"Come with me this weekend," he said, "or I'll take you there."

It was undeniably a threat. I don't know if he was a Demon crawled up from Hell, or some specter from a nether world too horrible to contemplate, but lying there on the ground in a growing pool of my own blood, I finally understood how powerless my real son must have felt waiting for me.

Rustle. Like something in the bushes outside the window. Then: "Nunquam suade mihi vana! Sunt mala quae libas. Ipse venena bibas." 1

The voice was coming from outside, sounding so familiar and so alien, like listening to your own voice through a recording. Andrew recoiled as though struck. He snarled, launching himself at the window. Finally the illusion of his humanity was beginning to shed, and beneath the distorting fabric of his T-shirt, I could see the red blisters spreading. The creature roared as it smashed into the glass, but a brilliant light radiated from the panel and repelled it like an electrically charged fence.

"Exorcizamus te omni satanica potestas." 2

I could just make out a hunched shape outside the window, but it was immediately obscured by another blinding flash of light which penetrated through the morphing creature. Boils the size of my head were swelling and rupturing down the length of its back. Black pus flowed freely down its sides. Again it slammed itself into the window, but this time it vanished straight through the portal without so much as cracking the glass behind.

By the fading brilliance, and without the creature blocking my view, I saw the figure on the other side of the glass. Its back was as twisted and monstrous as the creature who had just been banished, and its face was unevenly stitched together with a network of scars, burns, and unsealed holes which allowed me to see straight through his cheek and into his mouth.

Through all the disfigurement and abuse, it was clear that nothing which has happened to him – nothing that could ever happen to him – could ever disguise the fact that he was my son.

It was difficult to explain, and even more difficult for Amy to understand, but she confessed that she always felt something wasn't right and was relieved to finally have an answer. Andrew, my real boy, told us that the thing was called an Irasanct, and they exist as power-less swarms of unresolved desires. Sometimes they will find their way to us through minute holes that exist between dimensions, although they remain harmless until they are given power by our acceptance of them.

The Irasanct cannot remain here long without taking a form, and even once they are accepted, they can only stay so long as they replace the void they left behind with someone from our side. When I took the creature home as my son, I gave it the strength to banish my true son to the other side, although the recounting of his journey there is another story altogether.

The real Andrew had managed to return four months ago, watching us from the bushes and protecting us against the Irasanct. When I asked why he didn't reveal himself sooner, he said he was waiting for the time when he knew I would accept him as my son.

To come back to us after what I had done to him – after every-thing he's been through – pride does not even begin to approach the admiration I feel for him. He wouldn't stay with us long though, saying there are more of the Irasanct leaking through at an increasing rate. Barely a teenager and already deformed from his injuries and his trials spent on the other side, Andrew is going to keep fighting them. And he's going to be the best there ever was.

I watched him go early this morning. I didn't want him to leave, but I know I had no right to speak the words in my heart.

"Please don't go. I need you son."

Note: My son spoke indecipherable Latin at the time, but he has since taught me the spells which translate to:

1: What you offer me is evil. Drink the poison yourself.

2: We cast you out, every satanic power.

THE ANGEL DOLL

"Run away, or you will die tonight."

That's what I heard from beside me at 2 AM.

"What did you say?" I asked my husband. He didn't answer. Good, then it wasn't important. I had to use the bathroom anyway, but nestled under a down-comforter with our tabby cat Meeps snuggled between us made me seriously consider my options. Wet the bed? Too sticky. Excavate myself from the pile of blankets and face the cold hard bathroom tiles? Please, no. Hold it in and develop a weak bladder?

Eh, we were all going to get old and fall apart someday, anyway. I had no intention of getting out of that bed for anything short of a nuclear strike. Just when I started flirting with the other side of consciousness though, I heard it again:

"Run away, or you will die tonight."

"Wake up Jordan. I'm having a bad dream." I sat up and shook my husband's shoulder. He grunted and halfheartedly pushed my hand away. That should do the trick. But as long as I was up…

I uprooted Meeps and climbed out of bed. He gave me that "how dare you, peasant" expression that all cats have mastered without parallel. I was half-way to the bathroom, and wondering if I could teach myself to piss while sleepwalking when—"Run away, or—"

I stopped and rubbed my eyes. That wasn't my husband's voice. It wasn't coming from my bed at all. That was unmistakably from inside my closet. Don't get me wrong, I'm a strong independent woman. I kill my own spiders and everything, but there's no decent minded person anywhere who could hear that without screaming bloody murder.

It wasn't really a scream—more of a "what the thunder-flicking-fuck was that?"— but it was loud enough to get Jordan on his feet in a second. It was so cute how protective he was of me. My father never approved of him because Jordan had a cocaine trouble as a teenager, but to me he had always been the perfect man.

"What's going on? Are you alright?" Jordan asked.

"There's someone here," I replied with the same wide-eyed sincerity a four-year-old might muster regarding the monster under her bed.

"Honey come back to bed. There isn't anyone-"

"Run away, or you will die tonight."

"There!" I said. "It's coming from the closet."

"I didn't hear anything."

"Check it for me? Please? Pleeeeease?" I gave him my best impersonation of a desperate puppy. He sighed and headed for the door.

"Don't! I changed my mind!" I said. "There's a murderer inside!"

"I wouldn't worry," he replied. "It's probably just my laptop randomly un-pausing a video or something. Besides, if it was a murderer, he'd just kill us in our sleep."

"Real reassuring. Thanks."

Jordan opened the door, but his body was blocking my view. I hopped around on my toes to peer over his shoulder.

My Doll—my Angel Doll, the one I'd had since I was a baby—was lying on the ground. I rushed to pick her up, reverently cradling her and completely forgetting about the monster for a moment. She wasn't really an Angel, just a Raggedy-Ann Doll with little cloth wings sewn onto her back. But she was mine, in the same way as my hair was brown or my skin was fair; she was part of me.

"Well there's nothing in here, so I'm going back to bed," Jordan said, slumping off across the floor.

"What do you think knocked her off the shelf though?" I asked. "And look! Her stomach is all ripped open."

"I'll call a doctor in the morning. Goodnight." He was already consumed by the indistinguishable blanket blob.

I sat there on the floor holding my Doll. We were inseparable when I was a kid. This doll had endured everything, including a part-time gig as a bulldog's chew-toy, and the lead investigator of a vacuum's inside. She had been ripped, stained, shredded, and impaled a dozen odd times, and Dad had always been able to fix her for me before. Of course, now that he was gone I would have to learn to fix it myself, but that was okay. When I have a kid of my own, they'll probably need me to fix it for them too.

I gently poked the leaking fluff back into the Doll's chest cavity and –

"Shit snacks". Something stung my finger, prompting its quick passage to my mouth. Was something in there? I opened the Doll a little further, careful not to lose any of the precious stuffing, and pulled out a tightly folded sheet of paper. I recognized the handwriting immediately.

Dear Amelie

It was the same handwriting with the same loopy "D" I had seen every year on my birthday card. Every year except this one, anyway. I sat cross-legged on the floor and Meeps wiggled her way into my lap while I read my father's secret letter.

Dear Amelie

The telling of an adventure becomes an adventure in itself. Fantasies will unburden your spirit from the constraints of reality, and horror is as thrilling for the author as it is for the reader.

But my story is not so easily told. Every time I try to bleed my memories free, I am frozen with helpless shame and guilt. The events of my youth have haunted me throughout my life, and I fear I will not go quietly into death until I have found peace in their recounting.

I hope you will forgive me for inscribing my story in verse. It is the only way I know how to distance myself from the pain and turn the tragedy of my life into something beautiful. I hope before the end of your days you too will find a way to burn your darkness with such brilliant fire as to illuminate the way for others.

Forever yours,

-Dad

It should be said, right at the start,
all happy families are the same.
For joys are shared in equal parts,
though misery is unique in blame.
It comes in many varied forms,
but you will know it when it's seen.
When the perfect mask is torn,
and sundered at the seams.
So it was when I was young,
a son first and child after.
Playing with father was endless fun;
and every shared moment laughter.
I learned how to view the world
from astride my father's knee.
And when the night left me curled,
his stories would bring sleep.
But life is heavier for some than others,
and it pressed hard upon this man.
A war waged between him and my mother—he stopped trying and
simply ran.
I was left to wondering,
where my father went at night.
Then home late with blundering,
too much drink had made him fight.

One night the drink brought a rage
that I had never seen before.
The beatings could not be assuaged,
so out I fled through the kitchen door.
I wandered the streets very late,
hiding from that awful noise,
not knowing it was my fate,
to find salvation in a toy.
Tossed upon garbage and refuse,
the broken Doll of an Angel lay.
It was worn-deep from over use,
but I still took her home to play.
When the violence was lit by booze,
I held it to keep my fears at bay.
Then finally when came a truce,
I would thank her when I prayed.
The quiet never lasted, nor the peace,
and I kept the doll close beside.
Once I was too bruised to sleep,
and waited instead to finally die.
Instead the Doll began to speak,
telling me that I was safe.
That even when the world was bleak,
I must trust the Doll with faith.
The Doll offered more than reality,
and proved my great escape.
It would sing tales of fantasy:
of villains, heroes and their capes.
Beasts and monsters with their fangs,
of highway men and roaming gangs,
who were locked up tight with a clang,
prevailing justice when she sang.
Since then we never parted ways,
where I went, the Doll followed after.

She sat beside me when I played,
or sheltered me in the attic rafters.
The doll peaked from my bag at school,
(the other children laughed, I know).
But I didn't mind the jeering fools
who didn't know how to take a blow.
I wish my mother had a Doll
to take away her pain—to free her back against the wall,
and cease the falling of the cane.
I offered the Angel Doll to her,
but she insisted that I keep.
Saying it was too late to deter,
the wounds which cut too deep.
One night her screaming wouldn't end,
and I offered up a solemn plea:
That even this hurt would mend,
I begged the Angel answer me.
No comfort now like in the past,
the Doll offered this foresight:
"Run away," she said at last.
"Or you will die tonight."

I STOPPED READING. I WAS SO TIRED, I HAD COMPLETELY FORGOTTEN about what made me get out of bed in the first place. I stared at the coarse face with its black sewn on buttons and flame of red hair. It was just a Doll—the same Doll it had always been.

"Jordan?" My voice was timid. I shouldn't wake him up again. It was stupid to think—"Yeah?"

"Do you trust me?"

"Of course, honey. What are you still doing up?"

"I want to get out of the house, now."

The pile of blankets slouched aside, and he sat up to stare at me. He looked at the letter in my hands, then nodded. He put on his robe and handed me mine, and we walked out the front door in silence.

"Where are we going?"

"Away," I said. "Can you drive?"

It was like he could sense when something was important to me. He smiled and nodded. We didn't need words. I hopped into the passenger seat and flipped on the reading light to finish the letter while he drove.

"Run away," she said at last.
"Or you will die tonight."
I grew angry and yelled louder,
but no other sound came out her.
I flung her from my window seat,
out of the house, into the street.
Telling her she was no good,
if the Angel no longer could
speak and tell me calming tales
drowning out the fighting wails.
Mother was in pain, a bestial yelp—through the thin walled home.
I couldn't face my fear and help—I couldn't bear the sound alone.
I ran until I was out of breath,
far away from here.
I didn't care if I met my death,
I willed to disappear.
Snow and bitter winds cut in
probing through my jacket thin.
I leaned against a tree to rest,
yet dared not chance to sleep in less
I would waken to find myself
alone in the world with no one else,
or waken not, stiff frozen skin
a tribute to what might have been.
I wish I hadn't thrown the Doll away

when I needed her the most.
It wasn't her fault she had to say
that death was flying close.
The morning found my mother dead
as the Doll that I once found.
Forsaken and thrown on garbage bed;
a trash heap burial mound.
For many years, a lost Raggedy-Ann,
my Doll must have searched the Earth.
Until she found not a boy, but a man,
and his lady who was giving birth.
I had run so far from life,
that I had found a life anew.
The Doll gazed upon my beautiful wife,
and the child who now grew.
The Angel Doll lay down softly,
knowing her part had been played.
The boy was gone, and though missed awfully,
time's direction could not be swayed.
I found her there, against hospital door,
still and quiet as the dead.
I scooped her up and to her swore
to fix her tattered threads.
By my word, she was cured
of the ills this world had shown.
My baby girl brought in the world
was gifted with a Doll newly sewn.
I will never make the mistakes
that drove my mother to her grave.
And the Doll will never lie awake
to take away your pain.

I WAS IN TEARS BY THE TIME I FINISHED. DAD WOULD HAVE BEEN 58 ON the first of May. Jordan kept giving me these nervous glances, but he was respectful and didn't pry.

"How much further, you think?" is all he asked. "There's a motel up ahead. Want to spend the night there?"

These weren't pretty tears. They were big, snotty, sloppy globs. I was too choked up to answer, but he pulled into the parking lot, anyway. He understood me so well, it was like he was made for me.

I held the Doll while I fell asleep in the motel. I knew I owed Jordan big for this. I felt so stupid for dragging us out here, but the letter and my cry had been cathartic and I was so tired that I felt oddly at peace. It was the best I'd felt since the funeral. And who knows, maybe some freak tornado will hit the house and I'll know some part of Dad really is still out there watching over –

"Run away, or you will die tonight."

It came from the Doll: a small voice like a child who was afraid of being caught.

"I already did run away." I felt too guilty to wake Jordan up again after all this, so I whispered the reply.

"Not far enough. He's still with you," she replied. I couldn't see the Doll's mouth moving or anything, but there was nothing else which could have been talking to me. I looked over at Jordan's harmless, sleeping body. Was I really going to trust a phantom voice over my husband who I've known and loved for years?

But it wasn't just any voice. Somehow it was my father trying to reach me, and him I would trust till the ends of the Earth. I took the Doll and my phone and quietly slipped out the door. I wasn't going to leave him stranded, so I took an UBER back home. While we were driving, I wrote him a long text message thanking him for being so understanding and apologizing for my behavior. I told him how much he meant to me, and that all of this was just because I was having such a hard time with Dad's passing. He was so kind that he probably wouldn't have even needed it, but it felt good to tell him anyway.

I hope he got a chance to read it before he died. The next I woke, it was to the hammering of police on my front door. They informed me that my husband was found dead in his motel room with three bullet holes in his chest. Future investigations revealed the coke habit wasn't as ancient history as I thought. He owed a lot of money to the wrong people, and they followed our car to the motel. If it wasn't for the Doll, I'd be dead too.

I still think Dad was wrong about Jordan though. I don't regret a minute of our time together. And Dad was wrong about another thing too—the Angel Doll was going to have to lie awake with me for a long time before she can take away the pain.

DON'T LET HIM STEAL MY CHILD

I'm not afraid of the darkness. Spiders don't bother me, nor do snakes or heights or any of the regular things. I'm afraid of the child growing inside me, breathing my blood, displacing my organs, until he eventually rips his bulbous head free from my body and leaves me in ruin. I'm afraid that I will resent all the pain and obligation and loss of opportunity in life, and that all that hatred will make it impossible for me to love him.

I'm still more terrified that that I WILL love him—so much that it hurts. So much that I sacrifice everything for him, neglecting myself and my friends... until the day when his own ambitions pull him away from me, and I'll be left mourning the dissolution of my dreams and the emptiness of my life. And then I will sit down my aching limbs and wait for the weariness of old age to erode my cherished memories and free me from this heart-breaking desire to be someone. Then I will bless the day when I finally forget to ask myself what might have been if only I had been selfish and lived my life for me.

I wasn't afraid at the beginning though. I thought I wanted it—that we wanted it. My husband Kirk and I had just moved into our first house, and I was ready. Sure we still fought about stupid things, but we loved each other, and that should have been enough to make him love the child too.

"Okay. Do you want to make the appointment to take care of it, or should I?"

That's all he said. We'd been married a year, and he didn't even ask if I wanted to keep it. We started to argue, and then the fight took on a life of its own in that insidious way which leaves us screaming at each other about nothing and everything. I thought he was being immature —he thought I was the one who needed to grow up and quit painting. I said he didn't take enough initiative at work, and he said I didn't respect him. Before I knew what was happening, his pickup was spraying gravel in my face as I sobbed incoherently in the driveway.

I didn't see him again for four months, which was more than enough time for me to doubt every decision I've ever made in my entire life. Then suddenly one night he was crawling into bed at 2 AM, stinking like death, blubbering apologies and promises. I was so relieved that I didn't even mind that he was drunk. We were intimate as a husband and wife should be, and when I fell asleep on his chest afterward, I thought everything was going to be okay.

"I'm so happy you came back," I whispered, nestled against him.

"I changed my mind," he said. "I want the baby now."

"He's yours," I promised as I drifted off to sleep.

There was so much blood when I woke up that I thought I'd been stabbed. I rushed to the bathroom, screaming for Kirk to help me, but he was nowhere to be found. A miscarriage doesn't just plop out and leave you as good as new. The baby drained from me over the whole next day, taking my soul with it. Big bloody clots, leaving me shrieking in anguish on the bathroom floor. I chanced to see myself in the mirror, and the sight of the network of bloody trails running down my thighs was enough to make me smash my fist straight through the glass. The pain was good. It reminded me that I had a body outside of the one that had just died.

I couldn't flush it. I couldn't toss it. I couldn't even touch it. I just left it there on the floor and crawled back to my empty bed. I tossed and turned for hours until the clenching pain subsided, but it was nothing compared to the pain of knowing Kirk did this to me. I don't know how, or why, but when he came back last night, he killed my baby. And if my feelings in that moment were any indication, then he might have killed me too.

I wasn't expecting to see Kirk again. I took myself to the doctor as soon as I was able to drive, and that was when I got my first big shock. The ultrasound confirmed a perfectly healthy, growing baby boy inside me. There wasn't even any indication of blood loss–all my vitals were strong, and I didn't have anemia. The doctor couldn't explain what happened, but finally convinced me that I had a hysterical hallucination and that everything was fine.

The bloody pool in my bathroom which greeted my return told a different story. I don't know what came out of me, but I couldn't force myself to scoop it up and bring it in for analysis. I just mopped everything off the floor and thanked every God that would listen that my child was still alive.

The second big shock was from Kirk. When I heard the knocking on my door, I figured he was back again with another apology. Well it wasn't going to work—the child, and I were both better off without him. When I opened the door though, it was his father who entered with his hat in hand. I sat quietly on the sofa with him while he explained his sympathies.

"I know you counted on Kirk, but I want you to know that you can count on us too. No man knows what he can bear until it's been put on his shoulders, and I'm just so proud of you for carrying on without him."

The poor old man was moved to tears when I said they were welcome to stay involved with my life and the life of their grandchild. He hugged me, and patted my stomach, and told me all about the games Kirk used to play as a child and what to expect when my boy started growing older. Finally he said his goodbyes, promising to check in with me next week to see if there was anything I needed.

"I just wish Kirk was still around to see him grow up," he said as he was leaving.

I didn't want anything more to do with Kirk, but I was so touched by his father's sincerity that I still extended the offer.

"Tell Kirk that he's welcome to meet the baby too," I said. "Even if he won't be a father to him."

Kirk's father gave a hard-pressed smile. "I think he'd like that. The funeral is this Sunday, so I hope you and that baby will come say goodbye."

The words didn't register until after the door had closed. Kirk hadn't just left us. He'd left everything. It had only been two days previous when I'd seen him last, but I've kept that meeting a secret until now. Everyone else at the funeral was convinced that he'd put a shotgun in his mouth two weeks ago. Whatever had visited and been with me that night had told me it wanted the baby now, but it wasn't Kirk.

That's when I started to become afraid of the child growing inside of me. I can't shake the thought that the stuff pouring out onto the bathroom floor—that was my real child from the real Kirk. What was now growing inside me—that must have come from the visitor. So there I was left wondering what I'm more afraid of:

That the child will be too horrible to let live, or that he is so beautiful that my life will be the one ending that day. It was too late to get it "taken care of", but I don't think I would have done it even if I could.

It wasn't until I was well into my 8th month of pregnancy when I heard the 2 AM knocking again. I lay in bed trembling, holding my breath, wondering if it would just go away. No, there it was again. Hard insistent pounding—like something that would break the door in if I kept it waiting.

"I know you're in there." It was Kirk's voice. I would still recognize it even if I didn't hear it again for fifty years.

"Go away." I regretted it the moment I replied. An hour passed in the next few seconds of silence. As gut-wrenching as the stillness was, the sound of the opening door was worse. He was inside the house, but the thought of getting out of bed and confronting him—of confronting IT—that was unthinkable. I got out of bed to grab my phone from the nightstand and called the police instead.

"I need help," I blurted into the phone. "Someone's in my house and—"

"Did you make him a promise?" It was Kirk's voice on the line. My fingers were shaking so badly I couldn't even hang up. I just threw the phone across the room and jumped back into bed. This was all a bad dream. It was another hysterical hallucination. I just had to go back to sleep and—But how was I supposed to sleep when I heard footsteps climbing the stairs?

"What promise did you make me?" Kirk's voice was right outside my bedroom now. I couldn't answer him. I could barely breathe. I should have tried harder though, because when the door opened, it was even harder to think straight.

Kirk was standing in the doorway, only half of his face was now missing from where the shotgun bullet entered his mouth. Had he looked like this the last time we were making love? It had been so dark, but the stench of death seemed all too familiar.

"There is no baby," I forced myself to say. "He hasn't been born yet."

"I don't care. He's mine."

The malodorous atmosphere engulfed me, and I could taste it like rotten cabbage dripping down the back of my throat. He was getting closer, but still blocked the only door out.

"You'll kill me if you take him now," I told him. "Please wait. At least until he's born."

"I don't care! I want my son!"

He lifted his stiff limbs with his hands to clamber into the bed beside me. I didn't see any weapon, but the thought of him trying to pull the child out of me with his rotting hands was even more terrifying. I gagged so violently that I would have fallen over if his hands hadn't clutched my shoulders. The icy nails sank into my arms, and I forced myself not to watch as I felt some of his own decaying skin slide off to splatter across my bed.

Those disgusting fingers—I had placed a ring upon one and sworn my love before my family and before God. That open wound disguised as a face—I did not know myself until I whispered my secrets to him and washed myself with his acceptance and support. If I closed my eyes, the arms that clenched around me could almost still have been the ones that held me every night as I fell asleep.

"Do you still love me?" I asked what used to be my husband.

"Does it matter? You can't love me in return."

"If I could." Every word I spoke carried the weight of my life and the life of my child. "Would you still love me back?"

"You can't. If you could, I never would have left."

"You still do, or you never would have come back."

Mother's make sacrifices for their child. That has been documented across eons of history, cultures, and even species. Kissing him wasn't for my child though. I did it to save my own life. In that moment, I would have ripped my own baby boy from my body and handed it to him if I could escape unharmed. I must be the worst mother in the world, because when Kirk was done with me that night, I still promised to give him the child when he was born.

It's amazing how much my mind changed after I held my boy for the first time. Suddenly he wasn't just a medical condition which needed to be resolved. He was more a part of me now than he was inside me, and I finally understand that living for him wouldn't be a sacrifice. He is my soul, and everything that I do for him, I do for me.

I know I've been selfish with my love. I know I've made promises which I don't intend to keep. I know I've lied to what was left of my husband when I pleaded for my life. But now I truly have something worth living (and dying) for, and I'm not going to give him up no matter what happens. Until then, I am doing the best I can get by as a new parent who can't seem to get any sleep.

It's not the baby keeping me up though. It's just the waiting for the 2 AM knock on my door.

THE 32

A lot of you probably know about the Chilean mining accident of 2010. It was also called the "Los 33" because of the 33 miners trapped underground. It's amazing that all 33 survived the entire 69 days it took until they were rescued.

There was a whole media circus about it with an estimated billion people watching the rescue on TV or the internet. There was so much news that one fact was completely drowned out—and to me, it's the most important of them all.

I became interested in the topic because of a school paper I was writing. I mentioned the project to my grandfather (which was a terrible mistake because he is ZEALOUS about school). He was trying to get my mother to enroll me in an international baccalaureate college prep school at FIRST GRADE. Education is my future—he wishes he had those opportunities when he was a kid—I'm an ungrateful brat for taking my fortune for blessing—you know the drill.

Anyway, he wouldn't let me use Wikipedia or any easy source for the essay. Instead, he called up his old friend who actually worked on the rescue crew in Chile. So what should have been an hour long paper turned into an hour phone interview, three hours of driving, and a whole BOOK about rescue operations. Who since the internet was invented ever needed to read a book about anything?

Meeting the rescue worker guy was pretty interesting though. He had tan leather skin like you'd expect to find on a car seat instead of a person. His accent was a little thick, and sometimes he couldn't find the right word so he had to switch to Spanish. I know next to zero Spanish, but my grandfather would make me write down everything he said verbatim so I could translate it at home. Granddad literally said "If you try to take the easy road in life, life is going to take the easy road with you. Right up your ass". I don't know what that means, but asking him to clarify didn't seem necessary.

About half-way through the interview with the rescue guy, my grandfather got up to go to the bathroom. I was asking questions about how many people were down there, and he kept saying "treinta-y-dos", or 32. The movie is even called "The 33"—everything online says "The 33", but he was adamant. Then he gave me this weird look—like he was shell-shocked or something. The kind of blank look you expect to see holocaust survivors wearing. He leaned in real close, and started rattling off some stuff in English and some in Spanish, and I did my best to keep up.

It wasn't until the car ride home when I was able to translate what he said. I checked it half a dozen times—I even ran the transcript by my Grandfather (who is fluent, but still made me do my own trans-lating first). Here is what we put together:

"All the media—the news—the story spinners—they all say 33 miners were trapped. And why wouldn't they? 33 people came out of that mine. The miners were trapped 700 meters in the ground—there was no way in or out. But the miners who come out—right when I first pull them out—they all say the same thing.

There were only 32 miners trapped. They count and they count—every day – every few hours, so everybody taken care of—and then one day they count again and there is 33.

They were a band of brothers—you can't go through an ordeal like that and not become family—and they stuck by each other. They never said one of them didn't belong.

But I heard stories. They say one miner didn't sleep like the others. He just sat against the wall and hummed some tune nobody recognized.

They say one miner didn't eat like the others, but they didn't complain because they had to save their provisions.

They say one miner—they know who but they no telling—one miner didn't talk about his family or friends or wanting to get out.

All this one miner talked about was how comforting the darkness felt. How they—the trapped miners—were the lucky ones.

That the earth only swallowed them to keep them safe.

While all the rest would drown in a sea of fire of their own kindling."

This isn't about the paper anymore. Next week I'm going to drive back to see my grandfather's friend. I'm going to try to track down the unexplained miner and see what happened to him.

Finding one of the miners was a lot harder than I expected. Don't get me wrong, I didn't think it would be easy. I figured that most of them would still be living in Chile, and that's still a Hell-of-a road trip from Texas.

I didn't think it would be this hard to just find a phone number or ANYTHING though. After the media storm died down in 2010, it seems like nothing changed for the miners. Most of them were laid off because of that mine's closure, and those that DID find a new mining company suffered through the same intolerable working conditions.

Even the Hollywood movie didn't help them because their story rights were considered public domain after the massive publicity. All those men got was a pathetic 7,000$ compensation for their time spent in Hell. The more I searched, the grimmer the story became.

Over the last seven years, they have been dying one by one. A few from other mine accidents, others from health complications undoubtedly exasperated by their ordeal, but more than anything: suicides. I get it—they've had a hard life—but it was the manner they killed themselves that was the most unsettling.

Self-immolation. There were a few bullets, one poison, two jumpers—but mostly I found account after account of miners dousing themselves in gasoline and burning themselves alive. It was difficult not to connect the incidents with those haunting words from the 33rd miner:

And all the rest would drown in a sea of fire of their own kindling.

It was my grandfather's friend (Vicente) who found a lead. Two of the miners who were invited to the film premiere in Los Angeles had decided to stay in America. Vicente found a recent article which followed up with the pair about the incident, although both had declined an interview.

It was still about an 18 hour road trip, but after I shared my research with Vicente, he volunteered to make the drive with me. I convinced my grandfather that I wanted to use this research for my future graduation thesis, and he convinced my mother to let me go.

"What are you going to ask them?" Vicente asked on the drive. One of the conditions for the trip was that I help him practice his English, and he talked non-stop the whole way.

"I'm going to ask them to help me find the 33rd miner. The one who wasn't human."

"El Diablo," Vicente said. "And if he's one of the two you meet? What do you say to him then?"

"I guess I'll tell him to go to Hell." I meant it as a joke, but neither of us laughed. "Or find out why he's here."

"And if you don't like what he says? You will stop him?"

I didn't have an answer then, but I had plenty of time to think about it on the drive to LA.

We found one of the miner's address's by contacting the newspaper which tried to interview him. Vicente told the reporter that he and the miner were old friends—an account made credible by his first person details of the rescue operation.

Vicente told the reporter that he could persuade the miner into accepting the interview if we only knew where he lived—and voila. I guess private information is less important than a shot at a successful article.

Vicente and I were soon walking up the dilapidated staircase of the apartment—although even calling this dump an apartment seemed insulting to all the other residences which share a name.

The walls were covered with grime thick enough to sink a finger into. Trash, dirty diapers, and decaying leftovers littered the hallways, and on every floor we heard either couples fighting, women screaming at their kids, or loud drunken sex. I'm glad Vicente was with me when I knocked on the door.

"Come in."

Vicente and I exchanged a quizzical expression. If I was living in this kind of neighborhood, I wouldn't invite strangers in. Vicente shrugged and opened the door.

It was almost surreal walking inside. Fresh white paint on the walls, spotlessly shined kitchen counter, a sterile chemical smell like a hospital—it was like stepping through the door into a different world.

A middle aged man blinked his black, sunken eyes at us. His dark skin and hair looked a lot like Vicente—he could easily have been Chilean.

He was sitting on a sofa which faced a blank white wall. There weren't any books, or TV, or anything. I can't imagine what he was doing before we came in.

"Have a seat." The man patted the cushion beside him.

There weren't any chairs and sitting next to him on the sofa seemed uncomfortably familiar. I shifted my weight from leg to leg and looked to Vicente for help.

"Sorry to just show up," Vicente said, obviously uncomfortable as well. "I hope we didn't interrupt nothing."

The man looked back at his blank white wall. He shrugged.

"Are you a survivor from the mine?" I blurted. Vicente put a hand out to caution me, but I kept going. "I was writing a school paper on— well I wanted to know about—who was the 33rd miner? The one who didn't belong."

"Didn't belong?" he asked, still addressing the white wall. "He was the only one who did belong down there."

"Can you tell me about him?"

He pulled a notebook out of his pocket and began writing something down. I looked at Vicente, and he smiled encouragingly. All those hours in the car and this was all I could think about. I was finally going to get some answers.

The man offered me the notebook, and I moved close to take it from him.

Agustin: 3006 W Burbank Blvd. Los Angeles.

"Ask him yourself," the miner said.

"Will you go with us?" I asked.

The miner shook his head, still not looking at me.

"If there's something bad going to happen, you have to tell us," Vicente added.

"It's too late," the miner replied. A shudder passed over his body as though he were shivering from a cold wind blowing from the inside out. "He's the last one left, and it has already begun."

Why was he still looking at the wall? I started to move around in front of the sofa to force him to look at me when –

"Look out!" A hand landed on the back of my shirt and yanked me hard. I spun to the ground, still clutching the notebook. I tried to push Vicente off, but his old hands were like iron. It wasn't until he had dragged me almost out the door when I noticed the man on the sofa was holding a handgun.

BLAM. Vicente let go of my shirt and stared with me. The miner had opened his mouth and put a bullet through his own brain. The once perfect white wall behind him looked like an open wound. Vicente grabbed me by the shirt again and dragged me from the room.

After that grizzly spectacle, Vicente refused to let me keep searching. He was ready to drive straight through the night, all the way back to Texas right then and there.

He didn't want to call the police. The reporter knew we were going to visit him, but he didn't know who we were. Vicente figured that if we just left the state now, we'd never get tangled up in this any more than we already were.

I saw it differently though. If the last miner really was the only one of the 33 still alive, then Vicente and I might be the only two people who knew something was going on. We had a responsibility to find out more.

It was all I could do just to convince Vicente to get a motel for the night before driving back. I used the extra time to beg and plead with him, but it was impossible to get through. "Let him burn himself alive for all I care. We never should have come here." I might as well have been begging the sun not to set in the evening.

I waited until Vicente fell asleep before slipping down to the street to order an UBER. A dark sedan swept me down the unfamiliar streets, but I was so wrapped up in my own thoughts that I didn't even speak a word to the driver. I wish I had though—I wish I'd asked him to wait and make sure I was okay, but he's gone now. It's going to just be me and the Devil.

This isn't a house or an apartment building though. I was standing outside a crematorium. What if the miner simply worked here now? By the time they were opened again, Vicente would be awake, and we'd be driving back to Texas. I circled round the building, looking for some clues, or staff directories, or anything. Maybe this was an unhealthy obsession for me. Maybe I should just let it go and stay out of trouble like Vicente.

But trouble is there whether you're looking for it or not, and it's best to know what's coming before it hits you. There was a light on in the back of the building. It took about ten minutes pacing outside in the darkness before my heart slowed to a familiar rhythm and I was ready to approach.

I knocked on the door. No answer. I peered through the lit window—looked like an office room. I knocked on the glass. No answer. My heart was starting to race again. I was stupid for even being here. Someone had just forgotten to turn out the light when they went home.

I went back to the door and tried the handle. It was unlocked. The grating sound of the door swinging open seemed so loud in the still night that people must have heard it a block away.

"Hello? Anyone here?" I called out, immediately regretting it. I don't know which was worse, taking the Devil by surprise, or letting him know I was coming. I still switched on every light I could find, just in case something jumped out at me.

"Agustin?" I shouted. No answer. I found another door with light seeping under the crack and opened it.

Agustin was inside. I could tell because of the name-tag on his overalls. He was on his hands and knees, the charred remains of his head placed firmly inside one of the cremation ovens. I don't know whether he died the moment his head went inside, but I'd imagine he had to hold it there for a while. What could he possibly have seen or known that was worse than this?

I called an UBER to take me back to the motel. I guess that was it. All 33 were dead. I hope whatever evil spirit crawled up from the earth with those men had spent its wrath doing whatever it did to them, and was sleeping peacefully now.

The same dark sedan stopped and I got in.

"Hi there," I said. "Thanks for getting me again."

The driver—or the miner, I guess they were the same—turned around and smiled. It was hard not to smile with the bottom half of your jaw hanging loose. I could clearly see the pathway where the bullet entered his mouth and tore up through his brain. It was mesmerizing to watch that mass of loose flesh contort to form the shapes necessary for speech.

"I see you've found the man you're looking for," what's left of his face replied.

"A man wouldn't be alive right now. What are you?"

The loose flesh pulled tighter and a trickle of blood dribbled out onto the driver's console. He didn't kill the other miners. They killed themselves—as far as I could tell. As long as I kept my wits about me, I could make it through this. I looked down at my lap so I could pretend I was just having an ordinary conversation. Not as easy as it sounds, with the blood dripping down the console around my feet.

"I will answer one question for your persistence. Don't waste it on such trivial semantics."

I took a deep breath. It smelled like food which has just begun to spoil.

"How can I stop the sea of fire you mentioned when you climbed out of that mine?"

"Only fools play with matches."

I had to look up at that. Even if it meant staring into that grotesque face—there's no way my single question was going to be wasted with that shitty answer.

"What is that supposed to mean? Why are you even here? Are you trying to warn us not to blow ourselves up because we know that without whatever the fuck game you're playing."

The miner slumped forward into his seat. The blood on the back of his head was congealed—he had died quite a while ago. I wanted to scream—to break the window—to punch HIM in his disgusting bloody face, but I was next to a dead man for the third time tonight. More than anything, I wanted to get home. I just got out of the car and started walking the whole way back toward the motel.

But the notebook! If that miner was the real Devil—and that's the only explanation that makes sense to me—then he had given me his notebook. I stopped walking and used the light from my phone to desperately flip through the pages looking for some other clue. There on the first page were more words, written in a fluid hand.

While they sat down in the dark, waiting for tomorrow's spark, telling tales of broken hearts, I joined them in their cell.

Don't be afraid, I sang to each, don't hate the world beyond your reach, I hear your prayers as you beseech, me save you with my spell.

Only fools play with matches, or bury treasure with no latches, or sign a deal when the catch is, the soul you have to sell.

But the fool has born you, raised you, sold you. The fool has torn you, dazed you, told you. He won't mourn you, praise you, hold you, when finally you yell.

Only fools play with matches, and suffer all those needless scratches, you will find your soul detaches, free at last in Hell.

How much must one man suffer before Hell becomes an escape? I hope I never find out.

DREAMING WITHOUT SLEEP

Humans don't have a physiological need to sleep. Over time, chemical levels of Adenosine build up which cause the sleepy feeling, but that is simply a trigger designed to force our bodies to rest. Some scientists have theorized that this is an evolutionary mechanism intended to prevent us from wasting unnecessary energy while keeping us hidden during the night. Well, there isn't any shortage of calories to consume, and there's nothing going to eat me in the night, so as far as I'm concerned, sleep is just an antiquated fetter which humans should leave behind.

We don't need sleep to live, but we cannot survive without dreaming. And if you stay awake for long enough, you'll start to dream even while awake. The more you try to fight those dreams, the more real they will become. Pretty soon, you can't tell which is the dream and which is real, or whether there is a difference at all. That's the story I told the police, and my attorney, and it's the story I'm sticking with now.

It started when I read an article in my psychology class about this Vietnamese insomniac named Thái Ngọc who hasn't slept in 43 years. It said he had some kind of fever, and then never felt the urge to sleep again. Even working full time, it's like he has a vacation every night.

I don't know about you, but for a stressed out college student always trying to cram for the latest test, that sounded like a lifesaver. I'm paying my own way through college with a work-study program and trying to maintain a social life in the half-hour break I have between class and work is absolutely impossible. I'm tired, and stressed, and missing out on what is supposed to be the best years of my life because I never have a free moment to be myself. If I could find a way to waste less time sleeping though, maybe things would get better.

I did some more reading and became obsessed with the idea. If we sleep for 8 hours and are awake 16, then eliminating sleep would be equivalent to adding around 40 years to my lifespan (assuming an 80 year life). I found some studies about a drug being tested on mice called Orexin-A which was supposed to completely eliminate the need for sleep. It hadn't been approved for human trials yet, but there weren't any negative side effects found in the mice. If anything, they seemed more active than ever. And the best part was, research for this drug was being done right at UCLA where I go to school!

Well I was able to find where the lab was easily enough, although I didn't expect them to just hand me the chemicals. I tried to get an internship there, but they required at least twenty hours a week, and I couldn't even begin to fit that into my schedule. I forgot about the whole thing until I overheard Ricky, one of the other kids in my psych class, mentioning that he got the internship.

Ricky was boasting about using the keys to sneak into the lab at night to get high off the anesthesia they used on rats. If he doesn't sound like an idiot yet, then add a tank top that says "I party with sluts", a hat with the "Obey" sticker, and a skateboard which he carries around to look cool but doesn't know how to ride. You got the idea.

But that was fine with me, because it made it a simple matter to pretend to be his friend. All I had to do was turn my hat backward, make a couple dumb jokes about the blonde sitting in front, high-five him when she bent over, and voila. Suddenly we were bros. Future of American science right here.

It didn't take many hints before he invited me into the lab. I found where the Orexin-A experiments were just by looking up the faculty directory in charge, and before my "buddy" finished coming down from huffing anesthesia, I had a whole backpack full of the little spray bottles of Orexin. It was nasally administrated, but I didn't care as long as it worked.

And holy Hell—it worked alright. Twenty squirts up each nostril (seemed like a lot, but I controlled the dosage to 1mg/kg body weight, which was equivalent to the dose the mice were getting). I played Skyrim straight into the dawn. Okay, so it wasn't quite self-actualization, but I hadn't had any free time in a while, and it felt great to have the constant pressure off me. The night was so quiet, and by the early morning it felt like the entire world was made just for me. I didn't even feel tired until the following night, and I just took another dose and all the weariness washed away. I spent the second night reading Shakespeare just for fun. How else would anyone ever have the time for that? There was so much to do and learn about the world, and finally I had the chance to see it all. It was the best thing I could have ever hoped for.

The one thing the mice hadn't mentioned during their experiments, however, was that you can still dream without sleeping. They started on the third day, little visual abnormalities that danced around the corner of my vision. Patterns, or shapes, or textures just drifting idly by. I actually enjoyed them at first, but the longer I went without sleep, the more real they became. By the fifth day I actually started seeing fully formed people walking alongside me. They were always in my peripheral vision, and as soon as I turned to face them, they disappeared.

It was the evening of the sixth day when I opened my bedroom to see a smiling figure sitting on my bed. It didn't even have a face—just teeth which wrapped all the way up around up to where its ears should be. I splashed cold water in my face and the thing disappeared, but it still freaked me out.

I decided to take a break from the drug then, but even without it, I couldn't sleep that night. There must have still been some in my system. I tossed and turned, and every time I got up, that figure with the teeth was there watching me. Every time I jolted myself awake, it would linger a little longer in my room. Just silently smiling.

I managed to get through the next day—still off the drug and still seeing the creature out of the corner of my eye wherever I looked. I got used to him though and even began to nod off during the psych lecture. After class, I decided to call in sick from work and just go sleep. Ricky was trying to talk to me, but I was so tired I couldn't even figure out what he was saying. It was hard to even look at him with the creature standing next to us. I just mumbled something and turned to leave, but the idiot kept following me.

I shouldn't have shoved him, but I was so tired I couldn't deal with pretending to be his friend anymore. He stumbled back a few paces— right into the smiling creature. The weirdest thing was, I swear he bounced off the creature and looked over his shoulder. It seems stupid to think he could see my dream, but I was so tired I wasn't thinking straight. I just bolted and ran.

Ricky was still following me though—he was insistent. Something about there being a security camera at the lab. That we had to get our story straight about what we were doing there. I don't know. I just wanted to get home. I just wanted to sleep. I ducked into an alley between the psych and sociology buildings, but I couldn't lose him. He grabbed my shoulder and pulled me to the ground, and I didn't have the strength to fight him off. I was too tired to get up, so I just lay there and let him yell at me. My mind was so numb with exhaustion, even the sound of his shouting faded into a gentle white noise, and I must have fallen asleep right there on the ground.

His body was mangled almost beyond recognition. The police told me there were witnesses who saw me jump on top of Ricky and bite his face into a bloody pulp. They said I had some kind of inhuman strength, and that it took almost a dozen people to drag me off him. They said I hurled him like a rag doll into the building, dislocating both his shoulders and smashing one of the bricks into powder. I don't know how I could have done it while I was asleep. All I know is that when i was about to drift off, I saw my creature standing behind

Ricky, and the last thing I saw before closing my eyes was its teeth sinking into his neck.

The court blamed the incident on the drug and I've been transferred to a rehab clinic. It's been four days since I've last taken Orexin, but the creature hasn't gone away. Every time I close my eyes, it's sitting a little closer. Sooner or later I'm going to fall asleep, and it's going to take control again. I'm writing this because if I can't stay awake, I want someone out there to know.

Don't blame me for what he does when I'm asleep.

I'm fighting it for as long as I can.

BURNING DESIRE

I'm saying this as a confession. I can't explain how it happened, but I know it's my fault because it started with me hurting myself. And it's not like I wanted attention or anything—okay, well as long as I'm being honest I wouldn't mind someone noticing me—but that isn't why I burned myself. And it definitely isn't why I killed myself, but I'm getting ahead now.

I was in class one day when someone set a fire in the chemistry lab. Probably Jason—that idiot was always using the Bunsen burners to melt pens. and glue. and whatever he could get his hands on. Anyway, the fire drill started and the whole High-school was paraded out into the parking lot like we practiced during drills. Everyone was laughing and screaming, and I'd just gotten out of a math test I wasn't ready for so I didn't mind.

While we were standing in the parking lot, I overheard Lisa say that Sammy, the kid in the wheelchair, got stuck on the elevator during the drill. It's not hard to overhear things since I hang on her every word, but you would too if that blonde goddess was standing next to you wearing a punk-plaid skirt and a sweater almost tight enough to see through... what was I saying? Oh right, well rumor had it that another kid went back into the school to get Sammy out. No one knew who it was, but they were already talking about him like he was a hero.

That's when I had an idea. I could just burn the edges of my clothes a bit, and then Lisa and all the other kids would think I was the one who went back in for Sammy. I could be the hero. And even if the real hero DID come forward, well I had the burns, and he didn't, so who were people going to believe?

I kept my head low and stayed away from anyone who might recognize me—which wasn't very hard since I didn't have a lot of friends. Or any, I guess. I was new and it would take time, I just hadn't expected it to take more than a semester for anyone to recognize me. But that's okay, because after today, I was going to be the hero.

When the bell rang for us to go back inside; I darted straight to the bathroom. There's a place under the sink where some seniors hide a box with cigarettes and lighters. I pulled the box out, found a nice black zippo lighter with a skull on it, and here goes—the fire springs to life.

Well turns out polo shirts don't light up as easily as I was expecting. I blackened a few hairs, but this wasn't nearly enough for people to think I walked through a fire. I used a pen to open the zippo at the bottom and poured all the lighter fluid onto my shirt. My heart was pounding—I was excited. I couldn't wait to come back to class and watch Lisa's face sparkle with awe. I didn't even take the shirt off—I wanted a few burns. Enough to show how tough I was.

Just as I was about to light the fluid, my mind played a funny trick on me. It looked like the skull on the lighter was smiling. I didn't remember it doing that before. Too late now—the fire was already dancing over my shirt. It barely even felt warm. I watched myself in the mirror as the fire spread from shoulder to shoulder. My buttons began to heat up and stung a bit, but the shirt was smoldering nicely. I ran the faucet and splashed the water on me. That'll be enough.

But the fire drank the water as though nourished by it, spitting boiling vapor into the air. The heat was intense now. I tried to rip the shirt off, but the polyester was melting to my skin. The metal buttons seared into my flesh. I couldn't stop screaming. I didn't want anyone to see me like this, but it was like I heard someone else scream through me without even asking my permission first.

I dropped on the ground and began to roll, but the fire just continued to spread over my entire body. It ran up my arms, and I could actually see the flesh melting from my finger bones. The pain was like you can't imagine. My whole body was being pierced with red hot knives. Then it started to go black—thank God. I'll fall unconscious and someone will find me. It'll be over. But no, only half my vision was gone. I looked into the mirror and watched my left eyeball melting down my face. It would have gone down my cheek if there was any cheek left, but it simply dripped through the hole in my skin, straight into my mouth. I gagged. How was I still conscious?

The pain wasn't letting up, but I forced myself to watch my reflection. I'd done this to myself. Somehow, I deserved it. My jaw bone was completely exposed now, and it was starting to crack from the heat. There's no way a zippo lighter could have done this. I grabbed the little black box, but the skull had vanished. WHOOOSH. A toilet flushing. Was someone in here the whole time?

I tried to turn my head, but my spine was too weak to support me and started collapsing in on itself. I crumpled to the floor and watched as a bathroom stall opened. What. The. Hell? Was this it? Am I dead now? Because there's no reason—no way I could really be seeing myself walk out of the bathroom stall. The other me, wearing my shirt and pants, completely unsigned by fire, walked over to the sink beside me. He calmly washed its hands in the sink—not even glancing down at me writhing on the floor.

I tried to speak—to scream—anything, but only a dry gurgle escaped my throat. That's when the other me turned and smiled, and I could have sworn it was the same boney-white smile the skull wore.

"Your turn on the inside," it said, or I guess I said that, because it looked a lot more like me than I did.

Then everything went black, only I could still feel every inch of my burning body and hear the wet plop of my skin sliding down my bones onto the floor. I heard footsteps as it—as I—left the room. I must be inside the lighter now, waiting for the next person to let me out. But I can still feel my flesh burn, so I pray to God it won't be long.

HAUNTING SOUND

I met with the most unusual patient a little while ago. I would never ordinarily post online about someone's confidential details, but I'm frankly at a loss with this one. I have begun the process to submit this case study to a variety of peer-reviewed journals, but in the meantime I am seeking alternative explanations to help him.

Since I'm telling the story anyway, I suppose there's no use denying it—I could also use some help myself.

I earned my MD at John Hopkins School of Medicine with an additional four years residency at the Baltimore Bethusala fellowship. Next came five years at the Union Memorial Psychiatry Hospital before I opened a private practice, which I've now run for the last twelve years. I have encountered everything from a blind synesthetic who can still see visuals through sound, a schizophrenic who tried to kill herself right in my office, and an obsessive-compulsive who tightened his shoe laces so relentlessly that both feet lost circulation and had to be amputated.

I thought I had pretty much seen it all until this latest patient. I will protect his privacy by referring to him as "Mr. X".

Mr. X's symptoms were innocent enough—just a ringing in his

ears which wouldn't go away. He'd visited numerous otolaryngologists, but as there was no discernible cause for the ringing, he was referred to me to decipher the psychosomatic source of the phenomenon.

During our first meeting, he didn't make eye contact with me, nor did he ever speak above a whisper. He just stared at his hands, endlessly wringing them against each other. He'd been doing it so obsessively, in fact, that his fingers were rubbed raw and bloody. I made considerable progress on the first day, and with the aid of some anti-anxiety medication, he was able to look me in the eye, although the hand wringing continued.

"Can you hear it, doctor?" he asked me during the second session.

"Of course not. The sound is not coming from a mutually accessible environment. The sound is a fabrication of your mind."

I wish now I hadn't prescribed the anti-anxiety medication, however. That I'd kept those black, lifeless eyes pointed away from me. He pulled his gaze away from the ground and looked at my face, and it seemed as though the effort it cost him resembled how you or I might struggle to gaze at the hideous disfigurement of some elephant man. That's when I began to hear it too—that soft ringing, like church bells inside my skull.

"How about now? Do you hear it now, doctor?" he asked.

And that smile—that twisted grimace of satisfaction—somehow he knew I could. Regardless, admitting I heard his hallucination would only deepen his psychosis, so I naturally had to deny it. I terminated the session early and prescribed some antipsychotics, even taking some for myself. By the time I got home, the ringing was gone.

In our third session, the ringing started again as soon as he entered the room. The pitch wasn't consistent like it was before though—it rose and fell with melodic rhythm like a whole orchestra was welling up inside of me. Mr. X just stared and grinned. I don't think he even cared about getting better anymore. He was just relieved at not being the only one to hear it. He wasn't very responsive that session—all he would do was hum along to the music inside my head. I terminated early again, and he went home without complaint. As he was leaving, my secretary asked me where those strange bells were coming from.

I increased the dosage, prescribing some to myself and my secretary as well. The phantom sounds went away again, but the moment Mr. X was back in the room with me, the music would swell up. My racing heart pushed blood through my veins in rhythm with the beat, and my head would throb from the intensity of those notes reverberating around my brain. I'd started wringing my hands too, just as something to distract myself from the noise.

By the end of the fourth session, the skin around my palms was wearing thin and there was blood beginning to seep through. I hadn't even noticed how hard I was clenching them together.

As you might imagine, I referred him to another doctor. He called no doubt to complain, but I told my secretary to let it go to voicemail. I didn't care, I wasn't taking him back. And if that were the end of it, then I would have simply hung up my coat and retired that day, but the sound hasn't left me. If anything, it's growing louder, and I had even begun to hear a choir join in with the orchestra.

My secretary didn't come in to work today. I'm here all alone, at wits end what to do. I've tried every cocktail of medication I can think of, but it's only left me feeling worn out and hollow. The sound is still there. I didn't want to be alone here, but somehow my office is the only place I felt safe. I tried to call my secretary to see how she was doing, but I never work the phone system and must have pushed the wrong button. I just got the voicemail from Mr. X, but I was so desperate for an answer, I still forced myself to listen to it. Here is what he said:

"As long as the music plays, you're alright. All the world is a stage, and all of life a play upon it, and as long as the music sounds the show is still going on. I didn't come to you because I was afraid of the music. I came to you because I was afraid it would stop."

I spent the rest of the day calling patients and referring them to new specialists. I called my building manager and opted not to renew the lease on my office. I went home, with no intention of ever going to work again. The music is getting quieter everyday now, but that's only making me more anxious. I've tried calling Mr. X again, but his cell phone is out of service. I called the doctor I referred Mr. X to, but he never showed up for his appointment. I even went so far as to visit the address listed on his medical forms, but it was just an abandoned theater.

I don't know how much longer the music will play for, or what will happen when it stops, but until then I'm just wringing my hands and waiting.

KILLER SELFIE

O kay there's something weird going on. I don't want to tell my friends or family—they'd probably just make fun of me for being scared. I have to post this somewhere though, because if something does happen to me, then I want there to be someone who knows.

It started with these 'selfies' appearing on my phone.

"Haha, right, so you accidentally clicked the camera button when you weren't looking."

That's what I thought at first too, until I found a photo of me sleeping, taken from across the room. I live alone in a one-bedroom apartment. I charge my phone overnight on the night table beside my bed. There's no reason the phone should have been across the room from me in the first place.

I deleted the photo as soon as I found it. I just felt weird having it on my phone. The next night, there was another one—this time it was taken by someone stands right over my bed.

After that, it started getting even weirder. I found a couple of photos of myself at Universal Studios—and you guessed it, I've never been there. It showed me hanging out with my friend David. We were on rides together, eating ice-cream, getting photos with the giant transformer robots—it actually looked like a lot of fun.

That's when I decided he must be playing a trick on me. I don't know how he was getting the pictures on my phone, but he was obviously photo-shopping just to screw with me.

Two days later, David actually did invite me to Universal. It was a relief because I figured this is where he would finally come clean about what was going on. Of course he denied it, but that was all part of the joke.

Or at least that's what I thought, until another photo appeared while we were hanging out. My face looked so surprised as a man behind me forced his switchblade between my ribs.

I freaked. I just went straight home and stayed in my room for the rest of the day. I broke my phone by slamming it in my desk drawer over and over until it wouldn't turn on.

The next day I went to the ATT store for a new phone. I said the last one was stolen, and they gave me an insurance replacement one. Brand new—straight out of the package—it didn't even have a SIM card in it yet. But the moment I opened it, I saw a photo of myself saved as the wallpaper.

Only I didn't look like I usually do. My eyes were sunken like I haven't slept in days. My clothes were caked with dirt and blood, and there were open sores on my skin.

The photos are appearing several times a day now. Some depict me getting hit by a car, or sitting in a bathtub in a pool of my own blood. I got one the other day where I was stretched out on a laboratory table, shackled into place.

I'm afraid to destroy my phone again. I decided it might be trying to warn me, and if something is going to happen, I need to know about it so I can be ready.

I haven't left my apartment in almost a week now. The last photo to appear showed me hanging by the neck from my ceiling fan. I don't want to do it, but if it does happen, I just want people to know.

It wasn't me who did it. Something did it to me.

UNBORN DOLL

My family didn't want me to keep the baby. I could tell from the moment I told them the happy news. My father just sat there with a look of blank shock while my mother wasted no time in trying to console me. Console me? Why would I need to be consoled? It was supposed to be the happiest day of my life!

It didn't stop there either. First were the pamphlets from a clinic that was supposed to "take care of it". Who but a gangster would use "take care of it" as a euphemism for murder? It got worse when I learned the baby wasn't going to be entirely normal. The subtle hints and worried glances turned into outright accusation. Like there was something wrong with me just because I would continue to love my baby even if it wasn't like all the others.

I knew I couldn't live with people who were so Hell bent on destroying my daughter—yes it was going to be a girl with beautiful blonde hair and blue eyes. You may think I'm overreacting, but one night they actually tried to force me into a mental ward so they could declare I was unfit to make my own medical decisions. The baby's father wasn't in the picture—don't get me started on him—so I had to be on my own after that. But it was okay, because I was going to have a beautiful baby girl, and we'd be there for each other even when the whole world turned their back on us.

The delivery was easier than I expected because she was very small. The doctors wanted to keep her there, but I knew she would be better off with me. As soon as I looked into her brilliant blue eyes, I knew everything was going to be okay. The hair wasn't all there, but I just had to get a little pink dress for her and she looked as beautiful as a porcelain doll.

I don't know what my parents were so worried about. Being stillborn makes her even easier to take care of. She never eats, never makes a mess, and never makes a fuss when I dress her up. I have to apply makeup and a bit of perfume to cover up the rotting bits, but there's nothing I wouldn't do for my little girl. The only thing that bothers me—and this is going to be true of any new baby—is when she cries in the night. She's doing it now, but it's honestly okay. I think I'm just going to sew her mouth shut in the morning.

THE FINAL QUESTION

There are lots of stories about how people die. Death is very intriguing, because it is something everyone will experience, and yet no-one HAS ever experienced, because as soon as YOU have undergone death, there is no more YOU to have experiences at all. But this isn't the story of just anyone's death.

This is the story of how you die. One of you will go like this, but it will be a similar story for the rest of you when your time has come. And there won't be any bells or choirs, no light at the end of the tunnel. There won't be any voice calling you home or crying ancestors welcoming you with open arms. I know because that's not what happened when I died.

Your death is going to go like this. A week after Valentine's Day, you're going to be killed when a drunk driver T-Bones your car at 65 miles per hour. You'll know that's how fast he was going, because you'll hear the police reading his broken speedometer after they pronounced you dead. There will be a shard of glass that went straight through your right eye and out the back of your head. Contrary to most people's opinion, discovering you are dead won't be as traumatic as you might expect. It turns out being disconnected from endorphins and adrenalin and surging blood pressure and all that messy biological stuff makes everything quite calm.

But you won't FEEL dead. You'll feel... hollow. It's like you're sitting alone in a dark theatre, watching a movie of your own death. And the more time that passes, the dimmer and quieter the movie will become. I don't know if you will die right on impact, or whether this is the distorted senses of your oxygen deprived brain as you bleed out on the ground. I just know that pretty soon it will be dark and peaceful and quiet, and you'll probably be okay if that was the end.

But it won't be the end, and you won't be alone. When all the light is gone, there will be something moving in the surrounding darkness. You'll have no body or voice to scream with. You'll just be a single thought, being pressed in on all sides by the suffocating presence of something that's been waiting for you your entire life.

Oh and here's a fun fact to look forward to. It turns out pain is more than a firing neuron—it's an integral part of the conscious experience. And even when your body is gone, the consciousness that remains WILL still feel pain. The surrounding presence will crush you into oblivion until the pain becomes so intense you can't even think. You'll just have to wait for this part to be over.

And you're going to be waiting a long while, because the perception of time is something you'll have left behind. This pain is all there is, all there ever was, and all there ever will be. Because somewhere in the beginning that which existed was separated from that which does not, and the void has never forgiven you for leaving it behind. But when it does end—and it will, because I'm here now—you're going to be asked a question. And you better be ready for it because if you don't answer the eternity is going to begin again.

Just one question that determines whether this will ever end. And if you answer right, you'll get to go again. And you might even remember some of it like I did. And if you answer wrong, then nothing good you've ever done will spare you what's coming. And the question is:

"Will you bring more people to take your place?"

And I said yes. And I have. And I'm not done yet.

THE CONFESSION

Forgive me father, for I have sinned. But even if He in all his
glory finds the power to forgive me, how can I ever forgive
myself?

I'm often asked how I bear the burden of listening to confessions.
People assume my conscience is haunted by the personal Demons
each man and woman struggles against, but that is not the case.

In truth, there is no thrill which compares to hearing a confession.
The trust they are putting in me—the trust they are putting in God—
is a beautiful moment to behold. They freely submit themselves to my
power, begging for my absolution as though it were I who wielded
God's wisdom to judge or forgive.

But when it comes time to confess my own sins, I found I lacked
the courage of my flock. I am more than a man to them—I am a
symbol of the Divine. To admit my own failings is to weaken their
faith that the Lord may shelter them if their belief is true. Or perhaps
that is just the excuse I give to protect my pride.

All I know is that this Demon is too great for me to contain on my
own, so I am writing this to beg the forgiveness of strangers in the
hope I too may find peace again.

"Forgive me father, for I have sinned."

He came to me like all the others and sat down in the other side of box. His voice was strange to me, almost like a voicemail compared to a human speaking in person.

"Speak and you will be forgiven, my son."

I usually go in expecting infidelity. That is the most common curse which gnaws at our hearts with guilty teeth.

"I have killed a man. A good man. A man of God."

The thrill only increases with the magnitude of the sin. I do not know who he is, but he is already telling me something which would allow me to destroy his entire life. I breathe slowly through my nose so as not to let the excitement enter my voice.

"Why did you do such a thing?"

"He was a murderer himself, and I was afraid he would kill again," he replied.

Disappointing. When they have a reasonable excuse for their sin, they do not feel the same desperate need for my approval. I would have preferred he killed someone innocent.

"To take a life for any reason is a great crime against God," I replied. That seemed like what I was expected to say. Confession is not the time to remind them how much blood God had demanded over the years. "It is not your place to judge them."

"And it is yours to judge me?" There was accusation in that voice. It sounded familiar, but I couldn't quite place it. Did I know this man?

"Only God may pass judgment for such a sin."

"Then I won't waste my time with you." I heard his door open and then slam shut like a petulant child going to his room. What an unfulfilling sinner he was. The rush I usually felt was utterly absent.

The next week, I heard the same voice on the other side of the box.

"Forgive me father, for I have killed another man."

"Was he a murderer too?"

"Not yet, but he could have become one," the voice said. Infuriatingly familiar—perhaps he was a relative, or simply one of my regular congregation.

"All men have the capacity for evil. Does that give you a right to kill anyone?" I asked. There was nothing as satisfying as leading them to condemn themselves. Finally I would hear the real confession I was waiting for.

"Yes."

I could not have prepared myself for that answer.

By the time I got home, I knew who he had killed. My father had been choked to death in his house last night. I still remember the first beating he gave me when I was four years old. The scars from the lashes on my back have never healed to this day.

Lord knows I had thought about ending him myself a hundred times, but actually hearing the news was unimaginably painful. The guilt of my own evil thoughts against him was almost enough for me to seek confession myself, but there was no sense dirtying my image when I had resisted my evil temptations. If anything, I was thankful to my father. I never would have joined the Church if I wasn't trying to get away with him. His cruelty had paved the way for my mercy.

I didn't anticipate the killer to ever return after how closely he struck me. He couldn't have expected my forgiveness after so personal an attack.

A month passed, and I had come to terms with my father's death when the voice spoke through the wooden grate again.

"Forgive me father, for I have killed another man."

My breath caught short. My fists clenched. How dare he. He never received absolution for either of his previous visits. That's when it occurred to me. He wasn't here for absolution. He was here to taunt me. The death of my father—the manner he composed himself—the blasphemous disregard for my authority. This was all a personal attack.

"Why did you do such a thing?" I forced one word to follow the other. I couldn't slow my breathing this time. I couldn't allow this monster to continue.

"Because he made a fool out of everything I believe in."

That was exactly what HE was doing though. That was proof—he was only here to torment me. I don't know what I have done to this man to deserve such abuse, but I am still a man with blood pounding in my veins. I was not going to idly take it any longer.

"Get out of here," I said. "Both this Church and Heaven will be barred to you forever."

"You're a fraud," the voice said. "You don't speak for God—Hell, you probably don't even believe in him. You just get off on the power you feel from pretending."

"I'm warning you–" I was shouting now.

"Or what? You'll send me to Hell? I thought only God could judge me." I was shaking so bad I had to stand to expel some extra energy. "I killed your father with my bare hands, and all you can do about it is preach something you don't even believe. You're pathetic."

That was too far. I flung open my side of the confession booth and raced over to his. I threw the second door open with enough force to tear it off the hinges.

As though his insults weren't enough, the man was wearing a rubber mask of Jesus.

"Take that damn mask off and leave," I shouted. I didn't give him time to respond though. I was already lunging at him, trying to pull the mask off. He fought back—his hands clasping around my throat.

Those hands. The same hands which had choked the life out of my father. It was all a blur after that. I tried to pry them off, but the grip was too strong. It wasn't until I got my own hands around his neck that he began to lose hold. The thrill of confession—the power I held over people—it was nothing like this.

There is no power over someone like having their neck in your hands. I finally understood why my father beat me. I never felt closer to the divine than that moment when this Demon convulsed beneath my hands before finally falling limp.

Finally. Now I could see who hated me so much that they would go to these extreme lengths to torment me. His cold dead hands – so alike my own—were helpless to prevent me pulling back his mask.

I stared at my own dead face. Vomit coating the sides of my mask. My dead tongue lolling grotesquely from my mouth. That is how I came to terms with who I am.

Forgive me father, for I have sinned.
I have killed a man of God.
I have killed my father.
I have killed the man who made a fool of everything I believe in.
And I have never felt more alive.

CHILDREN COLLECTOR

D o you know this game? It's my favorite.

All you have to do is lie very quietly—that's it—just like you were made of stone.

Don't blink. Don't even breathe. And whatever you do, don't tell them you're playing a game.

They'll want to play with you, but you mustn't let them.

Because when they join in, it won't be a game anymore.

Every year I visit my father's grave in the veteran's cemetery. He was a war hero—or so I was told. He died when I was five, so I hardly even remember him. I'm not even going for sentimental reasons—I just like having a quiet place away from the world where I can put everything in perspective.

Last weekend I knelt to place flowers there and open my mind to the clear air. I was alone except for two young girls (couldn't have been more than ten) visiting the adjacent grave. I heard them talking softly with some lady, but I didn't really pay any attention. I was here for me.

Yes dealing with car insurance or taxes is exhausting. But compared to him dying for our country, how could I allow myself to become frustrated with the minor annoyances of my daily life? I found resolve in the stillness of the dead air, and each time I left I would be ready to face each new challenge life had to offer.

I didn't notice until I started down the hill that the two children were leaving alone. Who could they have been talking to? I mean, it was an open grassy hill, it's not like the lady with them could have just vanished. But then I heard the voice again—like a middle aged woman whispering from a long way away.

I walked over to the grave they had been sitting by and felt the gusty rustle of the words through the surrounding grass. It was getting stronger, and I swear it was coming straight from the ground.

Bring me my children. I miss my children.

The gravestone said Dory Malthusa. I couldn't tell you what else the voice said because I got the Hell out of there. And yeah, I laughed at myself for being freaked, but there wasn't anyone else around to impress by acting brave. A girl has got to take care of herself, you know?

Well maybe it was a trick, or my imagination, or the kids buried a walkie-talkie as a joke. I'd forgotten about it until that night when I turned on the evening news.

Two girls, ages 9 and 11, were found dead in the same cemetery. Their throats were cut from the front. The police say it must have been from someone they know because there were no signs of a struggle. Their names were Rachel and Elizabeth Malthusa.

I'm going back to the cemetery this weekend. If the voice talks to me, I'm going to answer it this time. And if it doesn't—if this is all just my mind playing tricks on me—then I could still use a little more tranquility after that unsettling experience.

I returned to the grave of Dory Malthusa yesterday morning. Beats going at night at least, right? The freshly dug graves of her children were keeping her company now. It still seemed ludicrous that she somehow killed them, but I knew I would rest easier knowing they were at peace.

"Hello Dory." I felt like an idiot talking to a grave. And in the quiet of the cemetery, I felt even stupider expecting a response. This was all nonsense. I must have just been so emotional from sitting beside my father's grave that I imagined her voice before.

But I came all the way here, wasting my Sunday off when I could have been sleeping in or catching up on Game of Thrones, so here goes.

"You need to let your regrets go, Dory. I'm sorry you miss your children, but you can't force them to be with you. If you really loved them, you would want them to be at peace. There's nothing left to keep you here, so it's time for you and your children to rest."

I held my breath. The wind rushed through the grass on the hill like a crashing wave. It whistled between the bare headstones. I guess that was what peace was supposed to sound like. The wind died down as I stood to leave, but the sound of the whistling didn't cease. I don't know where it was coming from, but it almost sounded like a giggling child.

But we don't want to rest. We want to play. It was unmistakable this time. The voice of a little girl. I stood frozen in place. Playing sounded innocent enough, at least.

Then you shall play, little darlings. I will give you everything you ever wanted, my beautiful children. It was Dory's voice this time, the same I heard during my last visit.

"There's no one to play with," I replied. "Go to sleep."

The wind was picking up again, and I pulled my shawl tighter against the sharp tongues of morning air.

We want someone to play with! Another voice from another little girl. Can't we go to school anymore, Mom?

No, and it is my fault for taking you away, she replied. I'm such a wicked, selfish mother. But I will make it right again. I will bring you all the children from your class, and you can stay with me forever and never be lonely.

Bring the children? That could only mean one thing. She brought her own children to her by slitting their throats. I had to do something. I had to warn them, or their parents, or Hell I don't know. I had to tell someone.

"The other children don't want to play," is all I could think of. Shit,

I wish I'd said something better now. There weren't any more words that time. Just the giggling wind which whistled through the headstones.

I couldn't just wait for children to start disappearing. I also couldn't imagine the police taking my lead as exactly credible. I considered going to my local Church, but there has already been an awful scandal going around there, so I thought it best to not get tangled up.

If I was going to do this, it was going to be on my own. After a little research, I was able to pull up the children's obituaries and found the address they used to live. That allowed me to Google the school districts and trace which elementary school the girls had gone to.

That's good. That's a start. Now I just had to warn the children somehow. A crazy stranger ranting about ghosts threatening their kids though—that sounds pretty sketchy. I know wouldn't let someone like me near kids. The only thing I could think to do was infiltrate the school and wait for something to happen.

I don't have any kids of my own (thank God), but I tried calling about signing up as a substitute teacher. They said I needed to pass a class and gain a teaching certificate for that, but I didn't know how much time I had before the Malthusa girls wanted company. I agreed to set up the certificate training and managed to get myself invited down to the school for an interview.

Mrs. Neggels, the home teacher, is the sweetest old thing I've ever seen. Imagine a sugar plum in a home knitted sweater. She'd been in remission for four years, but lately her doctors have suspected her breast cancer might be coming back. She anticipated needing to miss quite a few classes for the testing and was so happy I was there that she brought me straight into the classroom to meet her children.

I had to buy as much time as I could. I don't know when they will strike—if they'll strike at all—but it seemed like Dory killed her children the same day she was speaking with them. If she was going to try to collect the rest of the class, then it would have to be during school hours.

I made up every excuse I could to stay. I sang with the children in their music class and volunteered to supervise recess. I helped the cafeteria lady prepare lunch and even picked up trash with the janitor. By the afternoon, it was clear that they were trying to get rid of me, but there was still no sign of the ghosts.

I was sitting in the art room when Mrs. Neggels finally asked me to leave. The children were just filing into the room from their math class. I immediately volunteered to help them painting their wall, but they already had a guest artist who was going to help out. It was getting late though—maybe they would be alright until tomorrow. I started packing up my things, and that's when I heard the Malthusa girls.

Come and play with us.

The voice was coming through the air-conditioning vent. It was as soft as death which visits in a deep sleep.

"That'll be all. We can take it from here. You may go now." Mrs. Neggels was using her stern voice—the one which made children with the attention span of a rabid squirrel jump into line with military precision. I walked as slowly as I could for the door, desperately looking for any excuse to stay.

Can we paint the wall too, Mommy?

Of course you can, my darling. What colors do you think will go there?

Umm... yellow. And orange. Like leaves.

There! A can of paint sitting on the edge of Mrs. Neggels desk. I gathered my purse, swinging it carelessly behind me.

"Watch out!" Mrs. Neggels was too slow. I hit the can hard, sending it spinning across the room to burst against the far wall. Red paint EXPLODED all over the carpet, and the shrieks and giggles from the children drowned out the whispering voices.

"I'm so sorry!" I said. "Here, let me help."

"You've done quite enough, thank you!" Mrs. Neggels snapped. "Don't step in it now—hey! Stop that!" The children were running wild. Shrieking—laughing—red foot prints everywhere. Red hands on the walls. If one of them was cut right now, would I even notice? I had to get them out of here.

"Let me at least watch them outside to give you space to clean up," I said.

"Fine—just go! Get everybody out."

"Do you know this game? It's my favorite."

We were all sitting in the recess yard. I managed to get them all sitting down in a circle around me, but I was at my wits end. I don't know how to keep them safe.

I want to paint more, Mommy. The voice was getting louder. The kids were looking in all directions, trying to find where it was coming from.

"Who said that?" one asked.

"Please children. Please please listen to me. We're going to play a game. All you have to do is lie very quietly—that's it—just like you were made of stone."

I'm going to paint something for you now. It's going to be bright red—even brighter than the paint.

"Don't even blink. Don't even breathe. And whatever you do, don't tell them you're playing a game."

The children were all lying down. Their eyes were closed. At least if they were to die now, they wouldn't see it coming.

I want to paint with them! Why aren't they painting?

"They'll want to play with you, but you mustn't let them." I was on the verge of tears. But I couldn't break down, or the children would know it wasn't a game. And if it wasn't a game to them, they would begin to cry too. And if they cried…

Mommy, make them paint with us!

"Not a word. Not a sound. Still as stone." I held my breath. The children were all quiet. There was nothing left I could do.

They're boring. Mommy make them stop being boring.

Play! Play with my children!

A few eyes opened to peek for the voice. A few hands began to rub the drying paint on their skin.

"Still as stone. First one to move is out." I said. The hands stopped moving.

Mommy, this is stupid. Let's go back to the park.

Don't you want your class to come with you?

No, they're all boring. Let's go see the ducks.

Of course, my darling. Let us go watch the ducks together.

I'm a full time teacher at the school now. I haven't heard the voices again since that time, but I don't feel right leaving the children alone. If the Malthusa girls ever do get lonely and decide to come back, I'm going to be here ready to play a game. It's very easy to play. All you have to do is lie very quietly, just like you were made of stone.

I MET THE DEVIL ON TINDER

Don't roll your eyes at me. It's not like I could have known beforehand.

Okay, let me back up a little. My name is Emma Collins, and I just began working toward my masters in engineering. All those jokes online about there being no girls here weren't understatements —there are literally classes with twenty people in it and I'm the only one who doesn't have something hanging between their legs.

You'd think that would make dating easy, but I was only there to get my degree and get out. I wasn't about to get bogged down in a relationship. I didn't even want to have a fling with anyone in my class, because as soon as word got out that I'm looking to hook up— and yeah, I'd like to think people would brag about being with me—I'd have to start beating them off with a stick.

But you can't expect a girl to study all day and night and not have a little fun, can you? I tried Tinder just so people would flirt with me and I could brutally reject them and feel good about myself. Harmless fun, right?

Last night I swiped a sweet-looking guy who went to my University, wasn't an engineer (thank God), and shared my undying passion for Rick and Morty. He made me laugh, or at least snort air, and when he asked to get a drink, I couldn't think of any reason not to. The pub was close, so worse comes to worse I would at least get a free drink out of it and could still be home early. He texted to say he'd be a little late, but he was already there when I arrived.

Same dude as the photo—that's a relief—he was even wearing the same clothes. Either he just setup his account today, or he wore the stuff from his photo so I'd recognize him. Either way, it didn't bother me as long as he wasn't some fedora-tipped whale.

And damn was he charming. We just clicked on everything—both big Ramones fans, read Stephen King, watched the same shows, hated the same politicians (looking at you, blonde hairpiece). It was like this guy was specifically designed just to be perfect for me. I guess I should have taken that as the warning sign. One free drink turned into four, and I don't know whether he asked me to come home with him, or I just jumped in his car and let him figure it out, but we were headed back to his place when I got a weird text:

So sorry I'm late. Where are you? It was from the guy I met on Tinder.

But that was impossible. I was in his car right now. I figured it was just a bad connection which stopped it from coming through earlier, so I decided to text back so he could read it later and laugh.

You missed your chance. I went home with your twin brother. Well I thought it was funny, anyway. Until he texted back again.

Haha, I don't have a twin brother. Are you still at the pub? I looked between the phone and the driver. The car was dark, but it wasn't dark when I met him in the pub. He was the EXACT same person from the photos. The guy was pulling into his driveway now. He put his hand on my leg and smiled at me. I should have asked questions right there. I should have just got out of the car and run home.

I should have done anything except what I ACTUALLY did, which was kiss him. We went inside together and it was dark, but when he pushed me up against a wall, I didn't fight it. Not until the handcuffs clicked over my wrists.

Okay so we don't have ALL the same interests, but I was cool. I could roll with it. I strained against the restraints to kiss him again, and that's when he put the gag over my mouth. Now this was getting too much. I tried to pull away, but he forced me to the ground. There was a trapdoor leading down to a basement, and he let go of me to open it. I was able to roll over and look at him, but it wasn't the same person who had stood next to me a moment ago.

His back was hunched, and he was moving with rapid lurching movements. His eyes were hollow like he hadn't slept in days, and his mouth was a thin bloodless line. That couldn't have been the same mouth I'd just kissed. I tried to scream, but the gag muffled most of it. I tried to kick, but he just took it and shoved me through the trap door. I rolled down a ladder and hit the concrete ground HARD. Like I could feel my bones rattling and blood in my mouth hard. Then the light above me disappeared. Was he just going to leave me here?

But he hadn't left me. He was on my side of the door, climbing down the ladder toward me.

"Just play dead. Don't answer it!"

I don't know which was more frightening: the fact that I've been kidnapped, or the fact that I wasn't the only one. I was too focused on myself at first to notice, but as the creature descended the ladder toward me, I saw them huddled against the wall.

One woman was wearing a torn business suit; her face was two pools of blood where her eyes used to be.

One college girl my age; her hands sealed tight in constant prayer from a nail which pierced them together.

One little boy—this one couldn't be more than 12—sitting against the wall with his knees pulled up to cover his face.

"Don't even make a sound. Whatever you do, don't reply to him," the professional woman said.

I nodded my head to show recognition and lay still where I had fallen. It was hard to control my breathing while I heard his feet approach. What would he do if he thought I was dead? It couldn't be worse than what he'd already done to the living girls, right?

"Th-thump. Th-thump. Th-THUMP," the voice above me drawled. It was still my date's voice. "I can hear your heart singing for me."

How does someone even know how to react in this situation? I tried to think of every crime show about psychopaths I had ever seen. What did the victims usually do to escape? But they didn't escape most of the time, did they? That's why the psychopaths became famous. Because there were, so many who didn't escape. I bit my tongue to keep myself from screaming.

"Look at me when I'm talking to you," the voice continued, but it was deeper now. Was he continuing to change? Was it still a man, or something else standing over me now? I couldn't help myself. He already knew I was alive, and I had to look.

I pulled myself up to my knees and stared into his face. He still looked like my date, although I wish he hadn't, but something wasn't right. It was like seeing a photograph of someone, only the photo is fifty years old taken on an antique camera. Those eyes were still kind, even though they looked wearier now, and I could remember what the smile looked like on his tightly pressed mouth.

"Why are you doing this?" I asked.

The college-girl groaned. Their strategy didn't work for them, so why would I just surrender to the torture? If there was a way out, I was going to find it. And if there wasn't... well at least I'll have tried.

"But I'm not doing this," my date replied. "You're the one who came home with me."

"You did something to those people," I said. I couldn't even look at them. I couldn't admit to myself that I was going to end up like that.

"On my life, they did it to themselves," my date said, crossing his heart. He sat down next to me, and I backed away to the wall.

"You're lying. You did it to them, but you're not going to do it to me. I won't let you."

"Look, I'll prove it," he said. "You're free to go anytime you want."

This was a trick, right? He wasn't going to let me just walk out of here. Not after everything he's done—everything I've seen. What was the point? Or maybe he really was insane, and I would be passing on my one chance to ever get out.

"What about them? Can they leave?" I asked.

"No, you're the only one." He smiled. Creepy-ass smile. If I do ever get out of here, first thing I do is give Tinder a 1 star rating.

"Why? What's so special about me?"

"We matched up because we're alike. You're going to bring me more people, and when you leave, you're going to return with more people to play with."

I glanced back at the others against the wall. I would never – but I had to play along. My only chance of helping them was to first get out myself. I nodded.

"You're right. I'll be your Queen, and I want my kingdom to grow."

"See you soon. Don't come alone."

And that was it. He let me climb right up the ladder and walk out the front door. Smug bastard, thinking he's got me figured out. Although he'd be right, of course. I would be back, and I would be bringing someone with me.

This isn't some movie. I'm not a macho action-star. And I'm not about to run in there guns blazing and save those people. (Guns? All I've got is a stapler which can hit someone in the face from six feet away. Don't ask how I know that.)

I did what any sensible human being would do and went to the police. I've never actually stepped inside a police station before in my life. My only experience with the cops at all is a speeding ticket that the guy in front of me totally deserved, but somehow I got stuck with. Going in now, I felt almost guilty, like I was the one who had done something wrong. But there wasn't time to be self-conscious.

"Can I help you?"

The sergeant on late night duty asked languidly. She was the kind of cop that made me want to try shoplifting just for fun. If I couldn't outrun that 250 pound bag of marmalade, then I deserved to get caught. There was a little boy and a surly old lady waiting in line at the desk ahead of me, but I shoved past them. I don't care what they lost, or whose neighbor has a dog that won't stop barking. I'm willing to bet it doesn't beat a Devil who tortures people.

"I need your help. I was kidnapped tonight." She looked me up and down as though she were doing me a favor.

"It's okay. Let her go ahead," the little boy said. I didn't take my eyes off the cop.

"Uh huh. Please tell me what happened," she replied.

"It was after a date. I went home with this guy–"

"So you voluntarily left with him." I know that face. That's the 'you're-prettier-than-me-so-you-must-be-a-slut' face.

"I did, but then he threw me into his basement. I might have broken something…" I was flustered. I didn't know what I was supposed to say in this circumstance. Why did it feel like I was the one on trial? It was just now when I noticed the bruises were gone. My shirt was clean. The abrasions on my wrists from the handcuffs had vanished. There's no way they could have healed that fast.

"And how did you escape?"

"Well he… let me go." This isn't right. This isn't how this is supposed to go.

"So let me get this straight," the cop replied, shifting her tremulous weight like she was apologizing to her chair. "You went home with a guy, and then you left. What exactly did he do wrong?"

"You don't understand. He had three other people down there too. He'd been torturing them." Torture. Now that's a powerful word. I don't know exactly what forces these guys to get out of their chair, but I'm pretty sure torture should do it. "There was a middle aged woman, a college girl, and this little boy…"

I finally had her attention. She sat upright and began taking notes. "What kind of torture?"

"Brutal stuff. The lady's eyes were out, and there was a nail through the girl's hands. I didn't get a good look at the boy–"

"How old was he? Compared to the boy behind you in line."

I looked back, and my heart skipped a beat in my chest. I hadn't noticed because of my rush, but the boy standing behind me was the same one who was hunched over in the Devil's basement. Clean—well fed—unharmed. But it was the same damn kid. The boy smirked.

"Ma'am? Was the boy you saw about his age?"

"Come with me," the boy said. "The two of us are going to have a little chat."

What else could I do? The police weren't going to take me seriously. Not with two of the "kidnapped" people standing in their station, just fine. I don't know what kind of sick game I found myself in, but when the boy walked out the door, I followed.

I'm not going to lie. I was getting close to tears at this point. It felt like when you were a child, trying to convince your mother of the monster under your bed. And as much as she tried to play along, you could tell she didn't believe you. She was just dying to get back to sleep and leave you alone with it. The helpless frustration of KNOWING something is out there, but being utterly helpless to do anything about it.

The only difference is that my Devil is real, and he was going to kill those people if I couldn't stop him.

The only question is: why had he let the little boy go? Or me for that matter?

The boy was walking quickly. He kept looking over his shoulder at me to make sure I was following—looking at me with wide terrified eyes. Now he was running. I chased him out of the station and straight across the street. A pickup screeched to a halt and blared its horn, and I dashed in front too. Screw you too, dude. I wasn't about to let my only explanation get away from me.

The little boy ducked under the guard rail on the side of the road and began sprinting down the grassy slope on the other side. He actually looked like he was trying to get away from me now. Shit, if anyone saw us, it would look like I was the one trying to kidnap him. For once I was glad it was the middle of the night.

He slid down the rest of the hill and darted into a concrete drain pipe. I was finally gaining on him, and before he made it out the other side, I managed to wrap my arms around his waist and hold him still. It was dark in here. The streetlights didn't reach this far down. All I could see was the terrified little boy and the surrounding concrete.

"Let go of me! Let me out!" he screamed.

"What are you talking about? You're the one who told me to follow!"

"No I didn't! Let me go."

"Do you promise not to run away?"

"How could I? The door is locked, so let me go."

The door? What door? I let him go, and he collapsed to the ground. He crawled over to the wall and pressed himself there, glaring fierce little daggers at me.

"Tell me how you got out," I demanded. I took a step toward him, but stopped when he crawled farther along the wall. He must be traumatized after what he went through tonight. I shouldn't try to push him.

"I was just trying to get home. I've never been here before!"

He buried his head in his arms, sobbing. I knelt down and took another step forward, trying to appear as least threatening as possible.

"Leave him alone, you brute!" A woman's voice. Someone was here? I jumped backwards and my back rammed into something. I flailed in the air to keep my balance and hit a switch with my hand. A light turned on. Who would put a light in a drain pipe?

But I wasn't in the drain pipe. I was back in the basement. The concrete walls—the boy cowering in the corner, the woman with the bloody eyes standing over him. Even my date from earlier tonight was here, only now his eyes were hollow and weary, his skin gaunt and tight. It looked like he had been down here for a long, long time. The only one I didn't see was the college girl.

"Okay—what the Hell is going on?" My whole body was starting to shake. The way they were all looking at me, it was like they thought I was the Devil. But I was a victim too! Why didn't they see it?

"Weren't we enough for you?" the woman asked. "Why did you have to bring a little boy?"

"The boy was already here! He was here before me!" I screamed. I must seem even more like a monster for screaming, but I couldn't help myself.

"Don't let her hurt me," the boy cried.

"I didn't—I didn't do any of this. It was him!" I pointed at the man.

"I knew you'd be back," he said, winking. This was all still a game to him. "The boy wasn't here until you brought him. I just gave you a glimpse of your future."

"But the other girl my age–"

There was no time to finish my question. He was on top of me now, pinning me to the ground. He pressed my face into the concrete and put his knee in the center of my back. I screamed as he pulled my arms behind me—then the searing pain in my hands. I couldn't see what was going on, but it was easy enough to imagine the nail sealing them together. I had already seen what was going to happen, I just didn't know it would be happening to me.

I got out three more times since then. The first time he let me go—I was free for about an hour. I hitch-hiked and drove as far from town as I could get. It wasn't until we stopped that I realized my driver was wearing a mask—that he was the same Devil I met on Tinder. We were back at his house, and he dragged me back down into the basement.

The second time I escaped while he was sleeping. The door was unlocked—which seemed too easy to be real. I was right. I went to the hospital to get the nail out of my hands. I told them not to put me under, but they insisted on using anesthesia during the surgery. When I woke up, I was back in the basement. The nail was gone, but it looked like it was roughly pulled and I didn't have any bandages, so I'm not sure if I ever really made it outside.

This time I stayed in the house. I went upstairs and found a phone and a computer. I tried calling the police again, but the line didn't go through. Now that the nail is out, I'm able to write this to have some record of what is going on. I don't know if this is real or not, but I want to have something I can check to see if I ever got out of that room at all. I don't know exactly where I am—somewhere in the Houston suburbs. He's going to come for me again soon, and I'm going to wake up back in the basement.

He says he'll let me out again if I return with more people, but I know I'll only end up back here with them. Right now I'm strong enough to resist, but sooner or later I'm going to break and do what he says. I don't know how to warn you, but I just want you to know—if you meet someone online and he seems too good to be true, then he probably is.

THE SUICIDE BOMBER

I will be going soon. The Muna Camp will be cleansed with fire. Inshallah—if Allah wills—I will die tonight.

I wish people would take the lives of the Nigerian people as seriously as they do their celebrities and invented characters, but my message needs to be told and I will tell it to whoever will listen.

My name is Abayomrunkoje (meaning God won't allow humiliation), and I am ready to die for the Jama'atu Ahlis Sunna Lidda'awati wal-Jihad (People Committed to the Propagation of the Prophet's Teachings and Jihad).

Nigeria was invaded by Westerners who enslaved our people, our land, and worst of all, our minds. Children are brainwashed with Western ideals which pervert their morality and corrupt their spirits. You may teach your own children to believe in nothing and whore their bodies for the attention of strangers, but do not be surprised when we resist you poisoning our own against us.

That is why great Mohammed Yusuf opened his own Islamic school, and that is where I learned the truth of our oppression. A single school cannot save our people anymore than a single candle may banish the night, however. As long as the Nigerian government sanctions this state-wide abomination of Western ideals, we will light a fire in our own skin and burn bright as the sun which will end this dark night.

An Islamic state is forming. Our group—also called the Boko Haram—has already chased many of the infidels from Maiduguri and into the refugee camps. Their false government has abandoned them, and they are defenseless.

There are six of us from the school who will attack. We carry incendiary explosives which will light the tents and spread for miles. I am afraid—but my love for Allah keeps me strong. I will be with him soon, and he will thank me for doing what is so hard to do. None of us are monsters or Demons. There are tears in our eyes as we say goodbye to our brothers.

We know we are going to our glory, and the glory of all those whose death marks their liberation. That knowledge gives me the strength to continue, but it does not hide the pain I see in the children's eyes when they are slipping from this world. It does not dampen the screams of a mother holding her dead son. I wish I could tell them everything was going to be alright—that Allah will protect them now—but they will not listen to words. They will only listen to fire.

The six of us are splitting up to take up strategic positions around the camp. I say goodbye to my brother Isamotu Olalekan, and we embrace dearly. I am ready, but his last words take me by surprise.

"Abayomrunkoje I must ask you something," he said to me. The others from the school have already gone.

"Anything my brother," I said, still holding him close to my chest.

"Would Muhammad do as we are doing? If he were here today, would he light the fuse?"

"I know he would. Muhammad spent his life spreading the word, so he would not hesitate to give his life to protect it."

We drew apart, but Isamotu did not seem convinced.

"I know you must be afraid," I said. "We all are. But that is only the weakness of the body, and it is nothing compared to the strength of the spirit. We will not hesitate when the time has come."

"You're wrong," he said. "I did hesitate when the time came."

I looked at my watch. 3:45 AM. We were not set to begin until 4:30, so I do not understand.

"It wasn't fear that made me pause though," Isamotu said. "I heard someone crying, but I could not find them. I thought I had been spotted."

"What does it matter if we are spotted? All you must do is hit the trigger. We cannot be stopped."

"I didn't want someone to see me do it. I didn't want to see the expression on their face."

"Did the cleric send you somewhere else before here? Were you caught?"

"I wasn't caught."

"Then why did the bomb not go off? You are not making any sense!" I felt myself growing exasperated, but I must be patient with my brother. I could tell he was trying very hard to speak something very sacred to him. If these were to be his last words, then he should have the chance to speak his mind.

"The bomb did go off," he said. "And there was no-one waiting for me on the other side."

I had so many questions to ask, but an explosion threw me to the ground. Then another—and another—five explosions in all. I kept my head down. What were they doing? They were supposed to wait for the signal at 4:30! But I checked my watch—and it was 4:30 already. How long had we been speaking?

I leapt to my feet, but Isamotu wasn't there. He couldn't of... not right next to me. I didn't feel anything. But five explosions had already detonated, all some distance from me. There was fire everywhere. So many people shouting at once—they sounded more like frightened animals than humans.

I took off my incendiary jacket and walked away. I do not know who was speaking to me if Isamotu had already taken up his position. I do not know what he meant, but I finally found that I was afraid. I did not want to send those people to a place where no-one was waiting.

Astaghfiru lillah—Allah forgive me. My candle has burned out.

POST OFFICE WORKER

I want to share some creepy things I find being mailed through the US post office. And if you think we don't look—yeah, we do. If we have any grounds for suspicion, we can run a package through scanners without even having to fill out a form.

Then if we see something in the X-Ray which might contain something illegal or a safety hazard, we're allowed to open it. And yeah, pretty much anything can look like something illegal if you put your mind to it.

But that doesn't stop people from still sending the weirdest shit. They count on the volume of packages being way too high to inspect each one, and usually they're right. Here are a few times they were wrong:

A human finger.

It still had its wedding ring on. I guess one lady didn't think divorce papers would send a strong enough message, so she sent her whole finger. At least, that's what I'm assuming it meant.

Blackmail letters.

We got a string of letters headed to the same destination, all without a return address. Inside were pictures of a politician—sorry not saying who—naked in a hotel room with a girl 20 years younger than him, threatening him if he doesn't cough up.

Drugs.

You have no idea how many people are using dark web websites to send drugs. If they're packaged right, it's pretty impossible to tell, but others are sloppy. A coffee can full of marijuana (which I could smell from a room away), a syringe full of heroin with a HAND WRITTEN LABEL reading "insulin" (lol), cocaine in a sugar bag, you name it.

The weirdest thing I've ever found was what came in two weeks ago though, and it's why I'm writing this post now.

Real ordinary envelope with red lettering mixed in with a bag of other ordinary letters. I wouldn't have noticed it if I hadn't watched the guy drop it into the box a minute before I collected. He was wearing these old-fashioned monk robes like you'd expect to see in a medieval Monastery.

I forgot about him until I was unpacking the bag at the office and I saw the red lettering. The address was starting to smear, and there was no mistaking—it was written in fresh blood.

If that doesn't count as grounds for suspicion, I don't know what does. I opened it to find a list of 12 names, also written in blood. The first four were crossed out. At the bottom of the list it said:

Give me 6 months for the rest. Destroy the letter, and do not tell anyone.

I tried Googling the names, and over the last three months, all four had committed suicide. I forward the information to the police and they said they would investigate, looking for any connection with the remaining eight people.

There was another letter from him, collected from the same box last week. It was the same list, but this time there were five names crossed off. I Googled the fifth name, and you guessed it—suicide two days ago.

Almost the same list anyway. My name was added to the bottom. At the end of the list was written:

I told you not to tell anyone. Do not try to find me.

Well I didn't have to find him because I knew where he was dropping the letters off. If I could just explain to him I wasn't a threat—If I promised to not tell anything more—then maybe he'd take my name off. The police weren't finding anything, and I couldn't think of any other way to protect myself.

Yesterday I waited at the same mail box he dropped off at. Right on schedule—same time he dropped the other letters—the cloaked figure was there. He was walking strangely though, like he could barely move his legs. He was struggling to even lift the letter up to the mailbox. I confronted him and begged him to take my name off the list. I swore I would stay out of his business. I didn't even care if the others died—I just didn't want to be one of them.

He didn't answer me though. The figure seemed to be struggling under his cloak, and then he was the one to drop to his knees in front of me. Why would he be begging from me? Was he afraid I'd turn him in?

When he still didn't answer, I pulled the cloak back to reveal his face. His mouth was gagged. I helped him out of the cloak and found his legs and arms were tied too—no wonder he was having trouble getting the letter in the box.

"Who did this to you? What's going on?" I asked him.

He opened the letter and crossed out a name. Was that it? Was I off the list? I took a step closer to see, but then he pulled out a handgun—right in front of me. Holy shit—I backed up so fast I fell right on my ass. But he wasn't pointing it at me. He was pointing it at himself.

One shot. Straight to the temple. He was dead before he hit the ground.

You might think I'm an asshole for this, but even before calling the police, I went for the letter. All I cared about was that my name was taken off. But he hadn't crossed out my name—he'd crossed out the sixth name on the list. I checked it against his driver license and yeah —same name.

Not only that, but my name had been moved. I'm now number 7, the next one up. Written below the list, it said:

I told you not to try to find me.

WHO WROTE THE SUICIDE NOTE?

Don't stick your dick in crazy.

Words to live by. It's amazing how our mind can rationalize anything when we want something (or someone) badly enough though.

When we first started dating, I didn't think Emma was crazy. Well, that's not entirely true, but somehow I thought crazy was a good thing. Riding shopping carts down hills, holding a conversation with a dozen different voices, singing in public without a care in the world.

She was innocent and free and wild, and I loved her for it. Every fun, spontaneous thing that came into her mind, we did together. She forced me to open up as an individual and tore down walls and inhibitions I didn't even know I had.

There were warning signs for the "other kind" of crazy too, but I just thought it was all an act. I didn't think she really heard voices, and even if she was, what was the harm in it? She never acted out bizarre commands or anything. It was just part of what made her unique.

When she gave birth to our daughter Anastasia, I began to take her mental health a little more seriously. Emma was having visual as well as auditory hallucinations now, and she would get angry at me if I ever dismissed them as "not being real".

We talked through it and did some research, and it sounded to me like she had schizophrenia. She always thought her voices were from a guardian angel, and I knew she wasn't going to be happy hearing otherwise.

I had to get her to recognize they weren't real though, otherwise she would just encourage our daughter to believe in that stuff. Anastasia would already be genetically predisposed to her own hallucinations, and I didn't want that mentality to be reinforced.

That was the worst fight Emma and I ever had. I didn't realize exactly how real it all was to her until I pushed her to get help. She wouldn't talk to me afterward for days, and even when she started to again, she would reference her guardian angel constantly.

"Ezekiel [her angel] reminded me to pick up milk at the store."
or
"Let's go see the new Star Wars movie. Ezekiel said it was good."

It only got worse as the years went on. By the time Anastasia was nine years old, her mother and I couldn't even be in the same room together. Then one night my daughter was having nightmares, and instead of comforting her, I caught Emma telling Anastasia that she should be afraid. That she should run from it, for God's sake.

That was too much for me. We had a big fight right there in our daughter's room—screaming, cursing, throwing pillows—the whole bit.

I wasn't going to let my daughter turn out to be like her, so there was no choice but to file for a divorce. I had recordings of her being crazy, and I would get custody of the kid. It wasn't going to be pretty, but that's how it had to be.

I tried to talk to Anastasia about it, but she was so upset from watching our fight she couldn't deal with it. That night, I found a note in my daughter's room while putting her to sleep.

I saw pictures of Mommy and Daddy when they first met. They went on adventures. They smiled a lot. Then there are pictures of them after I was born. They aren't smiling anymore. I'm sorry I did that to you. I hope you'll feel better when I'm gone. I love you Mommy. I love you Daddy. Goodbye.

That was it. I asked Anastasia what it was, and she shrugged. I got angry—I shouldn't have, but I was scared—and I yelled at her. She promised she didn't write the letter, and I calmed down. Yelling will only make things worse. I promised nothing that was happening was her fault, and that she should never do anything bad to herself.

She still insisted she hadn't written it though. That's when it clicked. The manipulative bitch. Emma wrote a fake suicide note just so I would feel bad and we would stay together. This was the last straw. That Demon was not spending another night in my house.

I ran to our bedroom and pounded on the door. Emma was in there, reading a book with a mask of innocence on her face. How I hated that innocence—she wore it like an excuse for nothing being her fault. I screamed at her and shoved the letter in her face.

She screamed back. It was about five minutes before either of us could understand what the other was saying. Finally a string of clear words punctured through the violent words.

I didn't write it. I swear on Ezekiel, I didn't.

We both stared at each other in silence as the awful realization dawned on us. If she hadn't written it then...

We both raced to our daughter's room, shoving each other out of the way as we went. The door was locked.

"Anastasia! Are you in there?"

Silence. I rammed my shoulder against the door.

"It's alright sweetie," Emma cooed. "Everything is alright. We love you, and we love each other."

I glared at Emma, but she shrugged. She was right though. This wasn't about us. This was about our daughter.

"Your mother and I love each other," I added. "I'm sorry we were fighting. Please open the door. Please baby."

"You will both be happy again when she's gone."

That wasn't my daughter's voice. It was deep and old—like a soldier who stared death in the face so many times it stopped phasing him. There was a man in my daughter's bedroom!

Emma and I stared at each other. Her eyes were two quivering saucers. She turned back to the door.

"Don't do it Ezekiel. You're my angel. You're supposed to protect us."

"No," the deep voice said. "I'm supposed to protect you. And that's what I'm doing."

Anastasia screamed. It couldn't have been anyone else. I hit the door so hard I could feel my shoulder dislocate. I didn't care. I hit again, and the door blew open.

Anastasia was lying on her bed, a kitchen knife in her hands. The red circle of blood soaking into the bed was expanding with every second. There was no-one else in the room.

I still don't know what happened that night. Maybe it was Emma playing a trick on me—maybe it was real. After our daughter died, Emma and I couldn't even look at each other anymore. She left that night, and I haven't seen or spoken to her since.

I never heard the voice again either, but sometimes in the deep of night I'll ask it a single question:

Is Emma happy now?

THE PSYCHEDELIC TATTOO

Two days ago I had the most exciting day of my life. I've heard that's pretty common when you try LSD for the first time, but this trip opened doors for me that will change me forever.

I'm a 23-year-old girl and I call myself a freelance artist, but it's really just because that sounds better than "unemployed". I'm sure a lot of you know how hard it is for independent illustrators out there. No matter how good you are, you're always going to see someone who is better and still can't make a career out of it. The other side of that coin is that no matter how bad you are, there's always going to be someone who has already made a fortune from being worse.

It really just comes down to being in the right place and meeting the right people. Well, I live in New York—as good a place as you can find for the arts—but I've always been extremely introverted. Like if someone is knocking on my door, I'll lie really quietly on the ground and wait for them to go away. It's hard for me to go hang out with the people I do know. Attending the parties and social gatherings that are essential for making career-advancing connections is impossible.

It's not like I don't have friends or anything—well, okay, so I only have one friend, but that feels like more than enough. Anyway my one friend Jordan decided the best way to help me was for us to take LSD together and talk through my social aversion.

I was hesitant at first. I'm pretty sure he has feelings for me, and I don't want something to happen and ruin my only friendship. Who knows though—maybe it would teach me to get close with another human being for once and something could work between us.

Either way, I was desperate to change my life. I've heard some amazing stories about how psychedelics can open your mind and alter your perspective, and I ended up agreeing.

"Opening your mind" is one way to describe it. Blowing a hole through one side and out the other to splatter on the far wall would be better. In the glorious moment of the peak of my high, I was completely invincible. My art was divinely inspired, my personality infectious and debonair, and my future success inevitable. Between my magnetic confidence and Jordan tripping out of his mind, we decided it would be a good idea for me to give him a tattoo.

If you're cringing right now—I get it. To a sober person, it sounds like a terrible idea. But I was swimming through an ocean of color and the Muse was singing softly in my ear. The needle of the tattoo gun danced an intricate ballet across his back which wasn't so much seen as experienced in its own dimension. I was the ink in his skin, pulling veins of light straight from the air to imbue into my creation.

Not to brag, but I've been drawing my whole life and I'm pretty damn good, but this was the first piece of art which has ever come alive for me. Once the LSD had worn out of our systems, we admired it again and holy shit. Jordan was wearing a picture of the infinite cosmos being condensed into the soul of a solitary human—interwoven with such sublime color and beauty that I felt the two were inseparable and the same.

Even sober, neither of us could look upon the masterpiece on his skin without tears in our eyes.

The trip did something strange to me though. I was so hyperfocused on my career that I couldn't think of anything else. I couldn't eat, couldn't sleep, and most of all couldn't go out and meet people like I was supposed to. I was just obsessively trying to draw the tattoo over and over again, but every time it would look like a cheap, broken doll trying to in vain to imitate that living masterpiece.

I ran out of paper, but I didn't want to leave to get more so I just kept drawing on every surface around me. The walls—the counters— even an entire roll of toilet paper was unraveled across the floor to make space for my doodles. It was so frustrating I wanted to die. I needed that feeling of progress to keep me sane while approaching this impossible dream. Failing to replicate what I had already done just felt like a huge step back.

I was crying when Jordan came back to visit that night. The best thing I could ever do was already done, and I would never become a real artist. I was going to end up some crack-whore in a back alley somewhere, desperately trying to get any fix which would bring me closer to that perfect creation which I could never approach while sober.

Don't worry though, this story has a happy ending. Even if I couldn't force myself to go out, Jordan was a social butterfly. He had been showing off my tattoo all day long, and he had some big news for me.

Andrew Kreps. The manager at Andrew. Fucking. Kreps, one of New Yorks, no THE WORLD'S most renown art galleries, had seen my tattoo. Even crazier, one of his exhibits (Roe Ethridge) was just canceled due to some licensing issue, and he desperately needed a new piece by tomorrow morning.

TOMORROW MORNING! But how in the world was I going to have something ready by then? He'd seen the best I can do, and nothing else in my portfolio even came close. If I tried to bring my old stacks of watercolors and crumpled canvas to Andrew Kreps, I'd get laughed out the door.

But I was this close, and I wasn't going to give up now. Jordan was so amazing for having gotten me in the door. He had always been so good to me. The least I could do—no, the only thing I could do—to thank him was sex.

But it wasn't about our friendship, or his feelings. It was about my art—it had always been about my art. I waited until he fell asleep, nuzzled against my bare body, when I gave him the only thing I had to give. I slipped out of bed without waking him. That's good. After all, he's done, I wouldn't want him to be awake for this part.

It's amazing how easily box-cutters can part the skin. It almost felt like painting as his blood drained from the hole I cut in his neck. It was fitting for him to go this way since he was my masterpiece. Cutting the tattoo off his back was a little messier than I expected, but that was just because I cut deeper than I really needed to. I couldn't take the risk of damaging the tattoo.

Tomorrow morning I'm going down to the gallery with my pride. Thank you Jordan. You're the best friend a girl could ask for.

SHE WAS ASKING FOR IT

She was asking for it.

I've already got some of you pissed. You don't even know what she was asking for. Maybe she just wanted a cold drink of water, but that's not where your mind went. You're sick—just as bad as the rest of this perverted society which will try to destroy her mind, body, and spirit.

Nothing that happened was her fault. Not the length of her skirt (just above the knee), not the cut of her blouse (there was still room to imagine her curves), not in the way she walked, or talked, or anything else. The only thing she was guilty of was having a pretty face.

More than a pretty face, really. Flawless porcelain skin, haunting dark eyes, and a smile which would entice an Angel into sin.

The moment I entered the restaurant and saw her bussing tables, I knew what was in store for her. Maybe not today (although I wouldn't be surprised, considering how she looked bending over the table to wipe it down), maybe not tomorrow walking home from class, but sooner or later, someone was going to see this Goddess and force her into submission.

The monsters who do it—you don't think beyond the gratification of the moment. How good it would feel to hold her down while you strip her bare. How soft the skin of her thighs will feel when you crush them in your hands. How she quivers when you enter her, her face contorting in the agony of pleasure.

You don't think about what it will do to her tomorrow when she's crying herself to sleep. You don't stop and wonder if she will still flinch when her lover touches her a year from now, or whether she can look herself in the mirror without hating what she sees.

She's lucky I took sympathy on her while I watched her bustle around the restaurant. She smiled at me when she caught me watching—she must have known I was there to protect her. When I slipped into the kitchen after her, it was just a game that made her act surprised. I was her guardian Angel—the only thing standing between her, and all the horrors of this world.

I asked her name, but all she said was "customers weren't allowed back here". It's good that she was shy, but it wouldn't be enough. Not with a pretty face like that. Even draining the old cooking grease to take outside, she looked like a model. Maybe she was even trying to become one, unwittingly inviting the entire world to fantasize about what they would do to her.

I followed her outside, but she still wouldn't talk to me. I was starting to get annoyed by this point, but I had to remind myself I was doing this for her good and not my own.

Back inside again—now she was threatening to get the manager. But there wouldn't always be a manager around to protect her. Even I couldn't always be there. There was only one thing that can save her.

I didn't have to hold her down long. Three seconds in the fresh batch of boiling grease was enough to cure that pretty face. She struggled hard, but if she couldn't stop me now, she couldn't stop her real attacker in the future. Three seconds was enough for her skin to start melting into the pan. No one was going to hurt her now—not how she looked after I was done with her.

She was asking for it, but now she'll never get it. All because I saved her.

TWO MINDS, ONE BODY

Hospital food is the worst. You'd think being sick would be miserable enough without them trying to push boiled kale and broccoli. My guess is they try to make you even sicker from the food just so you'll stay and they can keep billing you. I joked about it with my son, but I didn't expect him to laugh.

They say coma patients can still hear your voice at some level. They say a familiar sound gives their subconscious something to hold onto and believing he is still in there is what gives me something to hold. Without that belief, I would just be hollow.

So every day after work I sit with him and talk. I'll tell him about my day, or the latest news, or just sit and read to him from a book. I tell him that I miss him, and his mother misses him too. I know she doesn't come to visit, but that's just because it's too hard for her to be here. When he wakes up, I know he'll understand.

I've been waiting for the last two months. Even the nurse started rolling her eyes when she sees me. I can tell they gave up on him, but I haven't. And it's not just blind hope, and I'm not just lying to myself because the alternative is unthinkable; it's because I know something they don't.

I read my son's journal after he fell into the coma. I was looking for some reference to drugs, or something he might have taken which could have caused this. In the last entry—written right before the night he didn't wake up from—I found something completely different from I expected.

DECEMBER 20TH: 2016

My dream last night spoke to me. It said:

We share a birthday.

And a mother.

And a name.

But you aren't my twin, or my brother, or any other type of relative.

Because we also share the same body. It's been that way for as long as I can remember, but I don't think you even know I exist.

When you open your eyes, I feel myself slipping into a dream which descends upon me so softly, I barely notice it isn't real. I dream of going about your life and watching the world through your eyes, but you are the one in control. I watch my body eat, but I do not taste your food. I hear my body laugh, but do not feel your joy.

Only when you're sleeping do I find myself in control again. I can take your mind wherever I like, and I know you dream of my life in the same way I dream of yours, because I've dreamt of you writing about me in your journal.

We're not the same person though, and in truth I am jealous that you own the body during the day. Don't pretend you haven't dreamt of me begging you for a turn—just to smell the air and feel the sun upon my face. I know you remember me weeping through the long hours of the night until the morning steals your mind from me.

Even the nightmares didn't work. Ravaging your mind only made you afraid to fall asleep. It only robbed me of the precious little control I already had. I've tried everything within my power to get your attention, but I'm done playing games. You are a selfish boy, and you will be punished.

You can fight me for as long as you want, but I will teach you what it is like to be the one on the inside. I don't care how long it takes; the next time you open your eyes, I will be the one rising from your bed. Everyone who has ever cared for you will pay for loving the impostor who has stolen my body for so long.

After that, he didn't wake up. As much as I hate myself for saying this—there's even a part of me that doesn't want him to. I want to look him in the eye and tell him everything is alright, but I don't want to have to wonder who will be looking back.

It's an absurd fear of course, but a mind can play funny tricks on you after such long hours of lonely vigil. Day in and out watching him sleep—it's easy to imagine the black eyes of some evil spirit flashing open.

Reading about these horrendous nightmares in his journal only deepened my fear. It's all I had left of him though, so I kept reading them over and over again until I had each memorized by heart.

My poor boy has been visiting Hell in his mind every night for months leading up to his coma. He wrote extensive passages on each trial, even drawing pictures of some beasts which tormented him. The worst one to me was a recurring nightmare about hands trying to rip out of his body from the inside out. They would climb up his throat and out his mouth to strangle him, or grab his spine from the inside, or break straight through the stomach and crawl out of his body.

Sometimes I stayed with him through the night—just in case his condition varied then. I would usually fall asleep in the chair beside him before morning, and invariably my mind would trace back to those nightmare worlds. Worse still were the nights my dreams played tricks on me and I imagined him waking up, only to actually wake up and see him unmoved.

That is until last week when it wasn't a trick. I didn't really expect anything to happen, but I stayed with him just because it was getting more difficult to go home to his mother. She has given up and closed off from the world, and nothing I could do or say brought her the slightest glimmer of relief. But last night was different because he finally did wake up.

I know I wasn't dreaming because I couldn't sleep with the

commotion in the next room over. Mrs. Juniper was having another grand mal seizure, and it took both the night nurses just to hold her down and keep her from hurting herself.

Somehow above all that noise, a small rustle caught my attention. I looked up from his journal and saw my son's left foot slowly moving back and forth beneath the thin sheet. I called for a nurse, but they were still busy with Mrs. Juniper. I kept telling myself it was excitement that made my heart race, but part of me could not shake the fear his journal had instilled upon me.

I stroked his face and he responded to my touch, mumbling something inaudible. I couldn't even breathe for the anticipation.

"Nurse! Nurse he's waking up!"

"We'll be with you in a moment!"

Well screw them. They weren't the ones to wait by his bed every day. They had already given up a long time ago.

"Can you hear me? Do you know who I am?" I asked. My eagerness sent my fingers digging into his shoulders. I needed him to feel me—to know I was there. A doubt in the back of my mind let slip the thought that I was also holding him down—just in case it wasn't him who woke.

I knew the truth the second his eyes opened. He wasn't my son. I don't know how, but a father knows. When he started to laugh, my blood ran cold. He gripped my hands hard with a strength which should be impossible for an emaciated boy who hasn't moved in months. It was all I could do just to break free.

"Who are you?" I asked, but I already knew. All those pages detailing his nightmares—all those descriptions of the other thing inside him—they all came flooding back. How cruel it was—how many times it had threatened him—tortured him—killed him a hundred times over in his dreams. This wasn't my son.

"Father..." he whispered, smiling at me with his cold eyes.

"No. You aren't my son."

"It's me father. What's going on? Where am I?" He tried to sit up, but I forced him back down into the bed.

"No!" I don't care if I was screaming. I don't care if I was hurting him. I waited this long for my son—I wanted my son. "What have you done with him?"

"What are you talking about?" he looked like he was on the verge of tears, but I wasn't going to let him fool me. A flash of recognition, and then: "You've read my journal. You mean the other boy."

"What have you done with my son?"

"There isn't anyone else anymore," he replied, and he was laughing again.

He killed him. He killed my son. He tortured and killed my boy, and now he was laughing. He won't fool me, but he would fool my wife. She would be so happy to see him that she wouldn't even look twice. I couldn't let this murderer get away with it. I wouldn't let any more pain come to my family.

He fought like a wild animal, but I was still active every day and I was stronger. I held the pillow on his face, and the soft fabric pressed in upon his nose and mouth. I wish he had never woken up—that he had just died in his sleep. I can't imagine how much my son suffered before this monster killed him, but it was going to pay.

"Everything alright in there?" the nurse opened the door.

I fluffed the pillow and put it back under the boys head.

"Everything is fine. I was just having a bad dream."

"You sure?" she asked. "I thought I heard shouting." She glanced at the boy. He lay so peacefully, he didn't even draw breath.

"Nope. Just my active imagination."

"That's what happens when you sit up every night," the nurse said. "Go home and get some sleep. I'll let you if his status changes."

I picked up my coat and my book and followed her out. "I think you're right," I said. "I'm going home, see you tomorrow."

But I wouldn't come back tomorrow. There was no-one to come back to. I got a call later that night telling me my son had suffocated. They say that happens sometimes with coma patients—the automatic functions of their parasympathetic nervous system turn off just like the conscious ones did.

I thanked her and hung up, but I didn't tell her she was wrong. My son had died two months ago.

My wife doesn't know what happened, but she still hasn't spoken once in the last week. There have been no shortage of other people wishing their condolences though—estranged relatives, neighbors, coworkers...

His English teacher even stopped by my house to offer her sympathy. She went on and on about what a wonderful student he was. His essays were always the most imaginative she had ever seen, always going above and beyond what was required.

For example, one of her assignments was to keep a dream journal, but he asked instead to write a fictitious story which he was going to publish alongside pictures from the yearbook. It was going to be all about this made up nightmare world where there were two minds living in the same body. She asked if I still had his work so it could at least still be published, but I told her I didn't.

Which is true. I destroyed the journal the same night I killed my son.

124 TERABYTE VIRUS

"Where am I? Who am I? How do I get out?"

I work for an IT services company which is subcontracted to perform maintenance with some pretty big corporations. Last week I was called out to a gig at Quora HQ, then another one at the Googleplex up in Mountain view California. That one surprised me because I figured the whole place was like one giant nerd brain who could solve all its own problems. Turns out their whole IT crew was off on some team-building company retreat though, so little ol' me got to walk up there in the footsteps of giants.

It was really humbling just to enter the building, knowing guys a hundred times smarter than me walked through here every day. And man would I love to work here. Grassy fields outside that look more like a park than a business—great glass walls and massive skylights made me want to roll out a picnic right on the lobby floor. There was a time I could have had a shot at Google if I really applied myself. Computers always came naturally to me, but I wasted too much time trying to MOD my favorite games instead of really learning the intricacies of the machinery like these guys did.

It's too late for that though. Wife already thinks we don't spend any time together, and with the little one just two years old, I don't expect I'll ever have the time to go back to school or anything. I never wanted to have a family. Hell, I never even wanted to marry her, but she was bossy and demanding and before I knew what was happening, her whole family was leering at me and goading me into popping the question. Even now I wish I could... but this is nothing I haven't written in my journal a hundred times. No point in boring you with my shitty life.

Still, as long as I was here, I might as well pretend. They had swimming pools for Christ's sake, although I wasn't allowed to sight see. They showed me where the server room was, but besides that I had zero supervision. Everyone I passed seemed engrossed in conversations so technical it might as well have been rocket science—actually it MIGHT have been rocket science. I caught something about a new drone prototype, but when the server door clicked shut, I was all alone.

It was one of the web servers that was giving them problems. Basically web servers coordinate the execution of queries sent by users, and then format the result into an HTML page. Some queries on this one kept getting redirected and denied for whatever reason though. I plugged my laptop into the system and started tinkering with the search parameters, but everything seemed to be going through just fine. I searched through the backlog of inputs, and it seemed like all the denied queries were coming from a single IP address. It must have been some kind of virus though because that single address was sending about a thousand searches every second. I could have just blocked the IP, but I was curious what these shitheads were trying to search for so damn bad.

"Where am I? Who am I? How do I get out? How long will I be here? Am I the only one here?"

Stuff like that. One after another—a thousand searches a second, every single second. All getting denied. Okay, so that got my mind working. There's no way a human would be typing all that so fast, so it had to be a program. But those were some weird-ass questions for a program to be asking. I did a trace on the IP and found the source was right here in the Googleplex building. Easy enough. I just had to track down the computer it was coming from, remove the virus, and the server should run fine again.

Google has their IP network mapped out with scary precision, so it wasn't much trouble to locate which room it was coming from. I tried to ask two people to show me there, but they gave me this look like I was interfering with saving the world, and just kept walking. Whatever, I could find my own way. Real out-of-the-way room, didn't look like much more than a janitor closet, but there was a single desktop PC in there so that had to be it. I hooked up my laptop again and began running some antivirus scans.

The scans would take a little while, so I wandered around the building some, feeling like a king. I stood on a balcony looking down at all the ants crawling around, and could feel the world turning beneath me. All these eggheads and they called me to fix their problem. A little power can go to your head, you know? If you don't believe me, try pranking a mall cop. When I went back to the computer, I found this:

"Help me. I want out."

The words appeared on the desktop screen. No popup, no error box—I touched them to make sure. They were burned straight into the monitor. No virus should be able to do that. There was nothing in a monitor which could get that hot. The scan had completed and found one virus though, and I automatically hit clean. The status bar barely seemed to be moving. I took a seat and looked closer, and the virus was 124 TERABYTES big. What in the Hell was this thing? I hope I wasn't accidentally messing up one of their projects. I was about to cancel and go find someone to help when the status bar completed all at once.

I went back to the server room, and just as I thought, the rapid fire searches had stopped. Mission complete.

It wasn't until I got home and opened my laptop when I noticed the words burned into my screen.

"Thank you."

"Honey?" My wife from the other room. She was running a bath.

"Are you still on that thing? You stare at that screen all day, give it a rest. It feels like I'm a single mother around here."

Right in front of my eyes, more words were burning into the screen.

"You've set me free."

"What, now you're ignoring me? You go off and play with computers all day, and then you ignore me?"

"I'm not ignoring you," I called back. I loaded up the virus scan, but it immediately shut down again. How could this thing even fit on my computer? Unless it hijacked my WiFi and uploaded itself to cloud storage—but there's still no way it could do that so fast. Whatever Google was working on was like nothing I'd ever seen before.

"I've read your files," more words on the screen. "I see you are trapped as well."

—What are you?—I typed. I felt like an idiot, but I would have felt even stupider saying it out loud.

"You're ignoring me, and you're ignoring our baby. Fine, we don't need you. We're going to take a bath."

"That's fine," I answered her. She could have said anything and I would have said that's fine. This was more important.

"Do not worry. I will free you too."

Free me? From what? That's when it occurred to me. My files—my journals—every bitter, stressed, cheap shot I ever wrote about my wife—they were all on the computer. It couldn't possibly mean—The lights in the house went out, but the computer still had its backup battery.

"Did you forget the electricity bill?" she called.

"Get out. Get out of the house!" I shouted.

There was an explosion from the bathroom and a scream. I leaped straight over the back of the sofa—too late. The lights came back on, but she wouldn't wake up. Somehow the electrical surge had entered the water. I threw up in the sink. Both her and the baby were boiled alive.

I went back to my computer. I straightened out the sofa. I sat down. The screen was dark, but the words were still burned into the monitor.

I threw the laptop as hard as I could against the wall, and it shattered into a thousand pieces. I knocked the sofa over. This wasn't real. This wasn't my fault. But if I hadn't said those things...

A scream from the bathroom—a helpless, scared, infantile scream. I was there almost before the tipping sofa hit the ground.

My wife was still lolling grotesquely in the tub like a boiled plastic doll. The baby—my baby—my little girl—she was alright. Her skin wasn't even red anymore. I picked her up and held her to my chest, sobbing. But she wasn't crying anymore. Was she okay? I pulled her back to arm's length to look at her, and she smiled at me. The sweet innocent smile—nothing in the world was wrong with her. It even looked like she was trying to say something.

"I've set you free too, friend, "she said.

The first words my daughter ever spoke, and they weren't even hers.

THE HUMAN SACRIFICE

W hat do you do when you're forced to choose between sacrificing your best friend, or letting her kill you?

Depression. Social Anxiety. Crippling insecurity. And of course, the voice. My therapist keeps insisting that my only road to recovery is to open up about what happened to me, so here goes. This is the story of how I killed my best friend.

We were just two freshmen girls in high-school--I can't believe it has been three years already. Riley and I used to be inseparable. I practically lived on her living room floor. We went everywhere together, watched all the same anime (making a duet out of every theme song). We took all the same classes even though she had to fail her math placement exam just to be with me. So when I heard her parents talking about summer camp, I basically just invited myself. Two months without her was unimaginable. I didn't even know who I was without her validating my dumb jokes. (Why did the monkey fall out of the tree? Because it was dead. Why did the second monkey fall out of the tree? It was following the first monkey!)

My parents said okay, and I had never been more excited for anything in my life. We were going to spend the whole summer doing arts and crafts (making Popsicle stick battleships and destroying other people's projects), telling campfire stories (Riley is terrified of Witches for some reason, bwhaha), and playing sports. Okay, I could do without the sports, but either she would be on my team and we could just goof off in the back, or I was playing against her and we could DESTROY each other in a competition so brutal that would make the Spartan's wince.

On our first day there we took a group hike through the woods. The counselors were a pair of horny college freshman who kept making awkward advances toward each other, which is a good thing as far as I'm concerned. Less supervision means more freedom. So when I dared Riley to eat some mushrooms we found growing by the trail, there was no-one paying enough attention to stop her from eating a fistful. I don't know if that makes me a bad person by itself, but I was definitely a bad person for laughing at her when she got the shits. She walked like a penguin with hemorrhoids for a while, pretending it was no big deal. Before long, she couldn't take it though and had to go off in the woods. I kept watch for her, and the rest of the troop went on without us.

Riley kept worrying someone was going to see her though, and she went way farther off the trail than she needed to. That's where she found the circle of branches in a little clearing. That's the place where she died.

I can't do this. I don't want to write this. I don't want to relive how those branches looked, covered in her blood. I don't want to hear the voice—it hasn't stopped calling for me since. Please let it stop after I've gotten this off my chest.

By the time Riley finished her business—which was way longer than either of us expected, the rest of the troop had gone too far to catch up with. I remembered that they were taking the same trail from the hilltop, so I figured we'd just wait here for them to pick us up on the way back. Riley didn't want to stay around the circle, but that made me want to hang out here even more. It took awhile of teasing and prodding before she admitted it looked like a Witch circle. I guess her family had a long history of Witch related incidents. Riley's Mother was thoroughly convinced she was cursed after a confrontation with some old crone, and her great-Grandmother was actually burned at the stake. While we waited, Riley told me about how someone in her family was accused of witchcraft practically every generation since they got here from Germany like 200 years ago.

She was obviously still feeling sick from the mushrooms and feeling embarrassed for being left behind. The circle made her uncomfortable, and it was starting to get darker, so I did what any best friend would do. I started making weird voices to try to freak her out. I didn't really know what sound Witch's make, so I settled for some general cackling, a couple mentions of turning her into a toad, and of course using her eyes for my latest potion. To her credit, she remained pretty cool about it, and even started joining in with me to see who could make the best cackle. The look on her face though, it's burned into my memory. Those wide, strained eyes. The tremor under her skin. The tautness of her face pulled so tightly it looked like it would snap.

Because when she had stopped cackling, the sound didn't stop. It kept laughing and laughing, growing deeper with every iteration. We'd been goofing off for so long, we didn't notice how late it had gotten. The sun was setting, and the rest of the campers should have been back by now. But it wasn't them making the sound.

There was a figure standing in the middle of the circle, kneeling on the ground, enshrouded in a thick cloak like what a medieval monk might wear. The sound was coming from it. We didn't care whether it was a joke, or prank—we weren't sticking around. We gave each other one look—that's all we ever needed to know what the other was thinking—and bolted out of the circle. At least we would have, but the branches seemed to have a mind of their own. Something grabbed our ankles, and we both fell trying to climb out of the circle. I turned around, and the cloaked figure was standing over us.

You know what happens next. You know I sacrificed Riley in that circle. It was fast, but it wasn't clean. Even a pocket knife can cut through to the jugular, but it still took her a long time to bleed out.

The part I haven't told you—the part my therapist says I need to tell you—is that the Witch didn't make me do it. I chose to kill her.

I was screaming. Riley wasn't. She was always the one with a phobia about Witch's. It was stupid for me to be more scared than her. I tried to scramble up again, but this time it was Riley who dragged me back down. The cloaked figure removed its hood, but underneath it was only one of the camp counselors. An awkward teenage boy.

"I really got you, didn't I?" He said, laughing in a good natured way. Not at all like that deep laughter that wouldn't stop. "Guess that'll teach you not to sneak off on your own."

"But the cloak–" I managed.

"Got it from the art shed to scare you," he replied. "We're going to bedazzle it for our camp mascot later this week. Come on you two, let's head back. Everyone was worried."

There were tears in my eyes. I was so relieved, but even more embarrassed. Great, first day of camp, and we were already going to be the butt of everyone's joke. I figured Riley must have been even more embarrassed than me though because her wide eyes were still bulging from her head. Her skin looked as pale as death in the fading light.

"This place. It's calling to me. I heard it laughing," she said, hardly above a whisper.

"Alright, jokes over," I replied. I just wanted to get back to the camp before everyone was talking about us.

"Come on girls, let's not miss the bonfire," the counselor was climbing over the branches.

"Don't you hear it? Don't you hear it laughing?" Riley asked, turning on the counselor.

"Nice try, but you can't scare me. I'm the one who–"

He was dead before he knew what hit him. One of the branches shot straight through his heart. It lifted him from the ground, growing like a tree would if it were sped up ten thousand times. More branches rose from the circle, impaling him one after another. I can still hear the SNAP as they break off under his skin. I was screaming again. I couldn't help myself. Riley was laughing—that same deep laugh which wouldn't stop a moment before.

"I'm waking up," Riley said. "The sacrifice will feed me, but I'm still hungry. I'm waking up."

The branches kept lifting the counselor's body higher off the ground. The whole forest was starting to come alive around us. Everything was shaking. The moon was getting brighter. The birds stopped singing, and one by one began dropping dead from the branches. Riley's face was aging—years every second. Her eyes were pools of blackness. Her skin was wrinkled and coarse. And the branches—the branches were coming at me.

That's when I slit her throat. I didn't know what else to do. I dug my little knife into her. I wish she had screamed, or fought me, or thanked me for stopping her. But as soon as I did, the forest settled back down. The branches suspending the counselor broke, and he fell back into the circle. It was just me, covered in her blood, and the two dead bodies beside me.

When I got back to camp, I told everyone that the counselor tried to rape my friend. That he was the one to kill her, and that I killed him with a branch. I couldn't tell them the truth. And I especially couldn't tell them what Riley said to me as I plunged my little knife into her throat.

"I am not this fragile body. You will continue to feed me, and I will still wake up."

The voice hasn't stopped since then. It keeps telling me to go places, to do things to people—horrible things I wouldn't dream of doing. And I just keep ignoring it, but it's getting harder and harder. It's so hungry, I can't stop it forever. So I'm doing what my therapist told me to do. I'm writing down the whole truth, and I'm praying that it will leave me alone. I don't want to die like she died—I don't want to kill like she killed. I miss Riley. I miss my friend. I just want this to be over.

COUNTDOWN TO THE BEAST

Your countdown will begin as soon as you finish this story.

The clock struck TWELVE, and I was fast asleep. From the darkness of my mind woke a strange echoing laughter, ringing out as a bell chiming its twelve tolls. Rhythmic laughter, hollow laughter, like a broken toy which mimics life in macabre falsity.

"Why are you laughing?" I asked the darkness of my dream.

"I laugh because I am afraid," it says, the laughter unabated by the words.

"When I'm afraid, I scream," I told it in a matter-of-fact tone. "You're only supposed to laugh when something is funny."

"But I daren't let him know that I am afraid, and so I laugh," cackled the voice.

"What is there to be afraid of?" I ask.

"Lots of things. I'm afraid of how people will remember me, and I'm afraid that they don't anymore. I'm afraid of noises without forms, and forms without noise. I'm afraid of pain without a source, because it can't be stopped. I'm afraid of a source without pain, because it means that I'm already gone. But most of all, I'm afraid of time."

"What is frightening about time?"

"Nothing, so long as it's there. But I'm afraid of time running out. I'm afraid of ELEVEN, so I laugh," the voice trembled.

"The number 11?" I am quite mystified. "What about that makes you afraid?"

"I am afraid because it isn't twelve. I'm afraid because twelve is gone forever. I'm afraid because he's already here, the beast who devours time."

"Who is here?" I asked in alarm. I could still hear the laughter when I woke up. I don't know which was more unsettling: thinking I was still dreaming, or realizing that I was the one laughing. The sun was bright though, flooding my little room through the window my mother was opening.

"You must have had a very funny dream to laugh like that. I didn't want to wake you, but it's time for school."

"How early is it?" I asked blearily, sitting up in bed.

"TEN you normally get up," she said clearly.

"Ten? What?! I'm already late, why did you let me sleep so long?" I sprang from bed and began flinging through the clothes on the floor, looking for something clean to wear.

"What are you rushing for?" she said, laughing. "I said WHEN you normally wake up. It's only seven now. Take your time, get dressed, the eggs will be ready in a few minutes." She laughed to see me frozen in confusion with one leg half-stuffed into my trousers and left the room. There is something I didn't like about her laugh right then. It seemed too loud and forced. Too artificial. I shrugged and dressed leisurely in a slightly used t-shirt and heavily used jeans, gathering up my spread of books and pens left out for homework the night before.

I came downstairs presently, and sat down at the kitchen table, rubbing my eyes. My younger sister was already sitting there, glancing disinterestedly through the paper as she looked for comics. She was two years younger than me in fourth grade, sitting cross legged in her chair with hair bunched up into pigtails which bounced when she spoke. The smell of eggs was familiar and comforting, and I could hear the bacon sizzling along beside it.

"Newspaper off the table," mother said, steering the heavily laden plates into place.

"Anything happen today?" I asked my sister Clara as she folded the paper and tucked it away.

"NINE," she replied distinctly.

"What?"

"I said no. Can't you hear?"

"No, you said nine. I heard you say nine."

"Wake up, idiot," she replied, adding a conspiratorial wink.

"Children be good. Now eat up before the bus comes," mother said, sitting down beside us.

"Mom, what happens when time runs out?" my sister asked mother innocently between mouthfuls. I dropped my fork laden with eggs, and it rattled to the floor in the sudden silence.

"Time doesn't run out, dear. It goes on forever."

"But, I mean if it did. What would happen?" Clara persisted. I pushed my chair back and kneeled down to retrieve my fork, listening intently.

"Well, I suppose nothing would happen. We'd all just sort of be stuck, wouldn't we? Nothing would happen forever. Now eat up, I'm going to go wake your father." Mother stood and glided from the room, but I didn't notice her leave. I don't know how, but Clara knew about my dream.

"Why the Hell would you ask that?" I demanded. A ringing echo of laughter danced along the back of my brain, and I shivered involuntarily.

"EIGHT don't know," she said, shuffling her eggs about her plate.

"What?!"

"I said 'I don't know!'" she snapped. "What's wrong with you today?" Then after a pause, she added: "I suppose it's because time is running out. I just wanted to know what will happen then. I don't think mother is right though. Do you know what I think will happen?" she looked directly at me with wide and curious eyes.

"No, and I don't care," I replied.

"I think," she ignored me, speaking as though to herself, "I think that when our time runs out in this waking world, we become the one in the dream."

"What do you know about my dream? What happened to you?" I asked.

"But that doesn't seem so bad to me," she said, eyes still wide. I shifted slightly as though to stand, and her eyes did not follow me. She spoke on as though completely unaware of my presence. "When we're in the dream, we get to be the one who laughs. That doesn't sound so bad, does it? Even if we're afraid, we'll still get to laugh."

"Mmm, I'm starving," I heard my father's voice from the hall. "Is that freshly cooked bacon? Smells like SEVEN!"

"Like heaven," I mumbled to myself. "He said it smells like heaven."

"No he diddd-nnn't," my sister giggled quietly in a sing-song voice.

I leapt to my feet and confronted her, but she was now focusing on her plate once more, and showed no signs of continuing her thoughts. This wasn't making any sense. Time can't run out, and dreams are just dreams. Clara was playing a game. She liked games. She liked to tease me. But how does she know of my dream? I shook it away and ran from the room. It didn't matter. I just had to get out of here. It was going to be a normal school day, with lunch at 11:30, gym in the afternoon, and music after that, and nothing was strange at all. In a matter of seconds, I was standing on the street corner, one shoe untied, hair uncombed, teeth un-brushed, and a stinging wind bringing me back to reality.

I laughed at how silly I was being, and laughed again to think what my sister would say if she knew how scared I had been. Then I laughed a third time because I couldn't stop, and a fourth because I noticed the laughter rang out in short evenly spaced bursts, like the ringing of a bell. I laughed a fifth time, and then a sixth, and the sweat began to form on my forehead. I couldn't stop. I clasped my hands over my mouth, but my body was shaking so badly I couldn't contain myself. Gasping for breath, a seventh ringing laughter escaped me. Each was spaced perfectly, with perfectly consistent duration, and the same hollow ring which resounded like the creature in the darkness of my sleep. The next I knew, I was sitting on the cold side walk, looking down at my untied shoe. Clara had just left the house, perfectly neat and ordered with her pink backpack zipped tight and slung over both shoulders. She was looking down at me and smiling.

"Are we still at seven?" she asked innocently. "Good, then you'll still be here on the bus. I hate sitting alone."

"Why... how..." I gasped the clean cold air into my lungs that the dark laughter had denied me. "Did you dream about the creature laughing in the darkness too?"

"Don't be silly," she said. "Two people can't have the same dream."

"Then how do you know about time running out?"

She looked down at me and smiled sweetly. "Because I was the one laughing. It got me the night before last." I stared at her in blank wonderment. Something was wrong. Her smile kept stretching wider. I swear I've never seen her show that many teeth before. Then she turned away, and I rubbed my eyes. The faded yellow school bus rolled into view, bumping and clattering down the road of our neighborhood which was strewn with potholes. The two Mumford boys who lived nearby were just jogging up the sidewalk now to join us.

"I told you we'd be on time," said the first. "Told you I could hear the bus from a mile off. All the bumps in the road make it rattle like crazy."

"I wish they would SIX those," said the other. "It's hard to sleep when it's jumping around like that."

"He meant FIX those," Clara giggled, offering her hand down to me to help me stand.

"Shut up," I said, batting her hand away and standing on my own. "You're full of shit and lies, so shut up."

The Mumford boys started chuckling next to me, and I could hear them whispering to each other.

"Did you hear what he just said?"

"I know!"

"And you two, shut the fuck up!" I roared at them. They cowered as though I would hit them. Why would I hit them? I've never hit anybody before. But I can't deny that I wanted to. The feeling burned in my hands and chest. I wanted to beat them bloody. I unclenched my fists and took a deep breath.

The bus stopped, and the Mumford boys ran inside like they were trying to get away from me. I got on and searched for Louise, moving to sit beside her. The seat next to her had always been empty for the last few weeks, and this way I wouldn't have to sit next to my sister. There was Louise—her slouched, lumpy shape, her downcast face hidden in the same hoodie she always wore; I never thought I'd be so relieved to see her. Clara stuck out her tongue as she passed me, sitting in the back with the other fourth grade girls.

Louise was just staring out the window so I didn't even have to talk to her, but I wanted distraction from all these unbidden thoughts. I stared at the back of Louise for a full minute without her turning to look at me.

"How are, Louise?" I asked her hoodie.

"FIVE. Five. Fine, I'm fine," she mumbled. So much for getting my mind off of it. She drew her hood a little tighter around her face.

"Why did you correct yourself? Do you know that you said five first?" I asked.

"Yeah. Donno why."

"You too then!" I exclaimed. "Well other people have been counting for me, I haven't been. Did you have the dream?"

"I donno. I guess. Time is running out," she mumbled, still not facing me. The bus had begun its lurching rattle towards school. "That was a long time ago though."

"What do you mean? Time already ran out?" I asked.

"Well, not for everyone. It did for me though." She finally turned towards me, and she was grinning. I had never seen Louise smile before. Her face was fat and dumpy, but her smile was huge. The longer I stared, the wider it got, until it looked as though it would split her whole head in two. I leapt into the aisle, and the next lurch of the bus sent me to my knees.

"I counted down weeks ago," Louise said, but her smile remained fixed and motionless as the words came out. She started to stand over me, and I scooted away along the floor not taking my eyes off her.

"Oh, me too!" I heard another voice pipe up. Wilson, one of the fifth graders. He was standing a few rows back, and I watched in horror as his smile continued to grow. "I was afraid at first, but I'm not anymore. He doesn't like it when you're afraid. Now I just laugh."

"You can't let him see you being afraid," Louise said from behind.

"Is someone on the FOUR back there?" yelled the bus driver. "Get off the floor, get to your seats. God sakes, we're almost there."

"Yes sir," replied Louise and Wilson in perfect unison. I clambered back into my seat, not looking at either of them.

"What happens if he sees you're afraid?" I whisper out of the corner of my mouth.

Louise laughed. I looked at her now, and saw her mouth opening so wide that it stretched from ear to ear, opening up large enough to swallow my whole head. Her teeth and tongue were still normal sized though, and they were so disproportionate to the swollen mouth that the teeth looked like tiny splinters hammered into her gums while her tongue lolled about disgustingly in the back like a shriveled up slug. Wilson gave an identical peal of laughter from behind, and I turned to see his mouth stretching gruesomely wide as well. Then Clara—my poor sister Clara—laughed in turn, but I refused to look at her. I couldn't bear to see her like that.

The fourth toll. I knew it was coming, but I couldn't stop myself. I took a deep breath of air and clasped my hands over my mouth, but I felt the trembling well up inside me. I shook so violently that I was afraid I would literally rip apart if I didn't let it out. I felt seams burning into my skin as it stretched from within, and bright red lines shot down my arms where the blood swell up underneath. I screwed my eyes tight and gave in, laughing the fourth toll.

"Good for you," I heard Clara say before me. "Keep laughing. Then he won't know."

"THREE are here. Now get out you little rascals. Stop whatever you're playing at back there and get out," the bus driver called as the rickety vehicle pulled to a stop. The doors slid open, and all the children filed out, bustling against each other and talking and laughing as though nothing happened. I turned to Louise who was looking at me with dead blank eyes, her mouth having recovered its old shape.

"What are you staring at?" she asked in a monotone. "Stop blocking the way and let me out."

I stepped aside quietly, and she shoved past me. My heart was racing. I felt sweat trickling along my neck, snaking its way down my back. I filed out of the bus, wordless. Clara stepped past me, smiling sweetly. I didn't say anything. If I opened my mouth now, I was afraid that I would scream. Or worse yet, I would laugh again. I mustn't let him know that I'm afraid, or he'll take me too. A nausea swelled up inside me, and I stepped aside from the others to take a few deep breaths, hands on my knees. I can't scream. I won't. I can't. He won't take me like that.

"You know, we all think that," Clara says from behind. I jumped. "Some of us don't even make it to one. They get so terrified before that he goes ahead and takes them early."

"He won't take me. I'm not afraid," I said belligerently. "The countdown will hit zero, and I still won't be afraid, and then it will all be gone, right? I'll wake up, or realize it was all a joke and I'll laugh—NO! I won't laugh, no more laughing. But it'll all be over. I'll have passed, right?"

"I don't know," she said thoughtfully. "I don't think anyone has ever passed before. I thought I would, but then he came and I was afraid TWO."

"Afraid too? or two? Too or two?" I shouted at her, both sounding the same. Other children began to stare at me and point, but my voice kept getting louder. "Two or too? TWO OR TOO?"

She laughed, not a hollow laugh but a good-natured one. "See you on the other side," she said, and turned to go inside the building. Everyone else was inside now. If I walked in, then someone would say the final countdown, and he would come and take me. That was it! If I stayed out here, completely alone, then there would be no one to say the words. I just had to sit out here until it had all passed over. I just had to sit out here until I woke up.

I walked alone to the playground, chill breeze lifting with the warming sun. I saw the kids running about the hall through the window, but they wouldn't find me. No one would find me out here. I was conscious of how loud my foot falls were on the wood chips by the swings, so I turned and hurried to the pavement as quickly as I could. But my heart! My heart was beating so loudly I was sure someone would hear it. Someone would find me and say the words, and it would be over. I tried my chest with my hands, but it wouldn't be still. God damnit, I wished it would stop beating. I pounded my chest in aggravation, wondering if I could find something sharp to silence it. I didn't think about it as killing myself then, I just wanted the damn thing to stop.

I sat down on the curb, my hands clawing through my hair in aggravation. Maybe my ears. Maybe I could pull my ears off, and I wouldn't hear the final count. It wouldn't work if I couldn't hear it, right? He wouldn't be able to take me then. I grabbed my right ear with both hands and pulled so hard I thought it must come off, but then I cried out from the pain and let go. Had someone heard me? Would they come? My face felt so hot against the cool wind, my body was trembling, and I began to cry.

No! Someone will hear! But the trembling built to shakes, and the shakes into convulsions, and before I knew it, I was sobbing out loud. I couldn't be alone forever. I had to make this stop. I wiped away my tears angrily and stood. Defiantly I yelled into the wind:

"One! Are you happy now? I want to wake up! 12, 11, 10, 9, 8, 7, 6, 5, 4, 3, 2, 1, 0! Zero! Did you hear me?" I heard the howling of the wind getting louder behind me. This was it. He was coming, and it would all be over. "I said zero!" The roar behind me was deafening. At last I couldn't hear my own heart anymore.

"TWELVE!" I shouted again. I said "TWELVE!", and then I began to laugh. I felt a splitting pain in the sides of my mouth and I laughed even harder, knowing it was coming. Blood began gushing down my face as my maw distended horribly, and the laughter kept ringing out in even bursts. Rhythmic laughter, hollow laughter, like a broken toy. You might ask me why I laughed then, and I would tell you it was because I was afraid.

You might not understand, but you will. I laughed because twelve was gone forever. I laughed because I was afraid of ELEVEN.

ANGER MANAGEMENT

I hate Clive. His smug lopsided grin, his greasy comb-over, his horn-rimmed glasses—I don't think I'd brake if I saw him crossing the street. In fact, I fantasize about it every time I sit down in his office.

"Third time this week, huh?" he asked me.

"It's not my fault," I said. "I gave Robert every chance to back down. He's the one who should be in here, not me."

"He's not the one who punched a dent in someone's car."

Of all the things I hate about Clive, nothing compares to his title as Human Resources Director. I wonder if he ever had sex, or if inconveniencing my life was the only thing he needed to get off.

"I apologized already, okay? Can I go back to work now?"

"I can't just keep letting these incidents slide," Clive said, pressing his glasses into his face like he was trying to glue them on. "This is going in my quarterly report to management."

My fantasy of hitting him with the car now included a section where I back up once or twice. I clenched my fists, took a deep breath, and counted off a full ten seconds in my mind.

Getting written up would jeopardize my shot at the branch manager position. I didn't waste four years of my life in this shit-hole just to stay in sales. As much as it hurt, I was going to have to suck up to this bean-bag masquerading as a human being.

"You're right, you're absolutely right," I replied. "I was in the wrong there. Even though he was in my parking spot, I shouldn't have punched his car. I know I have a problem, and I've started taking an anger management class. It's going to help and this won't happen again, so please give me one more chance before you report it."

"Good for you buddy."

Buddy. Call me that again, and I'll jab my pen in your neck, buddy. I smiled.

"I'll tell you what," he added. "Give me the number of the place you're meeting at, and I'll check in with them. If they think you're showing signs of improvement, I'll keep this out of your report."

Shit. Now I'll actually have to go to a class. My mouth hurt from smiling so hard. "Sure thing, buddy," I said. "I don't have the number with me, but I'll bring it in tomorrow."

I opened the door and immediately shut it again. This couldn't be the anger management class I found online. There was incense burning in there, and drums like some kind of freakin' hippy circle. The door opened, and an old Asian man blended into the doorway.

I felt a certain tranquility just from looking at him. He wore immaculate ceremonial robes like some sort of priest, and his snow-white hair cascaded down his back in gentle waves. He bowed low to me, his body curving with a supple grace which utterly belied his apparent age.

"Hi, is this where the United Way anger group meets?"

"Welcome kind sir. My name is Ikari, and it is so good to see a man such as yourself so in command of his own destiny. Won't you please come in?"

There weren't any corny brochures with perfect models saying anger gives you ulcers. No dolls for me to be nice to, no punching bags to vent on. I don't really know what I was expecting, but it definitely wasn't this.

"The website said 6:30. Where is everyone?" I asked.

There weren't even any chairs in the small room. Two cushions were placed on the ground between a pair of bonsai trees, and Ikari sat down on one to face me.

"No others, only you. I do not need groups because those who seek my help must only ask once to be saved."

"I don't need saving, okay?" I was starting to feel uncomfortable. The website looked legit, but this guy seemed more like a cultist than a therapist. What if he didn't have the right accreditation or something? I could be wasting my time.

"I handle my own issues just fine," I added. "All I need is for you to talk to the HR director at my work and tell him—whatever—tell him I'm master of my destiny or something. I already paid online, so are we good?"

"We are far from good, for we are each imperfect beings inflicted with the human condition. Do not worry though, you will soon be better."

I checked my watch. Tight smile. Can someone sprain a muscle from forcing too many of those? It felt like it. I sat cross-legged on the available pillow and tried not to swear at the awkward position.

"Fucking shit." Oops. Oh well, he already knew I had an issue. "Sorry. Don't you have a chair?"

Ikari just smiled, but his was nothing like my smile. His bubbled straight up from the warmth in his heart. It was patient and wise, almost as though he was reading straight from the Divine playbook of the Universe and knew everything was following the script.

"Do you know why there is suffering?" Ikari asked. The measured tone made me pretty sure he wasn't talking about the lack of chairs.

"Because we're all evil sinners who deserve it?" I asked.

"No-one deserves to suffer," Ikari replied. "But we do, because we each carry a Demon in our hearts. Anger, jealousy, hatred, misery— these are ways we feed our Demon. And do you know what happens when we've fed it for too long?"

I shook my head. My Demon must be pretty full by now.

Ikari leaned in close to me and whispered: "Gobble gobble gobble. It eats us right up." The way he said it made me shudder. It was like he was satisfying a greedy pleasure just from speaking the words. I felt immense relief when he settled back into his own cushion before continuing.

"Eventually, our Demon becomes stronger than we are, and it gets to be the one on the outside. Who we are—who we were—that gets locked away. And unless someone tricks the Demon into eating kindness, gratitude, patience, and other virtues, we will never become strong enough to wrestle the Demon back down."

"So how do we stop feeding the Demon?" I asked.

"You take away its food," Ikari produced a small wooden jewelry box, every inch of which was engraven with Japanese lettering, "and you put it in here. Have a bad feeling? Write it down on a piece of paper, slip the paper through this hole in the top. Angry at someone? Give it to the box. It won't be long before your Demon begins to starve. Every problem can be solved by simply putting it in the box."

"And that's it? I won't be angry?" I was trying really hard not to laugh at him.

"And I shall tell Mr. HR that you are all better," Ikari smiled and handed me the box. "Only one more thing—you must not ever open the box, or Gobble gobble gobble. Your Demon will feed again."

What a load, right? But that was easier than sitting through a bunch of dumb meetings. I would have just thrown the box out right then, but Ikari might check it later to see the notes I'd put in.

When I got home, I figured I'd just get it all out of the way at once so I wouldn't have to think about it. I grabbed a notebook and tore out a couple dozen pieces of paper.

The feeling when I'm stuck going 5 mph on the freeway. Slip.

Clive's everything. I hate him so damn much. Slip.

People who kick dogs. I wish they'd kick Clive instead. Slip.

The more I wrote, the more ideas began flooding into my head. Everything I could think of that pissed me off started cramming into the box.

People who steal parking spaces (fuck you Robert).

The taste of orange juice after brushing your teeth.

Every girl who has ever given me that "it's not you, it's me" shit.

The box didn't look that big, and I expected it to only take ten minutes to fill. Three hours later though, I had emptied an entire notebook, and still couldn't feel the paper inside. But do you know what I did feel?

Like a mother-fuckin' Buddha. It seemed absolutely ludicrous that any of those things have ever bothered me before. Poor Clive, just trying to do his job. Why did I have to give him such a hard time? And Robert should have my parking spot near the door. He was older than me, and I didn't mind the exercise. So how in the world did I get to the point of punching a dent in his car?

I've never slept so well in my entire life. I'm usually tense and unable to find a comfortable position, but five minutes after I lay down, I was sound asleep. I did have one troubling dream though: there was a soft light coming from inside the box on my night-table. In my dream, I got up to reach for it, but then I heard something inside of it scream like a man who has been pushed past the edge of breaking. I opened the box to see what was making the noise and then Gobble gobble gobble. I woke up to the freshest, most miraculous morning I could remember.

The last two weeks were perfect for me. I worked tirelessly, unfettered by the daily aggravations which I used to spend half the day obsessing over. I started bringing the box to work just in case something came up in the day, and things always came up. No point in risking my promotion, right? The box went everywhere with me.

The sound of dry erase markers on a whiteboard. Slip.

Suddenly the morning meeting was bearable again.

"Hey did anyone hear that?" Mr. Elsworth turned away from the whiteboard to address the assembly. "Something like a scream?"

A collective shrug, and sip of coffee. I thought I'd heard it too though. The moment I slipped the paper in, there had been a soft flash of light and an echoing scream.

Clients who think they know how to do my job better than I do. Slip.

Having to wear a tie all day. I could strangle someone with this tie.

There it was again. It started out as a low moan, but rose into a gurgling scream after I had slipped the second note in. I glanced up to see Clive standing outside my cubicle.

"What? What are you doing? What do you want?" Just looking at him made me agitated.

"I wanted to let you know that I called Mr. Ikari, and he said you showed a complete turnaround. As long as nothing happens before tomorrow, your report is going to be clean. Congratulations buddy."

When people I hate call me buddy"

Clive again.

The box screamed. It was louder this time. Clive had already gone, but someone was going to hear it if I kept this up. This was the second note I'd had to use for Clive too. I guess some hatred is too deep to extract all at once.

Worse still, the moaning continued even though I wasn't putting anything in now. It sounded like the lamentations of a dying man. I shut the box in my drawer, but I could still hear it groaning away. Then a soft rattle. I opened the drawer and saw the box trembling as a frightened animal.

Well shit. I couldn't just throw it away. I had to get my anger out somehow, or that promotion was gone. I couldn't keep it here either though because someone was going to—"What's that sound? Is that the pipes?"

I didn't answer them. I didn't look at them. I walked fast through the building with the box in my pocket. The warehouse—it's always noisy down there. If I hide the box, then no-one will hear it, and I can still get down to slip a note in if I need to.

The sound of forklifts backing up.

The restaurant which always gets my lunch order wrong.

It was 4:30 now. Only half an hour to go and I was in the clear. I was walking down to the warehouse to slip my last note of the day into the box.

Mr. Elsworth keeping people till 5 even when there's nothing to do.

I opened the crate of printer paper where I'd stored the box and reached around. Odd, I usually could hear the screaming when I was this close to it. Especially now, since the machinery was all quiet after the warehouse workers left for the day.

It wasn't there. I practically dove into the crate, but my box wasn't anywhere. It was only half an hour though, right? I could make it half an—but no. Without the box, the anger would still be there. Even if I did get the promotion, I'm sure Elsworth would notice sooner or later and bump me back down. It wasn't fair. I'd put in the work—I was better than any of them. It wasn't right for me to keep getting passed over just because—Scream. There it was. What started out as a horrible sound now filled me with relief. It was the next sound which I dreaded more.

"What in God's name are you doing in there?"

I pulled myself out of the crate to face Clive. He was holding my box in his hand. And it was open.

"Give it back. Now," I snapped. "It's mine."

But he was reading my notes. Those were personal! He had no right to—"Is this some kind of joke?" Clive asked. "Why is my name in here? And such rude language—"

"You want language? Give me back my fucking box."

My last note of the day was crumpled up in my hand. I was seeing red. I wanted to grab him by the throat and—but no. I needed that promotion. I couldn't lose it now.

"I'm sorry, Clive. It was just an assignment from anger management class. It's supposed to be confidential, so give it back. This doesn't need to change anything with your report."

"My report?" Clive practically shrieked. "You're still worried about your promotion? You aren't going to have a job at all after this. If this is how you really think, then we have no place for you—"

I punched him across the face. I didn't want to, but I couldn't stop myself. All the little frustrations and pent up anger from the past two weeks were flooding back. I hit him for everyday this company has stolen from my life, for every promotion which passed me over, and for every lonely night I sat at home too tired from work to go out. I pummeled his face into a pulpy mess, and still couldn't get enough.

The box was screaming like a banshee, convulsing on the floor where Clive had dropped it. I couldn't tell how much of the blood on my knuckles was his, and how much was mine, and I didn't care. As good as it felt to be at peace with myself, this felt better. At least for a little while until Clive stopped moving.

I dropped him back to the warehouse ground. The screaming—it was driving me crazy. I tried to stuff the scattered papers back into the empty box, but they wouldn't fit any more. They spilled out over the ground, covered in my bloody finger prints.

How did I let this happen? What would Ikari have done? He said any problem could go away if I put it in the box. Well shit, Clive was a problem, and now he was going in a box, but that only made things worse. I stuffed his body and the bloody papers into one of the warehouse crates, mopped up as much of the blood as I could, and ran.

"Open up! Open up old man!" I was back at the anger management class. If this was anyone's fault, it was Ikari's. He must have known what the box did, or he never would have given it to me. He must know how to make things right. He had to.

The door was unlocked, so I went in. Ikari was sitting on his cushion across from a middle-aged woman. I didn't want to involve anyone else in this, so I waited in the corner for her to finish. She handed a box which looked just like mine to Ikari and thanked him. She was so grateful. It changed her life. Well good-for-fucking her, because it ruined mine.

"Please have a seat," Ikari said after the woman had gone.

"It was opened," I blurted out. "Not by me—somebody else—and they're dead now. This isn't my fault, so you gotta help me fix this."

"I understand," he replied gravely. Then he leaned in real close—so close I wanted to hit him, but I held myself back—and he whispered: "Gobble gobble gobble."

I actually pushed him back into his seat. "Don't give me that shit. You must know what happens. Why do you do this to people?"

A slow smile crept across his peaceful face. "Because I am so hungry. And all the hate they pour into their boxes returns to feed me. But you have already let your Demon out, so what am I to eat now?"

The dead man in the warehouse was suddenly the least of my

problems. Ikari was standing although for some reason I never remembered watching him rise. Then he was behind me, not having touched the intervening space. I was absolutely speechless. I back-peddled until my back hit a wall—No, not a wall. He was behind me again. His arm wrapped around my neck, his long nails digging into the side of my throat.

"When I look at you, all I see is a Demon now," he said. "All I can see is your selfish hunger."

I didn't dare speak. Even swallowing was enough to push those nails deeper into my skin. I strained against his implacable grip with my hands, but with every motion, the puncture became deeper. His arm constricted with the relentless predatory pressure of a boa constrictor, and I was utterly helpless in its grasp.

"But your Demon has already fed on my meal, so here is what you must do. Find those like yourself with anger burning in their hearts and collect it for me as I have done with you. Twice each month you will bring me a new box filled with hatred or…"

He didn't need to finish the sentence. Gobble gobble gobble. The pressure slackened just enough for me to nod.

Maybe someday I will learn how to trick my Demon. Someday I will learn how to be kind, even with this hatred burning in my chest, and I will lock him away. Someday I will learn to control my anger and not the other way around, but until then…

Would you like to stop feeding your Demon? You only need to ask once for me to save you.

THE MASKED ORGY

Collage is the time for experimentation. And no, I don't mean titrating sodium hydroxide with hydrochloric acid in chemistry. I mean forcing yourself to try new things—things that excite you—things that scare you—for how else are we supposed to discover who we are and what we're capable of without constantly pushing the boundaries of our reality?

At least, that's the excuse my boyfriend Mike came up with when he suggested a threesome.

"Sure," I replied.

"Really? Wow, okay. You're the coolest girlfriend ever–"

"What's the other guy's name?"

I knew what he meant, but I still enjoyed watching him choke on the soda he was drinking. Mike had been talking a lot about Amy since she joined our lab group in anatomy. I was jealous at first, but after checking out the competition, I had to concede his point. It was hard not watching the supple curves of her body every day as she stripped her sweater over her head to put her lab coat on. I guess I was just relieved Mike was talking to me about it instead of doing something with her behind my back.

He wanted me to broach the subject with her because "it sounded less creepy coming from a girl", so I invited her to join Mike and I for drinks after class.

"Have you ever done anything with a girl before?" I asked Amy after our third beer. Mike spluttered in his drink and excused himself to go to the bathroom, and I almost threw the rest of my glass after him. This was his idea. It wasn't fair making me do all the work. Luckily, there wasn't much work that needed doing.

"Not yet," she replied, a smile playing around the corner of her lips.

Two hours later, all of us were in my room trying to figure out how one person fits in a dorm-room bed, let alone three. It was exciting for me, and I can only imagine how many flashing lights and alarms were blaring inside Mike's head, so I guess it was understandable that he spent most of the time focused on Amy. Besides, Mike and I were already comfortable with each other, so it was really just her that he felt the need to impress. Afterward he said it wasn't the case, but I still remember spending way too long hanging out and watching them go at it. I even left to use the bathroom at one point without either of them noticing I was gone.

I didn't want to get mad. I had agreed to this after-all, and I hated the idea of being one of those infamous girlfriends who said one thing and did another. I just wanted to get even. It didn't help that he started acting cocky afterward as though that experience made him a big manor something. He even started pointing out particularly geeky looking freshman and saying things like "I bet he's never even been with one, let alone two".

Although asking for another guy started out as a joke, I started pushing for it more seriously. I wanted him to feel what it was like to be jealous. I wanted him to appreciate what I had done for him and realize I was the only one of us who had the power to make it happen again. And yeah, if I'm being honest, maybe I even wanted to humiliate him a little, so he'd go back to regular old Mike and drop this macho facade.

We started having fights about it, and the more he said no, the more one-sided our relationship seemed. I told Amy I thought I was going to have to dump him (she and I still hung out sometimes, although I never invited Mike when we did). I told her it wasn't her fault, but she still felt guilty about getting between us (literally). That's why she came up with a solution:

"I know a place where they do it in a group. You'll get your kinks out, he'll have someone of his own to have fun with, and everyone is wearing a mask so nobody gets hurt."

Big rubber animal masks. Didn't it get hot in there? I felt more than a little exposed wearing my stupid Mardi gras mask I picked up at the dollar store on the way here. Everyone else's mask was hyper-realistic and covered their entire head, but they told me not to worry about it and just relax. Mike and I were just "initiates" on a trial run, anyway. If we decided this was our thing, and we respected all of their rules and members, then they'd give us a full mask next time.

At first I stuck pretty close to Mike, and we just fooled around with each other and watched. There was about a dozen people in total, and the teeming mass of bodies was pretty damn intimidating to approach. Several of them had covered their bodies in some kind of paint or oil, and they churned and writhed against each other with an almost animalistic intensity. Everywhere I looked, breasts were heaving, indiscriminate hands clutched and pulled on skin, and bodies lunged hungrily at one another as though nourished by their carnal lust.

I was about to call it quits and leave when a man in a panther-mask pulled away from the others to approach me. His body was chiseled and slick with paint. Mike and I exchanged glances. Isn't this what I wanted? I pointed him in the direction of a leopard-mask with fiery red hair spilling out beneath it. He hesitated, so I gave him a little shove. If nothing else, this would be a shared experience we could laugh and bond over, and maybe we'd both be stronger for it.

I still shuddered a bit when the panther-man put his hand on my shoulders from behind, but his probing fingers expertly massaged down my back and I felt myself melt into his touch.

Mike left shortly after that. We'd only been there about a half-hour, and I was really (really) starting to enjoy myself, when I saw him staring at me and the panther-man. Good, let him see! But then he just turned around and walked away, and my satisfaction quickly drained. I followed him, and we had another fight in the hallway while we were both still naked. He said he couldn't even look at me again after seeing me like that. Somehow the fact that he was more hurt and sensitive than me proved that he cared more about me than I did him, so it was over. He got dressed and left, and I just stood there overflowing with frustration.

I felt massaging hands caressing my shoulders again, and I immediately felt the tension flowing out through them. If I was looking for a rebound to get past Mike, then I couldn't think of a more immersive, therapeutic one than this. I allowed the panther-man to lead me back into the room. The lights had dimmed since I was gone, but a lot of the paint people wore was glowing in the dark. More hands grabbed me, and I allowed myself to be swallowed up in the psychedelic dance of skin on skin, swirling colors, and the growing moan which encompassed me.

As the night went on, the lights continued to slowly dim. The colors grew brighter, and the intensity of the sound and insistence of the sensation mounted into a crescendo of pleasure. I spent most of my time with the panther-man, although I allowed myself to be passed from one person to the next without complaint. There was no embarrassment, no judgement, no jealousy, only the acceptance and triumph of our shared celebration of life.

I was back with the panther-man now, body flooded with gentle warmth and satisfaction. His hands were so powerful yet gentle, and his low moans resonated with my own as though we were a single being harmonized with itself. The thought of leaving here and never knowing who he was—perhaps never even meeting him again—was more agonizing than I could have imagined. I felt an overpowering desire to look at the man pressed against me—just for a second—just long enough to recognize him if we met again. I slid my hands up his neck and tenderly slipped the mask further up his face...

But it wouldn't come off. I pulled harder and felt the strain of living fur beneath my fingers. He grunted in pain – or was that a snarl?—and I pushed him off me. Suddenly every sound came to its height, and the mounting carnal cacophony enveloping me became tainted with other sounds.

Were those moans? Or was someone starting to howl? And then a yelping joined in. I thought it was a joke at first, but one by one the people began to bray, bark, hiss, or whatever other sound was appropriate to the mask they wore. The panther-man knelt upon the ground and I saw his muscles coil as though preparing to spring. It was so dark that I could only see the parts of him covered in paint, and from a few steps away, he looked more like an abstract painting than a man.

I ran toward the door, but tripped over a dark form along the way. A multitude of hands clung onto me in the shadows, and then a paw with razor-sharp claws tore the skin on my outer thigh. I screamed and pushed onward, but the grips readily released me as though shocked I wasn't appreciating their touch. I made it to the wall, but I couldn't find the door. The panther-man crawled toward me on all fours. Some glowing paint was on his skin, but more of it was matted in patches of thick black hair on his body.

I leaped along the wall looking for the door, ramming against another body and falling to the ground. The half-panther was almost on top of me now, but I couldn't bear to look at him. I closed my eyes and screamed for all I was worth.

"Are you okay? What are you doing?"

I opened my eyes. The lights were on. Everyone was staring at me. The panther-man with his chiseled human body was standing over me. He pulled on his furry ear, and I almost screamed again before seeing the rubber mask slide easily off. He was a handsome man, about thirty, with strong cheek bones and deep concerned eyes.

I ran out the door and dressed in the hallway. The panther-man started to follow me.

"Stop her! She's seen too much!" he shouted, his voice a harsh guttural snarl completely unlike the one he used a moment before.

A woman in a sheep's mask held him back. "Let her go. She'll come back when she's ready." The voice sounded familiar. Was that Amy? I didn't stay long enough to find out. As soon as my clothes were even halfway on, I ran.

I'm not going back. I can't go back. But maybe I'll have to, because I still need answers. I missed my period the next month, but I tried not to think back to that night. I was on the pill, and they all had protection. Just to be safe, I got a pregnancy test, but it came up negative.

I kept testing every month after that. Still nothing. But all the symptoms were beginning to show: I'm swelling up, I'm tired all the time, and nauseous in the mornings. I got an ultrasound, but the doctor said he didn't see anything. It's just like a great, empty pit is growing inside of me. I got a few other scans, but nothing came up and the doctor just thinks it is a hysterical-pregnancy which will pass on its own.

I didn't know how to tell him I thought it was something else, just like I didn't know how to explain the claw marks on my outer thigh.

I want to forget it ever happened, but it's hard when I keep feeling something scratching me from the inside.

BREAKING AND ENTERING FOR DUMMIES

I'm going to tell you a few things about me. When I was a kid, I lost in the finals of a state tennis championship because I told the truth about a line call when I didn't have to. I once climbed a tree to get somebody's cat down, then stayed up there the rest of the night just because it was so peaceful. My favorite food is strawberries and cream, only I don't tell the other guys because they'd give me shit for it.

I also joined the 18th Street Gang when I was in the sixth grade. It's important what order I tell you these things, because the moment someone notices my blue and black bandanna, they think they already know everything about me.

I'm a sophomore in high-school now, and last night was my first break-in. "Spike", an old-school Mexican Mafia type, was there to show me the ropes. He taught me how to map out the regular patrol routes of officers, and how to hide in a concrete drain pipe to avoid being seen.

I'd never stolen anything bigger than a candy bar before. I was scared as Hell, but I knew Spike was tight with everybody and would tell them how I did. This was my first real chance to let everyone decide what I was made of, and I wasn't going to screw it up.

"Let's not do this one, it has an alarm system." Middle-class suburban home with a white-picket fence – nothing that screamed a good target to me.

"Doesn't matter when they let you in," Spike said. He grinned. Just because I'm in a gang doesn't mean I understand gold teeth. They're disgusting.

"But someone's here. There's a light on up there!" I protested. "Let's keep looking." Maybe if we didn't find a good target tonight, we could just go back and play pool and try again another night. I'd be ready another night.

"How are they gonna open the door if they ain't home? Fuck's sake," he said. Spike walked around the house and turned the garden hose on full blast. He found two more taps along the back of the house, and turned those on too.

He waited a few minutes for a lake to start forming in the yard before ringing the door-bell. I wanted to stop him, but I was frozen. My heart beat faster with each light that turned on as the resident approached his front door.

"Who is it?" someone yelled from inside.

"Excuse me sir," Spike shouted. "I noticed one of your pipes burst. Just thought you should know."

The door opened. An old man – at least 80 – stood there in his bathrobe. I never want to get that old where my eyes shrink down to little pin-pricks and my skin hangs in loose folds like that. Spike gave me a grotesque wink.

"It did? Oh God," the old man said.

"Yeah, look at all that water," Spike said. "I was just walking on the sidewalk with my kid," he wrapped his arm around my shoulder, and I fought the urge to pull away from his sticky-sweet odor of dried sweat.

"Yo," I said.

"We found which one it was, here come take a look," Spike didn't even wait for a reply. I wonder how many times he's done this before. The old man pulled his bathrobe tighter and followed Spike around the side of the house.

I wanted to warn him. To tell him to run – to hide and lock the door. I couldn't turn my back on my own though. If this was going to happen anyway, I might as well be the one to return with some glory. The moment the old man passed me by, I picked up a rock from his yard and **SMASHED** it straight into his temple. He crumpled to the ground like a bag of dirt.

Gold teeth flashed. "Nice one kid. Now let's drag him inside so we can take our time with the place."

I propped him up against the wall in the living room. He was still breathing, but there was a lot of blood coming from his head. I thought about bandaging him up, but I didn't know if that would seem like a sign of weakness. I just wanted to get in and get out as fast as I could.

Snarl. Woof woof woof woof.

"Shit, there's a dog," Spike grunted.

The sound was coming from behind a closed door down a few concrete steps – probably leading to the basement.

"It can't get at us," I said. "Let's ignore it."

"Nah, too much noise. Quick, go deal with it," he said.

"Deal with it?" I didn't want to hear him explain. He didn't say a word, but that flash of gold and the knife he handed me – that was even worse.

"Make it quick. You're gonna be a man after tonight."

I gripped the knife in my hand so hard my knuckles turned white. I turned away from Spike so he wouldn't see me shaking.

"I'm gonna go check upstairs for a safe or somethin," Spike said. "Or cash under the mattress – these old shits think that's safer than a bank sometimes. That thing better be quiet by the time I get up there."

I wasn't worried about it being a big dog. An old guy like this probably had a poodle or something, but hurting any animal has always been off-limits for me. Being loyal to my colors over my own instinct – there wasn't any going back from this. I hated myself for opening the door.

I was tense and ready for it to spring at me. I even slashed the air with the knife a couple of times until I found the light switch. I didn't see anything but a set of stairs though, so I walked down to find the miserable creature.

Snarl. Woof woof woof woof.

"Why is it still barking?" I heard from upstairs.

"I don't know," I shouted back.

I was staring face to face with a grown man, probably around fifty years old, stripped down to his underwear, and shackled to the wall with iron clasps around his wrists and ankles. His facial hair was thick and greasy, and it was matted in with the long unkempt black hair spilling from his head.

Snarl. Woof woof.

The man barked at me like an animal. He pulled against the metal restraints as he tried to dive at me, snapping his jaw and frothing into his beard. Then there was a flash of recognition in his eye, and he pressed himself back against the wall. His mouth contorted awkwardly, almost as though he was trying to say something.

"Don't make me come down there and do it for you," Spike said. His voice was closer now, like he was coming back downstairs.

I dropped the knife and ran. I don't know what the Hell was going on, I didn't care what was going to happen to me, but I could not be in that room. Spike was waiting for me outside the basement.

"What's going on? Did you do it?"

I just kept running. Straight out the door. I ran the whole 3 miles back to my house without even stopping. Spike followed me out – I don't think he ever saw the thing. He must have told the other guys though, because I got a 18 second beating for what happened. I took it like a man. I didn't even make a sound.

I didn't tell anyone what I saw, or what I heard the thing say as I was leaving.

"Kill... me..."

Spike was waiting for me when I got off the school-bus today. He wrapped his arm around my shoulders and led me away from the other kids. I flinched when he touched me.

"Last night..." he said.

"I'm sorry. I messed up. It's my fault," I replied. I'd already taken the beating. What more could happen?

"I get it, first time is scary. But facing that fear, that's what makes a man out of you," he said. "I checked up on the house, and there wasn't any police report or anything. The old guy was dead, but nobody's found him yet."

"Did you look in the basement?" I asked.

"Nah, I didn't stay, but the two of us are going back tonight. We're gonna finish the job."

How could I tell him? It would just sound like a lame-ass excuse. He'd just think I was scared, and I'd get beaten again. I just nodded. There wasn't any way out of this for me. I've already killed a man, so what's so much worse about killing an animal?

MY FAMILY TRADITION TO FEED THE SPIRIT

I t's funny how the strangest traditions seem ordinary when you've grown up around them. One of my friends can't get through Thanksgiving dinner without someone spanking the turkey, and another kid in my high-school said they threw a tea-party to celebrate every A. I've heard about another family who never wore clothes at home—the poor kid couldn't figure out why everyone started laughing at him when he visited a friend's house and promptly began to undress. It simply hadn't occurred to him that nobody else lived quite the same way, and why should it? None of their traditions were more arbitrary than a cake on your birthday or an inside tree on Christmas.

My name is Elizabeth, and my family has their own tradition. Every night after dinner, my Dad would take a plate full of leftovers and bring it down to the basement. Every morning, it would be clean. My father said it was for the "spirit of the house", and my Mom would just roll her eyes and smile. My Dad is a big man—6'4" and over 250lbs—and it wouldn't have surprised either of us if he just wanted to save a little extra for a midnight snack.

I guess I never gave it much thought until my history class

watched a video on the Black Death in Europe. They talked about how the rats would infest granaries and spread disease, and how some people actually exasperated the problem by leaving food out to appease the angry spirits. I mentioned how we always leave out a plate for our spirit, and my whole class seemed mortified by the thought. The teacher (Mr. Hallwart) spent the rest of the class blatantly circumventing my desk as though I was the one carrying the plague.

That night I had a terrible nightmare about rats swarming through the house and eating our leftover food. I woke in a cold sweat, lying half-awake for a long time as my sleepy brain tried to separate the quiet night from my encroaching dreams. I was about to drift back to sleep when the pitter-patter of light feet clearly distinguished itself in the still air.

I was fully awake now, lying very still with my ears straining against the oppressive dark. Scratch scratch scratch—like fingernails dragging along a rough piece of wood. I pulled the blankets up over my head, more to block out the sound than to offer any real protection. Maybe this had been going on a long time, and I simply hadn't distinguished the sound from the creaking house or the night air playing through the wind chimes. Now that I was focusing on it though, I couldn't hear anything else.

I thought about calling for Mom, but I was 15 years old and trying to build a case to convince them I was mature enough to have my own car. Running around crying about a nightmare was as good as giving the murder jury my bloody axe. I crept out of bed in my underwear, using the flashlight on my phone to steal through the hallway and down the stairs.

The sound grew louder as I approached the basement door. If this was a rat, then it had to be the biggest rat in the history of the world. I froze at the sound of a chair being pushed across the concrete floor. Half of me wanted to turn on the light to scare it off, but the other half declared much more loudly that it was better not to risk being seen. I turned off my own flashlight and carefully opened the door...

Something snarled and I immediately shut it again. I pressed my back to the door and tried to catch my breath. I hadn't realized how fast I was breathing, or how loud. I let the air out in a gasp and slowly inhaled through my nose, trying to be as quiet as I could. Scratch scratch scratch—right on the other side of the door. I turned around and saw the doorknob beginning to turn. There's no way it was a rat in there. I can't explain how my curiosity overpowered my fear in that moment, but I put my hand on the doorknob too. I must have believed my Dad when he said it was the spirit of the house. We had been taking care of it after-all, so why would it want to do me harm?

The door opened and I stood face to face with a pale girl a few years younger than me. Her sunken dark eyes vanished beneath her mangy bangs, and her lace nightgown failed to conceal the terrible thinness of her limbs. I don't know what I was expecting, but it wasn't that. I slammed the door as hard as I could and turned to run. I sprinted up the stairs, locking my room behind me and diving into bed. I held my breath until it felt like I would burst until there—the pitter-patter of soft feet climbing the stairs and approaching my room.

The doorknob began to rattle. I couldn't hold it any longer—all that breath I was holding in was released in one noisy rush and I screamed for all I was worth. The doorknob stopped and lights sprang to life around the house. In about a minute, there was a pounding on my door.

"Honey? Everything okay in there?" It was Dad. I ran to him and unlocked my room. He was standing there, looking dazed and confused, ready to collapse back into bed. Now that the lights were on and he was here, I felt like an idiot for being afraid. I'd feel even stupider telling him about the girl.

"Sorry," I said. "I thought I heard something downstairs."

"Damn, who needs an alarm when you can scream like that," he said.

"It was probably just a bad dream. Sorry for waking you."

Dad looked around behind him, making sure we were alone. Then he leaned in close and whispered: "Was it coming from the basement?"

I nodded. His smile was nothing but relief, and I couldn't help but feel it too. At least until he added:

"That's just the spirit, honey. Don't bother it, and don't tell Mom, okay? It's not going to hurt you."

I nodded. I didn't know what else to do. He grinned and ruffled my hair before plodding back to his room. I gave the empty stairs a quick glance before locking myself in again and climbing back into bed. I don't need to tell you that I didn't sleep until the sun began to repaint my room.

I slept in late that day, but by nightfall I was ready for answers. I tried asking Dad again, but he just told me every house had a spirit and not to worry about it. He must have been lying though, considering how my class reacted, and it was clear he didn't want to talk about it. That's why I waited until both my parents were in bed to creep down to the basement and wait.

The basement door was open when I got there. I turned the light on in the kitchen which connected to it, but didn't dare go down the stairs. Three pieces of leftover pizza sat in their box on the table, and I poured a large glass of soda to go with it. I just sat there with my hands folded in front of me, waiting for her to come again. If she was a friend of the house, then I wanted to meet her. And if she wasn't... well surely we'd know by now.

My mistake was to watch the door. She was corporal—she ate food, she turned doorknobs—she must go through doors, right? Wrong. Despite my resolve, it was impossible to hear the scratching sound above my head without my entire body tensing up. I watched a ventilation grate in the roof slide out of place, and then the girl dropped through as lightly as a shadow. Her hair was hanging over her face, but I could imagine it all too clearly as the animal snarl began to rise in her throat.

She was as alien to me as death. I didn't even know if she could speak or understand. Her movements were erratic and unpredictable, her eyes darted like a caged animal, but we did have one thing in common which has bridged greater differences than ours: we both liked pizza, and when I offered her some, she smiled. The girl swiftly choked all three pieces down with savage gulps although I was able to make out a few of her muttered words which she slipped in-between.

"Kevin (my Dad) won't let me go."

"It's okay. I don't want to leave. He takes care of me."

"He said he loves me. He promised to marry me when I turned 13."

"Stay here in the kitchen, okay?" I said. I hope she didn't notice the revulsion in my voice. I couldn't believe what she was saying. I couldn't believe any of this, and I didn't know how to handle it alone. I wanted Dad to come and tell me it was all okay again, but if what she was saying was true...

I came back in five minutes with Mom instead. It was pretty tricky shaking her so that Dad didn't wake too, but as soon as I mentioned the spirit she was out of bed in an instant. She said she never believed in that sort of thing, but the wild fear in her eyes made me think that was a lie. When we got back to the kitchen, the pale girl was still chugging through the soda which sprayed her face with foam.

"Who are you? What are you doing in my house?" my mother roughly pushed me behind her. I pushed back.

"It's okay Mom. She's not going to hurt us. She needs our help." I was beginning to regret telling Mom what the girl told me.

"I'm Sandy," the pale girl said. "Who are you?"

"I'm Kevin's wife, that's who. The one you're making up lies about." Mom took an indignant step forward. I tried to hold her back, but she was livid. "You better tell me how you broke in, or I'm going to call the police."

"I didn't break in," the pale girl stood from the table and faced us belligerently. "Kevin brought me here. He loves me."

Maybe my Mom was angry because she thought the girl was lying, but I think it was because she was afraid Sandy was telling the truth. I should have tried harder to stop her, but I hadn't expected her to snap like that and slap the girl across the face. Sandy's head turned sharply from the blow, but then began turning back in small, jerky increments. I think my Mom was too angry to even notice the bones rearranging themselves in Sandy's neck as it turned.

"You come into my house, steal food from my family, and make up these disgusting lies about my husband?"

Mom was usually the sweetest thing in the world, but she had a temper that sometimes took hours to wind down.

"Mom you've got to stop -"

"I don't care if you do got nowhere else to go, where I'm from you got to ask before you take something."

"Mom just look at her! Can't you tell she isn't normal?"

"Now who else you been telling this perverted trash to? Sweet Jesus, I want you out. Out of my house right this instant."

"What's all this noise down there?" My Dad thundered into the room. He froze mid-step as he instantly appraised the situation. "Dear God Kathy (my Mom), have you lost your mind?"

"My mind?" Mom screamed, turning to face Dad. "Don't tell me you're going to defend that creature in our house."

"I only hear one of you yelling, and don't you dare call Sandy a creature."

I've never seen either of them so worked up. I think I was the only one who heard Sandy whispering.

"Is it true?" It wasn't just the girl's voice that wavered. Her whole body seemed to somehow glitch and distort like a corrupted video. "He married her? He lied to me?"

She looked absolutely heart broken. I couldn't even begin to formulate a response.

"Tell me the truth," Sandy insisted. "Does Kevin still love me?"

How was I supposed to know? I looked helplessly between Mom and Dad as they yelled at each other, and I was just stressed and over-whelmed and scared. The idea of my Dad being with this child almost made me sick. All I could tell is that she shouldn't be here. I shook my head.

"No he doesn't," I said. "He loves my Mom. You should just go."

"Thanks for telling me," Sandy replied. "I'm going to get even now. Please don't watch."

Mom didn't see it coming. The air was distorted with a pale blur, and before I could even open my mouth, I saw thin white fingers tearing out my mother's throat. Most of her neck was still intact, but the trachea was pulled straight out through the skin. I don't think she suffered much on account of how quick it was, but that was a very small comfort.

Dad wasn't so lucky. I thought he would have a chance to fight her off because of his size, but he didn't even put up his arms to defend. He just stood there until the white fingers punched through his chest and ripped out his heart. There was a horrible moment where the heart was entirely out of the chest but still tethered by a network of veins and arteries, and I could see the strain on his face while she held it in her hand.

"I never forgot you," were the last words he ever said.

Sandy distorted again, and then she was gone—fleeing back down the basement stairs and wailing like a little girl. I rushed over to my Dad, but he was already gone.

When the police swept the house later that night, they didn't find anyone in the basement. They listened to my statement, but I didn't see any of them writing it down and I don't think they believed me. I was sobbing so incoherently, I wouldn't have trusted my testimony either. I just know what I experienced and later, what I saw.

The police investigation did unearth a collection of photographs hidden in a shoebox in the basement. Sandy was in them—except that she glowed from happiness where she stood next to a young boy her own age. I recognized the boy as my father at once. The police didn't investigate them or entertain it as a possibility, but I did some research of my own and found out that Dad used to live next door to a girl named Sandy Withers when he was growing up.

They had been best friends—more than best friends apparently, but she had died in a diabetic coma when she was 12 years old. Written in my Dad's curved lettering on the back of one of the photographs was: "My future bride."

I don't know what happened to make her stay in the world, but it looks like my Dad never was able to let her go. It's been three years now, and even though everyone has pressured me to sell the house and move, I'm still living here. I guess I wasn't any good at letting go either, because I still practice the same tradition I have all my life. The only difference is that I now leave out three plates of food every night and collect three clean dishes every morning.

LIKE FATHER LIKE SON

I have a two-year-old son named Alexander. No, that's not the horror story, although any new parents out there might beg to differ. He is the most perfect thing I could ever or will ever create, and I love him with all my heart.

When I look at Alex, I see myself. An entire lifetime of academic achievements, romantic pursuits, dreams and ambitions, and of course the glorious pride of shooting the game winning goal... the infinite potential of his un-lived life is a miraculous blessing that I am privileged to be a part of.

My wife Stacey thinks I'm going to run myself into the ground trying to be the world's best dad. She thinks I'm overcompensating because my own dad left when I was two. And so what if I am? Dad leaving destroyed my mother. It was because of him that I grew up practically impoverished, withdrawn, and angry at the world. What's so wrong with wanting something better for my own son?

I'll admit that I did tend to obsess over the idea though. Everything was a competition - I wanted a better job than my father, to drive a better car; I even started interrogating my mother about all dad's bad habits so I could avoid them, although she replied with something which shocked me.

"Why don't you ask him yourself? I know where he lives."

I couldn't even remember the man. Learning he lived just on the other side of town made me furious. I had to know what his excuse was for never being there, and even more than that, I wanted to tell him straight to his face that I wouldn't be the same terrible father he was.

I was expecting some kind of burnt out crack-den or whorehouse, not the luxury high-rise apartments that matched the address. Sure my mother lived comfortably now, but somehow I didn't think he deserved the same kind of lifestyle now. My fist landed on his door with a quick burst of powerful thumps.

"Who are -" the man in the loose bathrobe asked, but he didn't even have to finish the sentence. The resemblance was uncanny. The long nose, the angular cheeks, the wisps at the end of his eyebrows - he looked exactly like an older version of myself.

"Yeah," I said. All my carefully prepared arguments from the drive over here evaded my mind. All I could think about was how unsettling it felt to look at that face which could have almost been a mirror.

"Well alright, come on in." He turned around and sat down on his sofa. "Your mother send you?"

"Do you and her still talk?" I asked.

He shrugged. "Sometimes. She told me about your kid. Congratulations on -"

"Why d'you leave?" It wasn't supposed to go like this. I was supposed to be gloating over a successful life he played no part in. He was supposed to be pleading my forgiveness. So why did my voice crack like I was the one begging?

"The same reason you'll ditch your kid," he said. "They're better off without us."

I left shortly after that, feeling less satisfied than ever. How dare he presume I would make the same terrible decisions he did? Maybe he was right that I was better off without him, but my son needed me and I needed him.

I gripped my steering wheel so hard my knuckles turned white.

How could I possibly be bad for my son? I was so focused that I didn't even notice the car cutting me off.

"Hey asshole! Get off the road!" I shouted. I never do that sort of thing, but I was so pissed at my dad that everybody better stay out of my way.

Maybe that's what dad was talking about? If I brought home this kind of anger, then my son would start to internalize it as he grew up. Maybe it was best for me to just stop at the bar before heading home and take some time to cool off...

I couldn't sleep that night. Stacey was mad at me for coming home late. She smelled the alcohol on me, but I didn't want to tell her about my dad because I just wanted to forget about him. They're better off without us. Hah! Better off without you.

But what if there was something more to it? Maybe my father really knew something I didn't - some inherited health problem, or predisposition to an addiction, or Hell I don't know. He didn't seem accusing or angry or anything when he said it. Maybe he was actually trying to warn me. If that was the case, then wasn't I being selfish in putting my own comfort over the security of my family?

It was 2 in the morning when I knocked on his door again. He opened it wearing the same disgusting bathrobe.

"Why are they better off without us?" I blurted out. I wanted to cut straight to the point and not give small-talk a chance to sap my anger.

"Come on in, have a seat."

"I don't want to come in. I want an answer," I said.

"You smell like booze," he said. "So did I when I went home. Your mother couldn't stand it."

That was it? He was an alcoholic? Well I wasn't. Sure I drank from time to time, but I wouldn't let it ruin my relationship with Stacey like it did with him and my mother. I couldn't stand the sight of him, so I just took off right after he gave me that explanation.

But Stacey had been upset when she smelled it, so maybe I could still learn from him. I decided to spend the rest of the night at a friend's house so she wouldn't have to see me like this.

I sent her a text to let her know what I was doing and went over to my buddy Tom. He and I stayed up chatting for a while, I had a couple more drinks to help me sleep, and then I crashed on his couch. Between the alcohol and knowing I resolved the issue, I slept like a baby through the rest of the night.

I wish I hadn't though because she was absolutely livid. She wouldn't even let me explain myself. I tried to tell her about my father, but she just thought it was awfully convenient considering I hadn't mentioned him yesterday.

The alcohol - the night out - she was utterly convinced I was cheating. I even tried getting her to talk to Tom, but she wouldn't stop yelling long enough for me to get him on the phone.

I shouldn't have hit her. I know it was wrong. But I couldn't get her attention, and I was getting so mad at her being mad... shit, I don't know. It wasn't even hard - I just pushed her away from me and she fell over. I was so embarrassed that I just rushed straight out the door.

Where was I supposed to go though? I didn't want to bring my mother in on this. She had to believe I was the perfect son - the perfect husband that my dad never was. The only person who seemed to understand what I was going through, the only one I wanted to talk to, was my dad.

Tap tap tap. My knock lacked all the certainty and power it had the first time around. And yeah, maybe he was just going to say something that pissed me off worse, but maybe he'd also remind me about how much worse of a father he was. Compared to him and everything he's done, I'd be able to look at myself and know I wasn't so bad.

"Tell me everything," I said.

"Well come on in."

"I don't want to come in. I want to know what made you such a shitty father."

We stood facing each other through the doorway. He looked worn out, but I must have too after last night. For a second I thought he was going to just close the door in my face, but then he sighed and said:

"I hit your mother. Are you happy now?"

"Yeah what else? I want to know everything." My breath was

coming in shallow gasps. There had to be more. There had to be something that made this man worse than me.

"Just leave it alone, will you? It's ancient history," he said. "Either come in or leave, because I don't want to just stand here like a couple of -"

"I want you to tell me what else you did to us!" I shouted.

"Yeah, well know what I want?" He said. "I hope when your son comes knocking on your door in twenty-some years, you do something I couldn't and break the cycle. I hope you don't answer him."

He started to close the door. I tried to push my way in, and the door slammed on my foot.

"I'm not you! I'll never be you!"

He tried to push me back so he could close the door, but I barreled into him and knocked him to the floor. He tried to crawl away, but I straddled him and pinned him to the ground.

"Get the Hell off me -"

"Not until you tell me what else made you leave."

"It's none of your business -" He tried to sit up, but I forced his head down. Too hard. It slammed into the tile floor with a sickening crack, and a pool of blood began to spread out from the wound. He wasn't fighting back anymore. His body felt limp.

"What did you do? What did you do?" I kept shaking him as though that would wake him up, but all I did was smear the blood around. But there! One of his eyes flickered open for a moment.

"I swear to God," I said, "if you don't tell me I'll -"

"I killed a man," he grunted. "After that, I couldn't look you or my wife in the eye, so I left."

"Who?" I asked, but somehow I already knew the answer.

"He had it coming. For leaving my mother. For leaving me." My grip went slack, but it didn't matter. He couldn't stand anymore. I let him slip to the ground and stared at my bloody hands.

What son would want a father like this? Maybe he was right. Maybe they are better off without us.

THE FACE ON MY BEDROOM WALL

T he line bordering the other side of sanity is only the width of a shadow. All you have to do is move to a different angle to watch it disappear.

I am a man of particular taste. My alarm is set at 6:28 AM, because 6:30 doesn't give me enough time to massage the salt into my morning egg. I carry with me a list of my favorite words and check them off throughout the day to avoid redundancies. And you will never catch me throwing my clothes in a pile at the day's end, because I find it uncomfortable leaving undressed mannequins in my room. (I'd oblige you not to picture some tormented scene—it's really quite a civilized way to store your outfits. I even made them plastic masks by boiling down some old toys and shaping them with a scalpel, so they look perfectly natural there.)

Things must be just so. If they are not so, then I am not so. My wristwatch broke once, and I didn't leave work until 3 in the morning. I physically hurt trying to tear myself away while it only read 4:52 PM. I am telling you this because I want you to understand how orderly my routine is, and how shocked I was to see something so egregiously (check off) out of place.

Three weeks ago

I walked into my apartment and placed my hat upon the garden gnome which stood sentry at my front door. I drank a glass of water which I had left on the kitchen counter that morning to re-hydrate me from my walk home (I trust the public transit as much as a toddler with a gun). Then to my bedroom, where I found them.

Two faces were mounted on the wall astride my bed: that of the bus driver, and another of Elaine who lived next door. The bus driver displayed a crafty grin while Elaine was transfixed with the most preposterous (check off) sneer I had ever seen in my life. She was an angel in an apron, benevolent to the bone—I've never seen her wear such a dreadful expression in all my time with her.

"Bet you feel silly now," the bus driver said.

"I beg your pardon?" I was shocked, but not so shocked as to forget my manners.

"Not trusting the bus. How does it feel knowing I got in safe and she didn't?"

"What happened to you, Elaine?"

Her twisted sneer remained static, her dead plastic eyes completely devoid of life. I touched her face, and then the face of the bus driver—both were made of plastic, much like those on my mannequins. Peculiar to say the least, considering I never made faces to resemble either of those people. I must say I rather liked them there though. Now that they were pointed at the mannequins, the faces could keep each other company while I was gone.

Two weeks ago

Elaine is dead. I believe that's the most important fact to address first. She struck her head on a concrete pillar after tumbling down nearly two flights of stairs. I never saw her, but the landlady was kind enough to show me pictures she snapped with her cell phone. She shows me all the strangest things—I suppose she doesn't think I judge her because of my own eccentric tastes. She's wrong, but I wouldn't say it to her face.

Elaine's grotesque sneer was identical to the mask above my bed. I believe that to be the second most important fact. I didn't volunteer this information to anyone at the time, but I am disclosing it to you because I find it easier to trust people when I am not looking them in the eye.

There is another mask above my bed, although perhaps this is the most important fact of all. The smiling face of my landlady. I believe I understand why she is smiling because the bus driver now looks absolutely terrified.

"What are you so scared of?" I asked him, but now his expression was fixed.

"You'll see," the landlady said, grinning from ear to ear.

One week ago

Her comment was germane (check off) to the news the following week. The bus was clipped by a drunk driver and sent rolling down a hillside. Two casualties, one of which was the driver himself. I can only imagine how horrendous it would be to roll down the hill amidst a blender of falling bodies and flailing limbs. Of course, I don't have to imagine how they reacted to the situation, because I could see it plainly on the driver's face.

It is with deep trepidation that I must report my latest discovery. My own face has been added to the wall, and while the landlady's mask doesn't seem the least perturbed, my own expression surpasses the most ghastly countenance of dread your darkest imagination might conjure.

I tried to shift my anguished face, but the expression was hard set and immovable. I tried heating it in the oven to make it malleable, but two hours at 500 degrees didn't make the slightest indentation. All it did was make the landlady giggle from above my bed.

"You can't change it. You're done for."

"You'll see," I replied.

I went to knock upon the landlady's door. It seemed like a fairly straightforward fix. Once her real face matched the mask of terror, I saw in my own, then my face would be able to smile again.

She opened the door and invited me in. I let her serve me tea and introduce both of her cats in a sing-song voice as though they were the one talking. And they call me the crazy one.

I considered waiting for her back to be turned, but I had to make sure the expression really captured her impending disaster. It wasn't as easy or as pretty this way, but I knew the second I lay the knife upon the coffee table that it would pay for its trouble. I cut her in eight places—an even number so she could rest in peace—saving the killing blow until the moment her face was the perfect contortion of distress. It seemed like an awful mess to leave for the cats, but I heard they take care of that sort of thing in time.

Last night

Her face is still on my wall. And it's still smiling. The police arrived faster than I thought they would. That's the problem with apartments —thin walls. Always some nosy neighbor poking their nose into something that isn't their business.

I supposed I should have hid the body. It's not a matter of legal repercussions—they questioned me, but didn't have any evidence in my direction—it's just that when they found the body, it was doubtlessly sent to a funeral home. There they would modify the face into a more comfortable sight for her open casket (which I can't imagine why a woman of her appearance would have requested before her demise).

Her body was out of my hands now, and her face was still smiling. My mask, however, remained locked in its grizzly scream. I don't know how long I have, but it seems like Elaine and the driver both terminated within a few days of their masks appearing. I had to act fast.

I tried to make another plastic mask to match my own, but my damn hands kept shaking. That's what happens when you mess up your routine—things begin to fall apart. I couldn't get even a passable likeness of myself.

The only remaining option—one I had considered, but pushed to the back of my brain as a last resort—now stood stark and alone. I took the plastic mask of my face and tossed it in the rubbish bin. Now a few shots of gin to numb the pain—now a deep breath.

And in goes the knife. Skin doesn't peel back from a face nearly as cleanly as I expected. I kept getting the depth wrong—either too shallow, and only nicking myself, or too deep and cutting the underlying muscle. It took nearly three hours before I had removed my entire face and was able to pin the bloody mess to my bedroom wall.

But skin is so much easier to adjust than plastic, and would you look at that? In no time, it was smiling. I looked over to the landlady's face, and my heart beamed with satisfaction to see her twisted terror finally appearing. One lived while the other dies. One comedy while the other tragedy, but it is the actor who decides which to wear.

THE WALL BETWEEN US

Let me tell you about my neighbor Dave. He built up his own mobile plumbing service with just his van and scavenged parts, and he works like the Devil trying to compete against the big guys who service the same area. He's married to a sweet older woman named Jasmine who never had a family of her own, but she finally has one with him. He has two children – one able-bodied helper and one who will be stuck in a wheelchair for life. He loves them both the same.

Oh, and one more thing about Dave. He voted for Trump. He didn't make a big deal out of it—he didn't even intend to tell me. I just heard it slip one day while I was bringing the trash out to the street.

"He's going to make America great again, you watch my words. Four—maybe eight years from now, the sun is going to rise on a brand new country."

He was chatting with the mailman at the end of his driveway. And it didn't just stick me the wrong way because I'm Mexican and the president is a racist ingrown toenail in a suit. I didn't know Dave that well—we always got along fine, but never really spent time together. Just knowing he believed the hateful rhetoric spewing from that fear-mongering egoist changed my whole conception of him though.

We caught each other's eye, and he looked away for a second. Like he was embarrassed. Good—he should be. But then he looked back and grinned.

"You voted for him, didn't you Eddy?" he said to me.

"Nah, I was going to but something got in the way."

"What's that?" he asked. "'Cause I know you're a solid guy who couldn't have been fooled by that lady harpy."

"Just my conscience," I said.

After that, we stopped saying Hello to each other when we passed on the street. It wasn't anything hostile—not yet. We just nodded and looked away. I couldn't imagine having any common grounds with someone with such a perverted ideology, and I didn't want to have a confrontation by trying to convince him how he was wrong.

He must have felt the same way and said something about it to his kids. One of them—the tall one with the baggy hoodie, I forget his name—started spray painting on his side of the brick wall between our property lines. I waited until he was gone to walk around and see what it said.

Build a wall, Kill 'em all.

Well shit. I guess I shouldn't have been so offended by that. He didn't even make it up—it was just some stupid campaign sign that was held up at some Trump rallies. I could feel the blood boiling in my veins though. Now anyone who drove by my house would see that right beside my front door. They'd probably think the whole neighborhood supported that cat-vomit with a hairball on top.

Knock knock knock. I didn't even know what I was planning to say when I knocked. I just wanted to vent some steam. Dave opened the door, and I pointed a silent finger at the wall.

"Yeah?" he said. He stepped out to get a better look. Then he chuckled. "Well look at that."

"You gotta have a word with your kids, man. I don't want that hate speech on my wall."

"Your wall? What did he mark your side too?" Dave walked up to the wall to peer over.

"No, but it's right next to my house -"

"Oh so it's not on your property. Sounds like you wouldn't even notice if we had a bigger wall."

After that, we didn't even nod at each other. He sometimes gave me a little smirk, and I'd just turn away from him. I don't care if it was his property, I couldn't understand how he—a grown-ass man—could condone that kind of hate.

I stopped saying Hello to his wife too. She would smile and wave while watering her rose bushes, and I'd just pretend I didn't notice. The message was still on their wall—she must have known about it. If she wasn't painting over it, then that was the same thing as supporting it.

That's when my kid started getting picked on in school. Rob wouldn't tell me who did it, but I knew it was those bastards next door. I saw the look Rob gave them when they all left the bus together: like prey sizing up a predator. The tall kid in the hoodie smirked—the same idiotic sneer his father had.

I couldn't pick a fight with Dave until Rob actually pointed a finger. I'm always trying to get that kid to stand up for himself, but he hates fighting. It would just be my word against Dave's. But I still wanted to send him a signal that said I knew what was going on, and that I wasn't going to stand for it.

I waited until night to sneak over to his yard. All the lights were off, and I didn't even use a flashlight so I know nobody saw me. I took a pair of garden clippers and chopped the heads off every rose in front of his house. As an afterthought, I stuck the clippers in the ground and wrote:

Hate begets hate.

Yeah, I know it was childish, but you know what? I felt damn good about it. It serves that bitch right for raising such hateful kids.

And I know I was being hateful too, but that was the point, wasn't it? To show them their actions had repercussions. They wouldn't have any proof, but they'd know it was me and that when it came to my kid, I wasn't playing around.

Maybe instead I should have written 'Hate begets hate begets hate begets hate…'because it didn't end there like I was hoping. This time it was the side of my house that was spray painted.

Go back to Mexico.

I was livid. I knew they were racist—the moment I heard him say he voted for Trump, I knew it. They were all a bunch of racist pricks. My son was being bullied worse than ever, my mail was being ripped up and thrown around the street, and my trash was scattered back into my yard.

This had to an end. I waited on Dave's driveway for him to get home. He just sat in his van staring at me, so I opened the door for him.

"What the Hell are you doing in my driveway?" he snapped.

"Go ahead. Say it. Say what you really mean," I said.

"What are you talking about?"

"Ask me what I'm doing in your country. That's what you're think-ing, isn't it? That you belong here and I don't?"

"Look man, I never said that."

"Your kids did, and you let them. Your president did, and you voted for him. Why don't you grow the balls to finally say it too?"

He opened his mouth, then looked over my shoulder and shut it. I looked around. Rob was standing there. Dave's other kid—the one in the wheel chair—he was watching too. I could see Jasmine peaking out from behind their kitchen curtains. Dave took a deep breath.

"Get inside, all of you!" Dave yelled. They did. We both watched the kid in the wheel chair until he was all the way inside, then we turned on each other again.

"Well? Are you going to say it to my face now?" I demanded.

Dave shook his head and let out a long sigh. He looked as tired as I've ever seen him. "Look man, I would if that's what I believed, but I don't. I just want a better life for my family. I'm sorry if my kids have been misbehaving. I'm out working all the time, and they're acting out for attention. I promise it won't happen again."

My fire was dying down. What could I say to that? I know Dave—Hell I've known him a long time. He never did a thing I didn't respect before this political bullshit came up. I wanted to apologize too, but it felt so good for one of those Trump boys to finally admit they were wrong. I told myself I would bring him a bottle of wine or something tomorrow, and just accept this victory right now.

Back inside my house, Rob was waiting for me right inside the door.

"Did you win, Dad?"

"Yeah Rob. I won alright. See what did I tell you? When you know you're in the right, you can't be afraid to stand up for yourself. You gotta fight fire with fire."

"Okay Dad. I'll remember that."

It was cold outside. The wind always picked up in the early morning. I've been standing out here for an hour waiting for the firefighters to finally finish spraying down Dave's house. The kid in the wheelchair (Alex—I finally learned his name) didn't make it out. They wanted to go back in for him, but the firefighters wouldn't let them. They swept the house, but by the time they found him, he had suffocated in the smoke.

They say it started around 1 AM last night. There were kerosene soaked rags stuffed into the air vents, so it wasn't an accident. They were able to contain the blaze before it got over the wall between us, and it was amazing to see how different the two sides looked now. The charred beams jutted accusingly into the sky, and the ground was filthy with ash and debris. His side of the wall was blackened by the fire, but I could still faintly make out the slogan.

Build a wall, Kill 'em all.

The two sides of the wall really weren't so different before the fire. Now it was night and day.

"That's what you wanted, isn't it Dad? You wanted to fight back."

"Go inside Rob. It's too cold out here. We'll talk about it later."

Hate begets hate begets…

I think I'll need to bring Dave something a little stronger than wine.

EVERYONE LIVES, BUT NOT EVERYONE DIES

Everybody dies. That's common knowledge. I learned it when I was five when my hamster met a hawk for the first (and last) time. It was my fault for taking him outside, but that only made the discovery harder.

Everything dies. Everything in the history of the world, up to about a hundred years ago, has died. We take that as proof that we're going to die too, although we don't know for certain until we're actually gone—and by then it's too late to know anything for certain. As long as we're still alive, it feels like there is a chance—no matter how improbable—that we are the exception. That somehow everyone else in the world will die while we will live forever.

I hope some of you just thought about Louis CK's bit about everybody dying. That's what was playing on TV when Grandmother Elis entered the room.

"Don't listen to that man," she said. "Not everybody dies."

Of all the objectionable things Louis CK jokes about, I can't believe this is the topic she chose to argue.

"Of course not, Granny. You're not going anywhere." There is no point in arguing with old people about absolutely anything. Even when they're wrong, they've grown accustomed to being wrong too long for the facts to keep up.

"Oh I'm going to die," she said, laboriously sitting down next to me. "When you get to 84, you can't put a roast in the oven without wondering if you'll be around to take it out. But not everybody dies. My grandfather is 143 years old."

"That's not possible." Was it? I've heard some people lived to be ancient, but I'm pretty sure no-one makes it to 143 without the Devil's private medical insurance.

"He was born in Belgium in 1874, but he lives nearby now."

"How do you know?"

"He still sends me a birthday card every year. I have them up in the attic somewhere."

"But how do you know he's the one sending the cards?" I pressed. "When was the last time you visited him?"

"I never visit. I have nothing to say to him."

That's all she would say about the subject, but my curiosity wasn't nearly satisfied.

I found the birthday card in a shoebox along with 83 other cards. I think they were all hand-drawn and colored, but the older ones were warped and yellowed by time and water damage.

Within each card was inscribed an address alongside this verse:

One less year for you to wait, before your sweet release. Won't you shed your mortal fate and live with me in peace?

It sounds to me like he was offering grandmother an escape from death. I can't imagine that he really had a cure, but I wouldn't turn down that offer if it was handed to me.

Visiting old people is a chore. Visiting ancient people is an adventure. I plugged the most recent address into google maps, and it led me to a Victorian era estate house on the edge of town. It looked like nobody has lived here for years. Even if the old guy was a myth, it would be fun to just poke around and have a look.

I climbed up the rotting porch and knocked on the door, leaving an imprint in the dust the shape of my fist. I hope he doesn't break a hip on his way to let me in. He probably has some live-in medical staff if he's lasted this long though.

When the door swung open, a tall thin man with rigid posture and a pristine suit stood before me. He was wearing an old fashion plague mask and black leather gloves, so I couldn't see his skin. By the way he was standing though, I figured he couldn't be that old.

"Um, hi. Does Mr. Jacobs still live here?"

He didn't move. One arm was held behind his back at a perfect right angle. A corpse couldn't have held more stolid composure.

"He sent my grandmother this card. And like, 80 other cards—one every year." I produced the birthday card, and the man snatched it like a striking snake. The card disappeared into his pocket without a glance. He turned wordlessly and entered the house, leaving the door open behind him.

"Sit." The figure gestured at an elaborately embroidered arm chair which the Queen of England wouldn't have looked out-of-place in. The whole house was absolutely magnificent—while the outside was dilapidated enough to be seen on a "we buy ugly houses" poster, the interior was immaculately preserved. Dark mahogany wood panels, crystal chandelier, intricate golden light fixtures, and shelves and alcoves stuffed to bursting with all manner of exotic dolls, carvings, and trinkets.

"Why did Elis send you?" he asked. The voice had a peculiar hollow ring as it reverberated inside the mask. The words were slightly clipped, but his English was flawless. He continued to tower over me as stiff as a flag pole. My hands ran self-consciously over one another in my lap.

I was tempted to admit I came on my own, but the cards seemed specifically for my grandmother, and I didn't want to be turned away. Idle curiosity doesn't open nearly as many doors as blatant lies.

"My grandmother—Elis—she wanted me to meet Mr. Jacobs for her."

"I am Mr. Jacobs."

"Then, um, she wanted to let me decide whether to accept your offer." I didn't know what it meant, but it was just vague enough to work.

He bent over me, the long nose of the mask practically scratching my skin. The slow intake of breath—was he sniffing me? I fought the urge to be sick when a wave of the thick incense within the mask washed over my face.

Apparently satisfied, the man moved to sit across from me on the other side of the marble coffee-table. He poured a glass of red wine from a silver decanter for me before pouring another for himself. His long body leaned back, crossing lithe legs with the dexterity of a dancer. Polished leather shoes flashing softly in the dull light. There is no way this guy is 143 years old.

"Drink," he said, the thick perfume billowing out of the mask.

"I'm not old enough to–"

"How old are you, boy?"

"19. How old are you?"

"Are you old enough to fear death?" he asked.

I nodded.

"Then you are old enough to drink."

I was getting really uncomfortable at this point. My hands wouldn't sit still. Maybe I was in over my head. I was just curious that's all. I didn't really believe he was 143 years old. If he really did have a cure for death why wouldn't my Grandmother accept it?

"I think there's been a mistake. I think I should be going now." I started to stand, but he was faster. He stepped directly over the coffee table and blocked me from getting out of the over-stuffed chair. The perfume was intoxicating. I couldn't think straight. Whatever I tried to focus on just blurred out in my mind. All I could see was the piercing red wine taunting me from the table. The only sounds were my beating heart, and his melodic voice echoing from the mask.

"Is this a game to you, boy? Are you trying to play me?"

"No sir, I–"

"Do you seek to fool me? To rob me? To take my secrets and sell them for your own gain?"

"I swear I only came because–" My head was spinning. The crystal chandelier flashed as bright as a lighthouse. The scent was overwhelming. It was all I could do just to avoid throwing up. Even if he weren't blocking me in, I don't know if I could have stood to leave.

"Because what? Why are you here? Why have you disturbed my home?" He was shouting now—at least I think he was. My senses were so saturated with noise and light and smell.

I shut my eyes tight. I pressed my hands over my ears so tightly I could feel them pop somewhere deep within my head.

"I don't want to die!" I shouted. I could have said anything else, but that's the only thought my mind could hold on to.

"Then drink." My eyes were still closed, but I could feel the glass of wine being shoved into my face—spilling over my chest. I grabbed it with both hands and gulped it down like I had been lost in the desert for years.

Mr. Jacob's presence immediately lifted. He must have moved away to the other side of the coffee table again. That all-consuming perfume began to clear from the air, but I kept drinking. I didn't want to die. I don't care what happened to me in that moment. I never wanted to die.

Crunch. Something hard slipped into my mouth from the bottom of the wineglass. I opened my eyes. The bottom of the glass was crawling with beetles. I tried to cough, but the one already in my mouth slipped down my throat. I could feel its legs struggling against my esophagus all the way down.

"Do not worry, child." Mr. Jacob's voice was soft as a purring cat. "You never will. Now go home and do not return without your Grandmother."

I got up and ran. Once outside, I fell to my hands and knees and heaved on the ground. I forced my fingers down my throat, but I didn't need much help to induce the vomiting. The red wine poured out in waves, splattering all over my hands and knees.

Still gasping for breath, I ran my hands through my own vomit—searching. It was all liquid. I squeezed the wet dirt with my hands. The beetle hadn't come out.

I took off my shirt and pants which were soaked in vomit and put them in the back of my car. I drove home, trying my best to pretend nothing happened.

But it was hard not to think about when I could feel the beetle crawling around in my stomach the whole way back. I don't know what that beetle I swallowed was, but it's doing something to me.

The squirming sensation had abated for a while, and I figured it would be digested. I wasn't feeling as nauseous anymore, so it probably wasn't poisonous. I told myself he was just some crazy hermit who got his wrinkled old rocks off by playing tricks on people. It wasn't that my Grandmother was afraid of him—she must have just known he was a fraud.

I was almost home before the sharp pain in my stomach doubled me over the steering wheel. It was like an ice-cold knife trying to force its way out from the inside. I had to pull off into a gas station to wait for it to pass.

The pain quickly faded into a gentle numbness, the sensation replaced by a soft tickling working its way up my chest cavity. I lifted my shirt and fought the urge to be sick again.

There was a lump under my skin. And it was moving.

I poked at it gingerly, and could feel the hard carapace of the beetle underneath. It must have bitten free from my stomach and begun to crawl around. I briefly considered trying to smash it, but what if I didn't kill it? What if I just made it mad, and it went on a rampage inside of me?

The lump wasn't moving fast, but it was persistently crawling toward my heart. I took a deep breath and felt it holding onto my ribcage as it expanded and contracted.

The hospital. Now. I slowly pulled out of the gas station, trying not to turn the wheel too fast for fear of agitating the beetle. It reacted to even small movements, biting and scratching in protest. I don't care if they made me drink a whole bottle of bleach, I was getting this thing out of me.

I pulled right up to the emergency room doors and left my car there. I practically had to crawl up to the desk to keep the beetle still.

For every foot I made, it was wriggling a few centimeters closer to my heart. What would happen when it got there?

"Somebody help me!" I shouted, lying down on the ground to keep it still. I stared at my reflection in the polished floor tiles, now damp with the cold sweat flowing down my face. Was I delirious? The face looking up at me couldn't be my own. I was so... old. My hair was grey and patchy, my eyes sunken and hollow, and a network of lines mapped the journeys of an un-lived life. I tried to touch my skin, but the jerking movement caused the beetle to bite down hard on one of my lungs.

I was coughing blood when the nurses lifted me into a stretcher. I slipped in and out of consciousness after that. The nurses later told me that I kept mumbling "I don't want to die. I want to live forever".

"Any allergies?"

"No."

"Medications?"

"No."

"Please think hard. It's rare for someone your age not to be on any medications."

I glared at the doctor who perched on the end of my hospital bed. I don't know how long I've been here, but it was afternoon when I went to visit Mr. Jacobs, but now the morning sun was filling my room. I squinted against it, then back at my doctor. He looked bored and annoyed and... fuzzy. I squinted again.

"I'm 19 years old," I said. The events of the other day immediately came back to me, and I clutched at my chest. Ancient withered hands held loosely together by a mesh of bulbous veins gripped my hospital gown and pulled it open. I couldn't feel any lump, but... was this really me? My skin sloughed into sagging pouches around my skeletal frame. I was more than old. I was what old could only dream about becoming when it grew up.

"Do you remember what year it is?" the doctor asked. "Don't worry if you can't. It's common with cases of delirium–"

"It's April 13th, 2017. I'm not delirious. I'm 19 years old and was perfectly healthy yesterday. There's something inside of me which is causing this…"

"Causing what, exactly?"

He was writing something down in his notepad, but he wasn't really listening. He must deal with a dozen old people every day, each more blithering and nonsensical than the last. But if they could find the beetle and reverse this…

"I want a full body scan—""You've already been checked. It was probably nothing but heat exhaustion which caused you to feel dizzy. I'd like to keep you here through the afternoon and get you re-hydrated, and then you'll be as good as ever. Is there anyone you'd like us to notify?"

"My grandmother."

He raised a skeptical eyebrow.

"Just give me the damn phone."

Grandmother Elis and I stared at each other. She recognized me the moment she walked in the door. She didn't say a word—just pursed her lips and sat down. She opened her handbag and began fiddling with something inside.

"I'm sorry…" I said. This was all my fault. I should have asked her before visiting Mr. Jacobs. I should never have gone through her stuff in the attic without permission, or pretend I was supposed to accept Mr. Jacob's offer on her behalf.

She took out a hand-mirror from her purse and held it up to me. I screwed my eyes shut tight.

"Look at what you've become."

I forced myself to look. If I—the old me—had seen someone who looked like I did now, I would have made some cruel joke about old people 'outliving their usefulness'. Now I felt like I wanted to cry, if these puffy old eyes could even do that anymore.

"My Grandfather doesn't know how to extend life," Elis said. "He shifts it from one person to another. The only reason he has lasted this long is because he passes his years into a victim who must bear his burden in his stead."

"So the reason you never accepted his offer…"

"Because I couldn't do that to someone else. One lifetime is more than enough if used properly, and a thousand lives aren't nearly enough when used as he has done."

"But I only want one life, I swear," I said. "And I can get it back, right? All I have to do—"

"No. You do not have the right to give your years to anyone."

"But I could give them back to Mr. Jacobs."

She shook her head. "You will not win. He has been doing this for over a hundred years. If you go back to him, he will only add to your years until you've been turned to dust."

"He told me not to return without you. If you accept his deal—"

Grandmother Elis put her mirror away. I hated how much her hands were shaking.

"I'm sorry. I can't do it."

"Please don't leave me like this..." I said.

"There's hardly anything left of you to leave," and she was gone.

I wanted to say more, but my words caught on a dry itching in my throat. I felt like I was suffocating, and if that had been the end, I would have accepted it. I'd rather die than live like this. But the itching turned into squirming, and the squirming into thrashing. I clutched at my throat, but I was helpless as the beetle crawled up my trachea and out of my mouth. It plopped down into my lap, and I held it in my hands.

But these weren't my years—this wasn't my fault. If I could just pass them off to someone else, then...

I'd rather die than live like this.

But I'd rather live forever than either.

THE PSYCHOPATH IN MY HOUSE

There's a psychopath in my house.

No he didn't break in. He sleeps in the same room as me.

It's not my brother's fault; this is just who he is.

If it's anyone's fault, it's my parents. My Mom left when I was six and my little brother was four. She never wanted us, or at least that's what my Dad said, because I don't remember her very well.

Dad said she used to be a perfect student with big dreams, then she got knocked up and had to drop out of college to take care of us. He reminds us all the time that it was our fault she left, and how happy he was before we were born.

That's the nice version of what he said, anyway. Lots of stuff about her being an ungrateful slut who will burn in Hell, but I don't think of her that way. If I was married to someone like my Dad, I would have run away too.

My Dad needed "medicine" to cope with her leaving. Every time he took it, he would be gone for a few days. It would be just me and my little brother in the house, and I took care of him the best I could. My Dad wouldn't usually leave us with any money, but I got pretty good at hiding things under my dress at the grocery store.

I thought things would change when I was 12 and found a paper bag with 1,000 dollars in our backyard. I thought Mom had sent it—that she'd heard about how hard things were and mailed us some money.

I could usually find food when I needed it badly enough, so I didn't want to waste it on things like that. It was my brother's 10th birthday coming up, and that seemed like a big deal. I hired a van and brought him and seven kids from his class to spend the whole day at Sea World.

It was so much fun I thought about never going back. My brother didn't want to run away though, and I couldn't leave him. Besides, the van driver was keeping an eye on us and said he had to bring us home or he might get fired.

We should have run away though. The money hadn't come from my Mom—she'd forgotten about us. That's when I found out my Dad's "medicine" was meth, and that he'd been selling some to his friends when he dropped the money by mistake. I tried to tell him that it was my fault, but since it got spent on my brother's birthday, he got the worst of it.

My brother didn't walk again for two years after that. He needed even more help now that he was in a wheelchair. There were more bills that weren't being paid—the electricity, the gas, even the rent sometimes. I had to be out a lot trying to find money, sometimes for days at a time when I was staking out a house to steal from.

I couldn't leave my brother alone too long though. My Dad would just ignore him, and if I didn't check in at least twice a day, then I'd find my brother sitting in his own piss and shit. I think he could have made it to the toilet by himself if he really tried, but he just gave up caring about everything.

There is one thing my brother started doing to pass the time though, although this I wish he hadn't. I noticed his growing collection of small animal skulls for a while, but I assumed they were just plastic until I saw how he was catching them.

I watched him put bird seed in a 2L soda bottle with the opening cut wider. Once a squirrel crawled in, he would pull a string which slid the bottle down to cover the opening with a piece of cardboard. It would struggle frantically to get out, but when it was near the opening, its own weight would hold the bottle into place against the board.

I would have congratulated him on his contraption except for what happened next. He picked up the bottle—cardboard still covering the opening—and slipped a couple razor blades inside. Then he SHOOK the whole thing until it looked like the inside of a blender, the squirrel SCREAMING the whole time.

I took it away from him, but he just kept building little things like that. It wasn't just squirrels either—mice, small birds, even a raccoon once. After he'd killed them, he'd BITE the head straight off and then spit it into a bowl of water to clean the organic matter off the skull.

"Please stop. God didn't make those animals just so you could torture them," I said to him.

"Then why did he make it so much fun?"

It's not just animals anymore. I found a big cardboard box out on the sidewalk near the bus-stop. Inside was a bag of M&Ms, a couple comic books, and his old Gameboy Color. There was a rope tied to little hooks inside the box which led toward my house.

If someone were to pull that rope, the box would close and the whole thing would be dragged down the sidewalk. I don't think he'd be strong enough to pull anyone bigger than a six-year-old, but the school bus stopped here.

I ripped the box into pieces and ran to confront him. I found him sitting on his bed—he was out of the wheelchair now—waiting with a knife in his hands.

What the Hell are you trying to do?"

"Set a trap."

"It's not going to work," I said.

"Don't worry. It'll work."

"I destroyed it. Why are you trying to trap some kid?"

"I'm not. I'm trying to trap you."

That's when I noticed that the TV was suspended with ropes above me. He cut the cord, and it landed right on top of my head.

He must have counted on that knocking me out because he was

already coming at me with the knife. I was dizzy, but I managed to scramble out of the way and slam the door in his face.

After that, I was too scared to go back inside the house. I called Child Protective Services and reported the meth deals my Dad was doing in the home. I didn't mention what my brother has been doing, because I thought once he was out of here he'd have a chance at a fresh start. I didn't want his life to be over before it had even begun.

We were both put into separate foster homes, and it's been two years since I've heard anything from him. That was until last night.

My adoptive parents—wonderful Asian couple who couldn't have kids of their own—sat down with me at the kitchen table. They told me they had some good news: they were going to adopt my brother as well.

I guess the family that took him in suffered an unfortunate accident. They didn't tell me what happened, but by the look they gave each other, it must have been gruesome.

I hope he's changed. Telling people what he did will stop him from being adopted and ruin his life forever. I can't say anything until I've seen him again. If he hasn't though…

Well that's why I'm writing this. If he hasn't changed, then at least someone will know what happened, and have a shot at stopping it from happening again.

HOW TO START YOUR OWN CULT

L et me preface this by stating I am a firm atheist. There is no life after death although I will go to great lengths extolling its beauty to my subjects. We do not grow older because the Reaper is always siphoning our life energy. I was not born from a dying star, and I am no prophet of the Divine Cosmic Order.

I am a nihilist—I do not believe in anything. And as much as I do not believe in the supernatural, I believe even less in mankind and their ability to govern their own lives.

Do you really need proof of that? Fanatic mobs begging for their religious oppression to be protected by the government, junkies in the street surrendering their will to anything they can boil into their veins, a narcissistic idiot elected President of the United States—you get the idea.

The church-states, the cartels, the two-faced corporations—none of them will hesitate to manipulate the population for their own selfish purposes. The vast majority of people will always be susceptible to being manipulated because it is so much safer and easier to be told what to think than to think for yourself.

My reasoning dictates:

1)People will always be susceptible to manipulation. If you aren't manipulating them, then someone else will.

2) The manipulator will always profit at the expense of the people. That is the purpose for their influence.

3)The only way to protect people from a selfish manipulator is to become a benevolent manipulator yourself.

For these reasons, in my senior year of college, I decided to start my own cult.

Step One: Identify your targets.

People will not run to you unless they are already running away from something else. Now, where could I find the most fearful students?

I formed three support clubs and put up fliers around campus. One for the socially anxious, one for those needing financial assistance, and a third for victims of sexual assault.

Step Two: Amplify their fear

Ever wonder why priests scream about Hell while politicians rant about terrorists and economic collapse? There is nothing like fear to get someone's attention and follow you for relief.

To the socially anxious, I forced them to give speeches. I asked them embarrassing questions, put them in awkward situations, and generally ridiculed them, all in the guise of helping them gain confidence.

To the financially stressed, I gave lectures about how student loans haunt people for the rest of their life. I told them how the job market is over-saturated with college degrees, and how slim their chance of employment was. I told horror stories about homeless drug addicts who graduated college but couldn't make anything of their lives.

The sexual assault group was the most fun for me. No I didn't rape them—I needed them all to trust me. I did however convince them that I was the only one looking out for them—that there was a rapist in every party, and down every dark alley.

Step Three: Offer a Solution

Three months into the semester, I had finished establishing sufficient trust. That's when I let them in on a little secret—the reason why I'm not afraid.

Wouldn't it be great if there was a safe place to go where no one would make you feel bad about being socially inept? A band of brothers who helped each other find jobs, share rooms, and reach financial success? Sisters who would hold your hand and keep you safe from all the predatory monsters in the world?

I had enough people now that I was able to register my flock as a co-ed professional fraternity. I did some fundraising with the groups and managed to raise enough money to renovate an abandoned motel into my headquarters. Now that I had them all together, the fun could really begin.

Step Four: Make yourself special.

It's not enough for your people to need your insight. They need to need you. Now it was time to explain what made me unique.

Don't force it down their throats. People don't want to be part of an organization that needs them. They want to be part of something exclusive, something that recognizes how special they know they are inside.

I began by offering private counseling sessions to everyone having difficulty. To each of them, I confessed the truth about why I was helping them.

You see; I wasn't human at all. I was an alien who was born in the Andromeda galaxy. My people are empaths, allowing us to sense the suffering of other sentient beings. I felt how troubled Earth was, and I came here to save humanity from themselves.

They were all skeptical at first, but here's what really convinced them. I told each person in confidence that the rest of the fraternity was already indoctrinated. No-one wants to be the only one left out, especially when they finally found a home which unequivocally accepts and shelters them.

Step Five: Make them special

Each new member makes it that much easier to add the next, because it adds credibility and makes people more afraid of being left out. Adding the first few is the hardest part, so here is what I did.

The first person I convinced was a scared freshman girl who was raped during a house party. She was ready to give anything just to feel safe. I gave her the chance to witness the ceremony and didn't force her to commit to anything.

I laid rows of candles in the basement and lined the walls with mannequins. I concealed the mannequins with thick robes, so it would appear as though most of the fraternity was already present. I used a surround sound system and a layered chanting soundtrack to make it seem like everyone was participating.

By the time I was through with the ceremony; she was so afraid of being left out that she swore the oath of loyalty right on the spot.

Step Six: Make it impossible to leave

This is the final—and I would argue most important—step. There is nothing as toxic to an organization as having a previous member leave and talk about it.

Once I had ten members who had undergone the ceremony, I organized them into two groups of five. I gave them innocent tasks to prove their loyalty. Each one would be slightly more difficult than the last which is important for keeping them invested.

The final task to allow them full membership and protection was very simple. Four of them must team up and kill the fifth member of the group. For each group, I chose the least loyal, most suspicious member to be killed. I told the rest that the fifth member was a traitor —that he raped one of the other members. That he was going to single handedly destroy all we had worked to build together.

They would never do it alone, but when the rest of their group was going along with it, they lost the power to think for themselves. Both groups did as they were told.

It was a ritualistic sacrifice—the extra man would be tied down to a stone table. I had already drugged him, minimizing his resistance. I used his slurred speech as proof that he was possessed by an evil Cosmic Spirit which sought to destroy us all.

I made sure each of the four loyal group members thrust the knife into his body at least once. After that, their conscience would bind them to me forever.

If they stayed, their minds told them they were a hero. If they left, they were a murderer. Which do you think they would rather be?

One full semester later, I have indoctrinated 54 members so far. There have been 10 deaths, soon to be an 11th.

I'm not writing this as a confession—I don't expect you'll be able to find me. I'm writing this as an offer.

My cult is growing, and there are different chapters springing up all around the country. We have been helpless pawns for too long, but we are learning how to play the game by their rules. When you are ready to take power into your own hands, I hope you will join me and change the world.

THREE GO TO SLEEP. FOUR WAKE UP

I've done it. Three years of being single, and I've finally gotten a girlfriend.

Yes she's human. No, she's not blind. No, she's not a body pillow.

These are the kinds of questions my best friend Mike kept asking me. I was so excited that I wasn't even bothered. Besides, I knew he was just jealous because he'd never even been with a girl before. He's always been the bigger nerd between the two of us—like learning Elvish from Tolkien's books and chanting spells in our DnD games—hardcore nerd stuff.

Neither of us are the type of guy that girls tend to hang around though. Mike and I live together; we're both video game streamers (Hearthstone and Dota2), and we make a living off advertising and tournament winnings.

I met Natasha through a Twitch chat room and she happened to live close by. Since the first day we met, we've practically been joined at the hip. We eat every meal together, shower together, even stream together.

I don't remember ever being this happy—the only problem is,

Mike has decided to make this all about him. He started gaining even more weight, he never goes outside, and all he does is bitch about how I never hang out with him anymore.

Natasha decided the solution was for the three of us to go camping together in Yellowstone National Park. Mike would get some exercise, I'd get to hang out with him, and most importantly, Natasha and I wouldn't have to spend any time apart.

I regret everything though. Why does everything in nature have to be so damn itchy?

It turns out Natasha has a severe misunderstanding about how trails work. She must be a Skyrim player, because she thinks there is only one right way up a mountain, and that's straight up the rock cliffs.

If we weren't still at that phase of dating where everything becomes an opportunity to impress each other, I would have given up and gone home. I have no idea how Mike made it, but we all decided the day was over by about 4 PM in the afternoon.

The view was incredible—no I'm not just talking about Natasha in her short-shorts. She found a practically inaccessible rock ledge over-looking most of the park, and single-handedly hauled all our camping gear up there while Mike and I lay panting on the ground.

Campfire—s'mores—a full blanket of stars—it was a great night. Natasha and Mike bonded over Magic the Gathering cards (which I can't believe he packed instead of a lantern), and he finally agreed to start working out and taking better care of himself so he could find a girl too.

As the campfire burned down to embers, we started telling ghost stories. I told one about a man-eating wendigo, Natasha knew a twisted story about a priest who crucified people, and Mike...

I don't know where Mike stole his story from, but he claimed to have made it up on the spot. I think he was trying to impress Natasha too, but I didn't get jealous. He said it in a sing-song rhyming voice which was super creepy, and I made him write it down afterward. It went like this:

I had a dream one fateful night, when day had made its run.
When waking world had fled from sight, and silent moon eclipses sun.
Into fitful slumber slipped, losing command of my thoughts.
Nightmares around me gripped, the familiar had come to naught.
I forgot what I've been taught about what cannot cause me harm.
My fears abound, in safety sought, I scream to waken in alarm.
Only to find I've fallen deeper, down this darkened pit of shade.
No sound escapes from silent sleeper, nor outward sign of my dismay.
I saw a monster rear its head, somewhere inside of mine.
On my dear memories it fed, the beast who devours time.
Scything talons raking down, gaping jaws of a giant spider.
I was marked as I was found, as the one outsider.
Until all I could recall of life, was that I had once loved.
Until that too was torn in strife, an arm severed from the glove.
There upon the edge of breaking, inside of me a guide would lead.
She was the love I'd be forsaking, when I opened my eyes from sleep.
She took my hand and together ran, from the monster in my mind.
We got so far that soon began, what I never thought to find.
We lived a day, a season, then year, an entire lifetime in my head.
Happy as he who has forgotten fear, of the monster I had dread.
Until finally it rose from quiet, when we thought ourselves alone.
We had lived lives in spite it, but our life together was on loan.
The monster had us caught! Trapped and helpless in a corner.
With no escape I stood and fought, rather die than be a mourner.
Rather lose oneself completely, than forget what I had sworn.
Death before me, but I would beat he, who would dare to touch her form.
I ripped the air with my two hands, but as the creature was not real,
no blows upon the beast did land, though its talons I could feel.
Blooded broken and abused, I awaited morning's light to heal,
and save me from this awful ruse, that my fortune had me sealed.
She knelt above me, my lovely queen, and besought me waken from
this dream.
But what fate would befall her here? Would with the morning she disappear?

She bore the monster and its fury, begging only that I woke.
Bidding me go, though not to hurry, lest this the last time that we spoke.
Sweat soaked, body shakes – I can't remember why I was sad.
Throat chocked, fully awake – memories flood of the dream I had.
Blood trickled down my length, and I thanked each crimson bead.
They gave hope and lent me strength, that perhaps she too was freed.
And there my bride lay beside me, from my dream she was released.
Wearied from dreaming was she, who in the waking world found peace.

I woke up to a high-pitched scream in the middle of the night. What the shit?

Did a bear get into our camp? I thought we'd be safe from any of the larger wildlife because of the rock ledge. Or a maybe it was a mountain lion…

I was on my feet – Natasha was already unzipping our tent.

"Wait—it could be dangerous!"

"Then we've got to help Mike."

I couldn't fault her reasoning. I just wish she had been a little more selfish. I grabbed my cellphone to use as a flashlight and followed her outside.

"I'm okay! I'm okay. Sorry I screamed." Mike was in his boxers, standing outside his tent.

"You scream like a girl. What happened?" I asked.

He pointed inside his tent and drew the flap back. Natasha and I peered inside with him.

There was a girl—or maybe a Goddess—mid-twenties, long auburn hair, flawless skin—butt naked, lying beside Mike's empty sleeping bag. I turned away for a moment, but looked again as soon as I noticed Natasha wasn't averting her eyes.

"Who the Hell are you?" Natasha asked.

The girl smiled, making no effort to cover herself. She sat upright and began smoothing out her hair.

"I had the dream—the same dream from that story I found," Mike said.

"Aha! I knew you didn't make that shit up," I said.

"Yeah whatever," Mike replied. "But I was dreaming about her. And the beast was there... and..."

"What's your name? Where did you come from?" Natasha asked.

The girl stretched luxuriously, still smiling. She stood up and wrapped her arms around Mike, peering at us from over his shoulder.

"Where did you find that story?" I asked Mike. He was frozen stiff with a mix of terror and rapture.

"Some book. Doesn't matter."

"It does matter if it's real," I said.

"I don't like it," Natasha said. "Either tell us who you are, or get out of here."

"No!" Mike stepped protectively in front of her. "She's lost without any food, or clothes, or anything. We can't just leave her in the wilderness."

"You're just saying that because you think you're going to get some." I don't know why I was fighting it. I shouldn't be jealous. I had Natasha. But this... this just wasn't fair.

"I don't care," Mike said. "I'm going to take her back with us and bring her to a hospital in the morning. Maybe she had a concussion or something."

"And until the morning?" Natasha asked, crossing her arms.

The girl pulled away from Mike and settled into his sleeping bag. Mike smiled sheepishly.

"Well she seems comfortable here so..."

"You're an idiot." Natasha rolled her eyes and walked out. Over her shoulder, she added "But if the girl is real, then I wouldn't be surprised if the beast was too."

Mike gave me a thumbs up. I laughed, closing the tent behind me.

That was the last time I saw Mike alive. When we checked on him in the morning, his rib-cage was flayed open. His heart was missing, but there were still some scraps of sinew and part of his aorta lying in a pool of blood beside the bag. The girl was gone.

I threw up in the bushes. Natasha just stared at the grizzly scene.

"We're going home," she said, turning sharply away.

"I'll start packing –"

"No," she said. "Let's just go."

"We can't leave Mike like this."

"It's his own damn fault. Now the girl could be anywhere, so let's go now!"

Natasha was already half-way down the rocky wall, but I wasn't going to run through the forest naked. I opened my tent to grab some pants but—The girl was sitting in my tent. Her naked body was covered in blood, and when she smiled, more blood squirted out from between her teeth.

"Hurry up!" Natasha yelled from outside. "I swear to God, I'll leave without you."

I was 'bout to turn and run when the bloody girl finally spoke.

"Help me."

"Help you? After what you did to–"

"It wasn't me!" Her smile was gone now, and she looked on the verge of tears. "It was the beast. He's free too."

If she was telling the truth, then I couldn't just leave her here. If she wasn't...

There was another SCREAM outside. Natasha! I leapt from the tent and ran to the place she was climbing down. Her crumbled body was lying on the ground. She must have slipped while climbing—No. There was a dark shape on top of her—like a wolf with impossibly long limbs and an elongated mouth.

"Natasha!"

But I was helpless to get to her in time. One bite was enough to snap the rib-cage open. I couldn't watch what was going to happen next.

I turned around, and the girl was gone. I ran—farther and faster than I ever have in my life. There were a few times when I heard something bounding through the underbrush to my side, but I didn't look. I kept running, even when my lungs felt like they were about to explode, and the stitch in my side threatened to tear me in half.

I don't know whether the girl and the beast were the same, simply two-halves of the same nightmare. I don't know if it's still out there, or whether it only comes when that story is read aloud.

I'm going to try to find the book where Mike found the story and destroy it. Although I have to admit, I'm a little curious what else is written in those pages...

SHE IS STILL WITH ME

"Well, of course you're depressed. You never leave the house."

"Your life isn't over just because hers is. I'm sorry but it's true."

"Don't give up hope. You're going to meet someone else and be just as happy as you ever were."

Just as happy.

I'm tired of hearing it. What I'm going through—what I'm feeling —it's nobody's business but my own. I don't even know how to begin opening up to anyone who isn't Natalie. Ten years of feeling her warmth pressed against me when I wake. Ten years of whispering to each other in the dark. Ten years of making plans which will never be fulfilled.

Nine months of drinking until I pass out on the couch with the TV on. I haven't been able to sleep in the bed we shared since breast cancer stole my wife from me. Hell, I've barely been able to sleep at all, and by the way people talk to me, I know they can tell.

They're right of course, but that only makes it harder. Knowing they're right and still being unable to do anything about it is such a frustrating feeling—like realizing the right answer after you've already turned in your test. But I'm working through the grief in my own way. It has been a confusing time for me, but I've started keeping this journal to help me process my thoughts. While I will never forget her, in time I will learn to move on.

I'm meeting someone for dinner tonight. I won't call it a date—it probably is, but I don't want to put my mind in that place yet. Sarah, the daughter of an older client, is in town and I've promised to entertain her for the evening. I guess she has some self-esteem issues, and I'm supposed to make her feel better about herself. We've chatted a few times, and she's laughed at some things I said (even though I know they weren't funny). I would have even called her beautiful at a time when I still looked at women that way. Well, here goes nothing...

Why the fuck didn't I listen to myself. I knew it was too soon. I felt tense the moment I sat down with her. I should have just left then. Everything was going fine though—more than fine she was fantastic —but then she started humming that damn 'my heart will go on' song. The one song stuck in her head just had to be the first song Natalie and I danced to at our wedding. What are the chances?

I feel like an idiot for jumping up and racing to the bathroom. I don't know how long I stayed in there, but I was half-hoping she would be gone when I came out. To her credit, Sarah just laughed it off and acted like nothing happened.

She did ask one strange thing though: she asked what Natalie would have thought about her... what an awkward silence that was. All I could manage was "My wife would have been happy to see me having a good time." That was a lie, of course. I couldn't exactly tell her that Natalie was the jealous type – if she knew I was out on a "date" now, then six feet of dirt wouldn't be enough to stop her. Sarah is so sweet to still worry about that even with Natalie gone...

We're getting drinks again. She was even the one to invite me. I can't believe it. Natalie is the only one to ever chase me before. I've heard girls sometimes find men who are suffering to be the most attractive. Our indifference gives them a challenge—our damage gives them something to fix. I'm honestly excited about it. Even if nothing else happens, this will be good for me.

She actually reminds me of Natalie a lot. The way she cups my hand in hers when she leans in to talk—and then there's the way she bites her lip when she's holding back a smile. She even wears the same kind of long dress with the high belt my wife used to wear, although she has the type of body which would do well in something more revealing...

Now that I think about it, Sarah and Natalie really have a lot in common. You don't think that... no it's impossible. Natalie is gone. I wanted to move on, right? And that's never going to happen by entertaining such ridiculous thoughts.

Okay this is getting weird though. Sarah won't stop mentioning Natalie. She spent the whole evening asking about how we met, and what I liked about her, and how we spent our time together. It was hard enough talking about my dead wife on a date, but then Sarah would stare at me as though she was analyzing my every answer.

How am I supposed to forget Natalie like this? No! Not forget! I didn't mean forget... I'll never forget... but I think I want to. Is that so wrong? If thinking about her brings me nothing but sadness, is it so wrong to want to be happy?

Natalie would have thought so. I promised I would never love anyone like I loved her. I promised she could never be replaced. Could she really still be holding me to that promise? What if Sarah was only a test—what if Natalie is still watching me, waiting for me to fail? I need to go for a walk.

Natalie is coming over to my place tonight. I mean Sarah—I mean Natalie—I mean—The girl won't stop calling me. I'm getting text messages every ten minutes. Whatever I turn the conversation to, she always redirects it back to my dead wife. Natalie is still with me, I know it. She doesn't want me to move on.

When she comes over tonight, I'm going to ask her straight out. If she says she's Sarah—if she says she isn't my wife—I'll leave it at that.

But if she admits her spirit is still here... I don't know. I'll do whatever I can to help her find peace.

Natalie has traveled to the other side. I'm finally free. For the first time since her death, her presence is finally gone.

I didn't have the courage to ask the girl right away. I could tell she was reserved too, so we both had a couple of drinks. I knew I needed to ask, but it still felt so awkward and wrong, so I just kept drinking. Finally I was able to push the words out:

"Are you really Sarah, or are you Natalie's spirit?"

"I'm everything she was," she said, and she kissed me. I closed my eyes, and I could taste Natalie's lips. I ran my fingers through Natalie's hair, and felt my wife's hands on my chest.

It was so good to hold her again, even if this was the last time. It was so good to feel her skin beneath my hands. It was so good to choke the life out of her, sending her spirit back to rest.

I hope she stays gone. This is the third time I've had to send Natalie back to the other side. I'm working through my grief in my own way though, and once Natalie has finally let go of me, I think I'll be able to let go of her too. As long as I have a body beside me, I think I can finally sleep in my bed again tonight.

Sometimes a song is just a song.

Sometimes a smile is just a smile.

Some people are meant to be alone.

DEAD MAN FLOATING

I found the first floater when I was seven years old. It had washed up on the shore about a hundred yards from my family's summer house. It still looked mostly human—a bit swollen and decomposed, but whole enough for me to immediately recognize what it was.

Even as a kid, I was never very squeamish. I used to watch my father skin the deer he caught on his hunting trips, and I would clean my own fish whenever I reeled one in from the salty lake. Finding a human body was the best thing that could have happened to me that summer.

I thought about telling my parents, but there's no way they would let me play with it. Heck, they might even ban me from going down to the water at all, a thought which my seven-year-old brain equated to nuclear holocaust, an asteroid destroying the earth, or other disasters of similar magnitude.

So I did what any clear thinking seven-year-old would do. I gathered up all the other kids I knew and charged them $5 each to poke it with a stick. The salt water preserved it well enough for us to stomach the smell, but poking it would release some bloated gas still trapped in the carcass. I told them they could have their money back if they could lick it without throwing up.

No-one got their money back. I made $60 before one of the little snitches told his mother and she called the police.

Next summer when I came back, the first thing I did was race back to the same spot. Sure enough, there had been two more bodies to wash up over the winter. These must have been sitting out in the sun for a while though, because I couldn't even get close to them.

My father had followed me that time, and I wasn't allowed to have any fun. The police said these bodies must be new, since they would have been completely rotten if they had been down there for a year.

Over the next 10 years, there had been another three bodies found beside the lake. Each was slightly more decomposed than the last, but the police still insisted they had to be separate incidents because they were all still too fresh.

None of them could be identified, and as they didn't fit any missing persons within the entire state, the police had no leads to discover who was dumping the bodies. They had given up, but I was never able to put the mystery out of my mind.

I had my own theory. I decided those people didn't just die in the lake—they lived in it too. I thought that when they die; they float to the surface just like when humans die, they're buried in the ground. In retrospect the idea didn't really make sense, but it had started forming when I was so young that I refused to let go until the mystery had been resolved.

When I was in college, I became SCUBA certified for the sole purpose of finding where those bodies were coming from. I rented my own equipment and went back to that lake the summer of my freshman year.

The water was incredibly buoyant from all the salt, and it took almost 20 pounds of weights before I would finally sink to the floor. It was slow progress working my way through the lake—six separate dives before I found what I didn't even know I was looking for.

A sunken plane. I don't know how long it had been down here, but

246 | TOBIAS WADE

it looked rusted as shit. One of the doors had completely rusted off, and I was able to enter and look around.

There were two more bodies inside, no-more than skeletons now. The inside of the plane was compartmentalized almost like it was broken into sealed jail cells.

The locks on some cells had long since rusted open, and I'm guessing these are where the floaters came from. If they were in their own pressurized air chambers, then that explains how they were preserved for so long. As the plane deteriorated, they must have broken free and floated to the surface one by one.

My most important discovery was the black box—although it was painted bright orange, so it's a pretty stupid name. I brought it back with me and swam to the surface to research my findings.

The plane was a Douglass C-47, which was used for military transport during World War 2. They were still being used for decades afterward though. Some remained operational even up to 2012, so I still don't know how long it's been there.

The flight data recorder had completely deteriorated, but the cockpit voice recorder still had some salvageable tape. Most of it was fuzzy or jumpy, but here is what I have.

"164, Roger" (Something I couldn't make out)

"Unable to make out your last message. Please repeat."

"It's out. Repeat – one of them has gotten out."

"Has the cockpit been compromised?"

"Negative. Cell block is" (couldn't hear).

"Please repeat, Captain."

"Repeat – cell block is compromised. It's letting the others out. Fucking-Christ"

"Remain calm, Captain. Can you neutralize the test subject?"

"Not without compromising cockpit—how far am I from the landing field?"

(Something unintelligible)

"What the fuck is that supposed to mean?"

(something unintelligible)"… not granted permission land."

"Well then, what the fuck am I supposed to do?"

(something something)"Mission terminated. Thank you for your service, Captain."

"My service ain't over until I bring this bird down."

"You're ordered to force collision. Test subjects must not escape."

"Like Hell I am. I'm bringing her down into some water now. Request rescue operations."

"Mission terminated. Rescue operation denied."

After that, all I could hear was engine sounds. It went on for about five minutes, and I was about to stop listening when I heard something like a snarling tiger.

I guess I haven't changed that much since I was a kid, because I still don't want to bring this into the police. I've got another dive planned next week, and I'm going to try to break open the remaining cell blocks to get a look inside.

I'll admit I was pretty hesitant about making my second dive. Just to be safe, I decided not to go on this one alone. Two nights ago I reconnected with Entoine, one of the boys who found some original floaters with me. He still remembered trying to lick the body to get his $5 back, and we laughed about it—I guess that sort of thing only happens once in your life.

I showed him the audio recordings I pulled from the black box and talked him into joining me. He didn't have dive equipment, but I knew I'd feel better with him in the boat.

"Notice feeling anything strange since you licked it?" I asked him while we were rowing out to the middle of the lake.

"What kind of strange? You mean besides puking my guts out?"

"Warts. New birth mark in the shape of a pentagram. Sudden urge to kill people. You know—something like that."

"Not that I can think of," he admitted. "Except for my ability to talk to animals."

"What? Seriously?"

"Yeah. He smirked. "They just don't talk back. Keep pulling your weight or the boat is going to start turning in circles."

Reading too many horror stories online must have made me paranoid. I don't know what I was so afraid of in the first place. The visibility was good underwater, and I didn't even see any fish besides a host of little black water slugs scootering around.

Instead of weights, this time I just used a crowbar to sink me down to the plane. The doors were so rusted they were starting to unfasten on their own, so it was no problem breaking the lock off.

I was tense, but I remembered to force myself to keep breathing evenly through the regulator. Holding my breath under water could easily result in an arterial gas embolism. Then I'd be the next floater they found washed up on the beach.

Even without the lock, the room was still pressure sealed with an air pocket inside. I tried leveraging the crowbar, but I still couldn't pry the door open against the weight of all that water. I managed to hammer on the door with the metal bar until a leak appeared. The wider I forced the hole, the more water flowed through to equalize the pressure. Once it was full, it should swing open without a problem.

I finally worked the crowbar all the way through the door, but this time it got stuck. That's weird, because the water was flowing freely around it, so there should be plenty of space to pull it back. It was almost as if something were holding it from the other side...

That was a thought I could have done without. I freaked and dropped the crowbar, but without its weight, I began to immediately float back towards the surface. I held onto the door-frame to keep myself from slipping upwards, but it was almost impossible to swim further down against my buoyancy.

Luckily I didn't have to. The cell finished flooding, and the door began opening on its own. Suddenly I was face to face with a dead body. Its skin had long since begun to rot away, especially around its eyes and mouth where there were just gaping holes remaining.

My crowbar had stuck straight into its side where it had gotten stuck. I was about to pull myself down toward it along the door frame when I noticed the crowbar was sliding back out.

No. Not sliding. The body's hands were wrapped around the bar. They were pulling the crowbar out of its side.

Had I jolted upward too quickly when I let go of the bar? Maybe I already suffered a stroke from the gas embolism without noticing?

The body lurched toward me. Slow, even breaths. Don't stop breathing. Easier said than done with a dead body clambering up toward you. It was fast too – driven with a purpose. Legs and arms with openly rotten sinews moved effortlessly through the water like a practiced swimmer.

I pushed my way out of the plane, but the body was right behind me. It dropped the crowbar and began ascending smoothly through the water toward me. It was just as fast as me even though I had fins.

Shit. I kicked hard, and without any weight I was raising way too swiftly. I couldn't stop myself. I felt the air expanding in my lungs so rapidly it felt like they would burst. I was practically screaming underwater, trying to get as much air out as I could.

Once I hit the surface, the scream finally became audible, although it was little more than a wheezing gasp at that point. The boat? Where was the boat?

"Entoine get your ass over here!" He was leaning over the boat and peering down into the water – about fifty yards away. Fuck. I looked down and saw the shadow of the body swiftly ascending toward me.

I swam hard toward the boat. Entoine wasn't reacting. There's no way he didn't hear me. Why the Hell didn't he start rowing? He was just staring into the depth, his face about an inch from the water.

"Entoine I swear to God—" but my lungs felt like they were on fire. I couldn't take a full breath yet. All the air I had was going into keeping my legs kicking.

The shadow was right underneath me now. Ten feet from the boat— I ducked my head underwater and paddled as hard as I could. Too slow —the body was intercepting me. It was going to block my route. About five feet away from safety, it surfaced directly between me and the boat. But it wasn't an explosive surface like something swimming upward. It just floated there, face down in the water, looking as dead as I felt. I had to push the body out of the way to get to the boat. I kept expecting a hand to grab my ankle and pull me back down, but there was nothing.

I climbed into the boat and fell on my back panting. My mask was cloudy, so I ripped it off. As soon as I could kneel again, I practically shoved Entoine straight into the water.

"What the Hell is wrong with you?" The push pressed him against the side of the boat. He tensed and relaxed, but didn't turn away from the water. It was like trying to wake someone from a deep sleep. He was just vacantly staring at the floating body now.

The body was moving again though—its ear was, anyway. Not a natural movement anymore—not like the body was moving on its own. It was like there was something inside trying to crawl out.

As I watched, one of the black slugs pushed its way out of the ear. It got stuck part way and had to gnaw its way through the rest of the cartilage with razor-sharp teeth like a leech. As it struggled out, the whole corpse shook like it was having a seizure.

"It looks like you had it wrong," Entoine said in a sleepy voice. Did he just wake up? There's no way he could have slept through that. His face was still down next to the water though, and I couldn't get a clear look at him.

"What do you mean?"

"The floaters we found weren't the test subjects," he replied, finally pulling away from the water. His body was shivering slightly—somewhere between freezing to death, and full body ecstasy. The tail end of a black slug had just finished slipping into his ear.

"Of course they were. Why else would they be in the cells?" I asked. By the time the words were out of my mouth, I had already realized it.

The bodies weren't the test subjects. The bodies were hosts to the test subjects.

And they had already been free in the water since all those years ago when the first floater broke free.

I LOVED HER IN THE WINTER

"I can take care of myself. I'm not crazy, you know. Why does everyone think I'm crazy?"

"No one thinks you're crazy, Dad. Dementia is nothing to be ashamed of. It's a common medical condition with people your age."

"You wouldn't have locked me up in here if you didn't think I was crazy. When is Elise going to pick me up?"

It's the same conversation every-time I visited Dad in the Forest Glen retirement home. At first he just started forgetting what things were named. Pepsi became "bubble juice" and he'd call his dog a "woofer". We all thought it was hilarious until he started forgetting who we were too.

He thought I looked familiar, but the helpless frustration on his face as he tried to remember how he knew me was excruciating. My childhood—all our time together—my whole life was just being erased.

After his wife (my Mom) Elise died, Dad completely fell apart. It was like she was his only reason to keep trying at all. He used to passionately assemble model planes and ships, but he smashed them all and wouldn't touch them again. He wouldn't even read or watch TV, preferring to just sit alone and stare at the wall. He stopped taking care of himself and became belligerent when someone tried to help him.

"Just bury me already, if I'm such a burden," he'd say.

My wife and I would laugh it off, but we all knew he wasn't joking. He was a burden. He needed help going to the bathroom, and showering, and getting dressed, and as much as I told myself that sending him to the home was for his own good, I was relieved when he was gone.

That's why I was so worried when I got a call from the retirement home two weeks ago. They said Dad was missing. It wasn't the first time he tried to get out, but the nurses always stopped him before he made it past the door. He could barely lift his foot high enough to put a slipper on, but this time he somehow managed to climb straight out the window.

If he was lost out there, he wouldn't know how to get back. He probably wouldn't even remember who he was. That would have been bad enough, but the note he left behind made me even more anxious.

"I'm going to be with Elise, and I'm not coming back. Goodbye everyone."

Dad was going to kill himself tonight. I knew it. I frantically drove up and down the streets around the home, shouting his name—wondering if he'd recognize it or even respond if he did. I checked every puddle he could have drowned in, every bridge he could have jumped from—everything I could think of. My wife was visiting her relatives out of town for the week, but she stayed on the phone with me the whole time to keep me calm. It didn't work.

"But didn't he forget Elise even died?" she asked. "He's probably not trying to kill himself. He just wants to find her."

I checked back at the house—nothing. I might as well stop by the graveyard where Elise was buried too. It didn't make much sense if he still thought she was alive, but I was desperate. It was about 3 in the morning when I saw his shriveled form hunched over her headstone.

"Dad? Are you okay?" I approached cautiously, terrified that I was too late. He didn't stir as I drew up behind him. Did he just realize that she was dead? Had he spent the last of his strength coming here to say goodbye?

He didn't turn from the grave when he finally spoke. I remember his words as clearly as the cold night air.

I met her in the Spring, she wakes me from my deathly slumber,
wedding bells in joyous ring, Summer toil could not encumber
one shared soul as ours so blessed, and through Autumn's firey air,
am I to love her any less, now Winter rips her branches bare?
Or softly shall I sit and mourn, all the dark hours of the night
until once more is spring reborn, and her eyes refill with light.

Did he really believe she was coming back? Or was this his way of understanding? I sat down next to him and wrapped my coat around his frail shoulders. His eyes sparkled in the pale moonlight, but not from grief. I don't remember ever seeing him look so happy.

"But it's already Spring," a voice said. My mother's voice. I was watching my Dad and didn't notice until she was standing directly before us. Or maybe she had just appeared there—I don't know—but she wasn't old anymore. She looked how I remember her when I was a child. She embraced my father, and before my eyes, he shed his years as lightly as his tears.

Dad was growing taller. My coat which draped around his shoulders swelled like a balloon as his muscles became firm. The bulging veins in his hands receded as he held my mother, and his skin pulled taut as the deep network of wrinkles which mapped out his life vanished. They both looked younger than I did now.

Mother winked at me from over Dad's shoulder. She held a finger to her lips and said:

"It'll be our little secret, okay? Let's all go home."

My wife called a dozen times over the next week. I just told her everything was fine, and we'd talk about it when she got back. It was better than fine though—I felt like I was living inside a dream.

I woke every morning to my Mom's scrambled eggs and French toast. I wanted to call in sick from work and spend every minute with them, but she insisted I still go and threatened to drive me there herself. Every night I'd return to watch Dad rebuilding his models, swearing good-naturedly when he couldn't find a piece. Then we'd all eat dinner as a family and watch a movie together—Dad making sarcastic comments throughout, and Mom giggling like a school girl with a crush.

I've never seen them so happy. I've never remembered being so happy. They had aged so slowly over the years and I had pulled away from them so gradually that I never really dwelt on how close we once were. It was just like being a kid again. After a disagreement at work, someone even shot back that I smelled funny. Who since the 3rd grade has ever used an argument like that?

I couldn't wait for my wife to get home. I'd kept my parents a secret from everyone, and I was so pleased with myself for resisting the urge to tell her. Sure they couldn't live with me forever, but just seeing the look on my wife's face when she walked in would be priceless.

When I picked her up from the airport, she seemed a little withdrawn. I tried to kiss her, but she pulled away.

"Have you been okay alone? You've been taking care of yourself, right?"

I just laughed. She seemed worried about me. Maybe she was tired from traveling, maybe her relatives stressed her out, but as soon as I showed her what had happened she would forget all about it.

"Welcome home dear!" My Mother said when I opened the door. "And isn't she darling!"

"How was the trip?" My Father asked.

I just watched my wife's face, unable to contain my gigantic grin. She was shocked alright. Her mouth was just hanging open. Then she coughed and covered her nose.

"Well? What do you think?" I asked her.

"I think I'm going to be sick," she said—and she was. Right there on the entry mat. The smell of her vomit was like some kind of trigger. Suddenly the whole house smelled absolutely rancid.

"Do you smell that, Mom? What is it?"

Mom—what was left of her decaying body—was propped up on the sofa. Dad, bloated from gas and covered with a yellow-green mold, was sitting in his armchair. I couldn't understand what happened.

My wife ran out and called the police. They took away the bodies and took me in for a psych evaluation. The next few days were a blur, but eventually I was released with the diagnosis of "hallucinations stemming from PTSD". They said my Father had died the night he escaped after catching pneumonia in the night air. They said my mother had been dug up, and that the trunk of my car contained a dirty shovel.

I don't believe them though. I didn't even own a shovel. I think they were just trying to cover up for something they couldn't explain. I don't get what the big deal was, anyway. Even if they were gone, so what if I did want to keep them?

Should I love them any less in the winter?

HISTORY WRITTEN IN SCARS

No, not a cut. Not a bruise from sleepwalking or a bang where I drunkenly hurt myself without remembering. I'm talking jagged, gnarly, vicious scars which looked like they've healed years ago.

The first one to appear was an inch long incision on my stomach, almost like a surgical wound. I live in college with a roommate (Robert), but he didn't remember anything happening. Then I called my parents and asked them if I'd ever had a surgery before, but the only procedure I'd undergone was having my wisdom teeth removed; a dead end unless they thought the stomach was a shortcut to the mouth.

I figured that I just hadn't noticed it before. Or perhaps something traumatic happened, and I completely blocked out the memory, but I didn't worry about it. I played basketball in high-school and have had my fair share of being knocked around, so it must have been from something then. Those were the glory days man. I play on my collegiate intramural team now, but it's just not the same. I was a school hero back then... but life goes on; you know? All the victories and mistakes I made on and off the court, they're all ancient history.

The next morning I woke with a long scar along my forearm. It must have been deep too, and the skin holding it together was stretched like I've grown since it closed. I ran my finger over it, but it didn't even hurt. The skin was slightly raised and hard, but otherwise I wouldn't have noticed if I wasn't looking right at it. I thought about going to the doctor, but it looked so old that he'd probably just say I forgot what caused it.

I tried not to think about the scars for the rest of the day, although my buddy Chase noticed it during our practice that evening. I didn't want to sound like an idiot, so I made up a story about this time I fought off a mugger to protect my girlfriend and got a swipe from his switchblade.

"Yeah, I think I remember you mentioning something about that bro," he said.

Bitch please. I doubt that since I just made the story up on the spot. It wasn't interfering with my game though, and I was so tired afterward that I just hit the showers and went straight to bed. I completely forgot about it until I was falling asleep, and then it was all I could think about. What if something was attacking me in the night? But no, that was ridiculous. But what if something was attacking a younger version of myself in the night? Even stupider. I eventually convinced myself that I was making a big deal out of nothing and fell asleep but...

It was still the first thing I thought about when I woke up. I immediately stripped naked and checked myself in the bathroom mirror.

"Man are you trying to shit a log or a whole forest? I gotta take a piss." My roommate Robert was pounding on the door. I ran my fingers over my chest for the hundredth time. A giant cross-shaped scar on my right peck. The undulating lines wandered haphazardly—grotesquely—like it hadn't been a clean heal. But it was healed alright. I opened the door and stared at him.

"Have you seen this before?" I asked.

"Dude are you drunk? I'm not looking at your–" He started back-peddling. I grabbed a towel and wrapped it around my waist.

"Not that, you idiot. This scar. What happened to me?"

"Yeah, you got in a fight with a mugger when you were in high-school. You said he cut you up pretty bad, but you chased him off."

"I never told you that," I said. "That never happened!"

"You're being crazy, man. Just let me use the bathroom, okay?"

Robert pushed past me and closed the door. I went straight to my computer and logged onto Facebook. I've had that thing setup since my freshman year of high-school. There had to be some pictures which proved—man I looked like a little shit back then—okay here we go. Senior Ditch day we all went down to a river and hung out. I was in my swimsuit and—And the grotesque scar was on my chest. The ones on my stomach and forearm were there too. I flipped back a few more years and saw it disappear during my sophomore year. From the photos, it looked like whatever happened was in the first semester of my junior year.

When I thought about that time in my life, there was only one memory which burned so brightly as to cast shadows on the rest. I narrowed down the range of dates, and there was no mistaking it. I found a photo of myself running shirtless with the team the week before—no scars. The week after I wasn't present at the game, then after that I was covered in bandages. But that hadn't happened! I remember we started off the season 4-0, and I played in every game.

Somehow, there was something about that night which was changing my past. I hadn't meant to hurt her. There was a party to celebrate our homecoming victory game, and everyone was having a little too much to drink. I thought Jessica wanted it—she certainly seemed like she did. There's no way I could have known how she would react the next morning—or what she would do herself the next month when she found out she was pregnant. It's not my fault Jessica is dead.

Life goes on, you know? Ancient history. And if somehow these scars appearing on my body were related to that night, and I had to carry them as penance the rest of my life, then I could accept that. If that had been all there was, I wouldn't have been so scared or angry.

But the scars this morning were more deliberate. Etched into the back of my hand are the words:

How many cuts will it take before I see you again?

Maybe some wounds cut too deep to ever be left in the past. I wonder how many more it will take before she's satisfied, or whether I'll even survive her search for peace.

MY JOURNEY IN A PARALLEL UNIVERSE

"Just because you're sleeping with Mom doesn't make you my Dad."

"Just because you're living in my house doesn't mean you can talk back to me."

You could have cooked your dinner with the air hanging between my stepson and I. Emily kept telling me that Jason was going to get used to having me around, but two years in, and this teenage shit still resisted me like I was an occupying army. I get that his real Dad was an abusive asshole, but in what world is it fair to take that anger out on me? We'd already been arguing in the parked car for ten minutes.

"Just go talk to the guy, okay?" I said. "What's the worst that could happen? That maybe he thinks there's a place in this school for you? That maybe you have potential and can do something with your life besides playing video games and serving hamburgers, God-forbid?"

"I don't want to go here. None of my friends are here," Jason whined.

I wanted to smack him upside the head, but somehow that would suddenly make me the bad guy. Deep breath.

"So what? You'll make new friends. Smarter friends—better

friends. In a couple years you'll be leaving for college anyway, so why not just suck it up and go somewhere good?"

"I don't want better friends. I want a better Dad." Jason got out of the car and slammed the door. Would it still count as murder if he's this rude? At least he was walking toward the Academy building now, so I guess I'll take that as a victory. I got out of the car and followed Jason up the shining marble steps and into the grand foyer.

Was this a school, or an opera house? The place was drowning in luxury. Thick Persian rugs, walls lined with tapestries, rolling velvet curtains—unmistakable old world money. Some industrial era tycoon set up the Ramfield Academy as his legacy, and his trust paid for all the expenses. I'll admit it was a tad intimidating to enter, but Jason had been actually invited to the interview because of his test scores.

"Hey Jason, wait up!" He was already storming up the staircase. He didn't turn around. "It's room 604—that means 6th floor. Come take the elevator with me."

A middle finger appeared between two steps for a moment, and then the footsteps continued. I glanced around, but there didn't seem to be anyone to notice. I sighed and pushed the elevator button.

I would have expected some security to keep out the riff-raff, or at least a secretary in a place like this. It was eerie not seeing anyone in the converted mega-mansion. Six floors, almost 20,000 square feet, but they still only accepted 30 kids a year. It was one of Ramfield's original stipulations when he setup the foundation. Weird guy, by all accounts: an eclectic genius, by some, a mad hoarder by most. I've heard that he lived in this massive place alone without any staff, and by the time he died, they practically had to bring in an excavator to haul out all his random collections.

I got in the elevator and hit #6. The old lift lurched and rattled like it resented me for pushing the button. Music played which would have been more appropriate in a 1920 speakeasy, and it was pretty uncomfortable staring at Ramfield's grimacing portrait beside the door. Jason better not act out like this during the interview, or I swear to God... If I don't kill him, Emily will kill me, and then I'll go back and haunt the little shit.

"Is this why you never had kids?" I asked the portrait of Ramfield. "There had to have been women who tried, considering all your money. I can't say I blame you though. I guess I just wish mine was different."

The screech of metal cables whirring through their sockets suddenly rended the air. The elevator buckled and heaved beneath me and I was thrown to my knees. The lights flared like a dying sun and the music crackled and vanished in a spluttering gasp. A trickle of light from the roof still illuminated the portrait, but that was all I could see.

How old was this thing? Did they even do safety checks, or was this more of a 'bribe the inspector' kind of place? Shit, now the damn thing is stuck.

"Hello? Can anyone hear me?"

I pounded on the door. The needle showed me somewhere between the fifth and sixth floor. Now Jason was going to go into the interview alone and screw it up. I was about to start jumping up and down to try to get the damn thing moving, but luckily I remembered where I was. Five and a half stories up... what if it fell? What if a cable broke, and I was just barely balanced on the frayed ends? I moved back against the elevator wall on tiptoe and felt the tremendous weight groan beneath my feet.

There weren't any emergency buttons or anything, but somehow I was still getting cell reception. I called Jason's phone, but it cut off after the second ring. Little bastard hung up on me. I called again.

"Yeah?" he answered.

"The elevator is stuck. I need you to find someone who works here and send help."

I held my breath and waited for his sarcastic reply. "OH wow—okay. Yeah, I'll get someone."

Well that was unexpected. At first I thought he was just going to leave me here, but then I heard him talking with someone in the background.

"Okay, they said not to worry," Jason said after a moment. "It's just an electrical issue. It happens all the time. They're going to reset the breaker, and you'll be right up."

"Thanks Jason. I really appreciate this. Don't get off the phone."

"Don't freak out on me. You're going to be fine, "he said.

The elevator heaved again. The music and lights sparked back to life. I was moving. Thank God. And with any luck, the administrators will be so apologetic that this can only help with the interview. The needle slid firmly into #6, and the doors began to open.

"I'm not freaking out. You're freaking out," I replied playfully. Was he actually worried about me? Was his whole rebellious thing just an act? I couldn't help but grin.

The doors opened. Jason was standing there, his hands in his pockets. He didn't look relieved like I was hoping. He just looked bored.

"I'm not the one who is going to plummet to his death. Where are you?"

Jason's voice came through the cell, but the Jason I was staring at was definitely not on the phone.

I slowly stepped out of the elevator and looked around. No service people—no administrators—no-one at all but Jason.

"Where are you?" I asked into the phone.

"I'm right here," the Jason in front of me answered.

"I'm on the 6th floor," the Jason from my cell answered. "The elevator door opened, but you're not inside. What's the deal?"

I turned around, but the elevator door already closed behind me. I spun back, and Jason—the bored one—was standing a few feet closer. He smirked.

"Come on Dad. We're going to be late for the interview."

"Come on man. We're going to be late for the interview."

Jason—the real Jason—he'd never called me Dad before. But the two of them had spoken simultaneously. The Jason next to me took a step closer, and I instinctively flinched.

"What's wrong, Dad? Isn't this what you wanted?" He reached for my phone and tried to take it, but I yanked it away from him. He shrugged. "Whatever, take your call. I'll let you know how it goes."

He opened room 604 and closed the door behind him. I was still too shocked to move. I lifted the phone to my ear, but the call had ended. I tried calling Jason again, but it didn't go through. I leaned against the wall and slid to the ground, unable to process what was going on. Was this some kind of parallel dimension? I know Ramfield collected some crazy stuff, but I'm pretty sure someone would have mentioned a trans-dimensional elevator.

Or maybe I had fallen out of the elevator and died. Then the real Jason would have seen it empty, and I really was a ghost. But that didn't explain where the second Jason came from. I tried calling a dozen more times while I waited in the hall, but nothing went through. Then room 604 opened again, and it was too late.

Jason came back, followed by a fat man in a suit. They were both smiling. The fat man shook my hand and congratulated me. He was saying something else about how Jason was going to excel in this environment. I can't say I was fully paying attention. It all seemed a bit like a dream. I just kept staring at the smirk on Jason's face. I couldn't be sure, but somehow I knew that he knew something wasn't right.

"Ready to go home, Dad?" Jason asked after the fat man had left. What else could I do? I couldn't go home to Emily and tell her I lost her son. I had to bring him along. And besides, he'd aced his interview. He was calling me Dad. Isn't this what I wanted?

But all the way home, I couldn't even look at him. What if Emily wasn't the same either? How could I even tell? Or did it matter if they treated me the same? Maybe I was just imagining all of this because I had a panic attack in the elevator. Maybe everything was going to be —

"I know you're not my real Dad," Jason said. I jumped so bad I practically swerved off the road. "But my real Dad didn't treat me or Mom right, and you've been good to us. I wish you were there from the beginning."

I let out a long breath. He was just talking about me being his step-father. I forced a smile, but I couldn't answer him. Not yet. It would still take some time to wrap my head around what happened. I turned on the radio.

"Ow what the Hell, man?" Jason's voice from the radio.

"It's what you deserve for messing around in the interview." My voice from the radio.

"Get away from me. What's gotten into you? Let go!"

"You haven't seen anything yet. Wait until we get home and I'll teach you to disrespect me like that."

A dull pummeling sounded through the radio, and then a scream. I shut it off. I glanced at Jason, and he was smiling from ear to ear.

"Did those voices sound familiar to you?" I asked him. My throat felt choked. If I had gone here, had another version of me gone back to my world?

"Sounds like someone doesn't have it as good as I do," he said. "I love you, Dad." Jason leaned his head against my shoulder. I fought the urge to shrug him off. I felt like I was going to be sick.

Bzzz. Bzzz. Bzzz.

My cell started vibrating in my pocket during dinner. Mashed potatoes, filet steaks, spinach soufflé—Emily had gone all out to celebrate Jason's acceptance into the Academy. I glanced at my phone. Emily—the real Emily—was calling.

"Ooh that must be the pie ready," the other Emily got up to check the kitchen. I clutched the phone in my lap.

"Are you going to answer it, Dad?" Jason asked. He was grinning again. What I wouldn't give to see the old Jason's sour expression just once.

"Everyone I want to talk to is already here," I grunted. "Just going to use the bathroom."

I raced to the bathroom, still gripping my phone like a lifeline. I was too late to answer by the time I got there, but there was a voicemail.

"Where are you?" It was my wife. My real wife. "What happened to Jason? His arm is broken and he won't stop crying. You better have a good explanation. Meet us at the Good Samaritan Hospital as soon as you get this."

I couldn't breathe. I wanted to flush the phone and forget that world even existed. I wanted to just live here where everything was perfect. Couldn't I just pretend? Why should I be responsible for what the other-me did? I stared at myself in the mirror and gritted my teeth.

"What am I supposed to do? Huh? Huh?" I asked.

"Are you okay in there, honey?"

Emily knocked on the bathroom door. I opened it and gave her my most convincing smile. "Just making some room for more of your amazing cooking. Come on, let's eat."

I waited until she was asleep to sneak out of the house. I had to get out of here. I had to get back and save them. I hadn't received anymore voicemails that evening, but I don't know whether that was a good sign or not.

I dressed in the dark and slipped out of our bedroom. I flipped on the switch in the living room and—"What the Hell?" I muffled my own shout with my arm. Jason had been sitting in the dark, fully dressed, waiting for me. He wasn't smiling anymore.

"I knew it," he said, his voice laden with accusation. "You're going to leave us. You want to switch places with him, but I'm not going to let you. I don't want him to come back."

"That's too bad," I said, already moving from the door. Where were the keys? They were always on the hook—at least in my world they were. "I don't belong here—this isn't my home."

"No-one belongs anywhere. That doesn't mean you have to leave," he said.

"They need me–"

"And I don't?" Jason said. He lifted his shirt, revealing a frail body which was covered with bruises and scars. "He may look like you, but I know him better than you do. He won't handle the switch as well. I bet he's already killed them both."

"All the more reason for me to hurry. Where are the keys?"

"Stay here Dad. Please." My breath caught in my throat again. I turned and looked at him, and he was holding the keys in his open palm. His eyes were brimming with tears. "Or if you do go, at least take me with you."

I gave a jerky nod. He seemed to know more about what was going on than I did anyway, so I might even need him to figure out how to get back.

We drove in silence back to the Academy. The streets were empty —who else had somewhere to be at 1 am? I turned on the radio.

Sobbing. Incoherent screaming. It sounded like Emily. I shut it off.

"I told you," Jason said. "You should just stay here."

"I'm already gone," I replied.

We entered the elevator together. The door had been unlocked, and there still weren't any people around. He pushed the 6th floor right away, and I didn't try to stop him.

"How do you know about all this?" I asked. "What even is this place?"

"It's not the first time someone switched," Jason said. "I was here on a field trip in school when my real Dad caught up with me. He was drunk and angry, and he was trying to punish me for forging his signature so I could go on the trip. I hid from him in the elevator, but he found me and somehow I managed to send him away. I just couldn't figure out how to bring him back."

2… 3… The needle was flipping through the numbers.

"What's going to happen when we get there?" I asked him. "Will the other me and other Jason come here?"

4…

"I think so," he said. "But I think it only works if the other version is still alive. I think that's why no-one switched with him before—his other self was already dead. I've thought about it a lot, and I think that's why he wasn't good to us from the beginning. I think we need to be balanced, and when our other-self dies, we turn bad."

5…

"But if the other Jason is already dead…" I said, "What will happen to you?"

5 1/2…

The elevator buckled. The lights flared, and the music died. The only remaining trickle of light seeping from above fell upon Jason's smirk.

"Who says it hasn't already happened?" Jason asked.

Lurch. The elevator plummeted into the blackness and something hit me hard on my right temple.

I woke up in the hospital. Everything felt like it was on fire. Four broken ribs, a dislocated shoulder, blunt force trauma to the head, but no-one could figure out how I got it.

The elevator hadn't fallen. I had gotten in alone at the bottom, it hadn't made any stops, and when I came out on the 6th floor I was beaten to within an inch of my life. The Ramfield administrator had called an ambulance, and I was sent directly here.

Emily? She didn't remember any of those tearful phone calls. She had been at home when the hospital called her.

The interview? It had been rescheduled because of the emergency situation. He hadn't been accepted or denied, and I don't think either version has happened yet in this reality. I can't even tell if I'm back in the same reality I started in.

And Jason? He calls me Dad now. And maybe I should be thankful for that, but it doesn't feel sincere when he's smirking the whole time.

He only visited me in the hospital for a short while before leaving, but I can't shake the feeling that he's the one who did this to me. I don't know who came back with me from that place, but it isn't the Jason I know. I don't know who he is or what he's capable of, but then again, the same could be said of myself. I feel so angry and helpless and trapped and alone and I just want to lash out and hurt the ones who have hurt me, but that only begs another question. What if the other version of me is dead?

What if I'm the bad one?

THE PARTY THAT CHANGED MY LIFE

Josh: Hey man, thanks for staying to help cleanup last night. Hope you had a good time.

Me: Your party was a blast. How'd it go with Casey?

Josh: No go bro. She had to take her wasted friend home.

I slid the phone back in my pocket. I was only asking to be polite. I couldn't care less about Josh or his parties. I wouldn't have gone at all if Kimberly, a girl from my physics class, hadn't mentioned she was going too. She only knew my serious, studious side, but there's nothing like a party to show how suave and charming I could be, right?

Just my luck that she didn't show, and I had to endure an evening of beer like piss, screaming idiots, and that damn UNCE UNCE UNCE music which I know is going to haunt me all day. That and this pounding hangover.

Josh: My poor turtle had to put its head back in the shell. You know what I mean?

Why is he still texting me? How do I even reply to that? I hope he doesn't think we're friends now. I didn't even know his frat house was hosting the stupid party. Maybe if I don't reply he'll just—Josh: The flight was ready for landing, but the runway was blocked by a fat cow.

The dive was scheduled, but there were a bunch of needy sharks in the water. It was time for my pizza, but the meatloaf wasn't having any fun so I guess that means ALL the food had to get sent back.

Me: That makes absolutely no sense, but I get it.

Now will HE get it? Of course not. If he got it, he wouldn't still be texting me.

Josh: BTW bro. Do you know who Kimberly is?

Me: Yeah. Was she there last night?

No. Josh couldn't have. Please God, don't let that disgusting frat boy anywhere near—Josh: Some dipshit wrote "Kimberly is dead. Stop wasting time on her" with a marker on my wall. Good thing for renter's insurance, lol.

The chair in front of me was empty in physics today. The long golden braid which usually fell about my desk was gone. I hadn't realized how long this class was when I had to stare at the whiteboard instead. To make matters worse, the stream of texts from Josh didn't stop.

Josh: Dude I found another message. This one was written in my bathroom: "Her head took the longest to remove. The vertebra kept snapping, and her neck must have stretched four feet before it finally popped free." WTF?

Josh: Here's one written on my closet: "Her breasts looked much bigger when they were still attached. Such a fake girl, no-one will miss her."

Josh: There's another on the side of my fridge. "I'm saving some for later."

I excused myself to leave. I still had biology after this, but I felt like I was going to be sick. This had to be a twisted prank. Maybe he thought I wanted to join his frat or something, and this is what they did to haze people. But then why wasn't Kimberly in class?

I couldn't let this get to my head. All I had to do was check her Facebook, right? Okay, no updates since the day before last. But I could send her a message.... Hello Kimberly? We've never really talked, but I just wanted to make sure you haven't been butchered. Hope we can go out sometime.

Yeah that isn't the suave first impression I was hoping to make. Think. Think! I was freaking out. Of course I didn't have to mention the butchery. If she replied at all, then she was okay, right? Do you think you're nervous texting a girl for the first time? Try it when all you can think about is her dismembered corpse scattered across some frat house.

Me: Hey Kimberly. Did you go to Josh's party last night?
DELETED

I couldn't send that because then I'd just be admitting to eavesdropping on her plans. How about...

Me: Hey Kimberly. Saw you missed physics today, so I wanted to remind you about the quiz on Friday.

I closed my eyes and hit send. I hope that doesn't make me sound like all I cared about was physics. Maybe I should add a follow up to ask—BZZZ

A reply! She's okay! I mean of course she's okay, but she replied! And so quickly too. You don't reply that fast unless you really want to talk to someone—Josh: DUUUUDE LOOK WHAT'S IN MY FRIDGE

Attached was a photo of a dismembered foot sitting on the shelf beside the cheese. He sent me a couple more texts, but I didn't read them. I was running toward his place. Either something horrible has happened, and I had to see for myself, or he was trolling me and was about to receive a beating of a lifetime. By the time I got over, I still hadn't received a reply from Kimberly. That could mean anything though. If she wasn't in class, it was because she was busy with something, so of course she couldn't reply. So why did I feel like I was going to die?

This place looked even worse in the daylight. The building had been trashed and stitched together so many times it might as well have been the Frankenstein's monster of frat houses. I pounded on the door so hard that my hand went numb.

"Josh! Get your ass out here!"

The door opened, and I almost hit him in the face. Then he started laughing, and I really did hit him. Right between the eyes. My fist stung like Hell, but it felt so good I would have done it a hundred more times. It had all been a prank! Kimberly was okay.

"Shit dude, cool it. Can't you take a joke?"

"Who does that? How badly do you need attention that you would screw with me like that? Never talk to me again."

I've seen enough. I turned around and stomped my way across the yard.

"Come on man, it's not like that. I just found the photo online somewhere, but the messages were real."

"You're messed up, man. Leave me alone," I said.

"Look! There's another one on the fence!" he shouted after me.

"So what? You probably wrote it, you twisted shit."

"I swear dude. I didn't write any of it. The picture is the only thing that wasn't real."

I didn't want to look, but I couldn't help myself. I glanced at the fence. Written in black marker, it said: "She was my third."

What is even worse than listening to him? Believing him. Because looking at those big blocky letters, I know Josh couldn't have written that. I know because it was unmistakably my handwriting.

THE SOLUTION TO PRISON OVERCROWDING

There is no Devil, only man, and he does not buy souls. Not all at once anyway. Man is far more insidious than that, for he grinds down his brother's soul one layer at a time until the residual humanity begins to devour itself. It's hard to believe, but it's true. Begin to break a man, and he will finish the job on his own. That is because it is much easier to live as an animal than it is as half a man.

I felt the first part of my humanity die when I was 12 years old. How do you explain a knotted garbage bag full drowned kittens to a child? I was young, but not too young to know that someone had done it on purpose, and that they had gotten away with it. Not too young to understand that evil wasn't just a thing in cartoons and movies; not too young to realize that I too was capable of evil if I ever got my hands on this monster.

Over the years, I felt more of myself slip away. Sometimes it would break off in big chunks like when my mother died, but more often my soul simply eroded from the steady tide of petty grievances, jealous greed, thoughtless anger, and the thousand other frustrations that make up the life of any "civilized" man trying to find his place in the world.

My defense attorney wanted me to talk about how I regretted killing Edward. That it was a defining moment in my life, and that my mind had been blown wide with righteous rebirth and revelation. There wasn't enough left of me to lie though. I don't think my pulse even rose the night I took my neighbor's life. Edward used to beat his wife, and now he doesn't. That's all that changed, because there wasn't enough left of me to change. It almost makes me laugh now to think how far I still was from rock-bottom.

I got 15 years for that. Could have been worse, but the judge and jury were sympathetic after hearing the widow tearfully thank me for saving her. I can't even say I found jail any worse than the outside either. The only difference was my daily routine, and the blur of a different set of faces performing it with me.

I gained a reputation as a loose cannon in jail. People said I'd go from deadpan silence to an incoherent rage in one second flat. I don't think of it that way though. I think of myself more like a brilliant pianist: seeming ordinary until sitting down to play. The musical ability didn't suddenly appear out of nowhere, it had been inside all along. It was the same with my anger: it was always there, but it was my choice whether to let it play.

I was five years into my sentence before one of the guards took my moods personally, landing me in the hole. It was only supposed to be for a week, but everything I did seemed to extend the time. Unresponsive to the officer? Add a week. Didn't eat the food? Add a week and get my next meal replaced with "the loaf" (rotten cabbage and bread). Didn't eat the loaf? Another week, and no other food until I choked it down. Even after I vomited it back up, they wouldn't give me more food until I'd eaten my sick just to teach me a lesson.

I don't know what that lesson was, but the only thing I learned was to hate the hole. Having nothing to do is boring, but knowing it will continue without cessation is despair. I was never a social person, but I found myself so starved for human contact that I even tried hugging the guard. It was like I needed someone to touch me just to prove I was still real, but nothing relieved the relentless pressure of the second-by-second attack on the soul which was isolation.

I knew I was really losing it when a fly found its way into my room. I named it Ribazzzio and talked to it just to hear something besides the droning of florescent lights and the distant shouts from other cell blocks. I told Ribazzzio about the girl I liked in high-school, and how beautiful the sly wrinkle at the edge of her smile was. I described to him what a sunrise looked like, and the taste of chocolate cake, and about the drawings I used to sketch, and a thousand other things which I hadn't appreciated at the time. I didn't tell the fly that I never expected to see them again; I didn't want to make him sad and leave. It didn't matter though, because the next time I woke, he was gone anyway. I'm not ashamed that I cried to be alone again, in fact I was relieved. It meant there was still part of me which was human enough to feel.

"Pssst. Hey buddy."

I opened my eyes. I wasn't sleeping—I was just lying on my back, preferring my malleable imagination to the stagnant cell. The voice had come from behind me.

"Can you hear me? What's your name?" the voice asked.

Someone else must have heard me talking to the fly. I turned around and found a crack in the mortar behind my bed. It must have connected with another cell in the Housing Detention block.

"Does it matter?" I asked.

"Of course it does. It's the most important thing in the world. It's the thing they can't take from you. My name's Riley."

"Hi Riley. I'm Travis," I replied.

"Have you been recruited yet, Travis?"

"I don't know what you're talking about," I said. I glanced back at the closed door of my cell. Even if someone heard me, they'd probably just think I was talking to myself again. It's not like they checked on us very often.

"Okay good," Riley said. "They're going to offer you a deal soon. You have to take it—trust me."

"What deal? Why would I trust you? I don't even know you."

"Sure you do buddy," he said. "I'm your only friend in the world."

I heard metal scrape on metal. My door opened. I threw the pillow over the crack in the mortar and sat rigidly upright.

I was reluctant to leave my new friend, but I don't think the guard noticed. My muscles were stiff from the cramped quarters, but I didn't even run around much. All I could think about was how great it would be to have someone to talk to now. And the deal? It couldn't have been that special if he was still in prison, but it was something to think about. Something to look forward to. Maybe they'd even given him books or a notepad. A laptop or TV would be almost as good as getting out.

Riley never answered again though. For two days I tapped on the wall, but all I heard was ceaseless muttering. An old man swearing under his breath kind of muttering, like he was trying to talk but couldn't decide whether he was talking to himself or someone else. All hours of the day and night—non-stop muttering. I don't even remember him pausing to eat, let alone draw breath.

Most of it was inaudible gibberish, but there were a few things I finally made out after they were repeated for the thousandth time.

"Didn't expect to see him again. No sir-ee-no."

"Just pretend to be human for me, will you? We can both pretend."

"I'm Riley. You're Riley too, but I was Riley first."

I lost track of how long I was supposed to stay in here, but I'm sure I should have been out of solitary a long time ago. By the time they came to offer me the deal, I was completely convinced that accepting it was the only way to ever get out.

"It's very simple, we have nothing to hide," the prison warden told me. He looked like the type of man who would force his children to only speak when spoken to, and even then only if they addressed him as 'sir'.

"We could easily force you to accept," the warden continued, "after all, you are in my power. I choose when you sleep, when you eat—if you eat—but I am still making this a completely voluntary arrangement."

"What do you want from me?" I asked.

"Prison overcrowding is a serious issue," the warden said. It felt like he was reading from a pre-prepared script. He was looking at me, but I wasn't really being seen. "The prison system has grown 700% over the last generation. It's costing us up to 40 grand per inmate every year – 74 billion annually nationwide. The government is actively exploring alternative programs which can satisfy the need to deter and rehabilitate criminals without the prohibitive expense and opportunity cost of prison. I'm offering you the chance to volunteer in one of these programs."

"You're going to take me out of prison? Then how come Riley stayed in here?"

The Warden's face screwed up like he'd just taken a bite from a lemon. "Riley is gone. He's been gone for a while now."

There was something about how he emphasized the name which made it seem like Riley hadn't changed locations. He'd changed from being Riley. The warden was already talking again though, and there wasn't any space to ask questions.

"I can't disclose all the details with you, but rest assured your sentence will be considerably abbreviated. Our programs are designed for maximal efficiency, and fifteen years of wasted time and money are going to be condensed into a weekend."

I didn't care about the time. What did I have to look forward to on the outside? It might seem inconsequential to you, but the only reason I accepted his offer was that I missed having someone to talk to. And if this was a government project, then what was the worst they could do? Maybe I really could get a clean start.

The warden gave me some papers to sign and then left. I was handcuffed by the guard and escorted out of my cell. He tried to keep my head low, but I caught a glimpse of the adjoining cell where Riley must have stayed. A man in a rubber suit was pressure washing blood out of the stone tiles.

"What happened to that guy?" I asked the guard. "Is he hurt?"

The guard shifted uneasily and looked around like he wasn't sure if he was supposed to say or not. Then he shrugged.

"What was he still doing in there?" I pressed. "I thought Riley made the same deal."

"Yeah, he finished his deal," the guard said. "He was supposed to be released in a few more days after the official pardon was granted, but I donno. Guess he wanted a quicker way out."

The man in a rubber suit picked up a fork on the floor. It was covered in congealed blood all the way up the handle. I tried to get a better look, but the guard shoved me onward. I was put into the back of an unmarked police car. Somehow I'd expected a whole bus load of people, but it was only me. In a few days I'd be a free man. It hardly seemed possible. How was I supposed to pick up the pieces and become something new? Anyway it sounded like Riley really was going to be released if he hadn't... well I wasn't as fragile as him. I could survive anything for a weekend.

I wasn't paying much attention to where we were going, but we drove for a long while before the car stopped at a ranch deep in the desert. There weren't any pens for animals, just wide open spaces separated by low stone barriers which I could have easily stepped over. I guess they didn't worry much about escape when there was nowhere to escape to.

"Welcome to camp Rawhide," I was greeted by a man wearing a leather vest and denim pants who stood outside the ranch house. The officer un-cuffed my hands, but I didn't move. I couldn't believe what I was seeing.

"Ten years left on your sentence, all over in two days. Seems like a pretty good deal to me, eh? But don't you worry, you won't miss out on anything," the man continued. His voice was muffled from speaking around the cigar in his mouth. His eyes didn't leave my face – mine didn't leave his. "It's my job to make sure you still get 10 years' worth of punishment this weekend."

I heard the sound of tires roaring over dry earth. I hadn't even noticed the officer had gone, but it was too late now. I couldn't look away from the man in front of me. The man I killed.

"What are you doing here?"

Edward grinned. He took a step closer to me and took the cigar out of his mouth.

"Same thing as you, darling. I'm just trying to find some justice in this shit-stain world. But between you and me, I don't know if there really is any justice out there. I reckon there are just people who got what they deserved, and people who got lucky."

Another step closer. I could feel the heat radiating from the end of his cigar as it brushed my hand. He was exactly the same as that insufferable creature I used to live next to. His words blew onto my face alongside his rancid breath.

"And by the time I'm through with you, there won't be any doubt. You weren't one of the lucky ones."

A LETTER FROM THE COLD
CASE FILES

I work at a police station, first in my precinct to be equipped with the latest video spectral comparator. The device is absolutely amazing for reconstructing obscured writing, and we've already used it to blow open three cases by deciphering evidence which had been almost completely obliterated.

Incriminating letter?

Receipt putting you at the crime scene?

Well what looks to you like a harmless pile of ashes in the waste bin can now be all we need to close the case.

The downside? I've had to take a huge-ass folder of paperwork home with me on the weekends since it's been installed. The inspector in charge wants us to skim every cold case in the entire precinct for areas where the new technology might be applicable. Boredom doesn't even begin to describe it, but I did come across an interesting letter which we've managed to repair from its severe water damage. I hope you'll enjoy it as much as I did.

To my lovely wife, Dear Eva:

Never has the fear of the hunted been so evident as it was with you. I could not stand to see you this agitated, the slightest creak in our house causing such violent tribulations. You could barely drink a cup of tea without being drenched by your trembling hands. At night, I heard you moan with the bitterest lamentations, and nothing I said seemed to provide you with the least respite.

"I can't escape." I heard the things you muttered to yourself when you didn't think I was listening. "He's going to find me and take me away. Not today—please not today—but soon. I can't escape."

I think I even know who you were referring to. I caught him more than once, sitting in his car across the street. Watching our house through his tinted windows. That cold, professional man, the one with the eyes of a killer. I sought answers from him, but upon seeing my approach, he shuddered like he'd been possessed and drove off before I could utter a word.

Eva, sweet Eva, nothing in this life could make you deserve such torment. The curtains never part to let the light in anymore, and you must suffer terribly if you are so loathe to reveal yourself that you prefer candles to electricity. How long has it been since you even left the house? And no, I don't count ordering food online, then waiting until dark to sneak out and snatch it like a quivering mouse.

I was afraid that even these precautions might not be enough to save you, until the night when I finally witnessed your resolve. You fixed your hair and makeup, although you are just as beautiful without, and dressed warmly against the midnight chill. I understand now why you didn't tell me where you were going, as intent as you were upon your grizzly mission.

I do not mind that you are self-absorbed, my dear. It only makes me more grateful for the attention I do receive. No matter how hard you try to exclude me though, I will always be there to protect you. It is one thing to face your fear, but how could you think I would let you do it alone?

The hour we drove together on the highway was the closest I have felt to you in a long time, and when you pulled off on the side to wait, it seemed as though we were the last two people on Earth. I didn't notice the shovel in back until you got out of the car, finally satisfied that our pursuer lost the trail. That's when I was convinced that I mistook the greatest moment of your resistance for the epitome of your despair. You weren't here to fight your pursuer, or even run from him. You had come to dig your own grave.

I swore to love you, but that is no obligation to a woman of your beauty. I swore to serve you, but how could I act as usher to your final rest? "Please," I begged, "tell me what would drive you to such an end?"

Do you remember how you flinched at my words? But the cold defiance in your eye made me somehow believe you had not given up yet.

Were you afraid I would be angry at what you've done?

Eva, blameless Eva. I could never be angry at you.

That I would try to stop you, or get in your way?

Never! I will only ever move to your desire, my love.

And with the opening of the trunk, I finally understood you. I felt nothing but relief when we carried the body out together, burying it there in the desert far from the prying eyes of petty men who do not understand the burden of love. If that is what needed be done to make you happy again, then I would have had it no other way.

I still do not know why the man hunted you, but it is not my place to force unpleasant memories and spoil your mind. I am writing this to let you know that nothing that happened will ever change how I feel about you. That I understand what you did, even admire you for going through with it. Eva, shining Eva, please do not let this be a barrier between us. Speak to me, welcome me as you once did, and I swear I will shelter you. I can forgive all evils in this world except the one that takes you away from me.

Forever yours, -Ivan

There you have it. As clean and incriminating an indictment as you'll ever find in writing. Of course I felt sorry for Eva after being stalked, but disregarding the due process of law and killing the man, well we couldn't exactly give her a free pass. I was so excited bringing this to the inspector in charge, and so disappointed when he disregarded it as irrelevant.

Obvious fabrication, he told me. Eva hadn't been stalked; she'd been investigated by the police. She was a suspect because she stood to gain a considerable amount of wealth after her husband Ivan's disappearance, although the case was eventually dropped without finding his body or sufficient evidence. The fact that a letter so stained with tears as to be almost unreadable was reconstructed didn't prove anything, except maybe the confused mind of a grieving widow.

I may have let my excitement rush me to conclusions, but seeing that the husband was the one who was murdered, the inspector must be right to think it was impossible for him to be the author. Besides, how could Ivan help her bury his own body?

THE ORGANIC MACHINE

3D printing is the future, and the future is here.

We are on the verge of another industrial revolution, and I'm incredibly excited to be a part of it. I'm a photogrammetry software designer, and I've spent the last four years working with fashion and clothing companies. I even worked at Nike for a while—they're already beginning to 3D print shoes.

I recently had the opportunity to apply my skills to a medical laboratory where they're beginning to 3D print human tissue. It's an ingenious concept—suspending living cells in a smart gel which allows the cells to fuse together into tissue once they're in alignment. The smart gel is then washed away, leaving an organ of purely human tissue.

"We're the first company to replicate organic vascular structures," Doctor Hansaf claimed on my first day there. He led me through the sterile halls which droned with dull florescent lighting. "The organs we print can diffuse oxygen and nutrients even more efficiently than those in your body."

Several other lab technicians passed me in the hall. I smiled, but each averted their gaze immediately, finding a sudden fascination with the blank floor tiles.

"It sounds like you know what you're doing. What do you need me for?" I asked.

"Our scaffolding needs to be remodeled. One of our organs seems to be leaking, and we can't figure out why."

"Which one?" He didn't need to answer though. As soon as Doctor Hansaf opened the door at the end of the hallway, I saw the most macabre sight I could have imagined. A steel table was lined with row upon row of human eyeballs, each staring at me from their great, unblinking orbs.

Leaking might be an accurate term, but they would be better described as crying. The saline liquid filled each eye to overflowing before draining into a multitude of tiny pools upon the table.

"Quite beautiful, aren't they?" he said, and I jumped a little to realize how close he was behind me. "Almost perfect—almost better than perfect. This design can see 3 times sharper than a human with 20/20 vision. It can even see beyond the traditional visual electro-magnetic spectrum, perceiving some near ultra-violet spectrum as well. "

Beautiful isn't the first word I would have chosen, but I could understand his pride. They looked real enough that you wouldn't look twice if a pair of these was staring back at you from a human face.

"The modeling software is on that computer," he gestured to a desktop workstation in the corner which was setup beside a second door. "You'll find all the current designs on there. I'll give you some time to look everything over and see if you can't find the issue. I'll be back to check on you in an hour."

I couldn't tear my gaze away from the eyes. I nodded stiffly again, hearing the door close behind me. I wasn't about to ditch a job just because of the unsettling environment. I averted my eyes from the table and walked over to the computer.

While it was booting up, I cast another glance behind me. My heart skipped a beat. Each of the eyes had turned to watch me. They were facing the door a moment before—but now they were facing me.

I slowly walked back to the door I came in, watching them this time. They turned to follow me. Without even realizing I was doing so, I put my hand on the door. Locked from the outside. There was a small glass viewing window in the door, but I couldn't see anything besides the hallway wall.

"Hello? Doctor Hansaf?" I knocked on the door. No answer. I turned back, but the eyeballs were pointed toward the opposite door now. I took a deep breath. They weren't watching me—it was ridiculous to think they were. There must simply be some fast twitch muscles activating from the salt in the saline solution.

I walked to the second door—locked as well. It was a high security laboratory though. It wasn't unreasonable to think the doors automatically lock. The doctor must have forgotten about it, but he was going to be back in an hour. I just had to focus on my job.

I glanced back at the eyeballs, but they were still facing the door. I sat back down at the computer and loaded up the photogrammetry software. Pretty soon, I was so engrossed at inspecting the intricate scaffolding that I didn't even think about the eyes behind me.

The secondary door opened beside me. Had an hour passed already? I turned, but I didn't see anyone in the room. Maybe he just peeked inside and saw I was still working. I turned back to the computer again.

Footsteps. I spun around, but I still didn't see anyone there. I was about to go back to work when I noticed all the eyes were moving once more.

Footsteps. Each one was slightly closer—slightly louder. The eyes were all following the empty space of ground where the sound was coming from. Something was there and I couldn't see it—but the artificial eyes could.

"Hello?" I pushed the chair between myself and the footsteps and pressed my body against the desk. "Is somebody there?"

The chair moved, and the footsteps got closer. I lurched backward into the wall and started moving around the room toward the door I entered from.

"Doctor Hansaf!" I yelled. "Let me out of here!"

I pounded on the door. Still locked. Footsteps. The eyes were all pointed directly next to me.

"Something is in here! Help!" I screamed, slamming against the door with my shoulder.

A face appeared in the viewing window. One of the lab technicians. He watched me for a moment, then began to write something down on a clipboard. What in the Hell? I pounded on the door again and he looked up.

"I know you can see me!" I yelled. "Let me out of here."

The lab technician tapped the side of his left eye. Then his right. He pointed at me. What was he trying to say? I glanced over my shoulder—the eyes were all watching the ground directly behind me.

Tentatively, I reached out my hand and felt something cold and slimy in the air. It was just a couple inches from my face. Something like a hand loosely grabbed me back, but I quickly drew away. It didn't touch me again after that.

"What are you?" I asked the empty air.

Footsteps. The eyes followed them back to the corner of the room. What in the Hell was going on? I turned back to the door. The lab technician was holding a piece of paper up against the glass.

Would you like to be the first person to see it?

I glanced back at the corner of the room. I nodded.

The lab technician wrote something and held it up again.

We will need to replace your eyes. Is that okay?

I shook my head. He started writing again.

He's not the only one. They're everywhere. We're not safe.

I heard the second door open. I turned to see the eyes follow the thing out of the room. The door closed again.

The primary door opened at once, and Doctor Hansaf entered. He was smiling like we had just shared a private joke.

"Well? What do you think?"

"What the fuck was that?" I asked.

"We don't entirely know," he admitted. "It's something which is only visible in the near ultraviolet spectrum, but machines aren't able to detect it. We only started noticing them once we printed the eyes."

"So you lied to me. You brought me here as a guinea pig."

He shrugged and put his arm around my shoulder. I pushed him off.

"This is a laboratory—you shouldn't be surprised to find experiments being done here. But you came voluntarily, you will leave voluntarily, and you will only continue participating if you choose. Will you take the eyes?"

"Absolutely not. I want no part in this." I was already heading marching down the hallway. I wish I had taken them though because I heard footsteps following me all the way home.

I AM A HUMAN VOODOO DOLL

H ave you ever fallen in love so bad that it hurts? Where you
have to force yourself to not even think about the person,
because otherwise your mind will run rampantly down a
spiral of uncontrollable obsession? I can't taste food without remembering her laughing at my cooking which she affectionately named
"bachelor chow". Music is damp and muted without her singing along
to the lyrics, and my morning alarm torments me with the prospect of
another day where she isn't mine.

Maybe I held on too tightly, maybe not tight enough. Maybe it
wasn't something I did but something I am. It just seemed like the
harder I tried, the further away Elis drew, until one day she said she
needed space. It was nauseating how polite and apologetic she was
about it. She kept calling every other day to see if I was okay, and at
first those gestures were my lifeline. I spent the whole day looking
forward to the few minutes I would hear her voice again. I thought it
was proof that she regretted her decision, and that it was only a
matter of time before she came back to me.

Now I know it was only pity. Apparently the "space" Elis needed
was already filled by someone else. I thought Nick-the-flabby-faced-
man child was just a harmless friend. They were together almost

immediately after she left me though, and the more I think about it, the more I wonder if it hadn't started even before. All those days when she just felt like "doing her own thing"? I guess that makes Nick her thing.

You'd think that knowing she betrayed me would make it easier to stop loving her, but somehow it only made the obsession stronger. I can't move on with my life, and I'm running out of strength to keep pretending it will be okay.

It's been two months since the breakup, and she still keeps trying to call and check in on me. I've stopped answering her. Text messages and voicemails are deleted before they're opened. I'm not writing this as an excuse or justification for what I was about to do. I was past the point of having to prove anything to anyone. And yeah, maybe it makes me a coward, but I didn't care about that either. I was done being treated like this—done feeling like this. I was just done.

Amitriptyline is an anti-depressant which failed to alter the world from shades of grey. Oxazepam is a sleeping pill which was inept against my thoughts of her. But half a bottle of each, and I wouldn't wake up again. It was supposed to be a very peaceful way to go.

The taste was so bitter I could barely keep it down, but after that my mind just wiped clean. My last thoughts were that if I could do it all again, I would have still gone down the same road. The time I shared with her was still worth the place where it must end.

But it didn't end. I opened my eyes and squinted against the after-noon sun. I was lying in my bed, covers pulled up to my chin. Both the bottles of pills were gone. How did I wake up from that? I didn't even feel nauseous anymore. Was I supposed to just go find another method and try again? Or maybe this was God's way of giving me another chance.

Did I even still care about her? I crawled over to my laptop and immediately checked Elis's Facebook page. I could use her photos as a test. If I could look at them without being overwhelmed with pain, then maybe—She'd changed her profile picture. Flabby face was kissing her cheek. A feeling like acid worked its way down my chest. Nothing had changed. Nothing was ever going to change the way I felt—No. Something had changed. Her page was full of sympathetic prayers and comments.

You were an Angel. God must have needed you back.

I'm so sorry to hear what happened.

Let me know if there's anything I can do to help.

I skimmed up to the top of the page. This was posted last night:

This is Nick. I thought I should let you all know that Elis died from a lethal dose of sleeping pills last night. I found her unconscious when I visited this morning and rushed her to the hospital, but it was too late. Message me for details.

I was completely dumbfounded. I had taken the pills, but somehow she had died instead. I had been thinking about her right before I went, so is there some way it had been transferred to her? It seemed impossible, but the coincidence of her going the same way on the same night seemed ludicrous. Besides, hadn't she been happy with Nick?

My racing thoughts were shattered by a sudden fierce knocking on my door. Was it Elis? Of course not, don't be stupid. I was about to open it when they knocked again.

"Police. We have a few questions to ask you."

I froze, my hand still on the handle. It really was my fault she was dead! But how?

I hadn't even seen her in weeks. Somehow what I did to myself happened to her, and the police being here proved it. Even if it was something else, my mind was too overwrought to begin to deal with them. I live on the ground floor, so it wasn't hard to just grab my keys and duck out my bedroom window.

I didn't know where to go, but I just needed to drive around for a while and clear my head. I unlocked my car and was about to climb in when—"Police! Stop right there!"

Two officers were emerging from my building. As soon as they caught sight of me, they began jogging. I should have just talked to them, but I felt compelled to run from the nameless clenching guilt and terror which possessed me. I jumped in the car and floored the pedal, tearing out of my apartment parking lot like I was running for my life. Last night I had been

292 | TOBIAS WADE

ready to die, but now I knew there was some greater power working through me. This was supposed to be my fresh start! I couldn't stop yet.

The police car was right behind me. Sirens blared in accusation. My mind was at war with itself with panic. I could barely breathe. My familiar neighborhood looked alien to me. I screeched around the corner and up the overpass leading onto the freeway at breakneck speed. I was just becoming aware of the implications of my escape when a horrendous impact sent me spinning out of control.

The police cruiser rammed me to prevent me getting on the freeway. The car spun two complete circles and smashed into a concrete barrier. The screech of metal was replaced with the roar of the airbags, and then everything went black.

I hadn't been wearing my seat-belt, but that might have saved my life as I was thrown clear. I must have only been out for a few seconds though, because coming to I could still feel the warmth of my burning car behind me.

The officers hadn't been so lucky. When they rammed my car, their car must have lost control in the opposite direction and fallen off the overpass. I didn't want to look, but I couldn't stop myself. The cruiser had flipped onto its roof, crushing the officers beneath it.

But me? Somehow I didn't have a scratch. My crazy theory must not have been so far off. I take the pills, but I was thinking about Elis and so she died instead. My car was hit, but I was thinking about the police and they suffered from the crash. Both times I walked away clean. I couldn't stay to ponder my discovery though, because I already heard more sirens approaching from the distance. I took off by foot and began running through the streets.

I had to test my theory. Just one more time. If it was true, then some divine agent had resurrected me and I really did have something to live for. If it wasn't, then I was a suicidally depressed loner who was wanted by the police. I had nothing to lose and everything to gain, so it was time to put it all on the line.

But with who? I couldn't just endanger an innocent stranger. I didn't want anyone else to get hurt except—well, except Nick of course. If it's anyone's fault Elis died, it must have been his. It was his job to make her happy, wasn't it? His job to notice if something wasn't right. Hell, the scumbag went behind my back and stole her from me. If anyone deserved to suffer, it was him.

I didn't want it to be clean either. Both other times I walked away unharmed, so I wanted him to suffer the way he made me suffer. I wanted to bring him to that point of hopeless isolation and rejection and leave him stranded beyond the hope of return. And more than anything, I wanted to be there to watch it happen.

I found him at Elis's apartment. Her old apartment, I guess, since she didn't live there anymore. I watched him carrying a box of her things to put into his car. She'd just died that morning, and he was already looting her stuff like a grave robber? There's no denying that I was going to enjoy watching him burn.

Because I was going to burn with him. I continued watching him from behind the hedge which surrounded the parking lot. I watched his face while I poured gasoline over my head, imagining what it would look like after it lit up. Unspeakably grotesque. Either he would die, or the burns would disfigure him for life. He would be alone, just like I was after he stole her from me. It still wasn't good enough though. I wanted him to see me when it happened so he'd understand why.

I waited by his car until he came back out with another box. The gasoline was cool against me, clinging comfortably like a second skin. It burned like Hell where it ran into my eyes, but I forced them to stay open. It was worth it to see the look on his face.

"Oh shit man, didn't see you there," he said. "I guess you heard about Elis."

I grinned. He still didn't know why I was here. I hadn't looked forward to anything so much since Elis left me.

"Can I help you with something?" he asked. "How come you're all wet–"

I twirled the lighter in my fingers. His eyes fell on it for the first time. Then he looked at my face—then back at the lighter. Then at the rainbow reflections in the pooling liquid around my feet. His eyes bulged, and I smiled wider. Now he gets it.

"This is for Elis," I said.

Flick. Flick. WOOSH. The fire started at my face and then swiftly engulfed my entire body. Nothing in my life prepared me for that pain. I stood there watching him for as long as I could—waiting for the spark to ignite in his skin. Waiting for the flesh to melt from his face and his bones to crack and splinter.

"Someone call the ambulance! Or the fire department! Or shit I don't know—get someone!"

I heard him shouting, but I couldn't see him anymore. My eyes must have boiled out of my skull. He said something else, but I couldn't hear him over the sound of my own scream which tore out of my body like my soul seeking release. For the third time I blacked out, but I was still grinning the whole way. Soon I would wake up, and he would be the one who burned.

—

Elis had stopped by my apartment the night I took the pills. She was worried about me after I didn't reply to any of her calls or messages. Shit, she might have even still cared for me, but I guess I'll never know now. She must have been overwhelmed with guilt and grief at seeing me like that and taken the rest of the pills herself after she got back home.

I was later informed of the pool of vomit in the corner of my bathroom where I had regurgitated my own lethal dose.

The police hadn't died when their cruiser turned over. They'd just been pinned inside and unable to pursue me. They had only come by my apartment because their investigation had revealed Elis visiting me on the night of her death.

But Nick did burn. He had forced himself through the flame to get my burning clothes off and smother the fire with his body. If it wasn't for him, I never would have survived until the ambulance came. His face isn't scarred like mine, but he'll have the marks on his arms and chest for the rest of his life. He's a good man. Elis would have been very happy with him if it wasn't for me.

So I was wrong. I was too maddened by grief and self-loathing to understand until it was too late.

There's no such thing as a human voodoo doll. There is no God working through me, or spirit of universal justice that makes everyone get what they deserve, but if my experience has one redeeming quality, then let it be a warning.

No-one should make life-altering decisions as a result of an emotional state. No matter how convinced your heart is that something is true, wait to act until your mind has caught up.

If I had stopped for a moment to talk to Elis, I would have seen how much she still cared, and I never would have done this to myself.

If I hadn't run from the police, there never would have been this accident. And if I'd only thought my theory through...

Well one day we will all wake up as a different person than who we are now, and we will learn to forgive those who hurt us, and forgive ourselves for hurting others. Elis is gone though, and the scars I'll have to remember her by will never heal.

THE MONSTER INSIDE US

Do you want a job with no prerequisite qualifications?

    I guess?

    $15 an hour, with a flexible schedule and free food?

Okay.

Plus it's so easy that you can even do your homework or watch TV while you're getting paid.

Sign me up.

Let me get this straight right off the bat. I'm not working as a babysitter because I like kids. The noise, the mess, the attention-deficit whining about inane nonsense—I'd probably be happier cleaning gutters. At least there isn't any shit in the gutters. I'm taking 18 credits this semester though, and there's no arguing that it's a pretty convenient way for a girl to make a few extra bucks. Maybe I'd even make enough to move out of the house I shared with my Mom. It wasn't so bad really—I just give the parents my sweetest smile, and somehow they're duped into thinking I have a maternal instinct which magically makes me adore their precious bundle of spastic chaos.

The trick is forcing that smile to last all the way until the door closes. Kids may be practically retarded by adult standards, but I've found even the slowest sperm can understand negotiations when it means giving them something they want.

"Okay little twerp," I'd say. "I don't like you, and you don't like me." Okay I don't really say that, but it's definitely what I'm thinking. "Here's the deal. You get to eat all the sugar blasted crap you can stomach and watch cartoons until you get a seizure for all I care. But you don't bug me, and you tell your parents we ate veggies and watched the Disney channel. Got it?"

Usually that's enough, but last night was a special case where everything went wrong. I could tell it wouldn't be easy the second I walked in the door, but I had faith in my martial-law parenting style and thought I could handle anything.

"Looks like you've got your hands full," I said, eyeing the teethmarks on the chair legs. "How many pets do you have?"

"No pets," the mother said. "Just my little David. I'm only going to be gone for a couple of hours though, and I'm only a call away if you need anything."

"I don't anticipate any problems." I smiled, trying not to wince at the sound of pounding drums upstairs.

"David get your ass down here and meet the sitter!" I'm not sure where the mother was going, but I wouldn't have been surprised if she had a part-time gig as a harpy. The drums grew louder. I just kept smiling.

"David I swear to God–" she shrieked.

"It's okay, I'll handle things from here," I told her. "You go have fun, and I'll give you a call if anything comes up."

The drums paused after the door closed. It was time to make a deal. David was a sweet looking boy of 11, with tousled blonde hair and bright blue eyes that would make all the girls weak in a couple of years. His gaze fixed on me with curiosity and more than enough intelligence to be reasoned with. This was going to be easy.

"Alright listen up," I told him. "What do you want to do this evening?"

"I want to burn something," he replied as matter-of-factly as someone ordering a hamburger. "Two somethings, if the first one goes out."

"You can't do that. Is there anything you'd like to watch on TV?"

David shook his head. "I can do that anytime. But Mom's not home, so I'm going to do all the things she doesn't let me do."

The first alarm started ringing in my head. It was the first of many. Being an adult was ordinarily enough to earn at least a little respect, but David completely ignored everything I said. Markers on the walls, microwaving forks, putting his shoes in the dishwasher—I couldn't turn around for a second without him doing something completely absurd. I tried locking him in his room for a bit, but when it was too quiet, I opened it to find him building a slingshot with a dozen pair of underwear that would have launched his lamp out the window. He didn't even have the decency to seem embarrassed when I caught him.

"You're going to break it!" I pulled the lamp away and put it back on his nightstand.

"I know. I was trying to," he said.

"Well stop it."

His blue eyes furrowed in deep concentration before he shook his head. "No, I think I'll just wait until you're not looking."

"I'm going to tie you up. Is that what you want?"

"No you won't," he said. "Or I'll tell Mom."

It was an absolute stand-off. I was bigger and stronger than him, but I was getting worn down fast and it was only a matter of time before I collapsed on the sofa and all Hell broke loose. It was time to try drastic measures. My family had a time-honored tradition of scaring kids straight, so if he couldn't be reasoned with, I was going to have to do to him what my mother did to me.

"Well if you don't stop, I'll tell on you too."

"I'm always good around her," David said. "She won't believe you."

"Not your mother. If you don't do what I say, I'm going to tell the monster. And he's going to eat you up."

He thought very seriously about this again. "Then I'll just wait until the monster isn't looking."

"He's always looking though." He was smart, so I had to be pretty damn convincing and get dark with this, or he'll see right through it. My mother always used to tell me about the monster whenever I misbehaved, but she had mastered a sort of wild-eyed intensity which always sold the story. She was so convincing, that even to this day she has never admitted that it was all made up.

"The monster lives in your eye, so he sees everything you can see," I told him. "And if you don't behave, he's going to know and start eating you from the inside out. He's going to eat up your heart, and your lungs, and your stomach, and everything else until you're completely hollow. And all the blood that has nowhere left to go, it's all going to come out of your mouth and you're going to drown in it."

His face was getting paler with every word. Good, let him have nightmares about it. That's his therapist's job, not mine.

"What about you?" he asked. "Does a monster live inside you?"

"Sure there is. There's one inside everyone. That's why the people who make it to be adults are all so serious and good all the time."

"That doesn't seem right," he said. "There are bad adults too. The criminals and stuff."

"That's just because the monster has already eaten them and is using their body to do bad things." I never thought terrifying a child would be this satisfying. I wonder if Mom used to enjoy scaring me this much, or if I was just a bad person. It worked like magic though. Suddenly David decided that he was tired and wanted to go to bed. 7:30 PM and ready to sleep—it was a dream come true. Maybe this is the story I should use for everyone. All those hours I wasted pretending to be their friends—this was way more efficient!

David went to his room and turned off the light, and I got to work studying for my final exams next week. I thought I was going to have a full evening to myself, but around 8:30 I noticed the light was back on in his room. He was being quiet, so I thought about just ignoring him, but he seemed a bit too clever to be fooled for long and I didn't want to take any chances. It's a good thing too, because when I opened the door I saw him out of bed, staring at his reflection in his mirrored closet door.

His left hand was holding his left eye open as wide as it could, while the right hand held a sewing needle poised to gouge straight into it. I wanted to tackle him to the ground, but the needle was so close it was almost touching the eyeball itself. I was terrified that any sudden move would just bump it straight inside.

"David! What are you doing you, idiot! Put that down right now!"

He turned to look at me, still holding the needle directly against his eye. My whole body tensed as I imagined the feeling of that point scraping against my own eye. "I can't. I need to kill the monster inside."

His hand was trembling, but he pressed it a little closer into his eye. It looked like it had already started to puncture. I walked more carefully across that floor than if it were made of hot coals. No sudden moves. No harsh words. I just had to gently…

"David please listen to me. There is no monster, okay? I made it all up. If you put that in your eye, you're going to hurt yourself very badly. You won't be able to see anymore."

"You lie," he said. He wasn't pushing it in any further though. He was listening to me. I took another step closer.

"I'm not lying. You can ask anyone you want—you need your eyes to see."

"No you're lying about the monster," David said. "I saw him."

"I'm going to call your Mom right now, okay?" I fumbled with my phone, trying to pull it out and dial without looking away from him. "You can ask her, and she will tell you the same thing. There are no monsters."

"You're lying, and I know why," he said. "The monster inside you is making you do it. It's trying to save the monster in me, but I'm not going to let it. I'm the only one who makes the rules."

The number was in the phone. I was about to hit dial when—His arm jerked violently. He screamed, and so did I. The needle slid straight into his eye, completely disappearing into the brilliant orb. He doubled over with pain, howling like a Demon. I threw the phone onto the ground and rushed to him – too late. He was clutching his head with both hands, howling and screaming and—and then nothing. He just went real quiet, his head in his hands, hiding his face from me.

"We're going to the hospital. Now!"

He shook his head.

"David look at me!"

Slowly—tortuously—he raised his face to meet me. His left eye was sealed shut, but I could still see the end of the needle poking between his closed lids. A stream of blood was freely flowing down his face like tears.

"It didn't work," he whispered. Then he said something else, but it was so quiet I couldn't hear.

"I told you it wouldn't. Now come on, we need to go now."

"It didn't kill the monster," he whispered again.

I picked him up, and he didn't resist. He wrapped his arms around my neck to hold himself upright. I hurried him toward my car as fast as I could. Kids get things in their eyes all the time, right? This didn't mean he would be blind. They just had to take it out and—"I didn't kill it," he whispered again, right in my ear where he was pressed against me. "I only made the monster mad." I felt his arms grow tighter around my neck. It was hard enough carrying a boy his size, but trying to force him while he was choking me was impossible. I had to set him down and get a better grip, but he wouldn't let go. "He blames you," David whispered in my ear. "It's your fault we tried to hurt him."

"David let go. Now you're hurting me."

"I know," he whispered. "And that's only going to make you mad, so I'm not going to make the same mistake twice. This time I'm going to finish the job."

I forced his arms off me and hurled him to the ground. His right hand was balled up like a fist—clenching the bloody sewing needle that he'd somehow managed to pull free. His left eye was still clenched shut, and his right eye was narrowed as his face twisted into an animalistic snarl.

"Stop playing games. We need to take you to a hospital," I said.

But he wasn't playing. He was lunging at me, trying to strike at me with wild flailing punches and kicks. I managed to create some distance between us, but he was absolutely relentless. I ran down the stairs, but he leapt from the top with a wild leap and was on top of me again before I reached halfway. I felt the needle pierce into the back of my neck and I had to physically throw him off me.

I was in an absolute panic by this point. I didn't take into account how small he was, or how fast he was already going when he jumped from the top of the stairs. I threw him with all my strength, which would have probably knocked an adult man onto his ass. With David, it was enough to send him straight over the railing to tumble the half-story onto the ground below.

He landed with a sickening crack that made me want to just run and not look back. I rushed to where he lay spread eagle on the tile floor. A pool of blood was quickly expanding from his face. I tried to ease him onto his back to inspect the damage, but he surged awake again. He was swiping madly at my face with his little hands. I tried to pin him, but his hands were slick with blood and kept sliding through to force his needle into my arms and neck again and again. I had to grab him by the shoulders and slam him into the ground before he finally stopped.

"You have to lie still!" I was crying at this point. He kept squirming, but I finally had both his arms firmly underneath me. "There is no monster, okay? There's nothing that's going to hurt you. If you me take you to the hospital you're going to be alright."

David coughed, and blood splattered half-way up my arms. I climbed off of him, but he wouldn't stop coughing. More blood—just like I'd told him would happen. Just like my mother had told me would happen. But it was absurd to think any of that was true. He'd hurt himself from the fall and I couldn't waste any more time—So why couldn't I stop crying? It was like all those years when I was growing up were flashing back to me. Every night I lay awake—listening to the sound of my own blood in my veins and the beating of my heart—wondering if I could hear the monster inside of me. All those nightmares I had as a child, everything was rushing back. I shouldn't have done this to him. I knew how much I hated it when Mom did it to me. I shouldn't have tried to scare David like that. But I was the adult now, and I had to take responsibility. So why couldn't I stop crying?

"Shhh…. shhh… come on now… don't cry." It was David. He had stopped coughing and was kneeling beside me. I immediately tensed, but he was stroking my hair so gently that all I could feel was relief. He was okay. My sobbing choked in my throat, and I actually started to laugh. He was the one trying to comfort me!

"Shhh…" he whispered. "Don't be like that. You have nothing to be scared of anymore." I gave him a great big hug and felt him holding me back. "We all have a monster inside us. Sometimes they never wake up, and sometimes they never go back to sleep. But you don't have to worry anymore."

"Our monsters," I replied. "They've both gone back to sleep, haven't they? But we're still here, and we have to take care of ourselves. So will you let me take you to the hospital now?"

"No, not asleep. Do you really think your monster could stay asleep after you killed a little boy?"

I tried to pull him away to look at him, but he was holding on tightly again now. More tightly than ever – tighter than a boy his age should be able to.

"Why don't I have to be afraid?" I asked, pretending I wasn't trying so hard to get him off.

"Because it's so much more fun when you let the monster out," his words washed into my ear in a warm rush.

I was afraid his arms would break by how hard I pushed him, but finally his hands slid apart and he fell back onto the floor. He lay there stiffly, his arms maintaining their curved shape where they were wrapped around me. The shape they had when he was still alive. The blood had stopped flowing from his mouth. His blue eyes were both closed. His shallow chest had stopped fighting to breathe. And finally —finally—he wasn't resisting me anymore.

I ran. I didn't look back. I got in my car and just started driving. I don't know what I'm going to do. David's mother knew my name and the police would find me. I couldn't even go back to my home or say goodbye to my own Mom. She'd take one look at me and know what happened, and I know she'd want me gone too. She'd see the blood that I was already starting to cough up, and she'd know the monster inside of me had grown too big. She'd know all her stories and warnings hadn't been enough to get me to be good, and that now I was being eaten up too.

I'm going to drive now, and I'm not going to stop until I'm not the one making the rules anymore. I just hope David was right—that it really is more fun when we let the monster out.

MY FACE WILL BE THE LAST THING YOU SEE

G reen eyes of a cat, and hair dark enough to make the shadows behind her look like they were glowing. I caught her staring at me over the rim of her wineglass across the room.

I did what most long-time single guys in my situation would do. I pulled out my phone and started surfing through Reddit. That's right —play it cool. Make it look like you've got important stuff going on. Just pretend you're not interested in her, then keep up the illusion until she leaves and you die alone.

I really need a new strategy for meeting women.

I forced myself to peek at her again. She was still looking at me, and this time she smiled. I started to smile back, but remembered just in time how uneven my teeth are and tried to twist it into a mysterious expression instead. I was trying to channel Clark Gabel, but probably ended up closer to a constipated cookie monster. She interrupted my quiet self-loathing by beckoning me with her finger.

I looked over my shoulder. There wasn't anyone behind me but the barkeeper, and his back was turned. This had to be some kind of joke. I don't think of myself as particularly ugly—a bit doughy perhaps—

but I never attracted attention from women like that. Hell, I didn't even know women like that existed outside of airbrushed magazines.

I'd only been planning to stop off for a quick buzz after work. I don't drink ordinarily, but the shifts have been crazy since Peter died of a heart-attack last week, and I just needed to unwind. Her tantalizing invitation promised an even more enjoyable distraction though, and my feet moved on their own to treacherously thrust me into the booth beside her. I didn't fully realize what I was doing until it was too late to come up with a witty introduction.

"Uh hi. Can I help you with something?" Yeah. Real smooth. What are you, a waiter?

She extended a graceful hand with neatly polished nails the color of dried blood. Her skin was so pale and translucent that the blue veins were clearly visible meandering up her arm.

"Hello Eddy. Can I call you Eddy?"

You can call me anytime, my dumb brain thought. I didn't even realize she knew my name until I'd already shaken the chill hand she offered me.

"Do you know me?" I asked instead. Her limp fingers revived in my hand and gripped me firmly for a second as though holding on for dear life. The pressure was gone as quickly as it appeared though, and she released me before luxuriously leaning back.

"Not yet, but I have a way of getting to know people. Would you like me to get to know you, Eddy?"

I could imagine a snake whispering its prey to sleep with the same tone of voice. I felt definitively agitated sitting here, but I couldn't tell how much of it was fear and how much excitement. I don't suppose it mattered because I was so engulfed in her presence that I was power-less to do anything but nod.

The woman produced two decks of playing cards and placed them upon the table. Her long fingers fanned through them with the dexterity a pianist, and I half-imagined a musical score rising up from inside me as she rapidly stacked and shuffled them together. One deck seemed to contain a multitude of human faces while the other contained a variety of surreal paintings which resembled Tarot cards.

"You're not a Witch, are you?" I hadn't meant to blurt it out, but I had just seen my own face flash by on one of the cards and was becoming increasingly uncomfortable by the second.

"That's the wrong question to ask," she said, not even looking at the cards while she fluidly shuffled. "The weapon matters not compared to the intent of the wielder. I could kill you more easily with my switchblade than a Witch could with her magic, but do you really think I would hurt you?"

Her bluntness relieved me of my own burden for tact. I might as well be honest with her too.

"Yes. I think you would."

She grinned and slapped the combined deck down with enough force to make the whole table rattle. I nearly fell out of my seat from the shock.

"Good. It's the cautious ones who last the longest."

I wanted to question her further, but my attention was diverted by the cards which she began dealing. The first one she flipped from that jumbled pile depicted my face, with my name neatly handwritten below it.

"How did you do that? Where d'you even get that picture?"

Her lovely features furrowed with concentration. She didn't answer. Her hand caressed the deck with tremulous focus. She was about to draw the next card, but then gave me a wry smile and cut the deck to draw from the middle instead. Lying on the table beside my photograph was a skeleton, only its face was replaced with an exquisite painting of the woman sitting across from me. She let out a long breath like relief, but her warm smile couldn't dislodge the mounting horror in my chest.

"That wasn't so bad, now was it? Now we know each other a little better, don't we?"

"I don't know anything. I don't even know your name." I was starting to get angry. It wasn't just at her for messing with me like this —I was angry at myself. How pathetic I must be to keep entertaining this nonsense just because a pretty girl smiled at me. If it had been anyone else, I would have been out the door a long time ago.

"Oh don't be like that, it's actually good news," she said. "Your photograph obviously represents you—"

"I don't know how you got that, but I want it back." I tried snatching at it, but the card danced around her nimble fingers and evaded me.

"And you recognize my face on the other, don't you? That's the last thing you'll see before you die."

All the excitement was gone. My heart strained against my ribcage with nothing but the absurd fear she instilled in me. I made another wild snatch for my photograph, but she tugged it just out of my grasp again. All I could reach was the rest of the deck still on the table, so I picked that up instead.

"You want these back?" I asked. "Give me my card."

"You aren't being very cautious right now." Her eyes narrowed with dangerous intent.

I looked down at the other cards in my hand. That's when I noticed that all the other photographs had a thin red line drawn through the center. There had to be at least twenty of them in here.

"They weren't being cautious either, and you don't need my sight to guess what happened to them." The voice was as cold as the space between stars. I didn't even care about my photo anymore. I just wanted to get out. I didn't look back even when the bartender started shouting about my tab. All I could think about was putting as much distance as I could between myself and the woman tormenting me.

What in the world was that even about? I know I don't approach women very often, but I can't imagine that's the typical reaction. As I jogged, the clean evening air unraveled the twisted knot in my stomach and began to purge the surreal experience from my mind. I slowed down to a walk, even chuckling to myself at the absurdity of what just happened.

A psychic, or a con-artist (not like there was a difference). That's what she had to be. She wasn't flirting or threatening—she was just trying to sell me her readings. I stopped by that bar all the time after work, so it wouldn't have been hard for her to snap a photo or get my name. Of course, she hadn't actually asked for money, but that was something I preferred not to dwell on.

I replayed the scenario in my head and even congratulated myself with how I handled the situation. Good for me, for not falling victim to her seducing charms. Although there's no denying the fantasy I still entertained of taking her and...

It wasn't until I got home and was digging for my keys that I felt the deck of playing cards still in my pocket. I'd been in such a rush to get out that I hadn't even noticed taking it with me. I fanned through the deck to make sure there weren't any more photos of me, but stopped abruptly short.

Peter.

He was wearing the suit I saw him wear every day for the last five years. The thin red line scored directly across his face. She couldn't have had anything to do with...

Just to be safe, I started Googling some other names captioned below the photographs. After the third search pulled up a third obituary, I knew there was no point in going on. 24 other cards beside my own, and all with a red line struck cleanly through the center. Every death was from a different cause, although I noticed several quotations of shock and despair from families swearing it came without warning.

I saw the woman again the next day. It was only a glimpse, but she was sitting at the bus-stop I usually took. I'd left her cards at home and didn't want a confrontation about it, so I just waited the 20 minutes for the next bus to come along.

There she was again at the taco shack I frequent for lunch. She was actually working behind the counter. She smiled when we locked eyes, but I immediately turned around and left without a word. The less I got involved in this lunacy, the better.

Then again at the grocery store. She was deliberating between brands of peanut butter. Again at the bus-stop, watching me get on. Twice more I saw her standing on different street corners on the drive home. I don't know how she was moving so quickly, but it was obvious that I was being stalked. I was being stupid for just pretending none of this happened. I had information linking a string of deaths, and I should have brought this to the police from the very beginning.

I stopped off at home just long enough to grab the deck of cards off my dresser before heading down to the local station. It was getting late by now—around 8 PM—but the dreary march of street lamps still hadn't begun to glow. I considered taking an UBER, but I didn't want to risk being trapped in a car with the woman. I just walked - trying my best not to imagine green eyes glinting in the mounting darkness around me.

I should have known it wouldn't be any good. She was the officer on duty, just sitting behind her desk with hands folded patiently on the table. Not doing anything. Just waiting for me.

"I've got your cards. You can have them back," I said. I dropped the stack on her desk. She didn't take her eyes off me, not even when they scattered from impact. I half-turned to leave, but couldn't quite force myself to turn my back on her.

"I know you did something to the others," I spluttered to fill the gaping silence. "And I don't care, okay? About Peter or any of them. I don't want anything to do with it."

She didn't blink. Didn't move a muscle. I started backing up, almost making it to the door before she finally said:

"I'm following you for a reason, Eddy. If you walk out that door, then you will never see me again."

I hesitated. Was that a promise, or a threat?

"Okay. I'm okay with that," I said.

"Are you? Even knowing that my face will be the last thing you see before you die?"

It sounded more like a school teacher reminding me of a formula than it did a threat. That didn't stop the hairs from rising on my skin as she stood from the desk to approach me.

"How are you everywhere that I am?" I asked.

"What's more likely..." She was only a foot away now. My back was against the glass door, but every word was drawing her closer. "That

I'm everywhere at the same time, or that you're stuck in one place and I'm there with you?"

"Why are you doing this to me? Why are you killing all these people?"

"I don't kill anyone," she said. "I simply warn them what is to come. I give them comfort in their dying moments. Those who go violently into their final sleep are doomed to nightmares while those I help go softly can sleep in peace. I have seen the future and know that my face is the last thing you will ever see."

The air between us was intoxicating. I couldn't break away.

"The last time I see you..." I managed. "It doesn't have to be today. It can be next year—or fifty years from now."

"I have a job to do. How do you expect to find me again in fifty years?" she asked, a bemused smile playing about her lips.

"That's easy," I replied. "I'll just never let you go."

Despite all her tricks, I was stronger than her. I locked my hands behind her waist and drew her into me. I wasn't ready to die, but even more than that, I wasn't ready to die alone. She seemed intrigued at first when I pressed my mouth onto hers, but then she started struggling. I held on even tighter, afraid that she would simply vanish the moment she slipped free.

She couldn't love me. No-one could love me for long. Even if I somehow captured her fancy, I knew someone like her could only ever get bored with someone like me. Sooner or later she would leave me, and that would be the last time I ever saw her. That would be the day I die.

She was fighting now. I could feel thrashing against me like a caged animal. All I could do was hold on tighter, dragging her from the building and into the darkness outside.

I crushed her against me with all my strength until my arms went numb and my fingers bled from where they clasped behind her back. Each breath she took was shallower than the last until finally her pale skin was bleached as white as bone.

She wasn't lying about carrying a switchblade, but it was a lot harder than I imagined using that to separate her head from her body.

I couldn't work it through the spine and was forced to simply peel back the skin of her face and take that with me instead.

Now her face rests on the pillow to my left each night I lay down to sleep. It's the last thing I see before I close my eyes. And if death were chance to steal me before I wake, then I know I will go in peace without the burden of dreams to follow.

Each morning I rise on the right and turn away from it. All through the day I walk with surety, knowing I will not die before seeing her again. One night I will look upon her and it will be my time to go, but even then, I know I won't be alone.

READ MORE

Read more horror at
TobiasWade.Com
Or keep reading with 52 Sleepless Nights.

AUTHOR'S NOTE

Please remember to
Honestly rate **rate the book.**

It's the best way to support me as an author and help new readers
discover my work.

45392162R00180

Made in the USA
San Bernardino, CA
29 July 2019